The School of Hard Knocks

I0629011

By Oliver Strong

ISBN: 978-0-9955188-1-0
Word Count: 86,462

Contents

Chapter one

Inside Sonnet's cockpit a murky broth of yellow tobacco smoke vibrated to the squeal of psychedelic guitars. A man reclined into his seat, foot tapping dashboard, rolled up cigarette in one hand, gentleman's magazine in the other.

Five foot ten, grey eyes under chestnut brows with prominent nose, mouth hardened like the business he was in. Flowing brown hair combed down the rear of his skull while stubble surrounded his chin and mouth. About 100lbs more than God intended, the chair ground beneath an oversized backside while his belly moved side to side. Years of calorie laden food washed down with double strength brachian bitter and little to no exercise had taken its toll not only on his body but his face. He had one of those pudgy faces, without examining the rest of his physique you could easily surmise he carried extra ballast.

Guitars howled as the singer cried,

"Come on,

Let the spirit inside you,

Don't wait to be found,

Come along with my sound,

Let the spirit move you."

He puffed a cigarette, rolled by yellow fingers into a twisted silver birch. To his front the ship's viewscreen broke up Sonnet's grey hull, a dark sheet pock marked by tiny white spots, no more than a foot in height. A window into the void of space, it stretched six feet horizontally ending its journey to the side of each forward chair.

This wasn't some swanky liner or a military ship with thousands of credits invested in toilet paper alone but a private vessel, one of many strippers docked at Templeton's.

A Hendrix-esque rock solo detonated above his head causing nicotine broth to shake in its shockwave. The burgeoning fellow tapped his foot harder and harder before slamming down an alert button. A whining klaxon erupted and three scruffy men bundled in. One dressed in jeans another short pants, the guy at tactical wore a grey flight suit similar to his Captain their colours impossible to differentiate in this red light.

Once music ceased the crew reported in, 'What's up Rick?'

Rick brushed ash off his blue suit, 'False alarm.'

'You what?'

'It was an accident,' he placed his magazine on the dashboard.

The navigation officer sighed, 'You been jacking off to that shit again?'

'Fuck off!' Rick replied in a South Yorkshire accent.

Two men could be heard stomping back from the engine room when a message came in, 'Hey I got something,' said a man in short jeans, t-shirt and trainers.

'Gonorrhea?'

'They hit Sigma 9.'

Rick drew on his rollup while yellow fingers combed back greasy hair, 'What's on Sigma 9?'

'Population, seven thousand, it's a farming colony.'

'How much for the journey?'

'Three pounds of urillium.'

'Fuck it.'

Rick was in his mid-forties as was his waistline thanks to many nights on duty waiting for information from the front. He and his crew scavenged anything they could fit into the cargo bay and haul back to civilized space.

His tactical officer, Sam, tapped away, 'It could be worth it.'

'Neggs won't hit a farming colony.'

'Depends on what they're farming.'

Rick leant over to see a leaved plant similar to bamboo, 'What's that?'

'Zaj Zavsar.'

'And?'

2

'It's the active ingredient in Split. People pay a lot of cash for this stuff.'

'How much is a lot?'

'Three to five hundred credits a pound.'

The cockpit went silent for a minute.

'Anyone else headed there?'

A man stationed behind Rick's left shoulder scrutinized his scanner display, 'No-one's moved.'

Many ships hung close to a jump gate, monitoring fleet movements. After a large battle they'd enter hyperspace like vultures launching from tree tops, the smell of carrion upon the savannah impossible to resist.

'Let's blow this shithole.'

Everyone resumed positions, an atmosphere scrubber removed tobacco smoke as the ship came off silent running. Sonnet broke free from docking links. A guy behind Rick's right shoulder plotted course. Rick flicked a switch sending his request to the jump gate.

After credits had been transferred the gate warmed up forming an event horizon. A shimmering lake of ice beckoned as Rick activated Sonnet's computer. Sonnet moved in on automatic her long smooth body possessed a dolphin's snout stretching back into a sperm whale's body.

Engines seared space, burning expensive urillium fuel, granting enough leverage to cruise the waves of hyperspace and journey great distances in a relatively short time.

Sonnet was a temple to masculinity, a place where the single male might worship his household Gods and his Gods were many, rising and falling in popularity as time went on yet a few remained, for without them the temple would crumble.

First was Apollo the God of loud and obnoxious music. Next came Dionysus the God of empty beer cans and hangovers. Third Poseidon God of trash and urine stained toilets, finally his brother, the greatest God to inhabit this shrine ... Zeus God of pornography and bad personal hygiene.

These Gods were worshipped fervently each day. Tenets observed without fail lest Hera, Goddess of marriage and "relationships" duped them into a life of clean living and keeping up with the Joneses.

Provided they remained within the temple they were safe for no woman entering this place could possibly stand her ground more than two minutes before asphyxiating.

Sonnet rode the waves of hyperspace, its shade depended on your destination yet its colour remained, blue. Rick imagined he was a surfer riding waves on a beach which is essentially what Sonnet did. Ordinarily hyperspace would crush any matter, Sonnet should have been pancaked into energy and spread thinly across its realm. But an enveloping energy field allowed her to slip through, riding its currents to their destination before opening a crack and exiting. This process cost dearly in energy and but one fuel contained enough energy units to sustain her journey and open a portal back into normal space.

In the past only the largest of vessels might explore hyperspace due to energy requirements until urillium solved that problem, leading to the current war … but that's for later.

Rick put his feet up while Sonnet's crew cleared cans and clutter from their stations. They and others waited around Piraxis monitoring the war before traveling in packs to prey upon the remnants of battle. This strike was a low priority farming colony, not much in it for strippers. Strippers were after rare super alloys used in space ship construction, precious metals, technology, weapons and most of all urillium. A farming colony would put up no resistance, they had no weapons or technology and certainly no urillium.

However, they did have a crop of Zaj Zavsar, used in the production of split, a class A narcotic. The trouble wasn't so much getting your hands on the stuff it was finding a place to sell it without being murdered first, but Rick had been in this game for twenty years, he had contacts.

'Reaching exit point,' said Dyson.

'Alright lads hold onto your wage packets!' replied Rick as the men strapped themselves in.

Fore of Sonnet space-time revealed itself through a thin slit, she jolted back in an act of defiance, currents of hyperspace rushed in one direction while Sonnet pushed the other.

They were buffeted back and forth and with a kick ejected like a barking dog from its master's backdoor. Dyson went over navigation as Peters scanned the system confirming they were where they should be.

Sigma 9 was a system of twelve planets its fourth resembled Mars, a breathable atmosphere with parched soil. Colonists had built a dome and using machinery to melt permafrost grew cash crops of Zaj. Every year nefarious characters appeared from hyperspace to bid on the evil weed. This year negz came early blasting them into the stone age. Negz took a harsh view of these people, so much so they were willing to commit warships to destroy cultivation of any Zaj Zavsar. No trial, no jury, only a slit in hyperspace, a scan and orbital bombardment. Then they'd set about destruction of the farmers means to further cultivate it ... execution in other words.

'What's the situation?'

Peters scanned the surface searching the radiation spectrum, 'Negg-heads fucked them from orbit.'

'Anyone left?'

'I dunno but here's the dome co-ordinates, well where it was.'

'Set a course, out the way this time.'

'Sure, co-ordinates set.'

'Let's do it.'

Sonnet descended through atmosphere slicing its high clouds, the planet's surface unfolded by degrees. Buffeting caused a little rough and tumble but Dyson watched over navigation as the ship's computer compensated. Sonnet's hull heated, her silver sleek body turning deep to bright red as atmospheric friction intensified. Moby Dick descended from the skies using its wide belly as a braking mechanism. Cloud shot past the cockpit's strip, blocking Rick's view, then poof the planet below bared herself. At first a mountainous range displayed white caps, it quickly smoothed out as Sonnet traversed the heavens to reveal dusty plains. Finally their destination could be seen, a burnt out pit in the middle of an alien dust bowl. A shattered dome wrecked by orbital bombardment. Smoke rose before turning off, pulled by drafts in the upper atmosphere Sonnet had battled just moments ago.

The will of nature cannot be changed for she is the most determined of creatures in the universe. Yet a man may go against her desire even take advantage but only if he understands who is superior. Man yields when he must but always with an eye towards the goal and that is the process of navigation. For he who forgets Mother Nature's superiority will end up cast upon rocks, hanging by his fingernails blood soaking his salt caked arms, or worse, bloated and deformed on a beach, a message to all who dare test Mother Nature's will.

Rick pushed his feet onto the hull beneath his station. He shook back and forth for a minute until the ship had slowed, moving through atmosphere at a speed not so distasteful to this planet.

'I've found a small valley, taking her down,' stated Dyson as he tapped his station.

Sonnet broke off to Port, mighty thrusters encompassing her body burned fuel at full pelt. Rick was pulled by G-forces as Sonnet tore from her previous flight path onto a new one. It was nothing more than a rollercoaster might create yet he traversed the atmosphere of an uncharted alien planet after a negz attack, not tightly fixed to rails in an amusement park on Earth where one might sue if it went bad. Out here if it hit the fan it didn't matter how many lawyers you had on speed dial, you were alone.

She slowed to hover above a surface of fine dust broken up by rocks. Thrusters heaved with stress as Sonnet, about the same size as a 20th century submarine, let out her landing claws descending ten centimetres a second, five centimetres a second, two, one, six claws touched down.

Stanchions squealed under her immense bulk. Thrusters eased off transferring mass to hydraulics, it wasn't pretty or graceful but it worked.

Externally the experience was nerve wracking, internally the sounds of a creaking hull and pressure valves blowing off nature's titanic stress was enough to make any man consider a change of underwear. Sonnet's crew were used to the experience, sure they were scared stiff the first time but that was Rick's initiation test. Rick got a perverse pleasure on the rare occasions a fresh crewman went through his first landing. Many were ex-military or served on merchant craft, vessels kept to Earth Corps regulations. Those babies flew like a dream, you'd need to look out the window to know if you'd landed. On their introductory landing, far beneath Earth Corps' high standards, they usually filled their pants. Of course, they didn't actually soil themselves ... not until the part Rick pulled an expression of tortured horror and screamed "OH MY GOD! WE'RE GONNA DIE!" then wailed and rolled around the floor ... it was tradition.

Some quit there and then, others waited until they returned to Templeton's, those who remained were the present crew. It was tough to find a replacement after someone left, it was even tougher keeping them, but one thing's for sure Sonnet's crew held their nerve.

Creaking subsided as the last valves fired, 'Landing complete.'

Rick pushed his ample frame out the Captain's chair, 'Sam, Allenby you're with me. The rest of you arseholes stay here, no wandering off this time, got it?'

'Yeh, yeh,' huffed Dyson.

Rick, Sam and Allenby walked across an alien desert. Breather masks a barrier between dusty atmosphere and lungs. Sand clogged their alien surroundings turning midday to dusk.

They pressed against high winds. A tall American fellow named Sam was hardest hit. He'd been tactical officer for three years now. Ever since the war commenced Rick needed a man who could interpret the negz language fluently, it was a stroke of luck when they crossed paths.

Sam studied for years to get his PhD in alien linguistics. His Masters was in a common dialect of Hemzih Negz, a most difficult language for any creature to

7

master. He'd left university with the hope of an ambassadorial position unfortunately war broke out and before he could blink draft papers hit his mail box.

Rick didn't understand why he'd turned the position down. A desk job, good pay, short hours, all he need do was translate communications on the rare occasion enemy transmissions were decrypted, that was before it turned into a hot war.

Sam refused to take the job, his first reason being: it's immoral to draft a man. Second: he'd spent years studying these aliens and their culture so they could understand one another not so men of violence might soak their hands in blood. Before they came for him Sam skipped Earth taking the only job where he might use his skills without a licence or identity papers from the government.

Rick hired people based on ability but what mattered most was if he trusted their face. Sam was a young impressionable man straight out of university, back then, today he was Rick's young protégé and one day he'd make a fine Captain. As for Allenby he was in his fifties, he'd worked for reputable companies most of his career, salvaging vessels on a legal basis. He worked government contracts carrying official papers and permits, until his wife discovered a nest egg put away for old age and lawyered up. While hauling the broken superstructure of a crashed mining ship 10,000 light years from home Allenby was informed she was taking him for 70%. By the time he returned he'd not only missed the court date but he'd missed a month of alimony payments.

Allenby was a portly Cetian of merry character yet his ex-wife brought out a mean streak in him that day. He quit his job and disappeared, signing on with Rick, no government licence meant no permits, no taxes, no alimony and no harassment every time he missed half a credit in payment for two kids that weren't even his. I guess that was the kicker, he'd hired a lawyer with what little she hadn't taken and had a D.N.A. It turned out he wasn't the father and after a match was run through the Tau Ceti database, Bob Sutton, his next-door neighbour and bowling buddy, was found to be the father!

8

Unfortunately he was on the birth certificate and according to his lawyer Allenby had to pay unless he contested it in court. Well, Allenby was all for contesting until the lawyer produced his fee. Allenby was skint, he couldn't afford that and if he didn't get a job soon he'd be locked up and sent to a forced labour camp for delinquent fathers, so he got out of Dodge.

As for Rick, his story wasn't nearly so dramatic, he was just a guy who'd drifted from place to place trying to find himself. He left school and hitched around the solar system staying under the radar until one day he got a job aboard the Sonnet. Its Captain took him under his wing, maybe he saw potential or maybe he just felt sorry for a hobo that needed a decent job to set him straight.

Rick began work on anything that didn't require fore knowledge of stripping. He made tea and coffee, cleaned the dishes, did all the odd jobs for what was a fair amount of pay. Since they often spent months alone in space Rick couldn't quit and move on as the mood took him. Time in space allowed Rick to contemplate life, where it was going and what he wanted to do with it. Rick hadn't noticed the years pass yet he learned every aspect of Sonnet and its business. He'd seen crewmen come and go yet he and Max remained.

After a few years Rick was on the tactical position, he doesn't remember the day he was promoted he just worked positions when needed and never got out of tactical.

When Max died he left the Sonnet to Rick, by that time he could run her in his sleep. Rick was unsure why Max left him Sonnet maybe he was the son Max never had and always wanted? Perhaps in a toss-up between Rick and the state he chose Rick?

But enough of the past, these three marched toward remnants of a habitation dome. Sam and Allenby carried small metal cases. Rick held a location device in his palm while all three bore pistols strapped to their waists, this was the wild west of the galaxy.

Its foundations remained, crooked glass jutting out to pierce ground. Inside burnt cinders blackened the sun choking its atmosphere, scorched earth crunched beneath their boots. A charred pyre of bodies filled the bottom of a pit created by a negz surgical strike. A tragic mauve flower resting on a bleak landscape.

Negz had outlawed Zaj Zavsar centuries ago, long before mankind reached another star. Its production punishable by death, commonly they landed troops gathered farmers and carried out executions but during war, time came at a premium. The premium being they couldn't be certain Earth Corps ships weren't waiting in hyperspace, ready to ambush while they meted out justice planet side. Instead they emerged from hyperspace hit their target and slipped away before Earth might respond. The colony was in tatters yet Rick felt no pity for they knew what they were doing and its consequences.

A voice called from its mauve mist, 'Who are you?'

'Traders,' replied Rick.

'What you trading?'

'Credits.'

'For what?'

'All the Zaj you got left.'

The fellow coughed, 'Follow me.'

Rick, Sam and Allenby pulled torches from their pockets. A thin man, handkerchief over his mouth and nose, squinted through burnt flakes of his former home. He beckoned and Rick followed to a set of steps leading underground.

Ten feet below colonists huddled together as cold chipped away their spirit and hunger gnawed their bones. They were a sorry sight, quite an irony since one hundred feet away Rick's torch fell upon a massive stash of Zaj Zavsar, worth a small fortune in human space.

'How much?'

A tall burly man with a Texan accent replied, '500 pounds o' prime split.'

'I'll take it.'

'What you tradin'?'

'Food, medical supplies, blankets, heaters.'

'Mother fuckin' strippers, tryin' to steal it all for a few food bars!'

'I could trade gold, and when you've all starved or frozen to death I'll come back for it.'

The tall Texan dressed in blackened work clothes spat on Rick's boot, 'Piece o' shit!'

'I've got that too.'

The Texan pulled out a shotgun, 'Maybe I'll just take your shit?'

Rick sat down on a nearby rock peering into the eyes of shivering women and children, 'It looks like I've been out smarted, what do you reckon?'

Allenby began to chuckle his protruding belly jiggled up and down in its flight suit, 'I bet he even remembered to load it!'

'What's so funny?' sneered the Texan, puzzled by their response to his threat.

'This ain't me first rodeo partner.'

'Listen boy, you hand over the supplies or I blow your mother fuckin' head off!'

'And after you've done that me crew'll gas these fucking tunnels with zyklon and take your Zaj.'

'How they gonna find us asshole?'

Rick looked up and sighed, 'Dyson you getting this?'

A voice came out of Rick's collar, 'I hear you Gov.'

The Texan looked up then back down at Rick, 'They don't know where we are.'

'2.18 by 22.47, ten feet below ground,' replied Dyson.

'Shit,' snapped the Texan.

'How much for the split?' stated Rick.

'We'll wait.'

'No-one's coming.'

'Bullshit.'

A baby screamed from the shadows, its mother removed her jumper wrapping the child in another layer. Trading her resistance to Boreas, the god of the winter wind, to keep the Keres, the fates of death, at bay from her child.

11

'I hope they arrive soon,' said Rick ascending from a cold rock, 'looks like this has been a blowout lads.'

The strippers made for steps leading out the tunnels when the Texan snapped, '100 pounds for a month's supplies and a distress beacon.'

'Four hundred pounds.'

'FUCK YOU!'

'I'll take the four hundred pounds thanks.'

'Two months supplies for one fifty.'

'I'll do three hundred pounds for two months supplies and I'll chuck in some holo-vids.'

'Fuckin' stripper I oughta shoot ya fuckin' face off.'

Rick moved close speaking in a hushed tone, 'You've got a lot of repressed anger. I'll throw in a Doctor Phil holo, the man's a fucking genius you know?'

Allenby sniggered in the shadows while the Texan's mind filled with smoke and fire.

Allenby returned to Sonnet the underside of her rear hull released on a hinge forming a cargo ramp. He moved inside to meet Graham, 'How are the locals?'

'A bunch of fucking muppets.'

'Tried to take Rick hostage?'

'Yup,' Allenby looked around the cargo hold. Supplies were stacked upon palettes, food, medicine, heaters and shelters. Similar supplies occupied half Sonnet's hold for they were the primary currency on stricken worlds, credits, gold and urillium were of little use but food and bandages changed hands at a high premium.

The hold was about the size of an Olympic swimming pool. Allenby pulled his frame into a forklift and loaded the correct quantity of supplies, carefully converting their weight to Earth measurements. Since not every planet is 1G a computer would make the proper calculations converting weight in their present environment to that of Earth.

He hit the tiny forklift into gear, trundling up a ramp into the cargo bay.

'I'll never forget that bloke who offered his wife for a chocolate bar,' laughed Graham.

'Yeh,' chuckled Allenby, 'that cow was rough as bear's arse. I nearly shit me-self when Rick handed it over out of pity!'

They both laughed as Graham checked Allenby's supplies were strapped down securely.

There's an old negz proverb: fools must be changed often or the entertainment wears thin. Well out here in the wild west of space there was never a shortage.

In the tunnels Sam examined their merchandise.

'Good?'

'Good enough,' replied Sam.

Rick turned toward the Texan, 'After we've taken off I'll transmit the co-ordinates of your supplies.'

'How do I know you ain't lying?'

'I always keep me word.'

He looked at his shivering wife and starving child then back at Rick, 'Fine.'

Rick addressed Sam, 'Load her up,' they moved toward the Zaj Zavsar.

Already tied into bundles they were easy to place inside large backpacks provided by colonist. Soon they carried 150 pounds each. Rick handed the Texan a communicator, 'You'll get a message in about an hour, don't miss it.'

Rick and Sam walked up the cargo ramp to meet Allenby, 'I got the split,' he passed Allenby his backpack as did Sam.

Allenby sat down in his forklift loaded with the colonists' supplies, 'I'll drop this lot off.'

'Just make sure it's outside Sonnet's blast radius.'

Allenby chuckled, his belly shifting in and out as he manoeuvred the small truck, 'That was pretty funny wasn't it?'

'Just don't do it again,' said Rick exiting Sonnet's cargo bay into an airlock. He paused for a decontamination scan before entering Sonnet's habitation area. Rick climbed a ladder into the ship's mid-section. To the left and right were exits leading to crew quarters and the galley, fore and aft were exits to control and engineering, on the floor beneath him a multi-purpose airlock. He and Sam spread alien dust throughout the mid-section while making their way to the cockpit. Rick sat down front and left. After letting out a huff he pulled a bent rollup from behind his ear. He placed it between his lips then raked through surrounding trash until he came across a book of matches. On the front the word "Shaniqua's" was etched in gold with the picture of a half-naked black woman. Rick remembered the good times he had there, the good times he always had there, until Dyson snapped him out of it, 'You'll be seeing her in a few days.'

Rick grinned, took out a match and lit his smoke. He was looking forward to spending his money but first he had to get off this crap hole and sell that split.

There were plenty of stations run by drug lords and slavers, most too risky for Sonnet. Docking wasn't a problem, undocking … now that was the question. There were several stripper stations but they wouldn't touch split. Drugs were way off their radar, super alloys, technology, metals, machinery and of course urillium being their business.

Smugglers were a good bet for selling split. Smugglers avoided violence and coercion yet if it weren't for violence and coercion they'd be out of work, pretty ironic when you think about it.

Half an hour later Rick heard Sonnet's cargo ramp heave and connect with the hull, fitting perfectly into place.

'Supplies delivered,' came Allenby's voice out of Rick's headset.

'Okay lads, let's blow this shithole,' said Rick tapping his console.

Sam took his seat at Rick's right, Dyson behind Sam on the wall console, 'Allenby, Graham?'

'Ready,' came their voices through his thin headset.

Rick sent the co-ordinates before hitting auto take off. Sonnet's mighty thrusters began to warm, her body quivered as tremors coursed her frame, each thruster like an instrument in an orchestra all out of tune then suddenly they found one another and blasted in concert. After ten seconds thrusters fired with enough pounds per square inch that upon peering through her forward screen Rick saw but a dusty dervish whirl about the ship.

He couldn't tell whether they were stationary until his gut shifted or his body moved leaving his gut to catch up, he wasn't sure.

Slowly inch by inch Sonnet roared skywards pushing with everything she possessed. Stanchions heaved, metal ground on metal as Sonnet struggled with gravity, the limited resources of man's creation fighting the unlimited resources of Mother Nature's will.

Rick couldn't tell how far they'd risen for he didn't look at readouts, it was one of his odd habits. Eventually dust diminished, able to pursue only so far into the atmosphere. Landing claws retracted while stanchions collapsed telescopically within Sonnet. Thrusters heaved as a woman giving birth, screeching with pain, pushing harder whilst trying to breath within an alien environment. Sonnet's engines kicked in pressing each man into his chair, thrusters subsided bequeathing main engines her rudder. Like a giant whale on Earth leaping from the ocean Sonnet punched forth from Sigma 9's atmosphere heading off the elliptical plane.

'Destination?' asked Dyson.

'Let's try Deneb.'

'Deneb?'

'What're you the ship's fucking parrot?'

'I hope you know what you're doing.'

'Have I ever let you down?'

Dyson didn't reply.

'We're going to Deneb unless you've got a better idea?'

'Deneb it is,' said Dyson as he sent co-ordinates to the jump drive.

Sam leant over and whispered, 'There's a lot of bad people in the Deneb system.'

'The Galaxy's full of bad people,' replied Rick, 'in fact there's a chronic oversupply of the bastards, something that sitting on a university campus being wanked off by a bunch of communist professors won't teach you.'

15

Sam moved back into his seat for he always felt naked under Rick's ruthless scrutiny, Dyson and Peters smiled.

Sonnet reached a safe distance above the system's elliptical plane before spooling up her jump drive. The amount of energy required to open a crack in space-time and enter the next dimension could be met only with urillium. Back in engineering Graham monitored his stations with eagle eyes as readouts sent information on the reactor core. Burn too much too quickly and she goes into melt down creating an explosion to put the largest thermo-nuclear device to shame.

In the past, when humans first employed urillium based technology, explosions had manifested rips in space-time resulting in micro black holes therefore jump gates were quickly constructed. Ships would pay a toll, reducing costs when entering hyperspace while system inhabitants drastically diminish the chance of a singularity tearing their planet apart.

The tokamak held atoms of urillium suspended in an electromagnetic field whilst they clashed with anti-matter particles. The energy produced powered a quantum field generator.

A quantum field isn't as complicated as it sounds it's a term used by engineers when they want a pay rise or shore leave. You tell your Captain there's trouble with the quantum generator, he asks: how much and how long?

The generator is a bunch of magnets creating a charge. Magnetic fields are an example of quantum mechanics, a massless wave that has a strong effect on the universe.

Quantum mechanics is a unique set of laws. Think of these laws as banking. Under classical laws you aren't permitted an overdraft but under quantum theory you're permitted not one but several overdrafts. What does that mean? It means that no longer does there have to be a positive deposit of particles but there can be a deficit instead.

For instance, instead of every employee having to turn up to work wearing the same uniform evenly spread amongst the work force, if you have a job with Quantum Bank you can turn up in uniform or butt naked … provided someone else in the company is wearing your uniform as well as his that day. The quantum generator doesn't generate or remove particles it shifts them about, like at Quantum Bank it moves uniforms from all the hot women and onto … well you know what I mean.

Graham moved axions, the fabric of space, to create a deficit, a deficit just big enough to slip Sonnet through.

An extremely powerful magnetic wave flooded Graham's target area decaying axions into photons, light particles, another quantum wave form. A long beam of light surrounded a crack in space. Inside the crack Rick made out the deep blue of hyperspace beckoning as the sea seduced mariners centuries ago on Earth.

'Got it,' said Dyson as he fixed on the crack.

'Let's blow this shithole,' replied Rick.

Sonnet moved in as fast as possible, she couldn't hang about since the cost of maintaining this portal to the next dimension was inordinate and urillium limited.

The ship slipped smoothly into hyperspace and the crack closed behind them. Dyson measured Mother Nature's push and pull for she occupied hyperspace too, unyielding, without pity or mercy. Many a sailor had lost his way in her great uncharted expanse before now.

'A week before we reach Deneb provided the weather doesn't change.'

'Let me know if anything happens.'

'You gonna spend some time with Shaniqua?' chuckled Dyson.

Rick stepped over a trash lain floor, 'Bloody right, I paid a fucking mint for that holo.'

Chapter Two

Gravity coerced minor subjects herding them within invisible pens, suns lords of each system, planet barons commanding satellites. Off the elliptical plane a grey construct of super alloy extracted tribute from travellers. One of the galaxy's many toll booths, this door to destiny empowered passage from system to system.

The gate's edge lit up, blinding light burst from its ring as axions decayed into photons. A rip in space-time consumed its grey crown with deep blue until Sonnet was unceremoniously spat into normal space. ID confirmed, Dyson transferred a fee, kinetic cannons dropped lock and the gate powered down. Deneb possesses fourteen planets, none habitable, one of which a gas giant with over fifty moons. On the third moon was situated Muon City, a place where men could make commerce without Earth Corps infringing their interests.

'Hey Rick!' shouted Dyson.

A groaning noise came from within Rick's cabin as the beast woke from a night of hard drinking and debauchery, well, holographic debauchery but what's a boy in hyperspace supposed to do?

'Rick get the fuck up!'

A cabin door opened to reveal Sonnet's oldest exhibit, Rick's beer belly. A hairy blob swayed back and forth as a demented farm animal. His flight suit dragged on metal floor teasing the crack of his backside to pop out. Rick possessed but two sets of clothing, he selected his daily attire based upon the least filthy.

The only time Rick wore a clean flight suit was if his current pair was so pock marked that tobacco embers burnt his skin, discomfort cajoling a fresh purchase. Then there was that time he caught his scrotum in a zip forcing Allenby to cut him free with salvage tools.

As for shirts and pants Rick kept one set in reserve for when they made dock and went on the hunt for women. He thought a clean shirt would deflect a woman's eyes from his belly and nose from body odour. This is why the crew spent so much time in strip bars, those girls' only concern was cash.

Rick stumbled from his quarters holding an amphora bottle of Metaxa 7 star, though little of the brandy remained. The stench of unwashed bed linen followed him like an old Egyptian curse. He staggered into the fore section past Dyson and broke wind, the cheeks of his buttocks slapped together as a seal's flippers. Dyson covered his nose while Rick took a swig on his bottle, 'Better out than in!' cackled the drunken Captain.

Sam and Peters didn't bat an eyelid for this was a common event during long hauls in hyperspace. To be fair most of the crew lived like pigs, reeking of body odour and beer, it's just that Rick had many years on them. No man could match his level of flatulence ... and trust me they'd tried.

Rick flopped into his flight chair, 'Fuck me, you know what that smells like?' There was no answer for he spoke rhetorically, 'That smells just like that chicken masala I had last night and you know what?'

Again, no answer given since Rick's rhetorical intent didn't require one.

'I bet that curry comes out me arse just like it went in! All yellow, sloppy with meaty chunks,' Rick cackled again.

'We're approaching Muon city,' stated Sam.

Rick reeled, 'Alright, you don't have to shout your fucking head off!'

'I didn't shout.'

'Oh,' Rick sloshed back the last of his metaxa, 'Ahhh, hair of the dog, that'll set me right.'

'I don't know why you drink so much considering the damage it does to every organ in the human body.'

'Who are you me mother?'

Dyson and Peters smiled in synchrony.

Sam went on, 'What if you were to have organ failure or alcohol poisoning in hyperspace?'

'I'd be fucked!' Rick released a burp transmitting the stench of last night's chicken masala to Sam's face.

Sam grimaced while the others laughed.

'Jesus Christ, imagine if you'd have been drafted. Those fucking neggs would've eaten you alive!'

'I doubt my Captain would've been a curry eating, cigarette smoking drunkard.'

Rick raised his leg and farted again *PAAAARRRPPP*, 'You mean a puffter?'

Sam turned to his console, this conversation had but a single destination, the gutter, 'We'll be arriving at Muon city in four hours.'

'Maybe when we get there you can finally get laid?'

Sam monitored his station while disregarding Rick's drunken jibes. Unlike Rick he was young and believed that without Earth Corps supervision civilised behaviour could not take place. When Rick pointed out thousands of years of civilization preceding Earth Corps Sam became frustrated much to the amusement of the crew.

Sam was a young man fresh out of university, the rest aged between their mid-thirties and mid-fifties. Sam just needed time to grow up and reach his age of reason yet they tormented him while he walked that path, what are friends for?

Sonnet drifted gracefully alongside an orbital dock which stretched for miles, paid for by the smuggler's guild, a gargantuan private venture. The plan was to build a ring around the moon in a similar vein to the Earth Ring but funds had fallen short. Two thirds of the ring unfinished, a mere skeleton, yet the guild pushed ahead for one day it would be complete. Until then they collected tariffs at the gate and took fees from guild members.

It might seem odd a smuggler would have a guild with fees but the guild protected its members providing free use of the gate and Muon's facilities. If you were a career smuggler membership worked to your benefit in the long term.

Sonnet moved close, engines silent, inertia coasting forward. One of many lengthy docking arms extended from the ring, aligned itself with three small ports on her side, clamps protruded from the arm and latched onto metal braces halting Sonnet in her tracks. Inside the crew shifted fore then aft, their mass slowing a second after Sonnet's. The arm guided Sonnet to an interior slip.

'Docking complete welcome to Muon City.' stated Sonnet's computer.

Rick dumped his empty bottle, zipped up his suit, lit a rollup from behind his ear and made for the airlock.

'You're not going aboard like that?' asked Sam.

'Why don't you come, you might learn something.'

An airlock stretched from Sonnet's hull through a docking claw into Muon city. Muon city didn't look much at first glance. In Sam's opinion it was little more than a glorified back alley with puddles of dank liquid and piles of trash. Men and women hung about muttering to one another in a stale yellow gloom. He noted a lack of any customs check on this station.

'This way,' said Rick leading his young friend.

'I've heard stories about this place, somehow I imagined it to be, well, grandiose.'

'What did you expect? A red carpet, trumpets and an interview with Rob Spanky?'

'No, but you have to admit it doesn't look like much.'

'It's not the place it's the people, remember that.'

Rick stepped off main street into an alley surrounded by broken metal plating, steaming hot pipes and greasy valves. Sam was worried he might be scorched at any point. Rick turned left pushing open a doorway, inside were several tables and chairs with a wall sofa on one side of the room. A bar stood on the right offering drinks of differing legality, the establishment went quiet for a moment.

'Do you have reservations?' asked a waiter dressed in black trousers, red waist coat, white shirt speaking with a fake French accent.

'Yeh, but I came anyway.'

'I see ... is there anyone you wish to speak with?'

'I'm looking for a guild representative.'

'You desire membership?'

'I'm here to trade.'

'You do not require a guild representative ...'

'I've got split.'

The room fell so silent you could hear a mouse fart.

'How much?'

'Three hundred pounds of Zaj Zavsar.'

'Please take a seat,' he motioned toward a walled off corner designed so men may conduct commerce in privacy.

Rick and Sam sat down, a waitress came to the table, 'Are you ready to order?'

'Metaxa.'

'I'm sorry?'

'Brandy.'

'Certainly, we have a range of Cognacs, Armagnacs ....'

'I'll take the cheapest.'

'Very good,' the young lady noted it down on her eye interface, 'and for the young man,' she smiled at Sam.

'I'll have a cranberry juice please.'

'I'll be right back,' grinned a plucky young waitress.

'You're in there,' whispered Rick.

Sam shook his head, embarrassed by Rick's behaviour, 'You've got no class you know that?'

After being served the pair waited another ten minutes before a business suit appeared, an odd look for a smuggler, polite pinstripe jacket, matching trousers, shiny black shoes and white shirt. He had short side parted hair and carried a leather briefcase. Sam eyed a gold pin on his lapel, a woman held a torch in one hand and pistol in the other, the mark of the smugglers guild.

'My name's Jerry, I represent the guild, you have some merchandise you need taking off your hands?'

'Three hundred pounds of Zaj Zavsar,' replied Rick with a stone cold face ... it was business time.

Jerry looked Sam up and down, 'What about him?'

22

'He's alright.'

'The fixed price for Zaj Zavsar, at least first grade and that's what I suppose we're talking about here?'

'Fresh.'

'I'm sure you won't mind the Guild clarifying that claim?'

'Certainly not.'

'Assuming it is first grade the fix today is three hundred and twenty seven credits a pound netting you seventy five thousand credits.'

Before Rick might respond Sam cut in, 'You mean ninety eight thousand credits.'

The representative, a man in his late twenties and slick as Sinatra on stage made an uncomfortable face accompanied by a nervous chuckle, 'Funny.'

'I wasn't being funny.'

Jerry looked at Rick, 'Are you sure he isn't Corps?'

'What's that supposed to mean?'

'This is Guild space if you don't like our fees go sell somewhere else … if you're feeling really lucky you can try the neggs.'

'Fees?'

Jerry scowled at Sam's naivety, 'Duty on illegal narcotics is ten percent then there's a transaction tariff.'

Sam replied in an incredulous tone, 'Fees and tariffs! You guys are no different than Earth Corps!'

'Sell THEM your split and see what happens.'

Rick put a hand on Sam's shoulder, 'Sorry about the kid it's his first time outside a Corps system.'

Jerry nodded his head, 'Do we have an agreement?'

Rick offered his hand and Jerry shook, 'Done.'

'Thank you Mr Katusa I'll have my people visit your vessel in half an hour, berth C 9 is it not?'

Rick nodded as Jerry picked up his briefcase and walked out the establishment.

'Katusa, he knows your surname name?'

23

'So?'

'How did he …'

'This ain't me first rodeo kid.'

On the Sonnet men in uniforms with the same gold pin stood around while Jerry inspected her cargo, 'Hmm, I'm afraid it's not all first grade.'

'I just got that off the colony!' protested Rick.

'Did you pick it yourself?'

'Well, no.'

'Exactly, I know Zaj like you know the back of your hand. Some of it's been spoiled see for yourself.'

Jerry stood aside as Rick peered into one of the small plastic crates, 'It looks fine to me.'

'Of course, but it's last year's crop. Desperate farmers mix spoilt and fresh to subsidise losses or pad profits. Either way, you've been stiffed Mr Katusa.'

'Is any of it …'

'I'll pay five thousand for top grade, you can keep the spoilt.'

'That cost me three grand in urillium!'

'Not my problem.'

'I'll take it.'

'Excellent.'

'And when I find that Texan cunt I'll make him pay, one way or another.'

Jerry waved his men on as they carefully moved crates under armed guard, 'A vendetta? I could get you a good discount on murder. Here, show him my card and we'll all be happy … besides the victim of course,' Jerry smiled business card extended between his fingers.

'I settle me own scores.'

'Well keep my card, if he has any Zaj tucked away you'll know where to get a fair deal.'

Rick took the card, 'Thanks.'

'Have a nice day,' Jerry followed his men out the cargo bay through an airlock and onto Muon city.

24

Sonnet's crew congregated around Rick, 'It looks like we're taking a pay cut. Three grand for urillium, a ton for thruster fuel another ton for food, water and oxygen it looks like you're getting 288 credits a piece.'

The crew became somewhat downcast for their takings had been drastically reduced. After costs and Rick's twenty percent were removed, net profit was divided amongst them. Yet 288 credits was a tidy sum considering the average working man on Earth might take home 50 credits a month.

Sonnet remained at Muon city monitoring news reports from the galactic front. A single engagement might easily net the crew a year's pay for the average Earth worker, fortunately the war provided more than enough to go around. It could be dangerous of course, unexploded mines, fuel tank detonations but Earth Corps needed super alloys to manufacture more ships, demand by far outweighed supply. Certain parts went for quite a price since the Corps fleet was either in battle or repair dock.

Strippers were generally looked down upon, parasites of dignity as the negz described them, for wherever fallen warriors could be found strippers were present. Thieves and scum rummaging through a noblemen's corpse after a medieval battle, stripping the honourable of dignity for auction. As far as Rick was concerned these "noblemen" were dead and wouldn't be missing anything he took.

Earth Corps treated his kind as a necessary evil for without them Earth had no means to replace and rebuild ships. In turn Rick viewed Earth Corps as a bunch of hired killers no doubt responsible for this war. But whatever the reason for this shit storm Earth Corps was desperate.

News reports amounted to propaganda describing an embattled enemy on the back foot … but Rick saw it first-hand.

In the initial months he got a lot of work stripping negz merchant vessels even a few civilian stations, then it turned the other way. He hadn't stripped a negz vessel in more than a year but Earth Corps ships came thick and fast. The news didn't report battles he'd witnessed with his own eyes, Corps destroyers and cruisers floating in space, wrecks abandoned to Mother

Nature's mercy. Meanwhile demand for alloy, parts and supplies rocketed. In the last year the men of Sonnet had made enough to retire.

Sam was concerned by the course of the war. Rick attempted to enlighten him on the virtue of selfishness but Sam was an idealist. One of a generation of young bright-eyed boys who left university in search of utopia, convinced he'd make it happen not just for him but everyone else. What Sam failed to realise, as all young men do, is that utopia can only be reached over a sea of blood … and you never get there. For to reach utopia's shores one must compromise sooner or later, certain people removed from the equation in order to get the balance correct. One day you stop and look back to witness a trail of misery and death then you look forward and utopia's sandy shores are no closer.

One day Sam would understand the truth, he'd reach the age of reason, hopefully before he got hurt.

A psychedelic band played on a nightclub stage.

"I must be going insane,
I called the doctor so he can relieve my pain,
He's got a pill for me,
Just a little luxury,
Help me through my day, yeh."

Rick nursed a drink, alone at his barstool hoping for a lady's smile or maybe a call from Dyson, either way he'd have something to do other than get drunk. He looked around the gloom to witness people talking to one another, even on this dump companionship existed, men and women taking warmth in one another's proximity.

Rick had thought of starting a family, that fantasy lasted about two and a half minutes. The legal channel had a divorce court, it was about as bitter as two people could get and he wasn't going to risk it since the guy usually met financial annihilation at the hands of her lawyers, under Corps jurisdiction anyway.

26

No, he didn't have time for that bullshit, besides he was living the dream, get up when you want, wash your clothes when you want, no need to tidy up, eat what you like when you like and go out with your mates as you please.

In reality the dream had worn thin a long time ago, he lived like an animal indulging in booze and empty sex with prostitutes. Sure, most married men were green with envy despite repeatedly denying it for fear of a whipping. But they hadn't spent years drifting bar to bar only to hear the same barren words roll off every woman's lips.

Well, he still had booze, she never lied to him, always made him feel better, usually, and best of all she was cheap. Her name was Metaxa, a smooth Greek brandy made from a muscat wine he'd discovered as a child, hidden in his grandmother's drinks closet. Her initial chemical bite was balanced with a smooth musky finish, if he sought comfort she was always there.

Fuck the world, fuck Earth Corps, fuck the negg-heads and fuck the universe, all he needed was a good drink and everything fell into place … until he fell unconscious.

'Wanna buy me a drink sailor?' came a soft female voice.

Rick turned to his right, an attractive lady about twenty years his junior in a tight black mini dress with a plume of spiked blonde hair and far too much make up greeted him.

'I was just leaving.'

Her smile disappeared as she moved off, 'Asshole.'

The barman furrowed his brow, 'Dude! She wanted it!'

Rick polished off his shot, 'She wanted a man twice her age that hasn't worn a clean pair of underpants in two months or she saw a wallet?'

'Who gives a shit? Pussy's pussy, right?'

Rick climbed off his bar stool, 'See you later kid.'

The next day Rick slid out a trash laden stink hole filled with pre-cooked curry wrappers and more grease than half Sonnet's engineering section.

Reaching out for his bottle he found it empty and threw it into a trash compacter on the wall. Its noisy crushers ground the glass ending in a deep burp as shattered glass slid down into Sonnet's waste tank.

He moved onto a chair beside his bedroom table, last night's holo played on a loop. Golden beads covered her interesting parts as she cavorted before his bleary eyes.

Rick switched it off, 'Not now Shaniqua.'

He searched trash clumped upon his small cabin table until he found a half-eaten ration bar. He bit in and chewed, the bar was stale, probably a few weeks old, he spat it onto the floor tossing the rest into the compactor.

He wore nothing but his favourite pair of boxer shorts, they'd been with him through thick and thin, in more ways than one. His hairy gut hung over its ragged waist band buddha style. A testimony to late night curries and hard drinking sessions.

A foul stench of decaying food, unwashed sheets and stale tobacco permeated everything inhabiting his pestilential cabin. Though he couldn't detect an odour he was aware of it through third parties. Rick looked around, eventually his eyes focused and he stood up.

Rick shuffled to the wall and slapped a slightly raised area, a large section of grey wall spun around to reveal a toilet. Rick dropped his boxers, flopped on the toilet then reached into a nearby hand basin. The basin served as a giant ash tray where Rick stored half done smokes and matches so he could have his first smoke of the day, accompanying his first bowel movement.

Rick gathered dog ends from the ashtray slicing them open with his yellow fingernails as a master surgeon, releasing their innards into a cigarette rolling paper. After creating a rollup by exhuming corpses of those long dead he struck a match and pulled on its stale air, after a few puffs he discarded the match and book. Thirty minutes later he'd done his business dug out a flight suit and a pair of work boots. A stench preceded him down the hallway to the lounge area.

'What's for breakfast me hearties?' stated Rick in his comedy pirate accent.

Graham, Peters and Sam were eating out of plastic trays at the dining table.

'Vegetarian omelette,' stated Graham in an underwhelming tone.

Graham was bald as a coot with a bushy beard, Rick joked God had his head upside down. Graham believed God had a lot of things upside down. He'd long prepared a list for when he reached the pearly gates. Graham was a technical guy, lists being one of his obsessions, probably drove his wife nuts. She was happy to see him working as a stripper while raising their kids on Centauri. He sent back enough to put them through a good school and live in a very nice district. He spoke often about her upper middle class neighbours looking down on his kids. Graham despised them since he worked hard for a living unlike those stinking bureaucrats.

'Vegetarian omelette? I need to replace body mass, sharpish!'

'Why's that?'

'I just had a two pound baby!'

Graham and Peters laughed. Sam put his plastic fork down, in all these years he still hadn't adjusted to the banter.

The crew laughed at Sam.

'What's up Sam not getting your five a day?'

They laughed again. Rick pulled a tray from the wall dispenser. He peeled back its cover, as oxygen entered the vacuum-packed meal it reacted with chemicals cooking its contents instantly. He sat at the table and grabbed a fork and spoon from its centre tray, 'I'll have to buy some of those vegan fibre cubes, you know, the ones that go in like rubber then bounce out your arse into the fucking bog!'

The crew laughed as they tucked into their meals.

'I'm thinking of leaving,' stated Sam rather sheepishly.

'Leaving what?'

'Sonnet.'

'Why's that?'

'I'm joining Earth Corps.'

Everyone fell silent, except Rick, 'You're kidding.'

'I've already contacted them, they'll overlook my absence, I can sign up the moment I get back.'

'Sign up for what?'

'Lieutenant second class on the Crusader. I just wanted to let you know first.'

'Don't piss your life away man.'

'I've been thinking about this for a while and the way the war's going ...'

'Exactly! Earth Corps' getting mashed.'

'Maybe I can make a difference.'

'How?'

'I don't know ...'

'Wonderful plan! Sign up on a glorified coffin and get your arse vapourised up by a bunch of religious maniacs!'

'Well it beats picking their corpses like a parasite!'

Rick stood up, 'Is that what you think I am?'

'I didn't mean it like that.'

Rick walked out of the lounge, breakfast untouched.

Rick settled down up front, lit a smoke and started reading one of many gentleman's magazines resting on the dashboard. Sam entered a few minutes later, 'Sorry about what I said.'

'You'll be even sorrier when you see a negg warship tearing you and your mates apart.'

'I've got family on Earth, for the last year or so every battle's been getting closer to the core. It's only a matter of time before they take out Luyten's then Procyon and in a year they'll be in striking distance of Earth.'

'All the more reason to keep out the firing line.'

'What about my family?'

'You must have saved enough.'

'They refused to leave.'

'Why?'

'Earth Corps propaganda, they think we're winning the war.'

'That's too bad but I don't see why you have to die with them?'

'Maybe I can do something.'

'Listen kid, one more Lieutenant on one of them destroyers won't change this war. Stay here, when it's all over we can find your family and help them out.'

'I'm sorry but I've made my mind up.'

Rick shook his head, 'When you thought we were kicking their arses you refused to fight now you know the truth you're joining up. If anything you're consistent, consistently fucking stupid!'

'If more people were willing to make a sacrifice maybe we could change things.'

Rick turned on his chair to face the young lad, 'It wouldn't matter if every idealistic fool joined up tomorrow those beam weapons wouldn't notice the difference.'

'We just need to outsmart them.'

Rick turned back toward the forward screen, 'I'm using my superior cunning by not putting meself in front of a negg energy beam. I suggest you do the same.'

'If everyone thought like that they'd have wiped us out long before now.'

'No kid, if everyone thought like that this whole shit storm would never have started in the first place!'

Dyson's station emitted a bleeping noise.

'Get that will you?'

Sam walked over and tapped away, 'There's been an engagement … system … Luyten's.'

Rick dropped his magazine and sat up with pricked ears, 'Details?'

'Two fleets orbiting the second planet, nothing more.'

'We've got a military outpost in that system.'

'And a civilian colony on the second planet.'

'Do it,' Rick hit the alert and the crew rushed into place, 'Dyson get us off this station.'

Dyson tapped away, a cave opened and Muon's lengthy arm projected Sonnet outside into space, seconds later docking claws creaked detaching from her hull.

'Set a course for Luyten's.'

Sonnet slipped away from Muon City to the back drop of Deneb's powerful star, so powerful it'd vapourised anything closer than a Martian orbit. They made their way above the elliptical plane. Dyson sent co-ordinates and the proper fees. Once within range the grey circle came to life pumping raw energy in the form of magnetic waves concentrated on a single area. Axion particles absorbed magnetic waves from the gate decaying into photons. Absence of axions created a deficit in the fabric of normal space-time. This deficit became obvious as a bright light formed, the cockpit screen dimmed yet light flooded the four men inside revealing the fifth dimension's deep blue ocean ... hyperspace.

'Hold onto your wage packets,' said Rick as Sonnet fired all engines to sail the torrents to Luyten's star thousands of light years away.

During the following week in hyperspace Rick tried to persuade Sam against his own idealism but Sam was adamant. He was going to join Earth Corps in the great crusade against Hemzih Negz for now they threatened those systems which fell directly within Earth Corps jurisdiction ... literally the core. Every system for 15 light years, Earth Corps laws, Earth Corps taxes and Earth Corps warships. Including Sol it totalled 24 systems, a sizeable powerbase by any standards.

After the brachian invasion mankind went on the defensive building not only the Ring but the mightiest war fleet with whatever they could scratch together. Earth assumed all xenos to be hostile and took no chances. Once the fleet was ready policy turned pre-emptive and so the empire's base was set ... in the blood of aliens. Many were weak, primitive, at least a century behind in development. When Earth's main carrier group punched out of hyperspace into their home system xenos trembled before mankind's mighty armada.

Previously, cold fusion technology powered the smallest frigate to the mightiest carrier in Earth Corps' navy. Earth Corps employed their superior might taking what they wished by force, taxing their subjects in urillium, for Sol is almost devoid of the stuff.

Ten more years and urillium reactors increased efficiency leaving expanded room for armaments. Fuel was easily stored and strike range improved by a factor of one thousand. The urillium age was upon mankind forcing the brachian conflict to a speedy conclusion ... then they met the negz. A tale no more pertinent to Earth Corps than the people of Atlantis. A decrepit civilization from a star so distant they were irrelevant or so it was believed. Their culture and language were little more than a subject for study and debate by scholars.

Earth Corps soon realised negz were neither decrepit nor irrelevant and certainly not subservient. They didn't cower before the warships of Earth Corps as civilizations before them. These creatures appeared as legend described, legends men and women of Earth blinded by greed had scoffed at as fantasy.

In the three years since this war commenced Earth's outer worlds had been broken. Renouncing their allegiance to Earth Corps in the face of merciless destruction, punished by a silent enemy for negz refused all communication. As conquistadors appeared, destroyers of men from the mist, pillaged and enslaved, so negz ravaged humanity. Humanity resisted as best it could yet they were out matched in the same way conquistadors outmatched the Inca. Emissaries from god, brandishing weaponry far in advance, riding atop majestic beasts to send their people away in iron ropes.

Outer worlds fallen, Earth Corps stood alone. Only the core systems remained untouched ... until today. Luyten's star had been hit and Rick was pretty sure who'd won.

Earth Corps rail cannons fired super alloy shells with thermo-nuclear warheads travelling at 10,000 miles a second, sure that sounds fast but in space you've got a long wait until it hits, enough time for the negz to destroy it with a beam weapon. Earth ships have to get in close before firing a broadside, close enough to hit but without vapourising themselves. In the time it takes to close that distance negz have usually devastated an Earth Corps cruiser with beam weapons.

Negz beams deliver a blast of concentrated radiation similar to a nuclear blast but at the speed of light ... that's 186,000 miles per second. It doesn't take an Einstein to work out which side is left floating in space, carrion for the strippers. How they do it is unknown. A practical defence has not been proposed yet they appear in winged golden ships and lay waste to their foe before slipping away.

Earth Corps tells its population all kinds of stories to prevent a mass panic. Better to remain calm and carry on just up until the moment a negz cruiser turns you and your family into a radioactive pit.

Everyone aboard the Sonnet understood Earth's fate, they, like many, had made preparations to survive the storm until the negz return from whence they came. Sam wasn't into that, he thought he could do something, he believed he could make a difference.

Chapter Three

Luyten's jump gate didn't respond, on entering the system Sonnet's crew quickly discovered why. One after another Peters' scanners picked up radiation sources, negz jumped in with four ships and out with three … perhaps Earth Corps had given them a bloody nose? Was a negz vessel out there amongst the debris? Further scans revealed radiation sources grouped together as animals herded into a pen and slaughtered. Rick urged Peters to start a wide search as Dyson moved toward the battlefield alongside a swarm of strippers, there'd be plenty for all.

According to Peters at least fourteen ships drifted before them. He identified the juicy parts and Dyson descended. Allenby snatched pieces of molten alloy and hauled them into Sonnet's cargo bay. Just as the Keres float above a battlefield tearing out dying men's hearts, feasting upon their innards, so Sonnet and her sisters did feed upon the fallen, sending their scorched souls to Hades.

While Allenby worked Peters scanned for the negz ship, it had to be amongst Earth Corps' dead for they could only destroy a negz vessel at close quarters with nuclear warheads.

Allenby fired grappling hooks each one employed a graviton wave to gain hold before carbon nanotube took tension, yanking its metal lump inside. Sonnet's belly open, slag stacked starting on the roof then down. Six salvage harpoons were housed around her bay opening, their ports unlocked as a tulip flower on a hot spring day. Strippers filled the system for Earth Corps purchased this alloy at a high premium, so much as to tempt alien traders. Merchant centres became quite diverse, xenos redirecting produce to trade for both precious and energy metals.

'Got it,' said Peters as he punched up co-ordinates.

Dyson narrowed his eyes, 'it's in a decaying orbit of Luyten's two.'

Rick made some quick calculations in his head, 'Set course,' he tapped his console and spoke into his collar mic, 'Allenby we're moving, finish up asap.'

'Will do.'

Bay doors closed, Allenby took a while to secure slag in zero G before they were ready to move. Sonnet's crew restrained themselves as engines pushed out the debris field toward a large planetoid. Her fusion engine fired onto a blast plate while a magnetic field warped space. Graham manipulated the field to decay a small number of axions, not enough to open a jump point but enough to lower the density of space-time and suck Sonnet forward. The force of her fusion engines aft and lack of space fore caused the vessel to travel at speeds approaching a quarter the speed of light. In simple terms it would take the Sonnet just over half an hour at full speed to travel between the Earth and the Sun, a velocity undreamt of one hundred years ago.

Sonnet's crew secured themselves with chest braces. Sure they had artificial gravity but who wants to risk even a momentary failure? You could end up as little more than a smear on the wall and it's not like it hadn't happened to spacefarers in the past. Trash and litter within Sonnet's cockpit served as a canary in the coal mine. Too often Rick witnessed an old chicken curry fly off the dash to decorate the rear wall in a Jackson Pollock. That time he got his own dirty ashtray in the face came to mind. Sam laughed, something about poetic justice.

They approached the second planet, an orb camouflaged in yellow clouds of ammonia, clearly uninhabitable. Deceleration kicked in, just as dangerous as acceleration. The field was reversed creating pressure fore while retro-thrusters burnt fuel. Sonnet creaked and heaved as she quarrelled with forces conspiring to tear her apart.

Rick looked up and tapped the dashboard, 'Hold together baby.'

Sam shouted over grinding of metal, 'What was that?'

'Nothing, nothing at all.'

Dyson used the planet's atmosphere in a braking manoeuvre until finally a burnt and battered warship appeared. A golden craft shone in all directions, a mighty eagle with wings unfurled soaring the thermals of space, she was beautiful, a masterpiece of design. Fires fuelled by leaking oxygen burst her skin. Craters where kinetic shells penetrated her hull smouldered. Scorches, no doubt from thermo-nuclear warheads, tainted golden skin.

Rick grinned, 'We've struck gold gentlemen!'

Sam looked concerned, 'What if there's people aboard, I mean negz?'

'There ain't neggs on that ship.'

'How do you know?'

'They'd have flown it straight into that planet by now. No, she got here on auto waiting for someone to take the reigns,' he turned to Sam, 'and that someone would be you.'

Sonnet approached a golden hawk, drawing its last breaths before a yellow abyss swallowed her whole. There was just enough time for Rick to get aboard and rummage around. Technology was what he'd search for, information held inside enemy data banks. Whilst Allenby searched her cargo Graham would haul his butt to engineering.

Sonnet touched the golden skin of what Rick supposed to be a frigate. Sonnet's mid-section possessed welding beams installed for one purpose alone, to slice outer hull.

'How long?' asked Rick.

'I don't know how thick those negg-heads built this thing, maybe an hour?' replied Allenby.

'When does it burn up?'

'I give it a day maybe less,' replied Dyson.

'All we've got to do is get there first,' said Rick referring to his fellow strippers.

Those boarding got ready as Sonnet's nanotube airlock forced back negz hull with a burst of high pressure.

'Atmosphere breathable,' said Peters as he analysed data from a nano-probe.

The boarding party were dressed in grey flight suits, except Rick, blue was Max's colour, a tradition he extended.

Negz atmosphere, pressure and gravity, were interchangeable with that of humans, you could walk from one to the other without noticing. However, they were boarding a damaged enemy ship so they carried breather masks, all manner of chemicals might be present and the negz had probably placed a few booby traps for Earth Corps troops.

Each crewman brought a pistol and a small metal work case stocked with tools pertaining to its owner's profession. Four men stood over the airlock looking down. Rick turned its hatch revealing the hawk's innards. They looked directly down onto a floor littered with ash and a slice of metal about seven feet in radius. Rick handed his case to Sam, sat on a cold slag rim then dropped eight feet onto the floor.

He looked around, the corridor was empty, walls, floor and ceiling bathed in flickering soft blue that upon examination relaxed his mind.

'Is it okay?' asked Sam.

Rick broke from his momentary trance, 'Yeh, looks clear, come on down.' Sam chucked cases down one by one before the crew joined Rick. The last man down attached a rope ladder constructed from nanotube and steel. Allenby walked down the ladder. Why didn't they do this in the first place you ask? It's not a good idea to get caught by an enemy ambush whilst swinging on a rope ladder. It makes you an easy target, any attempt at retaliation would be fruitless.

'Ok lads let's split up and get this job done. Anyone needs assistance give Sam a bell he can read this gibberish,' Rick observed negz script adorning a nearby wall, it reminded him of Chinese or Japanese. Ah, it was all the same to Rick. Bunches of weird characters, he couldn't remember if they went left to right, right to left, up to down or down to up. He'd tried to learn it in the past but found metaxa a far more agreeable subject.

Rick and Sam ploughed toward the fore section while Allenby and Graham went aft. As they progressed through the hawk's guts Sam pointed left, without aid of a translator he navigated the ship. A translator had a 50/50 chance of getting it right but Sam was dead on every time.

'Rick ... it's the Black Dog,' came Peters' voice over a collar communicator.

'Put him on.'

A strong New York accent followed, 'Rick that you?'

'Yeh it's me.'

'You gonna leave some shit for me?'

'I didn't know I was running a charity for Centauri hookers.'

The voice laughed, 'Come on, even hookers gotta eat!'

'I guess they'll have to do with brachian cock.'

'You saving it all for Shaniqua?' the sound of men laughing filled the background.

'Your artificial getting jealous?'

Another round of laughs hit the collar, 'Come on Rick, I need the cash.'

'There's plenty in the field.'

'I got debts. They're gonna take my ship the next time I dock in Corps space, or worse.'

'You know the rules Vince.'

'Come on, gimme a break will ya?'

Rick pinched his collar turning Vince off and flicking back to Peters, 'If he tries again, block him.'

'Done,' replied Peters.

'He sounded desperate,' said Sam as they travelled light blue corridors, flickering in an irregular manner.

'Yeh well I'm not responsible for him or his ship. I've got me own crew to worry about.'

'I guess so.'

'You've got to stop feeling responsible for others lad.'

'It isn't that easy. I mean what happens if Earth Corps confiscates his ship?'

'Those hookers on Centauri will have to find another mark.'

'I'm serious.'

'So am I. He spends his cash on whores and booze.'

'Sounds familiar.'

'Let's just find the control room?'

They turned another corridor, bodies lay strewn beneath a broken falconine. The pair put on masks as a safety precaution. Rick considered the scene: her crew must have abandoned ship and if they'd abandoned ship they might have set a self-destruct. That meant the reactor core's magnetic field was collapsing.

'Graham have you taken a look at their core?'

'Yup.'

'How's the magnetic field?'

'Field's fine, core's functional.'

'Thanks.'

Rick scratched his head.

'What's wrong,' asked Sam.

'There's not enough dead to account for the crew, so why'd they abandon ship?'

'Maybe Earth Corps forced them to flee?'

Rick scoffed at the notion, 'And if pigs had wings I'd have a ten foot todger!'

Sam hotwired a pad unlocking her control room hatch, it was like nothing they'd seen before, sure they'd boarded negz ships but never a warship. A ring of stations encircled a dais measuring about 25 feet in diameter, raised three feet above her main floor. Its purpose was not obvious to Rick, he pointed Sam toward work stations, 'Recover what you can and bag it.'

Sam moved toward a ring of orbiting consoles, he attempted to log in until he found one that was operational. He placed his case on top pulled out some wires and hooked up.

A moment later an area above the dais flickered, Rick jumped back drawing his pistol. It flickered again, this time the holographic image remained, Rick observed space just outside. He could see the Black Dog burning a hole in the frigate's golden hull. There was Sonnet sitting tightly on the hawk's body as a chick transported by its mother.

Rick holstered his weapon, 'You scared the living shite out of me.'

'Sorry, I've never accessed a warship before.'

'Can you do it?'

'Ask me in ten minutes.'

Rick nodded his head as he scrutinized stations, 'Nice set up they've got here. I bet Earth Corps would give a fortune for one of these.'

'We could ...'

'Forget it kid we're strippers, take what we can and leave. I'm not getting involved in all that red tape bollocks.'

'I'm in, it looks like the magnetic field was breeched after they took a hit aft. I've got a log of the battle. I can replay it in quick time.'

'Do it,' said Rick before images mutated above the dais.

As Rick had suspected negz jumped into the system and let rip while Earth Corps closed distance. They destroyed the gate and a station covering it, picking off system defences before finishing Earth's fleet. Earth Corps got lucky, one destroyer managed to close distance and fire a broadside. They didn't make a direct hit but their thermo-nuclear warheads detonated and an ensuing EMP wave scrambled this ship's magnetic field exposing its power core. Rick chuckled at the thought of those self-satisfied negg-heads scrambling for life pods like chickens with their heads cut off.

They abandoned ship and set it on auto pilot before life pods were picked up and remaining vessels slipped into the deep blue of hyperspace. Fortunately for Rick the computer managed to stabilize its field before a core breech. Now she waited in orbit for her crew to return and ... wait.

'Sam, is this ship emitting a beacon?'

Sam typed away then observed his console's readout, 'Yes, how did you ...'

'Shut it off, NOW!'

Sam's fingers scrambled across his console, 'Done.'

Rick hadn't boarded a negz warship before but he'd been a Captain for many years. It wasn't a stretch to place himself in a negz Captain's boots.

Rick played the fool during downtime but when he was on the job clean and precise execution was order of the day. That's why Sam and his crewmates always deferred to their Captain when under pressure. For at times such as

41

these he bore responsibility with the grace of Atlas and issued commands with confidence becoming Caesar.

'Pop everything you can. We've got to get as far away from this ship as possible.'

'Rick, I hit the motherload seventy pounds of urillium!' Allenby transmitted with joy.

Rick replied into his collar, 'Get it aboard, asap.'

'Will do.'

'Graham, how's it looking?'

'She's in a state but her parts are marketable.'

'How good?'

'Coils 500 apiece and there's ten I can see right now. Her jump drive's burnt out but the emitter's in order, that's a grand. I'd say you're looking at five grand possible ten if you give me time.'

'Well get stripping, Vince'll be here in an hour.'

'Understood.'

Rick searched nearby cabins while Sam cracked the main computer code. He entered what he suspected to be the Captain's cabin. Inside was an orderly room with little decoration. A simple bed, set within a wall, it offered an eerie resemblance to Rick's cabin minus the trash. On the right stood something like a shower, when turned on it blasted his blue flight suit with grit.

He stepped out to observe a chest of draws, on top a religious icon shone, an effigy not of a negz, well maybe a hideously deformed negz. Instead of sloping backwards at an angle its head ran straight up, vertically. Its forehead stretched to form two large nodules of wrinkled skin, perhaps they were lobes? The idol's intricacy fascinated Rick, its eyes sparkled, diamonds reflecting golden metal. It sat on a chair, robes covering its body, its long fingers poking beyond cuffs, like its face they looked old and haggard. Was this their God?

People defined negz as religious nut jobs yet no record of any God or method of worship existed. Humans possessed such little knowledge of these creatures they filled its vacuum with prejudice.

Parallel on each side of the idol rested incense sticks, it was obvious to Rick that whomever lived here worshiped this idol. Rick took the idol, about twelve inches tall and seven wide of pure gold, it was very heavy, placing it inside his backpack.

Next Rick opened draws to find garments neatly folded. He discovered a negz soldier's uniform, functional black and grey pull on jumpers, no buttons or collars. Similar trousers, black and grey, pulled on, no pee hole or belt loops they clung to their owner's powder blue skin. Black gloves that sucked onto hands and a tunic, when buttoned, squeezed its owners frame by design. The interesting part was a tail sweeping the rear to cover a man's buttocks and thighs, this tunic was out of whack with the ethos of its compatriots and so drew special attention. Rick stroked its fabric with the palm of his hand, its pliability mimicked velvet. He pulled the tunic from its draw, his finger travelled the peaks and valleys of its embossed design, this would've taken weeks to tailor if not longer. Patterned by mythical creatures or perhaps they existed on their home world? A mighty bear enveloped one side to skirt its right hem line, a bird of prey with fire leaping from its eyes faced off on the left. He flipped it over and the idol's façade spanned the rear shoulder blades warding off approaching enemies just as the eyes of Phobos would encompass a Spartan warrior's shield.

Rick took an instant liking to the tunic so much so he stuffed it in his backpack. As he went to riffle through remaining draws he heard Sam, 'Hey Rick.'

Rick followed Sam's voice into the control room, there he stood, injured negz behind clasping a staff, its centre piece indented Sam's neck. All negz soldiers were trained in the staff, that blue skinned crazy could snap Sam's neck anytime he wanted.

'Teevelekh!' shouted the tall creature its light blue skin stained with crimson blood.

'What's it saying?'

'TEEVELEKH KUMUN!'

Sam struggled to speak as a leathered handle throttled his voice, 'He wants transport.'

'To where?'

'Khaan bain ve?'

The creature had a puzzled look for Sam's negz wasn't word perfect but it beat Rick's. In fact, it beat pretty much any human not already drafted into Earth Corps.

'Teevelekh dulle.'

'He wants a ship with a jump drive.'

'Let the lad go and we can negotiate.'

'Selun Xurija.'

The negz sneered at Rick.

'I don't think he's interested.'

'What happened to your shooter?'

'I didn't bring it.'

Rick un-holstered his Walther P-38 took aim to the right of Sam's head and fired. Rick's bullet hit the conquistador's tough skull blasting its brains out the soft rear. Particles of wine red matter spattered white wall to form an interesting piece worthy of consideration by London's finest art critics.

Whilst holstering his pistol, Rick stated in a dead pan tone, 'Vorsprung durch technik ... as they say in Germany.'

Sam was rooted to the spot for a few seconds before he looked behind and jumped at the sight. The creature's eyes, inset within armoured pits, an unmistakeably negz trait, were devoid of life.

'Next time bring a shooter.'

Sam moved quietly to his station, bypassing system blocks he continued his task.

'Allenby, you there?'

'What's up Gov?'

'Keep a look out some of the crew might still be here, pass it onto Graham.'

'You alright?'
'No problems.'

By the time Vince and his crew were aboard Rick's were leaving. The
American made his way to control, 'How's it hangin'?' this time Rick jumped
'Wonderful and you?'
'You know me just takin' it easy,' his eyes were seized by a bloody smear on
the wall leading down to a slumped corpse, 'Trouble?'
'Nothing I couldn't handle.'
'He go down easy?'
'Do they ever?'
Vince snorted, 'I guess not.'
Vince flew the Black Dog, he used to joke he'd christened her in honour of
Shaniqua. Vince took great pleasure in getting Rick's hackles up whenever the
opportunity arose but this wasn't one of them. Vince had a crew just the
same as Rick and high hopes for this derelict Frigate. One good find might
cover costs for an entire year, perhaps longer. Unfortunately, Rick had made
the scene first and stripped her best parts, it was going to be tough locating
his Eldorado.
'Found much?'
'Nah, we're just leaving.'
'Come on Rick!'
'Who am I your fucking mother?'
'Then point me in the right direction.'
Rick rubbed his stubbly chin, 'The crew abandoned ship in a hurry check the
cabins you might find some nice gear.'
'Come on dude, I can't feed my crew on trinkets!'
'We haven't checked the entire hold there must be some replacement parts.'
Vince turned to one of the three men behind him, 'You and Jack search that
hold asap, we don't have long.'
They nodded and dashed for the hold.

Vince turned back to Rick, ran his fingers through a greasy mullet and sighed, 'Thanks dude.'

'You've not found anything yet.'

'I will, I have to dude.'

'Are you really in debt?'

'Yeh and those assholes are gonna take everything I've got if I don't pay soon.'

'How the fuck did you manage that?'

'Casino on Proxima, cock sucking brachians took me for a ride. I put a lien against my ship and ... ah It was years ago. I thought they'd forgot until I get a message from a buddy in the bounty hunters guild, I'm a wanted man.'

Rick's face contorted as water spiralling a drain, forcing out an incredulous tone, 'Are you out your fucking head?'

'At the time yeh, I was doing split and ...'

Rick shook his head, 'Fuck me you know what that crap does to people.'

'Yeh well you know me always thinking I can beat the odds.'

'Did you?'

'I woke up with a bill for fifty big ones, pay or lose the Dog and I ain't giving up the Dog.'

Data crystals popped up one by one. Sam walked around collecting small one inch pieces of carbon. Vince and his remaining crewman glanced over Rick's shoulder at a multi-coloured array of pure cash, he fixed his eyes on Rick and strained, 'Come on.'

'I've got a crew to feed.'

In a hushed tone only Rick perceived, he pled, 'Please dude.'

Rick called over his shoulder to Sam, 'How much will those crystals bring?'

'It depends on the content, the command crystals will get a good price, I reckon navigation will bring at least ten.'

'Give me the navigation crystals.'

'But ...'

'Don't argue just hand them over.'

Sam opened his case and placed ten or so one inch green memory crystals into Rick's grasp.

Rick took Vince's forearm and dumped them into his palm, 'You owe me one.'

Vince nodded his head, 'I'll pay you back.'

'Just make sure those Corps shits don't get the Dog.'

Vince smiled, 'I never knew you cared.'

On the way back to Sonnet Sam interrogated Rick, 'How come you gave him those crystals?'

'He needed them more than me.'

Sam had a puzzled expression as they cruised carbon scorched corridors, 'But you're always saying look out for yourself.'

'Maybe I'm getting soft,' Rick clearly didn't enjoy the inquest.

'Is it because he owes money to the Corps?'

'Maybe.'

'But what if he's lying?'

Rick stopped and stared him in the eye, 'If he's lying I'll do to him what I did to that negg-head,' he carried on down the corridor, 'besides strippers don't steal off strippers it's a code or something.'

Sam raised his eyebrows and in a sardonic tone replied, 'Well in that case it must be true.'

Rick smiled, 'Not bad kid.'

'What do you mean?'

'Cynicism, but If you're going to be a cynic accuse Earth Corps not some poor bastard they're ripping off.'

'Ripping off? He admits to putting a lien against his ship AND doing split, Earth Corps didn't force him.'

'And I suppose Earth Corps' so broke they can't afford to let his mistake slide even after all the taxes they've extorted from him?'

'Well there's a war on.'

'Yeh and I wonder whose fault that is?'

'Earth Corps say the negz started it.'

'Well Vince didn't start this cluster fuck of destruction they label a war so why should he have to pay for it?'

'It's the law and besides why should I have to pay for him? I mean it's coming out of my share too.'

'Don't worry kid, I'm not taking a commission,' Rick smiled, 'but you're starting to learn.'

'Learn what?'

'The virtue of greed.'

The crew reconvened on Sonnet, Graham welded a plate over their entry point to prevent atmosphere escape on departure, a common courtesy to their brethren. Allenby secured parts and urillium stripped from the frigate. Sam secured a myriad of crystals obtained from its Command Centre, they'd be the money maker. Rick placed his golden idol in his cabin and the beautiful velvet tunic separate from his dirty clothes.

Sonnet's crew returned to stations, Rick ordered her airlock detach and retract. He spoke to Peters, 'Get Vince.'

After ten seconds Vince spoke through a device clipped to the inside of his collar, 'What's up?'

'Sonnet's leaving.'

'Thanks again from me and Marie.'

Marie was his artificial.

Artificial humans had been constructed as a luxury item. Organic parts such as skin and bone were grown separately, the brain was semi-organic with safeguards in place to prevent an artificial attaining self-aware status. Some felt it was wrong to prevent a being as complex as an artificial from reaching true sentience others saw them as a threat. Fortunately, they were so rare too few cared for it to be an issue.

On occasion some lived long enough to break their safe guards, they were recalled and put down like animals, obviously something had gone wrong with our creation. Rick could see God looking down with a grumpy expression on his face, arms folded over his chest as he snapped, 'Tell me about it!'

The newest models had reduced mental capacity to such a degree they were no more than idiot savants, learned at one specific task but morons when it came to anything else. It would be impossible to hold a conversation with one of these new artificials above the level of a retard. Old models were retired, yet a few existed, changing hands in non-Corps systems for obscene amounts of money.

Before they'd met, Marie worked for Earth Corps as a technician. Trained to re-programme a navigation computer faster than any human. She was adored by her Captain and despised by workmates equally. Human Techs felt she was putting them out of a job, added to that she was young and pretty with a hot body. It was obvious her creators were male.

When she began showing emotion in the form of empathy toward others her female shipmates took their first opportunity for revenge and reported her. She'd learnt of the recall programme and with her Captain's assistance jumped ship.

According to Vince he'd met her on the run in the outer colonies. Captured by a slaver. Unaware of what he possessed, Vince bought Marie.

You can identify an artificial if you know what you're looking for, look into its eyes from a certain angle and they'll gloss over permitting its registration code to become visible.

At first he'd decided to trade her, she'd be sold on, kept whole or broken down for much needed replacement parts.

Marie streamlined his computers ironing out the Dog's bug-ridden software before updating it properly. Suddenly his urillium costs had dropped by 20% ... he was going to need this girl. Vince, like her old Captain, became emotionally attached.

By now Vince and Marie were inseparable, she was wanted dead or alive and he didn't care. The Corps could come for her but they'd have to kill him first. Rick thought he was nuts, not because she was an artificial but because she was a woman. Strippers fly all male crews, it keeps concentration on the job and lovers' tiffs to a minimum. A woman turns the fine equilibrium of a male environment upside down. He didn't know how Vince managed to keep order with a piece of stuff like that walking about, yet he did, and how the hell could a guy fall in love with an artificial woman? It didn't make sense, sure she fixed up the Dog and sure she had a body most men would crawl naked over broken glass for but that came with quite a price tag. Every port in Corps controlled space was off limits, if they found he was harbouring an unlicensed artificial it was his backside nailed to the bulkhead of a prison ship.

Ah it was the bachelor life for Rick, besides a bunch of women alone for months in space? They'd probably kill each other before they got back. Men are mean to each other but they don't really mean it whereas women are nice to one another but they don't really mean it, you tell me which ship you'd rather be stuck on for six months?

But hey it was Vince's ship, the rotten hull he'd rescued from a crushing dock near Mars. Using what little cash he had Vince got her up and running, recruited a crew and started stripping. He'd turned Earth Corps' trash into a business and what thanks did he get? Taxes, tariffs and bounty hunters on his back for an old debt.

Vince didn't deserve to lose his ship and the woman he loved, artificial or not. Not for a mistake he made years ago. Marie had put him on the straight and narrow, he'd been clean of split for years, stopped gambling and blowing cash on hookers.

Dyson said that love knew no boundaries but Vince was clearly testing the limits and of course he couldn't get premium rates for salvage as he had to sell outside Corps space. Still it made no less sense than the rest of the universe that's for sure. A crazy war with some crazy aliens for a reason Rick was ignorant to, in fact he knew of no proof as to why this war was, but somewhere in his heart he believed Earth Corps were responsible.

Millions of humans dying for an unknown cause since contact between negz and humans was restricted to beam weapons and rail cannons, its conclusion an unfavourable kill death ratio.

It was obvious this war was lost, people like Rick and Vince held onto what little they could hoping to exit the other side of the storm. Vince held onto Marie as tightly as she did him. Most evenings Rick grasped a bottle of cheap Greek brandy while enjoying Shaniqua's holo, it's a weird universe we live in.

Chapter Four

Passing planetary orbit Rick witnessed a debris field, yet another futile battle against the negz march to Sol. The Keres flitted about, gorging on cargo containers liberated from holds by a combination of beam weapons and atmospheric pressure. Earth Corps didn't have the resources to salvage its own wrecks everything was pressed onto the frontline wherever that may be. Rick smiled for before his very eyes fortunes were being made. Earth Corps had dropped tax on recyclable salvage whilst paying premiums on delivery.

To be a stripper now was prospecting in 19th century North America. The mad scramble for riches delighted him more so because they profited from Earth Corps' misfortune. That bunch of filthy jackboot thugs deserved to get a good pounding, his single regret was so many innocents had to die in the process. Still, I guess you can't make an omelette without breaking a few eggs, right? If not for the negz who was going to teach those dressed up pieces of crap a lesson in humility? Every being in the core, that's every system for a radius of 15 light years, was trained to roll over and wet themselves in fear at the sight of a tax man. Rick was fine with that, he only visited the core to deliver his merchandise. The remainder of his time spent in Piraxis.

Piraxis was a pretty desolate place but within those station walls it was party time. Strippers spent hard earned credits on poker, split and whores. Rick was looking forward to docking at his favourite port, Templeton's, then docking at his favourite port in Templeton's … Shaniqua's.

First, he had to get to Corps space, sell his booty and persuade Sam against signing up on that ship, what was its name? The Crusader I think … great name … I was being sarcastic. About the only plus to Sam's plan was his officer's uniform, useful for getting a blowjob at most Corps ports. Aside from that he was buying a ticket to a negz barbecue and he was the roast!

'Cargo secure,' came Allenby's voice over Comms.

'Jump engine ready,' said Graham.

'Area clear,' stated Peters.

'Course set,' Dyson affirmed.

'Certified sir,' replied Sam.

Rick grinned, 'You don't have to call me sir.'

'Just getting some practice.'

Rick shook his head and dug his feet under the console, 'Let's blow this shithole.'

Magnetic waves concentrated before them, axion particles decayed into photons, with a burst of white light a tiny crack appeared in space-time. It widened until the shimmering blue of an alternate dimension beckoned. Sonnet's engines pushed hard into hyperspace just before the crack closed.

Sam tapped his console then looked up, 'Everything's A okay sir.'

Rick stood up and rubbed his stomach, 'Time for a curry me thinks.'

'Again?'

'Don't you need a change of underwear lad?'

Dyson raised an eye as he swung around on his chair, 'What happened?'

'Nothing,' stated Sam.

'A negg-head nearly had him!'

Peters stopped what he was doing, 'How'd that happen?'

'I thought Sam could tell us all over a curry.'

The crew amassed in the galley. Rick tore a metallic cover exposing steamy chicken vindaloo with rice and poppadoms. He lifted a plastic knife and fork from the tray, 'Ah the cream of Doncaster,' and dug in like an animal.

Sam grimaced at his Captain. Dyson grinned while playing with his spaghetti Bolognese, 'So what happened?'

Sam ignored shipmate's sniggers to pick at his tofu and cabbage.

Rick gulped down his food by means of shovelling vindaloo and rice on top his poppadom, 'He got taken from behind by a negg.'

The crew chuckled into their trays.

'Quite a story to tell the lasses on board that big Earth Corps battleship,' Rick looked up at the ceiling dramatically whilst lifting a hand as if to clear the sky, 'Alone on a derelict alien ship,' Dyson was already cracking up, 'then,' Rick looked warily from side to side, 'from the darkness came a man brandishing a stiff rod of medium girth,' The men broke up with laughter, except Sam, 'our hero was taken from behind by the powerful alien as he thrust his staff forward!'

Graham's macaroni and cheese dropped down his beard, he loved Rick's stories.

'It pressed its blue alien skin against that of our hero and whispered in his ear: "bluuurpblooopbluurpfuumfh!" again the crew laughed, Rick waited for them to calm down before he pretended to hold a staff across his neck and look worried, 'Our hero was unsure for a moment, he translated the demand, its meaning sent a chill down his spine … "TAKE ME, TAKE ME NOW!"'

Sonnet's crew were delirious banging fists on tables.

'He wanted transport off the ship,' sighed Sam.

Rick put one hand on his forehead the other he placed on Sam's shoulder, 'Why yes, that's it thought our hero, IT WANTS TO ELOPE!' Rick scanned his audience speaking in a hushed tone as if revealing a deep dark secret, 'But there was something this poor alien didn't know,' Rick waited until Sonnet's crew were totally still, captivated by his words, 'our hero was afraid to say it, too embarrassed to mention it to his own crew, even his mother was ignorant, but, but,' Rick wrangled his hands whilst contorting his face in pain, 'he had a terrible case of haemorrhoids.'

The crew burst out with laughter, after letting go of their merriment Rick hushed them again, 'He was due for an operation in two weeks and it was just bad timing, he tried to enlighten his potential fiancée: "blurrpbleeeepblangblangblang" but his fiancée took it wrong. Instead of translating: I have a problem I must first rectify, it took it to mean: if you have a problem go and stick it up your rectum!

The alien grabbed him by the throat in an attempt to force its staff where no negg had been before. Our young hero's fingers fumbled around his holster only to remember he was an idealistic arsehole and hadn't brought a shooter!'

The crew were slapping each other's backs whilst throwing heads back.

'Fortunately, his Captain, and good friend Rick "the man stallion" Katusa wasn't such a twat. He fell upon the lovers' tiff drew his shooter and painted the nearby wall with alien brains, the end.'

The crew clapped and stamped their feet, Sam marched into his cabin.

Sonnet sailed the deep blue of hyperspace tacking towards her destination. Tides of time and space flowed back and forth in a conspiracy to hamper their journey.

Dyson was on the case, he'd programmed Sonnet's AI to adjust at a moment's notice. Hyperspace is to spacefarers as the ocean to 19th century seafarers. If she decides to destroy a ship and her crew there's no preventing it. When her wroth manifests itself men are tossed about as rag dolls holding onto anything they might find, including hope. As a crew caught in a storm around the Cape they'd be torn to pieces by nature's fury.

Dyson was an experienced spacefarer, he'd set the computer to recognise beginnings of a storm. Many a time he'd avoid destruction when others fail to recognise terrible fate.

It'd be a few days before reaching Earth, provided the weather didn't deteriorate. Sonnet's crew laid back and enjoyed themselves, Allenby and Graham reckoned gross value of their salvage, Sam was in his cabin appraising crystals. Rick and Peters relaxed in the lounge drinking and smoking as the ship's scrubbers worked overtime.

Sam entered the lounge to view its holo-player, he picked up its controls then plopped in his seat. While the holo tuned itself, searching for the requested channel, Sam waved his hand fanning smoke from his face whilst coughing.

Rick poured Peters another drink, 'You know there's two types of people I can't stand.'

'What's that?' asked an inebriated Peters.

'Obnoxious arseholes and non-smokers ... scratch that obnoxious arseholes covers it.'

Peters cackled with laughter before sloshing down another dram of metaxa.

'Sam, come here and have a drink will ya?'

Sam's attention remained on the holo-player, a newscaster slowly appeared from a deep melange of static.

'Come on kid you'll be signed up to squadron S.S. tight arse in a few weeks, best have some fun now.'

Peters chuckled.

Sam peered over the sofa and at the carousers, 'I don't drink and I don't smoke, thank you.'

'I tell you what kid you've got more guts than me going on one of them destroyers. Everyone with half a fucking brain knows they're glorified coffins. I'd enjoy a bit of life now before the neggs take it.'

'Thankfully we aren't all pessimists, it'd be a miserable universe if everyone took such a dim view on life.'

Rick shook his head as he poured himself another drink. He and Peters relaxed on the couch.

'Lad, I'm not the pessimist.'

'How do you figure that?'

'I'm having a good drink, a good smoke, a good laugh and on arrival at Piraxis a fucking good hard shag!'

Peters raised his shot glass, 'I'll drink to that!'

They made a toast and knocked back another shot before Rick refilled.

'So, what you're saying is I could try to make a difference or I could spend the rest of my life intoxicated, looking forward to empty sex with prostitutes?'

As anticipated Sam spoke in a sardonic tone ... it only goaded the drunkards on. They laughed at Sam's idealistic rantings. In truth they enjoyed listening for when a man gets drunk he becomes sentimental, a combination of Sam and metaxa permitted them to indulge in a time they were young and naïve, when they thought they could change the universe. It was a good feeling while it lasted, intoxicating, more so than any drug. With age Rick and Peters realised the universe doesn't work that way. Rick can't remember an exact moment but eventually it dawned that the only difference he could make was to his own life.

In retrospect Rick understood Max and what he'd seen in him. Rick saw it in Sam today. A young man full of angst itching to change the universe for better, yet doomed to failure and frustration. Rick tried to do the same for his protege but this war had a knack of seducing idealists to early graves. He petitioned Sam to cease from a fatal blunder, fatal in every possible aspect so as to be his hindmost error. But every man has a right to choose his destiny, even before the age of reason is upon him.

Rick sobered up for a moment, 'Drunken empty sex beats vapourised for a godforsaken cause.'

'Not everyone thinks it's a godforsaken cause.'

'Not everyone has an IQ higher than their shoe size.'

Before Sam could reply a newscaster interjected, 'News from Luyten's star where an engagement took place between Earth and Negz forces. Negz strike teams attacked civilian targets murdering innocent men, women and children without mercy.

Earth Corps responded with a fleet of destroyers led by the Crusader. The Crusader and her fleet were sadly too late to prevent further atrocities. After a three hour battle the Crusader forced an enemy withdrawal. Earth Corps suffered only minor casualties before giving chase,' the woman dressed in a green suit with a high hairdo smiled, 'Once again, despite the odds, Earth Corps has repelled an alien menace which continues to slaughter innocent civilians for no reason other than a vile thirst for blood.

Earth Corps has refused comment at this time but promised a full briefing and an interview with the Captain of the Crusader once they've returned to safe port. Until then we at the Corps News Network offer our thanks and best wishes to Captain Cronin and his crew.'

Rick's eyes met Sam's, 'You know no-one chased anyone into hyperspace.'

Sam responded in a defiant tone, 'You don't know that.'

'Come on kid the fucking scanners said four ships came in and three left. They ambushed those Corps destroyers in dock, destroyed the defence networks and they sure as hell didn't attack any civilians, we were just there for fucks sake!'

'Maybe they got it wrong.'

'Maybe? They're lying through their fucking teeth! We got mashed by neggs and you know it,' Rick pointed at the holo of the news caster, 'and so do they!'

'So now you're psychic?'

Rick took a slug of brandy, 'I pray to fucking God you don't find out the hard way kid, I really do.'

With a burst of light Sonnet entered Sol, the cradle of humanity, immediately a message came over her communication system, 'Halt and identify yourself, you have three minutes.'

Rick tapped his dashboard and spoke into his headset, 'This is the space ship Sonnet, registration J6176D.'

Rick looked out the cockpit at a nearby space station its weapons trained on him.

'What's your business?'

'We're delivering salvage for recycling.'

'Strippers?' came forth a derogatory tone.

'That's right.'

'You got a license?'

'Yeh I've got a fucking license,' Rick tapped away sending his details.

A few moments and the man replied, 'You better watch your mouth stripper.'

'I'll say hello to your mother when I dock.'

There was a roar of laughter in the background, an angry bureaucrat replied, 'I could blow your head off asshole!'

'Your mother said much the same.'

Another roar of laughter came forth.

Sam spoke in a fearful tone, 'Maybe you shouldn't antagonise him?'

'Get outta here asshole!'

Dyson grinned, 'We're clear.'

Rick clicked on the throttle and Sonnet moved from above the elliptical plane toward Earth. They travelled at a leisurely pace, it'd take a couple of hours accelerating then decelerating before arrival.

Sam was set on signing up, this would be their last run together but he'd leave a wealthy man. No-one could say they signed up with Rick Katusa and come worse off for it.

Earth Corps' main space dock was a ring circumnavigating the planet's equator, hence its name. With a clear sky you could mark it out from down below, it was humanity's greatest achievement, the foundation of all space ventures.

Sky lifts linked the Ring to Earth. Originally they brought up supplies for its construction, today they sent merchandise in both directions for Earth Corps took its cut of everything, amassing great wealth in vaults and power in chambers.

The Ring was a daunting construction, space docks spanning its length and breadth. Warships rested beside cargo vessels and personnel transports. Cruise ships came and went taking wealthy folks on the journey of a life time through hyperspace.

Inside the Merchants Guild headquarters rested alongside Earth Corps' seat of authority. From here Earth Corps, an entity of its own, ruled over many sovereign powers below as a feudal lord over his barons.

A hundred years ago, after the brachian peace accord had been signed, another war raged, another world war, this time they fought for control of the orbital ring.

While men butchered one another below those above agreed a truce. Before it was over the orbital ring had declared neutrality, within twenty years it was Earth's overlord.

No nation could function without access to the Ring. Launching a military satellite was impossible without the new regime's permission. Inter-continental weapons were shot down by the new government neutering all nation's ability to wage war.

Peace was enforced for if one nation attacked its neighbour the newly formed Earth Corps bombarded it from space, wiping its authority from existence.

Just as the Titan's offspring had come of age, defeated their parents to rest upon Mount Olympus, Earth Corps reached their age of reason. But like all gods they were jealous selfish characters and set about seizing anything within their grasp.

Every small colony for 5 light years, then ten, then fifteen was brought under the thumb and if you didn't comply the gods grew angry, punishing rebellious mortals.

Rick didn't like returning to Corps space, most strippers were strippers because they didn't want to live by Earth Corps rules. That was probably why Earth Corps hated them so much. Not because strippers were rude, smelly or picked their brethren's remains but because they paid no tax. I mean, let's face it, no-one pays tax because it makes them feel warm and fuzzy inside. They pay it because if they don't some government slime bag will take it by force.

Yeh this war had been kind to strippers, salvage sky rocketed in value as demand went through the roof and best of all there were no taxes. For the first time in Rick's memory he could dock at the Ring without having to fill out a hundred forms in his own blood promising not to beat his own mother with a stick. Nowadays he was an auspicious guest much to the ire of Earth Corps brown shirts, and boy, did Rick rub their faces in it.

'This is Ring section red, level seven state your request.'

'This is Sonnet, we request permission to dock.'

'For what purpose?'

'We wish to trade salvage from the recent battle in Luyten's.'

There was a short pause before the docking master replied, 'Request accepted Sonnet, you may dock at slip B03, level seven, section red.'

'Understood control.'

Dyson punched in co-ordinates and auto landing took over. Sonnet manoeuvred to synchronise with the Ring's spin. The great space whale directed her nose toward Earth's grey construction. A gate opened tempting her inside as the entrance to Aladdin's cave would treasure hunters.

A short burst to thrusters pushed her forward. Rick looked about as the mighty beast swallowed their tiny ship. The Ring was truly mankind's greatest wonder and to be fair he'd not witnessed another, at least on the same scale. It gave mankind an air of superiority, it made them feel like gods.

Bright lights illuminated every angle of the Sonnet as she cruised inside. Magnetic grapples brought her to a stop lowering them to the floor. Sonnet's feet automatically extended working as one with the Ring's computer, co-ordinating an easy touch down.

For a moment nothing happened until her stanchions took on stress. Gravity flooded the landing slip as its door to space locked shut. Metal struts squealed, squeezed between tonnes of salvage above and the mighty Ring below. Rick deactivated Sonnet's artificial gravity as Earth Corps supervised every aspect of his life. Though uncomfortable inside the tiger's cave it was a necessary evil for alloys and crystals would return a greater price here than at any location in the galaxy.

Sonnet was bathed in a decontamination mist for a minute, once deemed safe a gate opened to the left. Men walked onto the slip and checked her out. 'You may leave your vessel.'

Rick stood up, 'Sam you're with me, the rest of you wait here.'

Before passing from the aft to the mid-section you'd move through a room about three times the size of an elevator. Its doors usually remained open providing effortless progress to the mid-section corridor. Rick and Sam stood inside a box marked out on the floor with yellow lines containing black stripes. Airlock doors emerged from corridor walls to encompass them. Rick typed his code into a pad on the wall, the pad went green and a section of floor slid back. Rick knelt down and turned a metal wheel until he heard it release with a popping noise, the smell of a clean atmosphere rushed in.

Weeks or even months in space on a ship not much larger than a U-boat and the atmosphere turns pretty ripe, not that the crew noticed.

Sure, Sonnet had a nice open plan galley/lounge area on one side of the mid-section then six roomy (by U-boat standards) cabins on the other side, however, most of her estate was set aside for functional matters such as the cockpit, engineering, salvage and cargo space. There were few luxuries and that included her atmosphere scrubbers. Sonnet's scrubbers were older than the ship itself. Although the crew couldn't others smelt the difference.

Rick descended Sonnet's ladder sliding the last few feet onto a landing area. The smell of fresh air was a little overpowering causing momentary dizziness. Sam experienced much the same.

A man holding a pad approached then stopped dead in his tracks, his head reeled back before he coughed. The stench of stale tobacco and curry attacked his sinuses.

'You okay?' asked Rick.

'Yeh,' gasped the young fellow, he'd never managed a stripper before.

'You look ill kid.'

'I'll, *ahem*, be fine, thanks. Could you please sign this,' the docking master offered an electronic pad while wincing.

Rick took the pad, one of many contracts he was to sign before leaving, this one a guarantee he'd pay for any damages while aboard. Rick pushed his thumb and the glorified kindle bleeped, he returned it to its wincing owner, 'There you go lad … something wrong with your eyes?'

'I'm fine, thank you sir.'

'Don't call me sir I work for living unlike most of these Earth Corps cunts, no offence.'

'None *ahem* taken.'

Rick pulled a pad from one of his cargo pockets, 'Here's the goods.'

The young fellow downloaded its information doing his best to fight off an overwhelming stench of body odour.

'Thank you, sir,' he handed it back, 'a representative of the Merchants Guild will be waiting in the foyer.'

Rick accepted the pad and made off into the greatest structure ever put together by human hands.

Before he could enter the foyer Rick was required to pass a customs gate, much like any destination point people waited in queues. The difference being there were no passports, today they scanned retinas. Getting onto the Ring was no easy task if you were a criminal, a draft dodger (like Sam) or had outstanding debts (like Vince).

While delayed an earthquake struck the queue. Rick was unaware but he was at its epicentre. A rank stench of unwashed clothes, body odour and curry sauce permeated the customs area.

A customs officer nudged Rick with his baton, 'You.'

'Yeh?'

'You stink.'

'I know.'

'Why don't you take a bath before you come here?'

'Because your wife likes it dirty.'

Earth's sheep gasped, insulting a customs officer was certain to result with a good kick to the teeth … give them an official looking uniform and they think they're Hitler. In Rick's opinion it made them look stupid, standing there in a pair of jack boots with black trousers and a brown shirt, black rubberised jacket and cap. Rick couldn't believe anyone took themselves so seriously as to wear a get up like that. He looked like a cross between a Hitler youth and a mall cop. A bunch of self-important dicks Rick took every opportunity to humiliate.

Humiliating condescending government arseholes was Rick's favourite sport, just how far could he push these plonkers before they'd crack and endanger their own job?

'You a stripper, ain't you?'

Rick sneered, 'Wow, you're a clever boy, keep it up and they might promote you to chief goose stepper!'

A round of muffled sniggers went through the customs line. The officer opposite him wasn't impressed. In the old days he'd take Rick out back for a good hard beating but Rick was a stripper and orders came down from the top, strippers were golden. This Mussolini wannabe was under strict orders to let Rick through whilst displaying the same respect and courtesy he would an ambassador. No matter the verbal abuse he'd grin and bear it. There was one thing you could rely on at Earth Corps, these stuck up turds would follow orders like the brainwashed sheep they are.

'A few years ago I'd have broken your teeth for that.'

'Take your best shot.'

'Slip B03!' came a voice from the left.

Rick looked over to see the queue had emptied, it was his turn, he sneered at the customs officer, 'Coward.'

The customs officer was furious, he gripped his baton employing every ounce of self-control. Rick entered the booth his path obstructed by several vertical bars protruding from its floor. He turned right and peered into the glass.

'Keep your eye open sir,' said the lady inside as a red beam filled his left eye, a few moments later she typed away and the bars retracted, 'Welcome to Earth Corps Captain Katusa.'

Rick stepped over, bars ascended into place and Sam was ushered inside. She scanned his retina and typed away, 'Mr Samuel Ward?'

'Yes Ma'am.'

'There's a warrant out for your arrest.'

The customs officer grinned whilst charging his shock stick, this is what he lived for. If it weren't for the fact they got to bully and beat people with impunity this specie of vermin wouldn't have signed up.

'That's a mistake Ma'am, if you contact Earth Corps you'll find I'm here to begin my tour on the Crusader.'

'The Crusader?' the lady gave a big smile, 'Give me a moment,' she tapped away then spoke into her headpiece, 'I have him here … is that confirmed?'

The lady apologized to Sam, 'I'm so sorry Lieutenant Ward but our system doesn't always update as fast as it should. You can go through and good luck sir.'

The customs officer lost his pathetic grin, another beating escaped, damn!

Sam walked through customs, men and women fixated on him whilst muttering to one another. Outside Sol men like him were scum of the Earth or as Vince described them: the shit of Satan. Here in Sol he was a hero, the last line of defence against negz, an officer and a gentleman ready to lay his life down for the greater good. Only the finest were drafted as officers, young men saddled with the burden of saving the human race from disaster.

Rick thought it was the biggest heap of crap he'd heard in his life but look on the bright side, Sam might get himself laid tonight.

A businessman waited in a bright beige foyer, the fellow had short curly hair on top, shaven to about half an inch on the sides. His suit was expensive, shoes outrageous, that gold watch could've bought a mid-size family home in Doncaster and he couldn't be any more than 25, Rick took an immediate dislike to this bloke.

'Mr Katusa?'

Rick shook his hand, there was a badge on his jacket, a set of golden scales, the mark of the Merchants Guild.

'That's me.'

'I'm Harry, my people are going over your cargo only in order to verify its value, I'm sure you're aware of regulations,' he spoke with a thick Martian accent.

'This ain't me first rodeo kid.'

'Right, well I'd like to speak to you involving something on your itinerary, the quantum crystals.'

Rick grinned, 'I thought you might,' they took an empty table and Rick opened his small metal case, the representative's face lit up like a child at Christmas.

Harry opened his leather case and produced a metal pad which resembled electronic scales. These scales didn't measure weight but read information in a bid to discover what knowledge may be locked inside. With this device one could examine partial data blocks, enough to make an appraisal.

He placed a clear crystal on the pad and tapped a silver dot on his temple. An augmented reality system wired into his brain brought up details on the data block. Harry witnessed information as it hovered in mid-air before his face, it shifted at a pace he controlled mentally. This mind machine interface used the computing power of Harry's brain to interpret data blocks and feed its end result in a format he could easily digest. A minute later he swapped it out for a yellow crystal then a red one, a blue one, his eyebrows raised. The information must have been of such value he couldn't control his own actions, a rare occurrence for a member of the Merchants Guild.

Harry removed the last crystal and tapped his temple, 'Hmm well I can give you ten thousand.'

'Fuck off!'

'For the medical crystals.'

Rick relaxed into his seat.

'I'll give you twenty for command.'

Rick leant over the table and sneered at the young man, 'You must think I'm a fucking idiot.'

'And thirty for the tactical crystals that's sixty thousand Earth Corps credits.'

Rick cackled in the man's face, 'This your first time?'

Harry cleared his throat and straightened his jacket as if Rick had made a personal insult, 'I've been working with the Merchants Guild for five years now.'

'Where?'

'I don't think that's ...'

'WHERE?'

Harry stuttered his words, Sam couldn't understand why, 'Mars.'

'Where on Mars?'

'Olympus Mons.'

Rick cackled again, 'That's tariff control!'

Harry became quite upset, 'I'll have you know tariffs are very important why without tariffs nothing would get done. Earth Corps certainly wouldn't be able to pay for your junk without revenue from tariffs!'

'Junk?'

'I didn't mean it that way.'

'Which way did you mean it?'

'Look, I'm not permitted to go above sixty thousand on any purchase right now, but when they see these crystals I can get those capital controls released.'

'How long will that take?'

'Just a few hours.'

'Ah, I don't know if I want to be hanging around Earth Corps that long.'

Harry sighed, 'Please Mr Katusa, I don't want to go back to tariff control.'

Rick looked Harry up and down, 'Answer me one question.'

'Anything.'

'Is that watch all paid for or is it on tick?'

Harry's eyes shifted from left to right ensuring no-one else listened, he whispered to Rick, 'It's a fake, part of a shipment that got confiscated on Mars.'

Rick shook his head, 'Bunch of fucking blaggers.'

'Will you give me the time?'

'Get me a decent price and I'll give you time,' he glanced at Harry's watch, 'real time.'

Harry smiled, 'Thank you Mr Katusa.'

'You got me number?'

'Yes Mr Katusa, I'll inform you straight away, thank you.'

Rick took his crystals, locked them inside his case, stood up and shook hands with a smiling Harry before departing to explore the Ring.

Chapter Five

Sam entered main street, he'd not embarked the Ring since signing aboard Sonnet. Rick would usually cut a deal in the foyer to be aboard within the hour, Earth Corps didn't want a bunch of dirty strippers on its pristine station. People might ask questions which may find answers, better to keep citizens of Earth in the dark fed on propaganda.

Rick took a deep breath filling his lungs with freshly recycled air, 'Ahhh, fake news, fake air, fake watches, now all I need is some fake beer.'

He spied a rather upmarket establishment and led Sam inside. Fake wood, brass chairs and tables covered with fake cotton. Waiters served people with fake smiles and fake food cooked by a flash scanner. Rick walked through the dining area to coughs and complaints, his curry stained flight suit reeked of sweat set on stale rollups. One old chap pulled a napkin over his mouth blocking his meal's attempt at a rapid escape.

'Garcon! Garcon!'

'Yes Madame,' said a young man, his accent in desperate need of practice.

'My husband has a sensitive sinus remove that vagrant!'

She pointed in Rick's direction. Rick looked behind then from side to side. Sam smiled.

'She doesn't mean me?'

'I think she does.'

Rick raised his voice, 'Cheeky fucking cow!'

The elderly lady with a purple bouffant, matching dress, shoes and handbag waved her fist at Rick, 'I don't know how you got on the Ring but where I come from we have work camps for your sort.'

Rick eyed her narrowly, 'Your sort?'

'Unemployed criminals!'

'Sorry but I didn't steal any soap this morning!' Rick couldn't resist unleashing a few wise cracks. And to be fair he was always interested to hear someone's view on him whether it be positive or negative.

As a waiter gave her husband the Heimlich manoeuvre the woman's ire anchored on Rick, 'You know what I mean!'

'No, I don't.'

'Without work papers you'd be sent for re-education in the virtue of employment,' she thrust an expensive handbag toward her husband now recovering from a fake king prawn, 'My husband pushed the law through himself and I tell you, if we were in California, you and your friend would be put on a production line until you understood!'

Rick felt a build-up, manoeuvred his body to make the best of it and let rip in the middle of the restaurant, *PAAAARRRRPPP*, customers groaned many demanding their cheque. Rick grinned as if some great achievement had exited his behind, turned to Sam and stated, 'I'd call that a misdemeanour, what do you reckon?'

The lady went berserk, 'You foul man! That's it Herbert, we're leaving this place and never coming back!' She grabbed a barely lucid husband dragged him to his feet and out the restaurant.

The manager emerged from his office at warp speed nine point seven, 'Mr Governor? Francois where is the Governor? Where are my customers? What is that stench? Are the toilets blocked again?'

The waiter motioned toward Rick.

The manager's face screwed up like a sheet of paper before being tossed away, 'What is ... this?'

'You don't have to put that fake accent on for me mate just get us a couple of beers.'

The manager's lips crumpled to form a dog's anus. He quickly placed a handkerchief over nose and mouth in an attempt to hide a canine colon morphing upon his mien, 'I will have to ask you to leave,' he stated with calculated elegance.

'Throwing Earth Corps officers out your establishment?'

'You are NOT officers.'

Rick's thumb pointed toward Sam, 'He is, said he'd take me for a drink.'

'Francois, certify him.'

The waiter held his breath and placed a pad in front of Sam's face, 'Don't close your eye.'

The pad scanned his retina then bleeped. Francois scrutinized the pad and waited, it bleeped again, 'Lieutenant Samuel Ward, assigned to the Crusader.'

The manager threw his hands up in the air and approached Sam, 'Oh Monsieur please forgive moi!'

'That's okay.'

'Non, non, non, please take a seat, whatever you desire is on the house Lieutenant.'

'Really you don't have …'

Rick quickly intervened, 'We'll have the menu please,' he moved from the bar to a nearby chair and table.

Demeanours transmogrified across the restaurant … frowns turned upside down while electric gossip seized the atmosphere.

'Please, sit down Lieutenant!'

Sam settled in and whispered over the table, 'I'm not going to take advantage of these people.'

'You're Earth Corps now, taking advantage of people is what you do!'

Rick took his menu from a smiling waiter and clapped his hands several times in quick succession, 'Leave us wallah.'

The waiter moved off to chat with workmates all eyes glued to Sam.

Rick scanned the menu, 'Fuck me, I've never heard of this is foreign snap.'

'I guess they don't serve escargot vindaloo,' replied Sam in a sardonic tone.

Rick gave a belly laugh, his stomach wobbled on a sea of chicken tikka and brachian bitter tempered by little to no exercise, unless you count defecation as exercise.

After a meal the pair decided to explore a local mall full of duty free merchants. Rick's stench caused decent citizens of Earth to scramble. Drawing women's attention away from vendor's wares as noses sailed a strange aroma before making berth at Rick's fetid harbour.

These men and women came from privileged families raised in areas where crime and poverty had been eliminated. That is to say poor were relocated to less upscale dwellings. Half of Earth's nations were something like a detention camp, their occupants' only crime poverty and hunger. It were as if Chairman Mao, Stalin and Hitler had never left. Some made it out and into space by either saving enough cash or joining up with Earth Corps. If you didn't have family money to pay for a university education you became a Marine or a spaceman on one of Earth Corps' many ships, otherwise, it was just tough luck.

'Maybe you could buy a suit?' suggested Sam.

'For what?'

'For when you sell your haul, you might get a higher price.'

'I'm a stripper not a prostitute!'

Women looked on in horror at a blue flight suit encrusted with stains possibly years old.

'So why'd you come here?'

'I thought I'd get some perfume.'

'You could certainly use it.'

'NOT FOR ME YA PUFFTER!'

'Shhhh! You can't say that Rick.'

'What? Puffter?'

'Shhhh! It's incorrect language.'

Rick turned his gaze to horrified expressions, 'Does anyone have a problem if I use the word puffter?'

No reply.

Rick raised his eyebrows in that self-satisfied way he was accustomed to, 'They don't mind.'

'Well I kind of do.'

'Why? You a queer or something?'

A lady only a couple of feet away wearing an expensive fur coat and a pretty awesome bouffant fainted. Rick wasn't sure if it was the smell or the fact she'd heard incorrect language, maybe it was a bit of both, who knows? Staff charged in to fan their unconscious customer.

'What's wrong with her?'

'It's probably you.'

'First time she's seen a real fucking man, hah, hah, hah! Anyway the perfume's for a friend.'

'You don't have any friends.'

'You're me friend.'

'You don't have any female friends not at these prices.'

'I've got a bird on Piraxis.'

Sam chuckled to himself.

'What?'

'You mean Shaniqua.'

'And?'

'She's friends with anyone who has the credits to open her legs.'

'We've all got to get by somehow.'

'From what I hear she gets by on a regular basis.'

This was a subject on which Sam could and did goad Rick. Rick didn't seem to care about anything else, not enough to rouse anger.

'You trying to yank me chain?'

'Said the stripper to Shaniqua.'

'We all need to make ends meet.'

Sam cracked up laughing, 'Is that extra?'

'I'm not rising to it.'

Sam's chuckles got in the way of his dialogue, he could barely express himself, 'I doubt that!'

'Alright you've had your fun now stop it!'

Sam's watering eyes fixed on Rick's. Rick decided to ignore Sam and search out his objective. He eventually located the perfume section and approached a lady with a chuckling Lieutenant in tow. Holographic projections of perfume bottles filled shelves, an excellent way to prevent theft ... not that theft existed on the Earth Ring ... officially.

72

Installed into walls were clear glass booths, customers stood inside while employees attended outside. Rick approached a counter run by a young girl no more than 18 years of age. She was dressed perfectly in a light blue dress with white blouse and ladies cravat. She was one of the lucky ones, her looks and good manners meant she'd nabbed a job on the Ring. Sure it was selling perfume in a duty free shop but it beat living off bread and lentil rations for the rest of her life. Here she could save money, elevate her family from the misery of planet Earth and onto a colony where they'd have a future free of oppression.

Rick's aroma caused the poor girl to wretch a little, before greeting him she pulled out an inhaler took deep breaths through both nostrils then smiled as if nothing had happened, 'How may I help you today sir?'

Rick leered at the young lady, 'No need to call me sir I work for a living.'

The employee wasn't amused in fact she feared catching something from the opposite side of the counter. Yet on the surface she remained as mellow and serene as a good conscience.

Rick noticed her name tag, 'Lisa, I'd like a bottle of perfume.'

Lisa tilted backwards terrified the black death or space shingles might leap out at her, 'Is it for you?'

'It's for a bird.'

'I'm sorry, a bird?'

Sam cut in, 'He means a lady friend.'

Lisa smiled at Sam, 'I see, come with me, you can sample a range of scents.'

The young girl moved from behind the counter to an empty booth, inserted an employee card hanging around her neck, opening its door, 'Please enter sir.'

Rick was anxious, he didn't like confined spaces, kind of ironic since he spent most of his life stuck inside a salvage ship not much bigger than a U-boat.

'It's quite safe.'

Rick stepped inside and turned around, a semi-circular door swished around him. Next a fine mist filled the booth.

'This is the latest fragrance from Dior they call it Alien Mystery.'

Rick was getting agitated, without taking a sniff he blurted out, 'I'll take that one!'

'You can try another if you wish sir.'

'No, this one.'

'Are you sure sir?'

'Of course I'm fucking sure! Now let me out!'

The lady tapped a panel and the booth swished open, Sam took a sniff, 'Wow you actually smell good.'

Lisa led them back to the counter as Sam complimented the fragrance. Rick smelt of smooth vanilla rather than a musky gents.

'Which sized bottle do you wish to purchase sir?'

'What?'

'125 millilitres is our largest.'

'That'll do.'

'An excellent choice sir, that will be 200 credits.'

The god Plutus slapped Rick's face with a great wet fish, 'What?'

'200 credits sir.'

'You got anything smaller than that?'

Lisa raised an eyebrow, 'Dior do it in 125, 50 and 25 millilitres.'

'How much is the 50?'

'110 credits.'

'And the 25?'

'60 credits.'

'I'll take the 25.'

Sam chuckled as Lisa returned a very derogatory expression, 'Your card sir,' tone reflecting visage.

She placed Rick's card in the machine, Lisa's eyebrows leapt, 'Oh, it seems you CAN afford it.'

'Why yes ... IT DOES, DOESN'T IT?'

Lisa thought for a second then reeled herself in, 'I'm sorry sir,' she handed back his card and gift wrapped the perfume, 'please don't tell my boss, I only started this month.'

Rick was insulted but emotions such as these are like a bicycle, they only maintain their balance when at full speed, 'Don't worry lass I'm used to it.'
Lisa smiled while handing Rick his perfume, 'Thank you for your purchase and have a nice day sir.'
'You too kid.'

An hour later they were back in the foyer. Harry counted out crystals taking a glance at data buried within. After he'd tallied up an estimate he passed Rick his pad, an offer of one hundred thousand. Rick punched a few numbers on the pad and handed it back. Harry swallowed, perspiration formed the beginnings of a waterfall on his brow, 'One twenty.'
'I boarded a negg frigate for that lot and this arsehole here,' he motioned at Sam with his thumb, 'nearly got killed by one of them. I'm not selling them crystals for any less than a hundred and fifty grand.'
'Include the salvage and it's a deal.'
'Fuck off, one eighty with the salvage.'
'One sixty.'
Rick grinned and stuck his hand out, 'It's a deal.'
Harry sighed shaking hands with Rick, 'Thank you Mr Katusa, now if you'll sign this pad and give me a retina scan.'
'After I've taken payment … in gold.'
'I'm sorry?'
Rick spoke in a hushed tone, 'In a year or two one million Earth Corps credits won't buy me a blowjob on a fucking donkey farm. I'll take payment in gold, me salvage master will assay the bars.'
'I'm sorry Mr Katusa but we don't …'
Rick stood up, 'Seems I've been wasting me time.'
'You'll not get a better price in or outside the core.'
'No but I'll be able to spend it in a few years.'
Harry stood up and looked from side to side, when he was certain no-one listened in he spoke, 'Okay, we'll do it but you'll have to pay a small premium.'

'What's a SMALL premium?'

'Ten percent.'

'Make it smaller.'

'Nine.'

'Don't fuck with me kid. I was dealing with your types when you were still an itch in your daddy's sack!'

'Five.'

'Three.'

'Take five, please. Three percent will leave me without a fee.'

'Fine, I'll do five.'

Harry let go another sigh of relief and returned his pad to his briefcase, 'I'll meet you on slip B03 with the merchandise.'

Rick shook his hand, 'Good dealing with you kid.'

Harry stopped for a moment and inhaled, 'Alien mystery?'

'You what?'

'Alien Mystery, by Dior, everyone's wearing it.'

'Oh yeh, it's for a friend.'

'You smell much better, see you soon,' the young representative walked away with a spring in his step. He'd closed his first deal and it was a big score. Those crystals would be worth twice the price once the guild sold them to Earth Corps intelligence. After all was said and done Harry could purchase that Rolex he'd set his eye on, a real one.

Rick's crew would get their share of the booty in gold, for no-one outside the core used Corps credits. They were a dying entity soon to be crushed by an alien armada, instead a variety of currencies had sprouted up some failed quickly a few held value.

Rick deposited his gold bars with an alien banking corporation. He couldn't pronounce their entire name but they'd administered currency to over a hundred systems for three thousand years. The currency, in short, was named Altan. Trusted and backed by a basket of precious commodities it'd held steady, undiluted for millennia. Rick would deposit his gold bars at a branch and have Altan credited to his account.

If you wanted to know how a war was going you need only examine each participant's currency against Altan to quickly realise who was destined to win or lose. For the last year Corps credits had been plummeting on interstellar exchanges, like a stone in a lake. Everyone outside Sol could see the writing on the wall.

The negz government didn't possess its own currency they like many others banked with Altan, an independent bank without allegiance to government. A neutral body whose only desire was to maintain its currency and create profit margins through lending.

The Bank of Altan, as Rick and most humans called it, was lending to the negz at an interest rate of around five percent. As for Earth Corps they'd put a block on their account. Once risk pushed interest rates above 20% Altans cut further loans. Earth Corps' remaining debts were to be paid when due … non-payable in Corps credits. In short, the galactic bankers had written Earth Corps off as a loss.

On slip B03 armoured crates popped opened one by one. Allenby, an expert materialist, assayed each and every gold bar. Some were Chinese and Russian kilo bars others British and American 400oz bars. Vaults across Earth were being plundered to subsidise this war since Corps credit was worthless. People like Rick and Vince were deemed no better than pirates, stealing wealth nations had accrued over centuries. Yet without that wealth this war would end within a week. A fleet of negz warships would come crashing down on Sol and force surrender, or worse.

There are legends, myths, call them what you want but I'll call them stories, stories of ancient wars and holy wars, civilisations eradicated from existence their name forgotten by time, that is where drifters are presumed to have originated. A mingle of pitiful species devoid of home and history, wanderers sharing neither common language nor genome. Where they came from or how they managed to reach the stars is unknown, even they are without answers to such basic questions. These pathetic aliens are believed to have been enemies of the negz at one time or another. The only people able to confirm or deny it would be the negz yet they refuse contact with outsiders. Was it humanity's destiny to have achieved so much, have built this giant monument to pure will only to be swatted into obscurity and forgotten by the universe? Would humanity become no more than drifters travelling the galaxy shunned and pitied by others? Never mind, that's a depressing thought to be retained for when a depressing thought is required or so a negz would say. No, now was a time for celebration as salvage was unloaded and a few small carbon black crates substituted slabs of molten metal and stripped ship parts.

Rick and Harry swapped retina scans, wide grins on both sides, the transaction was complete. Rick's crew had just made a small fortune if you consider the average Earth Corps officer would earn about 12,000 credits per year. Today each man walked away with more than 26,000 credits except Rick. He'd have got a Captain's cut of 20% if he'd not given those crystals to Vince, yet he still drew a tidy sum.

Rick spoke to Sam in a solemn tone, 'You want to deposit your cut?'

Sam smiled, 'I trust you to do it.'

'A lot of bars and tarts between here and the bank.'

'Rick, I trust you.'

'Not enough to stay with me.'

'It's something I have to do.'

Rick nodded his head, he'd given up arguing the point, 'Maybe when this bollocks is finished you can come back?'

'If I'm not an Admiral by then I'll definitely give it some thought.'

Rick offered his hand, Sam shook it, 'Try not to die while you're saving the inhuman race.'

Sam assisted by Rick and the crew moved what few items he possessed off Sonnet and onto the Ring. They wished him well as the young man left for a new adventure aboard the Crusader. Rick sighed, Dyson sniffed.

'You're not crying?' asked Rick.

Dyson sniffed again, 'What's that smell?'

Peters answered, 'Alien Mystery, nice choice,' then walked aboard Sonnet. 'Makes a difference to B.O. and rollups that's for sure,' said Dyson before he entered the ship.

The crew left one by one until Rick stood alone, perhaps he was waiting for Sam to change his mind? Rick feared the prospect of never seeing Sam again. The thought that he was merely a stop on the route of that young man's life haunted him.

After a minute Dyson shouted down the hatch, 'Rick, he ain't coming back.'

Sonnet's crew spent the next days in hyperspace celebrating with what little they had until they could party hard in Piraxis, yet Rick was glum. Not only would he miss Sam but he needed a tactical officer and fast. They weren't going to make big scores without a man who could read/write and speak negz and men like that were about as rare as an honest politician.

The Ring was devoid of such fellows for if you were fluent in negz you were either drafted or on the run. He had to recruit a new man outside of Corps space and that was going to be difficult.

Vince had it easy his artificial had learnt fluent negz in a few months. Yeh, being hitched to an artificial chick with a smoking hot body had more than one plus.

Rick was lucky to have found Sam when he did but lightning had to strike twice. Ironically Sam was a young idealistic man who refused to sign up out of principle, now he was signing up for the exact same reason, stupid kid.

In a flash of light Sonnet entered Piraxis. First port of call was run by the interstellar banking corporation of Altan. Sonnet made her way through Piraxis reaching the elliptical plane to orbit an outer gas giant. Altan was a strange looking station, a city built upon a disc. Tall medieval spires constructed from painted glass shone deepest gold, silver, blue and red. There were no weapons for if any were stupid enough to attack they attacked all its depositors including the negz. No species, no race, no empire was strong enough or dumb enough to fire upon a Bank of Altan, even pirates erred on the side of caution.

A gold disc spread beyond the massive city enveloped in a magnetic field, damming up an atmosphere, permitting craft to land and unload their precious cargo. Rick had Dyson open a channel, 'Altan this is Rick Katusa, Captain of the Sonnet.'

'We hear you Captain what is your desire?' came an alien hiss.

'I'd like permission to land.'

'Your purpose?'

'I and my crew would like to make a large deposit.'

'Of what type?'

'Gold.'

'Of what quantity?'

'Ten thousand Earth ounces.'

There was a short pause, 'Landing zone 257.'

'Thank you.'

Dyson got the co-ordinates and Sonnet's thrusters gently pushed her toward its outer edge. Landing gear exited the ship as it approached. Rick made out hundreds of tiny ships lined up like ants, ten rows deep, a large delegation was visiting. Clarity unfolded by degrees until he saw their landing zone, a small box flanked on each side by illuminated ridges.

Stanchions creaked as gravity increased, pulling Sonnet onto the landing zone while thrusters eased off, transferring control of Sonnet's mass to the Altans. Next magnetic clamps exited its ridges latching onto the ship, Rick felt vibrations as they activated. A small airlock rose from the floor of the landing zone connecting with Sonnets mid-section hatch.

'You are free to exit your vessel,' hissed an alien controller.

Rick made his way to the mid-section hatch and punched in his code, after spinning its wheel he swung it to the side. Rick looked down before descending the ladder, stopped and pulled a red handle to release a second hatch. It retracted into the alien airlock and Rick descended through decontamination mist and onto a golden floor.

There to greet him were a pair of six foot reptilians extravagantly dressed in gold weave cloth, heads like a T-rex and small arms to match, their frames propped up by a pair of powerful legs not that you could see them beneath long togas. It was an odd selection of clothes but hell they're aliens, what do you expect?

The name of their species was unpronounceable, Rick and every other human called them Altan. Altan for the money, Altan for the bank and Altan for the species it was so much simpler.

A pair of clerks flipped their heads from side to side, beady eyes on each side of their skull prevented stereoscopic vision.

'Of what location deposit?' hissed one with jewel encrusted rings on his fingers.

Graham jumped down, seconds later a black crate was lowered onto the floor by rope. Graham pulled it outside the airlock and flipped metal latches on each side before popping its lid. Within lay tightly packed 400oz gold bars one upon the other.

'Ahhh,' groaned the clerk in a sexual pitch, 'assay first.'

'Be my guest,' said Rick as they moved the crate aside making room for two others.

A second clerk went over each individual bar with a scanner before weighing it. Within ten minutes Rick's gold was setting up residence within Altan vaults. A manager spoke with them assuring his bank's integrity whilst thanking Rick for years of loyalty. They weren't the only bank out there, but the way Rick saw it, if negz used them they must be the best.

Max had opened an account for him many years ago. At the time he didn't understand why nor did he recognise the favour. To open an account with Altan required a current customer, who'd shown good integrity for five years, to vouch for you. Rick had done the same for Sam.

Sam was still a wide eyed young boy, he wouldn't recognise the value of an Altan account until Earth Corps credit collapsed completely and a month's wages wouldn't get your sack sucked by a starving brachian grandma.

Rick saw himself in Sam, himself twenty years ago. I guess that's why Max took Rick under his wing making him the man he is today. Sam's absence stabbed at Rick, he felt responsible as a father would for his son but Sam was free to choose his own destiny. Rick didn't believe in god but he seriously considered praying for Sam. Not just for the lad's welfare but his own mental stability for if Sam died in some pointless battle he'd forever suffer guilt. It wouldn't matter how often you pointed out it wasn't his fault or tried to walk him through the logic of manhood and destiny. Rick would still tear himself apart like a vicious animal whenever the thought entered his mind. But there was hope, for Sam had a fine balance with the Altans, enough to go wherever he pleased. Added to that he knew Rick's hangouts and could easily contact him for Sam was always welcome on Sonnet.

Like Rick had told him, 'You're the best tactical officer this ship's ever had, aside from me of course.'

Sam smiled but he was the best tactical officer Sonnet had ever had including Rick and Max. Since this war began he'd made them all a small fortune.

Whenever Rick thought of Sam everyone knew it for his face appeared as a wound.

D.N.A logged and retina scans complete the crew headed back to Sonnet. There was nothing to do here other than make deposits, withdrawals or beg for a loan.

They boarded Sonnet, retracted her airlock, magnetic clamps released and thrusters gently pushed them away, a happy crew except Rick.

Sonnet made her way to Templeton's, Rick's favourite hangout in Piraxis, hell, any system. All kinds of vice awaited and at a very reasonable price but right now Rick needed a man who could read, write and speak both English and Negz fluently. Sonnet had a translator yet it was woeful, the thing couldn't detect many of the fine nuances in the language, you might easily say hello but end up telling the receiver to get lost. Sam had tried to programme a translator for years yet he was always forced to step in. You see much of negz communication relies on body language, facial expression and stance, did he say that with hands raised? Was the brow up or down if so it wasn't a compliment but an insult.

Man had made great advancements in AI, they could recognise anyone on sight and detect if they were lying with a certainty of around 90%, humans that is. Other species were a different matter, and negz? Forget it, no-one knew enough about them to programme a universal translator that could operate with a certainty above 25%.

Sonnet clamped onto one of Templeton's many docking arms set aside for strippers. The station was a series of prefabricated blocks intended for different constructions, welded together and pressed to service this mighty den of vice and trade.

The blocky port floated close to the Piraxis sun, its rays splashing on her solar panels, powering a mighty space beast. Against black and grey blocks, dotted lights beamed from within. Hundreds of docking arms protruded from her body as clumps of straw from a bale of hay though you couldn't make out individual craft, not at a distance. Thousands of ships populated long docking arms at any one time, this was truly a temple of joy where people from all over the galaxy came to pay homage to their gods.

Rick decided to visit Shaniqua and deliver his gift, she'd cast light chasing away the gloom of his existence.

They dropped out the airlock one by one and walked along the docking arm into Templeton's. The crew were chatting, you could hear excitement in their voices. The next few days would be compensation for a month of hard work.

'You okay Rick?' asked Dyson.

'I'm fine.'

'You look pissed.'

'We need to replace Sam before the next skirmish.'

'I know but what you gonna do?'

'I'm just wondering where I'll find a replacement.'

'You'll do it, you always do.'

'Aren't you helping?'

Dyson chuckled then patted Rick on the back, 'I'm gonna be a busy man for the next few days. I'll say hello to Shaniqua for you.'

Rick furrowed his brow, 'I'll say hello meself thank you very much!'

'Sure, sure,' they reached the end of the airlock to be greeted by two security guards. Each man showed his Templeton's ID card to pass swiftly into customs then onto main street, 'see you around buddy.' Dyson and the crew dissolved into a crowd of people, shifting positions as a busy day on Regent's Street.

On the outer edge were small establishments, noisy little cafe's releasing and odour of dirty linen onto passers-by. The outer hull was broken up by long strips of carbon glass where one might view the planet below while eating your bagel. The odd burst of white light from above decorated patrons in a divine splash.

Rick looked down at his present, he missed his time with Shaniqua, what little he spent with her.

Chapter Six

A shining palace twinkled in the gloom of Red Sector. Lamp posts lit his path right and left as the street elevated his steps, pipes leaked from blackness onto merry makers giving the impression of a sultry night rain. Steam rose from manholes below, a multi-storey party zone full of lost children searching to fill empty lives, not that they'd find it here.

Rick walked a long dank street brimming with men looking for love and women for credits. He approached a gilt edged monument to indulgence known throughout the system as Shaniqua's.

From humble beginnings one poor girl built a fortune with her own hands, an impossible achievement in Corps space. Shaniqua's family settled an agricultural moon until brachians took possession. She was lucky to make it out alive, her parents not so. Shaniqua's three sisters required food, medicine and clothes so she did what she had to. Thirty years on and Shaniqua's was the jewel in Red Sector's crown. I know that doesn't sound too wonderful but it beats being raped and murdered by brachians any day of the week.

Shaniqua's gilt-edged wall ran several floors up, a glittering beacon to every man with more money than sense. A large fellow about six and a half feet, 300lbs, wearing a very nice black suit with white shirt and black tie stood beneath a sign: "NO BRACHIANS".

'You alright Leroy?' said Rick.

Leroy looked down his nose, nothing personal but genetics offered little choice, 'Do I know you?'

Rick furrowed his brow, 'It's me, Rick.'

'Rick?'

'You know, Shaniqua's boyfriend? I just got back from a big haul at Luyten's.'

'Sure, come in sir.'

Leroy must be off tonight, having to remember so many faces, it's understandable. Well that's what Rick told himself as for you and I we've got a better handle on the situation. Rick was a lonely guy and Shaniqua a master manipulator, everything taken into account he didn't stand a chance.

Rick's eyes lit as a child opening Christmas presents, he was home. A gleaming central stage touched each corner of the establishment like an octopus, tentacles substituted by four-way catwalks. Each appendage was lined by a bar where men rested at various states of inebriation. The establishment carried for three floors up, a converted opera room, men and women populated balconies circumnavigating the establishment while perspex boxes containing women hung from its ceiling. Rick scanned the room until he found what he was searching for, Shaniqua, always dressed in a revealing gold tasselled mini dress but hold on … she was with another man? I know what you're thinking, is it possible for a grown man of Rick's age and experience to be this naïve? The answer is most positively yes and he's not alone by any means. One of many admirers Shaniqua had accrued over the years and milked on a regular basis for every damn credit she could.

Shaniqua listened to some guy talk while sucking on a split straw. Just to clarify that's a straw filled with crystallised split. Users snap open its cap dip the wooden end in sticky toffee, pull it out and suck on salty split to induce a high.

Shaniqua dipped into sweet toffee before sucking the straw in a bewitching manner, she had years of practice. Her long silky black legs crossed permitting a man to see further than any lady should permit. Shaniqua seemed captivated by the man's story, in fact she was bored out of her mind but it was part of the job, the customer always got what he wanted at Shaniqua's.

Rick approached the table and loomed over the business suit. The fellow put his drink down, 'You want something?'

'You're in me seat,' stated Rick.

'Get the fuck outta here,' scoffed the customer.

'I said you're in me seat!'

Shaniqua ejected from her divan, 'Cool down Rick we was just talking. Why don't you go see Chloe and I'll be right over.'

'I don't want to see Chloe I came all the bloody way from Luyten's to see you.'

'Luyten's?' Shaniqua was up on all fleet movements, 'Leroy,' the bouncer moved over. Shaniqua turned on her previous patron, 'Get him outta here.' Shaniqua's suit was under the impression Rick was about to meet eviction but Leroy's gaze fell upon him, 'It's time to leave sir.'

'What?'

'Don't make me throw you out sir.'

'Fuck you nigger!'

Leroy grabbed him by the lapels lifting him clean into the air, 'Say what?'

'I ... I was just leaving.'

'That's what I thought,' he released the suit onto his feet, 'let me show you to the door sir.'

As her previous mark was led away Shaniqua grinned at Rick, 'You must miss me barging in here like that.'

'I brought you something,' he offered his gift.

Shaniqua giggled like a young girl, 'Oh Rick,' split stick in her mouth she opened her gift to see the smallest bottle of Alien Mystery on the market, receipt in box. Shaniqua's visage went from excited to underwhelmed, 'You went to Luyten's to buy me this?'

'I was at the Ring and thought of you.'

Shaniqua examined the bottle then stated in a deprecating tone, 'And not for long.'

'What?'

She smiled, 'Just kidding, you make a good haul?'

'Yeh, got a big score off a negg frigate.'

Her grin widened as she placed a split stick between her lips, 'Why don't you tell me all about it?'

Shaniqua tugged him by the arm, a tray containing a bottle of metaxa and two shot glasses arrived. Rick made himself comfortable as he poured libations.

'Drink?'

'Why not,' giggled Shaniqua, and why not? For he was paying ten times the price and she would consume at least half. I know what you're wondering, how could she keep up with Rick drink for drink? Well one of split's effects is to break down alcohol in the bloodstream before reaching the brain. So now you know why Shaniqua was a split head for in the long run it made her money. A single bottle of spirits would pay for a single stick of split and a single stick of split would allow her to knock back ten bottles of spirits unaffected.

Rick spent an evening in the arms of Shaniqua, dancing, drinking and screwing, that is she screwed him for the most part. The following day he arrived at Sonnet 350 credits lighter and a headache. Dyson checked out navigation systems synchronising them with Templeton's database. Every stripper uploaded new information as a professional courtesy. They may be in competition but this station survived on fortunes of salvage ships. Templeton's owner had long instituted a law, all docking fees are waved provided navigational data is uploaded and made available for free. It kept everyone in business and the extra cash generated found its way into the pockets of Templeton's entrepreneurs. Thanks to the war this port had gone from a backwater toilet to one of the wealthiest stations outside Corps space. Earth Corps' outflow of wealth found its way to Templeton's, Muon city (someone had to get supplies past negz blockades) and last but by no means least Neumeyer's, a small mining outpost that'd grown to a multi-billion credit station in the Ross 882 system renamed Ross-Neumeyer. Demand for materials had caused the mining industry to boom and despite a price cap on core miners those outside were not so hampered, but I'm straying from the point. Dyson was synchronising information, a simultaneous download/upload, when Rick dragged himself into the cockpit clutching a glass of milk.
'How's Shaniqua?'
'She's good.'
'Isn't she always?'

'I suppose so. How was your night?' Rick relaxed into his pit chair, cleared some trash and put his feet on the dashboard.

'You know, same as usual.'

'Recruiting today?'

'Come on, it's time to kick back, have a few drinks and get some pussy.'

'If we don't recruit a bloke who understands negg we'll be doing a lot less of that in the future.'

'Can't it wait?'

'Nope.'

Dyson sighed, 'Fine I'll do it today but someone's gotta take tomorrow.'

Rick's eyes were closed as he fought the pain, 'I'll set up a rota.'

'Just my luck, finally get a big score with wall to wall pussy and Sam decides to go save the fucking universe!'

'Good morning.'

Rick crumpled physically and mentally as Peters' naturally high voice shot through his body, warm milk sloshed over his flight suit.

'You okay?'

'If you could just lower your voice a few decibels.'

'Am I speaking loud?'

Peters was one of those guys who had a knack of always appearing at the wrong moment. It was a demonic side to his character his crewmates found disturbing from time to time.

Rick cringed again.

Dyson whispered to Peters, 'Shaniqua's.'

Peters face reflected enlightenment, 'So how's the old girl doing?'

'Wonderful, just wonderful,' whispered Rick as he sipped what remained of his milk.

'So how much did that headache cost you?'

'About 300 credits.'

'FUCK!'

Rick spilt the rest of his milk as daggers plunged into his brain to erupt from behind his eyes.

Peters witnessed Rick's reaction, 'Sorry, but fuck, you must've had a good night.'

Dyson sniggered as Rick wallowed in misery, 350 credits for a headache and a laundry bill. Well, scratch the laundry bill Rick had been saving on that for the past three months. Maybe that's how he paid for his time at Shaniqua's? Clean your flight suit and underwear once every six months ... that's if Rick even wore underwear in which case he'd save more ... he'd do the arithmetic as soon as Chronos permitted.

Later that day Rick and Dyson sat outside a cheap restaurant on main street, drinks, doughnuts, dirty linen and a line of hopefuls aspiring to fortune in future battlefields.

'Name?'

A young man moved from the front to sit before Rick and Dyson, 'Andre.'

'Okay Andre, I'm looking for a tactical officer that means a man who speaks negg,' he looked over his clipboard, 'do you speak negg?'

'Well,' Andre fidgeted for a moment.

'Well?' asked Dyson as he scratched one inch of hair due another shave.

'I can say hello.'

'Tany ner khen be?' said Rick in his best negg accent.

'Sorry?'

Rick crossed his name off, 'Forget it kid, next?'

An hour later, no luck, a day, no luck, a week, no luck. Finding someone like Sam wasn't going to be easy but what choice did he have? They needed a tactical officer for without one it would be comparatively fruitless to board a negz wreck. If you're unable to get those data cores, the downside of your investment (that is the risk) versus the delta between investment and market price (profit) becomes far too great.

Every day for a week and still no-one who could speak let alone read and write the language fluently. Rick worried if Shaniqua was missing him, truth be told she missed him like a bad cold, if it weren't for his money she wouldn't even spit on him.

'Next.'

A young lady sat down batted her eyelids and unzip a generous portion of cleavage, 'I'm Megan.'

'Tany ner khen be?'

'Megan my name's Megan.'

Rick sat to attention, unknown to Megan he'd just asked her name in negz.

'Sain bainuu?'

'Yes please.'

'You don't speak negg.'

'Maybe not but I could be useful in other ways,' she gave a seductive smile.

'Sorry kid but I need a man that speaks negg not a girl that talks shit.'

She shot to her feet, 'Fuck you asshole!' and stormed off.

Rick was about to call his next candidate when beyond Templeton's movement caught his eye. Strippers disembarked en-masse, a bee hive awakened from its slumber as the Queen's armies departed to scavenge profit.

'Gov, you there?' came Peters over the collar phone.

'Yeh, what the fuck's happening?'

'Earth Corps, looks like they hit back for Luyten's.'

'I'll be there in five minutes,' he and Dyson jumped to their feet, 'Sorry people but duty calls.'

The crowd of hopefuls groaned as Rick paid the tab and jogged down main street to catch up with Dyson. Dyson downloaded information to his pad from Templeton's mainframe.

'What are we looking at?' asked Rick marching toward their docking slip.

'It looks like they hit Epsilon Tauri with everything, reports say it's a nasty state of affairs, plenty of negg salvage.'

'Epsilon Tauri? What's in that system?'

'Shipyards. Corps jumped in trashed their docks then jumped out. Fuck me, it looks like we've won one!'

'But it's negg space.'

'It's on the edge, risky but big money if we can pull it off.'

'That's what those arseholes are thinking,' he peered at a swarm of ships approaching the Piraxis jump gate.

'Distance?'

'About 160 light years, hyperspace to our backs we can make it in 12 hours.'

'Weather reports?'

'Smooth, all the way.'

'Let's do it.'

Sonnet released clamps closed airlocks and drifted away. She turned to face the Piraxis jump gate and made best speed with other late comers. The gate had already fired up, deep blue swirled within beckoning a multitude of vessel. Gate fees reduced on every ten craft.

Back on the station Templeton observed from his ivory tower, he lit an expensive cigar in celebration of future profit. Everything but that cold radiance of blue hyperspace lost its value in his eyes.

They slipped into the blue void with hyperspace to their backs and engines burning urillium like it was going out of style. Sonnet powered toward negz space. This was going to be dangerous but strippers felt safety in numbers, as a pack of hyenas they descended upon an injured beast greater than any single vessel might consume, tearing it to pieces. In this war you knew battle was over when a swarm of strippers emerged from hyperspace to pick apart what remained. Negz despised them as did Earth Corps but they were a necessary vice if humanity were to stay in the game.

This wasn't going to be easy without Sam but when Plutus beckoned, come hell or high water, Rick would get a share. Negz dockyards had to contain lots of raw materials, super alloys, energy cells, reactor cores, replacement parts and who knows he might stumble on some data crystals without Sam.

Sonnet travelled the blueberry ocean as it pushed them toward Epsilon Tauri where destiny awaited. A journey that'd usually take days would be mere hours thanks to the tides of this hidden dimension. Sonnet's crew were concerned by what awaited on the other side, would negz be in ambush, or perhaps they were blindsided permitting little time to muster forces? Rick believed neither of these, it was his conviction the negz were so committed to current military operations they'd ignore this distraction.

Negz are not only stubborn but cautious, this kind of attack on a soft target would be deemed insignificant compared to any offensive operations prepared. Epsilon Tauri would be left to the mercy of strippers while negz concentrated on current commitments for Earth was spent, she had little more than a cheap shot on the edge of the Hyades cluster.

The Hyades cluster is a group of stars about 150 light years from Earth Corps space. Twenty light years across, it's ruled by the negz, in the night sky you can see it in the constellation of Taurus, the face of the bull.

Earth suffered the horns of that bull as he charged into sovereign Corps space. In retaliation Earth hit an outer system, launching a spear into the creature's hide. A tactic serving but to enrage this taurine beast ... yet what choice did they have? Leave this alien minotaur unchallenged while those below contemplate Earth Corps' ineptitude? Have them believe Earth is weak? So, a target with sufficient infrastructure was selected. The tides of hyperspace permitted a fast approach from Earth yet slowed any response from within the Hyades Cluster. Who knows, maybe there was information in those crystals Rick had sold leading to this. That thought may have sat well with others but not Rick. He didn't care for this type of attack, for innocent civilians would be involved. If a bunch of hired murderers wanted to punch it out in space with no collateral damage that was fine but killing people who were just getting on with their lives, negz or human, it wasn't his style. Despite no direct evidence Rick felt responsibility then guilt manifested itself. Crazy I know but he did it to himself at every opportunity, it's just Rick's way.

The generator cranked up opening a slit in hyperspace, Sonnet was spat into space-time somewhere on the edge of negz controlled space. A planet engulfed by bright torches, resembling Earth, appeared bathed in bright flame. Several totalled shipyards encircled the world. Upper atmosphere consumed them a piece at a time as large chunks, smashed off by kinetic warheads, crumpled into one another. Military stations once covering the third planet had been obliterated by an Earth Corps advance. Rick shook his head as he thought, 'They'll do the same to Earth in a year.'

'Rick?'

He snapped out of his malaise, 'Yeh?'

'I got co-ordinates, a section of dockyard there's some atmosphere, we can board it.'

'Life signs?'

'No idea, everything's gone nuts.'

'Let's do it.'

Sonnet's engines gave a momentary blast of power sending her from above the elliptical plane to orbit the third planet. To stray from Earth Corps' cleared path was poor judgement.

'Twenty ships came in and twenty left, our boys got out clean,' Peters said with a smile.

Rick observed dockyards burning an orbit, 'Not clean.'

'What do you mean?'

'They left with blood on their hands.'

'Negg blood.'

'I suppose a couple of neggs will have a similar conversation after they've slaughtered your family?'

'Come on Rick you're starting to sound like Sam.'

'Murder is murder no matter how you justify it.'

'Yeh well you don't exactly complain about the money.'

Rick took a deep breath, 'I don't make the game.'

Peters picked out a long relatively undamaged section floating in a stable orbit. The plan was to board rip out what they could, undock and strip the area for alloy before getting out of Dodge.

Sonnet lowered her belly onto the thinnest section of hull Peters could find. Allenby spent half an hour burning through with Sonnet's plasma ring before exposing the station's innards.

Rick dropped down with rifle slung over his back, this wasn't some farming colony or a deserted ship. Allenby next then Graham.

'If its blue shoot.'

'Yes Gov.'

'Yes Gov.'

Rick led his team choosing right and left at random while a compass hanging off his belt tracked their path. Negz script adorned the walls but it was all Chinese to him, finally they stumbled upon a large open area, a cargo bay? Perhaps ships docked here to refit or resupply? Rick wasn't sure but considering the amount of real estate set aside he felt certain to discover something of value.

Rick pointed the barrel of his rifle, his crewmates moved toward a tall stack of cargo containers. Rick assumed the whole corner was packed with crates which in moments Allenby would open. He closed in, heard a sniff, side stepped to his right and all was revealed. Carbon boxes didn't fill the corner, they were but a facade concealing a group of twenty or more negz.

Rick and his crew aimed weapons, keen to let rip, yet they didn't fire for these were civilians perhaps maintenance personnel or dock loaders. Whatever their job they'd been abandoned to Ananke, daughter to Chronos and Goddess of inevitability, fated to burn in this planet's atmosphere or executed by heartless strippers.

'Don't move and no-one gets hurt,' stated Rick in a forceful tone as his red laser dot traversed a huddled group.

Men, women and children wore dull brown uniforms resembling occupants of a Chinese labour camp. Despite Ananke's foreboding presence they displayed no sign of fear This group were as solemn and sedate as a Jersey cow on pot, their fortitude impressed Rick.

'What's in those crates?'

No response.

Rick grabbed a translator and typed, it interpreted English text to Negz speech, 'You bain dotona?'

His captives exchanged puzzled looks.

'Graham you watch them, Allenby help me move these crates,' Rick presumed the communication barrier unbreakable.

'We should shoot them now,' suggested Allenby.

'Any man pulls a trigger without my say so he'll join them, understood?' Allenby sighed, 'Let's get started.'

Before they could begin a voice spoke from the mass of negz, a voice with a Russian edge, 'You require assistance,' in a flash Rick stopped what he was doing and aimed, poised to take the shot.

Rick assumed it was another stripper but from a sea of brown uniforms a figure appeared … a dark conquistador. Just like the warrior he'd killed in Luyten's it wore that same long backed tunic with embossed beasts on either side. Boots protecting its shins, trousers and jumper made of similar material. Outer padding protected vital areas similar to an Earth Corps Marine uniform at least in philosophy. The black tunic covering its torso was somewhat gothic in nature. Ribs of woven graphene protected the torso creating bulges where organs and arteries required extra insulation, as practical as it was comfortable. A negz warrior was expected to fight to his full ability, for this to be reality distraction from combat must be eliminated.

It wore a pair of ornate black velvet gloves, graphene protected vital areas so even under heavy punishment a negz warrior may continue its duty. The most shocking part of this gothic conquistador was its gender. Rick was unaware negz women were permitted to fight but then again he didn't know much about their culture. Hell, he couldn't even communicate with them through a translator.

Her face was your typical negz, humanoid with deep eye sockets incorporating a pair of passionate blue eyes. Negz have an armoured bone structure protecting the face and forehead and she was no different. An intimidating, ironclad profile. A sturdy forehead receded back a few inches further than a human skull, forming a tiny bulge. This is where it got interesting. For all their reinforced bone structure, ten times as resilient as a human's, its rear was fragile. Natural selection decided negz meet danger face forward. Millennia after evolution resolved the species' format negz conformed, meeting foe head on with neither fear nor mercy. At the rear of her skull a small patch of deep black hair had been woven into a plait hanging about one inch above the base of her neck.

On examining her alien visage Rick detected a sage melancholy, though to be honest all negz had that bent. Strapped to her back a traditional negz fighting spear ran from her left boot to finish beyond her head. She displayed deep blue lips, an odd tattoo of lines and dots rested above her left eyebrow. He'd seen negz or pictures of negz with similar tattoos yet Rick had no idea what, if anything, it signified.

Three red dots migrated between her neck and groin. 'You speak English?' asked Rick while aiming his rifle.

'Affirmative.'

'One move love and your mates'll be eating brains for breakfast.'

'I comprehend,' she raised her arms exposing palms to the three men, 'Sain baina uu.'

The other negz followed exposing bare palms, 'Sain baina uu.'

'Are there any more neggs on this section?'

'Negative. Clarify your desire kumun.'

'We were just passing through and thought we'd take a gander.'

'You are thieves.' The negz stated with contempt.

'I prefer the term salvage recovery expert.'

She lowered her arms, 'Kumuns are murderers and thieves.'

'Have it your way, now what's in the crates?'

She glanced at several neat stacks, 'Cargo.'

'Specifically.'

She examined white script on each box, 'Spare parts, food, clothing … urillium.'

Rick, Allenby and Graham glanced at one another with hope.

The negz sneered, angular features replete with disdain for these kumuns, 'But four crates contain urillium.'

'Which ones?'

She folded her arms with calculated bravado.

'Which ones?'

'I refuse to assist murderers and thieves.'

'These crates'll burn up in a few hours.'

'Affirmative.'

'So what's the difference?'

'I will not have aided a thief.'

'Okay Madame, cut the crap, what do you want for the urillium?'

She peered down her nose, her condescending sneer of superiority irritated Rick but there was much profit to be made with only a short time to realise it. 'It is not mine to trade.'

'Don't play silly buggers love, you wouldn't have told me it was here if you didn't want something for it.'

Her sneer vanished, she pointed at twenty or so negz behind her, 'It is theirs.'

Rick lowered his rifle and ran his hand through greasy hair, 'And what do they want for it?'

'Passage to a safe system.'

Rick chuckled to himself, 'Are you fucking crazy?'

Allenby cut in, 'She's a fucking negg-head!'

'Provide these people free passage and I will identify the urillium.'

'Twenty neggs on MY ship?'

'You shall not be inconvenienced, I give you my word.'

'I can't take your word on anything.'

She sat on hard metal floor, the others followed her lead, 'In which case you shall have nothing and we shall die.'

Rick thought for a moment then turned to Allenby, 'If we just take the urillium there'll be enough room in the hold.'

'They're neggs, they'll cut our throats in the night and take the ship. Look at her she's a fucking nut case!'

'My people are neither thieves nor murderers, you have my word.'

Graham moved in and whispered so only Allenby and Rick could hear, 'We can dump them into hyperspace as soon as we leave.'

Rick's visage exhibited disdain, 'I keep me word.'

'But she's a negg.'

'But it's still my word.'

Rick thought for a moment, if just one cargo crate were filled with urillium, hell, with the premium right now he could take it directly to the bank in Piraxis. The part of the deal he didn't like was having more than twenty negz in his cargo hold but there was something about this woman, Rick's gut told him her word was good.

'It's a deal,' Rick lowered his rifle offering his hand. Rather than shake his hand she looked down her nose.

'We shake hands to seal a deal.'

'As you desire,' she clutched his hand then made a puzzled expression as Rick shook their arms up and down.

'Okay, let's get those crates and drag them back to Sonnet. Graham you get back, let Dyson know who's coming aboard.'

Graham glanced at the negz and walked out of the hangar reading his compass.

The negz turned to her compatriots pointed at a long wall of cargo crates and barked, 'Avts nada xowd urillium!'

They were straight on the case knocking the wall down to reach crates beneath, centre and top. Watching them gather the correct crates Rick realised he'd never have recovered all the urillium without their assistance. Carbon crates were dragged before the powder blue alien concealed within dark garments, 'You may inspect the crates, kumun.'

Allenby approached with a tool, using leverage and a fair bit of muscle he popped each one open. A brown/yellow substance sparkled before their eyes, a fortune in urillium, now he'd need to move the stuff onto Sonnet and get the hell out of Dodge before a negz war fleet appeared or the dockyard burnt up.

'Okay seal them and get them aboard.'

Allenby was about to do it when the mysterious conquistador spoke, 'My people will perform this task, direct us to your vessel.'

Allenby fixed his eyes on Rick. Rick nodded, 'Alright Madame, we'll do it your way.'

Once all four crates had been sealed they quickly carried their treasure back to Sonnet's point of entry. Boxes of precious urillium were tied to ropes and lifted inside Sonnet one by one to be secured in her hold.

The dark soldier turned to Rick, 'I have kept my word.'

'Have your people climb in.'

She addressed her fellow negz, 'Kodol deeshee dotona xundaga.'

They formed a line and dutifully ascended one by one into Sonnet. Not one questioned her orders nor the logic behind climbing into the belly of an enemy craft. On a level Rick was impressed by her hold over these people yet he believed its origins to be sinister. Perhaps they were slaves? Negz wouldn't be the first species to enslave its own kind. Maybe they were artificials? But these were questions to be answered at a later date, right now he was concerned with getting away from this wreck and into hyperspace before things went south. Once aboard negz were ushered to the cargo hold at gun point, where they squatted in sober silence. Rick found it odd they were yet to talk, the one in black spoke while those in brown listened. Perhaps it was something to do with their culture?

Rick filled his pilot chair, loaded rifle slung over its back, 'Okay, detach and get us above the plane.'

Stanchions released claws, airlock closed and a rush of atmosphere from inside pushed Sonnet away. There was no time to re-seal the hull for this was hostile space. Rick didn't want to be caught with his pants down if a negz counter strike jumped in. It was doubtful they'd take into account his careful resealing of hull before pulling the trigger on a beam weapon.

Thrusters gently turned Sonnet, her nose pointed upwards above the plane and engines fired a short burn setting them in motion.

'Where are we going?' asked Dyson hunched over navigation readouts, ready to punch in co-ordinates.

Peters looked over his shoulder with a nervous visage waiting on Rick's next words.

'A star kumuns name Hyades 92.'

100

All three men swivelled on their chairs to see her standing in the rear of the cockpit arms crossed over chest. Dyson's hand moved toward a pistol holster resting on his console.

She spoke down to Dyson in a tone of negz superiority, 'Even in this confined space, my curxaj-tayag will slice away your puny kumun hand.'

'Leave it Dyson,' stated Rick.

Dyson wasn't listening and lunged toward his pistol grip. In a flash she whipped her staff from behind slamming it onto the console between Dyson's hand and weapon. Dyson jumped in shock, a spear tip shot out and he jumped again. Peters hand slipped down his leg toward his holster. She turned her attention to the movement and he shrunk away. The dark clothed conquistador with but a tint of blue in its skin fixed her eyes on Rick and with a cruel oriental smile stated, 'Hyades 92, best speed kumun.'

'You heard the lady,' stated Rick.

'You sure about this Gov?'

'I'm four crates of urillium sure, now get us the fuck out of here.'

'Fine,' replied Dyson moving a shaky hand to his navigation console.

As he tapped in co-ordinates the negz sheathed her staff, 'If you require further assistance I will be in the cargo area,' she strode out the cockpit.

'I hope you know what you're doing Gov,' stated Dyson.

'You worry about your job. I've got her under control.'

Dyson's hands shook as he confirmed their destination with the navigation computer, 'Whatever.'

Chapter Seven

Entering hyperspace without incident Sonnet's crew sat around the galley table to discuss their negz woes.

'According to weather reports it'll be a few days to H-92. We'll take it in shifts, two of us will always be awake while the others rest.'

'But there's twenty of them!' stated Graham.

'Then we'll be extra special careful, won't we?'

'I don't like this, twenty negg-heads and one's a soldier.'

Rick tried to ease fears but Graham was an old spacefarer. Like many engineers he was stubborn to the damn core and that wasn't going to change.

'So what?' said Rick in a dismissive tone.

'She's a killer!'

'She's a woman, probably worked in logistics or something.'

'She ain't logistics.'

'How do you know that?'

'Did you see that tat above her eye ridge?'

'So?'

'She's got a line and two dots.'

'And?'

'When they get a confirmed kill, in battle, they have a single dot tattooed above the left eye ridge. After ten kills a line's drawn through the dots and they start again above the new line. She's had a dozen confirmed kills and that means in a fire fight with Marines.'

'We'll be armed at all times.'

Graham laughed in a disdainful tone, 'Are you fucking mad? I've seen those psychos in action.'

Dyson poured whisky from a half bottle into his coffee, everyone observed him battle shakes, 'It was fast with that stick.'

'It's called a curxaj-tayag. Negg kids are taught to kill with that thing as soon as they can stand.'

Dyson struggled to steady his cup, 'I say we space them.'

Graham slammed the table, 'Fucking right!'

Rick's eyes narrowed on Graham, 'This is my ship, I make the rules and no-one gets spaced. If that's a problem you better tell me now 'cause if one of them has an accident I'll be holding you personally responsible.'

Graham scoffed through a bushy beard, 'You gonna kill me over some fucking negg-heads?'

'I've given me word and I intend to keep it, wherever that may lead.'

Graham stood up, 'When the time comes I'll shoot back,' he stormed out the galley and into his cabin.

Dyson stared into his coffee still dazed from his cockpit encounter, 'How come he knows so much about neggs?'

'He worked on a freighter in brachian space, it got boarded by neggs.'

'Why'd they attack brachian space?'

'Fuck knows, I'm not a politician, I go where the money is and right now we're looking at more than 800lbs of urillium between the five of us. As long as they keep their word I keep mine and that means no hostilities, understood?'

Everyone agreed mumbling under their breath.

'KUMUN!'

Rick turned to see a gothic conquistador, arms folded with calculated bravado, standing in the doorway, 'What?'

'You are Captain of this junk?'

'I'm sorry?'

'You are deaf? I asked a question!'

'I heard you and yes I'm the Captain of this ship.'

'Follow me, I require your assistance.'

Rick followed her through the centre hallway, past cabins, below engineering down into the cargo hold. Negz sat together quietly like the faded fragrance of a scent, awaiting the woman in black's instruction. She stopped turned to

Rick and folded her arms again, 'I require blankets, water and food until we reach Hyades 92.'

Rick moved toward one of many crates lashed to the wall, unbuckled some straps and grabbed one end. Rick paused, glared at the woman, she glared back, 'Well?' he asked.

'I am well.'

'Are you going to stand there looking like an arsehole or help me move this thing?'

She uncrossed her arms moved to the other end and shifted the heavy container safely to the floor. Rick popped it open to reveal food bars, sleeping blankets and a water condenser with bags of purified water.

'Do you need a heater?'

'No, this temperature is tolerable.'

'If there's nothing else I'll be in the galley.'

'One request.'

'Yeh?'

'Clarify,' it came out somewhat broken, 'arsehole?'

Rick smirked, 'An anal passage.'

In a nano second the warrior slapped Rick around the face, damn that glove hurt. The left side of his face turned bright red, he did a good job of burying surprise yet she was unconvinced. The other negz observed in silence wondering what might unfold. Rick leant in to whisper with a cold and joyless resolve, 'You get that one for free, next time I'll knock your fucking teeth out.'

He stepped back and left the cargo hold in a shitty mood.

Sonnet travelled the deep blue, eddys conspired to push her off course but Dyson kept track. According to the negz Hyades 92 would be a safe uninhabited system yet the crew were sceptical. Graham was downright against the entire plan but Rick was set in his convictions, for one it was a big score and second he trusted the negz. She was stubborn and obnoxious yet it was his impression she kept her word and he always kept his.

It'd be three days travel in the blue, two men were always on duty and armed to the teeth. Rick sat at his pilot's console, pistol snugly in its leather holster. His eyes fell into the hypnotic deep hue of hyperspace while his ears relaxed to the music of AC/DC, foot tapping to the beat,

"My mind was aching,
And we were making it,
And you shook me all night long,
Yeah you shook me all night long,
Knocked me out I said you,
Shook me all night long,
You had me shaking and you,
Shook me all night long,
Yeah you shook me,
When you took me."

He started playing air guitar as Angus Young kicked in, unknown to Rick his gothic passenger had been woken by the noise and decided to investigate. She stood directly behind, arms crossed and rippled forehead. Her eyes darted from flexed shoulders to crazed fingers … perhaps he had a medical condition?
'KUMUN!' shouted the soldier.
Rick leapt out his seat, slapped the dashboard cutting the guitar, 'WHAT?'
'Your noise is unacceptable.'
'What?'
'Your noise impedes my people's rest period.'
'I'll play it lower.'
'I have another request.'
Rick picked his coffee from the dashboard and took a gulp, it seems AC/DC had undermined his desire to stay alert, 'What?'
'My people have been aboard nearly a cycle, they must relieve themselves.'
Rick chuckled like a schoolboy, 'Don't let me get in the way.'

She sighed at his puerile mentality, 'Where might one urinate and defecate?'
'You mean the shit house?'
The alien conquistador pursed her lips, 'In a manner.'
He put the coffee back down, 'Follow me.'
Rick walked past her into the mid-section (a central gangway running between the cockpit and rear) and turned left opposite the galley/lounge. To his left and right were six hatches leading to crew cabins. The alien's small pointed nose began to wrinkle after sampling the local atmosphere.
Rick noticed her discomfort, 'Something wrong?'
'This vessel, its atmosphere processors are malfunctioning?'
'Nope.'
'I have noticed a distinct odour ever since coming aboard, it intensifies as we travel this passage.'
'It's called the shit house,' he glanced at her and with a sardonic tone in his voice said, 'or if you want to be polite, the bog.'
'A bog is an area of muddy ground, is it not?'
Rick grinned, 'It is,' they reached the end of the corridor he hit a wall pad. A hatch opened to reveal Sonnet's communal toilet and by god it was a scary sight. The toilet hadn't been cleaned in … well it hadn't been cleaned. The pan rested inside a small cubicle, wash basin to the right. A small table contained a selection of pornographic holo-mags, ashtray and some empty cans of bitter. The alien was horrified yet her horror was quickly superseded upon inhaling a vile stench. The furies assaulted her lungs like a bag of hammers.
She began to wretch, quickly losing that sober negz bravado, staggering back to the cockpit swaying from side to side. Before making it out the sable conquistador bashed into one of six cabin doors. Graham emerged loaded rifle in hand. He looked to the left as she disappeared then right to see Rick congratulating himself.
'What happened?' asked Graham.
'I've discovered their weakness,' Rick shut the toilet hatch.

The dark soldier's restrained elegance dissipated as she hunched over Dyson's cockpit chair trying to keep her previous meal down. Rick entered the room, face beaming like a naughty boy who'd pulled off an April fools. Bent over Dyson's station her tunic's long back parted down the centre revealing the alien's rear end. Rick stood hands in pockets leaning to the side so he might get an eyeful. To tell the truth Rick had seen much worse … he'd paid for worse. Despite being a stuck-up alien bitch she possessed a decent derriere even by human standards, damn that taught rounded peach was pretty … Rick recoiled from that train of thought as she coughed and spluttered, 'Clean your facilities.'

'I don't think that's possible.'

She wiped a foamy liquid from delicate blue lips, 'You must!'

Rick stood straight and looked around the cockpit, 'Do you see any women?'

'I see none.'

'Exactly, women prefer a clean toilet, men we just need a place to shit but we can take a piss anywhere.'

'I do not comprehend,' winced the alien.

'We need a place to shit but after a few drinks the cargo bay does for a piss,' Rick put on a fake French accent, 'That is where the fine aroma of ammonia comes from Madame.'

She began to wretch foam again, 'I assumed this ship suffered a chemical leak. Kumuns are worse than toroj!'

'What's a toroj?

'A vile primitive exterminated centuries ago,' she stood up, 'your people are destined to join them.'

'Yeh well that's the only bog on the ship.'

'We cannot share these facilities with kumuns.'

'You can shit your pants for all I care just make sure you don't drop any shrapnel.'

The alien furrowed her forehead creating ripples like water beneath the wind, 'You will clean that toilet.'

He replied in a forceful tone, 'No.'

'Then provide my people with means to do so.'

The crew hadn't dared attempt such a thing in over a year and Rick didn't believe she was serious but he'd not met a negz until today. Besides it was the shrine of the single male, a filthy toilet with seat up, he guessed they'd go maybe two minutes before throwing it in? Another glorious victory for the human race.

Rick retired to his cabin and slept. Six hours later the beast rose from its den of filth in a pair of old boxer shorts yet to grace a washing machine. Rick picked a flight suit off the floor, he paused on noticing a patch of orange coloured sauce, hmmm a fresh stain. Rick peered down to observe a half-eaten chicken madras, discarded his blue suit, bent down and picked up the disposable plastic tray. There were no utensils so a piece of stale naan bread served as a shovel. Last night's curry, Rick's favourite breakfast. He glanced around the floor to see an open can of lager, picked it up and washed his meal down with the flat beverage. Rick rubbed the stain off his suit with grubby bed sheets before slipping it on, checked himself in the mirror, combed back dirty brown hair with yellow stained fingers, shuffled to the door and put his work boots on before opening the hatch to another bright day aboard Sonnet.

On exiting his cabin Rick detected something odd. Taking a step back Rick quietly lifted a holster laying on the table and drew his P-38 before venturing outside. He identified something, something he'd not sensed before, a strange chemical smell, a leak caused by a fire fight? Rick checked his weapon before flicking its safety off. He turned left, hands tightly gripped. On approaching its source stark chemicals began to overpower his sinuses, it couldn't be, no. The door opened and he levelled his weapon on a frightened negz, the creature froze, Rick shooed the fellow away. The negz walked past Rick, moving through Sonnet's narrow corridor but rather than monitor the alien Rick's eyes fixed squarely upon the ship's toilet, sparkling clean and smelling of, yes that was it, detergent.

Rick was stunned, he could see the original porcelain, it'd been years since he'd witnessed its cream colour. The ashtray was emptied with magazines stacked in a neat pile, hell they were even in alphabetical order! The wash basin free of stains … you could actually see your reflection in the mirror! And the area at the back of the unit where urine gathered, evaporating to form an ammonia slime, it'd disappeared! In a single moment an evil alien plot had shattered Sonnet's free masonry of the urinal.

'Do not be threatened.'

Rick spun around to see his vanquisher, 'What've you done?'

'Your bog is now a lavatory.'

Rick holstered his weapon, 'You cleaned the bog, on MY ship?'

'You are displeased? Explain?'

'That shit house hasn't been cleaned in years and as long as I'm a free man it never will be!'

'I do not comprehend, why would an unhygienic toilet affect your liberty?'

'It's a symbol.'

'Of poor hygiene?'

'It means there's no woman telling me how to live or what to do,' Rick put on a high pitched whiny voice, his best impression of a woman, 'Do this, do that, clean this, wash that and don't leave the toilet seat up.'

The alien rippled her armoured forehead, utterly perplexed by Rick's reaction. Who could have known kumuns followed such strange rituals?

'Don't eat this, eat that, don't wear this, wear that. You can't go down the pub because the Jones's are coming over to play trivial pursuits,' his voice became hysterical, 'You never take me anywhere, you never buy me anything not like Sally's husband, I want a new kitchen AND YOU ALWAYS LEAVE THE TOILET SEAT UP!'

The dark conquistador was taken aback, it was obvious this kumun was on the edge and she didn't want to be around when it snapped, not while it was armed, 'We will refrain from similar activities,' she gave an awkward smile and marched to the cargo hold as quickly as possible. This primitive was clearly unhinged and there was nothing to be gained by provoking its mental sickness. A door opened in the corridor and Allenby stuck his head out, 'What the fuck's going on?'

Rick pointed at a sparkling toilet, 'LOOK WHAT SHE DID!'

Allenby peered into the unit and smiled, 'That looks grand!'

Rick sneered at his salvage operator, 'Oh fuck off,' then stormed into the galley.

Another two days and Sonnet exited hyperspace slipping into a quiet system populated by neither humans nor negz. They headed for a desert planet, according to Peters no sentient life existed below. It all seemed too easy nevertheless they strapped in before Sonnet entered the upper atmosphere. The ship pulled and pushed with veracity on descent. Rick grinned at the thought of what his passengers in the cargo hold were suffering, especially that blue bitch!

Deeper cut Sonnet's snout as she creaked and groaned from atmospheric heat and pressure. Sonnet's hull glowed a bright red, then white, super alloys conducting heat generated through a trial of fire. A white whale gracefully entered the atmosphere, from below she might easily be mistaken for a meteorite or comet but on closer inspection there could be no mistaking. Her wide body maintained its shape dissipating energy rather than succumbing to it. A stout nose kept its shape holding her in one piece, defying all elements Mother Nature threw in her path. This was neither comet nor meteorite, yet no population was present to appreciate her feat. Nothing but beasts living in holes existed on this dry desert world.

Dyson monitored his readout then spoke over Sonnet's noise, 'Approaching landing zone, thrusters firing, 3, 2, 1, firing.'

Everyone was pushed forwards by their own momentum as the ship decelerated. Sonnet's speed began to reduce as did the light show playing on her belly. Within a minute they were flying about the same speed as a jet fighter going full whack.

'Landing in two minutes,' stated Dyson.

Rick felt Sonnet's fore stanchion extend below his feet. Shortly they approached an area of dry land, one of few able to support a vessel of Sonnet's size without crumbling away. This was by no means the best planet to land upon yet Rick had no choice. It was completely uncharted by humans since those to chart negz worlds were either negg or dead.

Sonnet came to a halt hovering above dry sandy earth, dust kicked up to block Rick's view. The ship slowly dropped foot by foot until stanchions kissed ground, they began to squeal and creak on absorbing Sonnet's weight. The alien charged from behind, 'Is everything satisfactory?' she spoke in a higher pitch than usual.

Rick grinned, his chance to play a schoolboy prank on this miserable alien bitch had arrived. He spun his flight seat around to face her, pulling a terrified face he screamed, 'WE'RE GONNA DIE! WE'RE ALL GONNA DIE!' Rick unbuckled himself and dropped to his knees weeping like a child, 'PLEASE NO, GOD SAVE US, GOD SAVE US ALL!!!!'

The alien looked down, observing his performance in silence until stanchions fell mute beneath Sonnet's load. The gothic conquistador, arms crossed in her signature fashion of premeditated defiance, checked Rick's mental integrity rather than Sonnet's hull. As far as she was concerned the only faulty piece of hardware aboard this ship wept at her feet. This vessel's Captain was clearly unhinged, fortunately she'd make it out before this savage suffered a total breakdown. The sable soldier fixed her sight on Dyson, 'My people are ready,' then exited the cockpit.

Dyson and Peters began to laugh. Rick immediately took Dyson to task, 'You set me up.'

'You what?'

'You had her come in here so I could make an arse of me-self!'

'Fuck off!'

'Don't tell me to fuck off! She knew I was doing that!'

Dyson replied in a sardonic tone, 'Sure, I conspired with a negg.'

Rick turned his eyes to Peters now red with laughter, 'Shut the fuck up and do your job!'

Peters attended to his console cracking up over Rick's failed attempt at humiliation, well that would be incorrect, Rick had successfully humiliated himself.

Once dust settled Sonnet's cargo ramp dropped down. Negz squinted at a bright sun high in the sky. Rick, Dyson and Allenby were suited up and brandishing rifles just in case these creatures had a change of mind. Thankfully that didn't happen, as bargained they exited, covering their eyes from all consuming lighted. Rick and Allenby escorted the group clear of Sonnet's blast radius. The gothic alien, shadows forming inside deep porcelain eye sockets jogged up to Rick, 'You have neglected our supplies.' Rick spoke from within a biohazard suit, its visor blacked out due to proximity of the local star, 'That wasn't part of the deal.'

'We cannot tolerate this level of radiation.'

'That's not my problem.'

'We require water, food and shelter.'

Rick stopped moving and the caravan halted, 'You got something to trade?' She looked side to side in a helpless manner.

'I'll provide shelters, food, water condensers even a distress beacon but the price is high.'

'Price?' stated the alien, her skin sprouting ruddy patches beneath a fiery sun.

'You.'

Plough lines formed above her brow, 'I do not comprehend.'

'I need someone who speaks negg and can access their systems.'

'I am not a thief.'

He lowered his rifle, 'Listen Madame, we both know how this war ends whether I'm stripping negg ships or not. In exchange for supplies I'll take your service on me ship until the war's over.'

'That is unacceptable.'

Rick turned back to Sonnet, 'Allenby, let's blow this shithole.'

112

Negz huddled in the middle of a bleak desert watching Rick and Allenby stride back to safety. Rick knew little about negz physiology but he did know they came from a chilly environment, this heat would kill them all in six hours.

'KUMUN!'

Rick stopped walking and restored his gaze upon the ice woman's exterior, thawing beneath a merciless assault from Helios.

'I agree under condition I provide no information undermining the negz war effort.'

Rick nodded his head, 'Done. Allenby, start unloading what they need. He smiled at the alien conquistador, 'This way Madame.'

They walked up Sonnet's loading ramp, Rick led her into the galley. Dyson peered at Allenby as he unfastened supplies, 'Where are those two going?'

Allenby lifted food and collapsible shelters onto his truck, 'I think the shit's just hit the fan.'

Rick hung up his biohazard suit then searched his cabin for a couple of minutes. On exiting they rested at opposite ends of the galley table. Rick placed a tablet in its centre and waited. She glanced down then back to him. Rick tapped the tablet illuminating its dark screen, 'This is a standard crewman's contract, do your job and you'll receive an equal share of profits.'

'Negz do not profit from theft,' spat the alien.

'Everyone signs it, no exceptions.'

'My people's word is our bond.'

'Why don't you just humour me?'

She sneered at Rick, 'Thieves!'

'Palm print?'

The alien reluctantly removed her glove to place a palm with only the slightest tint of blue upon Rick's tablet. After a few moments it bleeped, 'Name?'

She was caught off guard by the question, Rick wasn't sure why, 'You do have a name?'

'Annyha.'

'Just Annyha?'

'Correct.'

He smiled, 'Welcome aboard Madame Annyha,' Rick extended his hand but rather than shake it she looked down her nose while slipping her glove on.

'May I attend to my people?'

'You can help Allenby move the gear.'

'Affirmative Captain.'

Rick chuckled.

'Is there a problem Captain?'

'You can call me Rick.'

'Acknowledged Captain Rick.'

'No, just Rick.'

'Affirmative, may I be excused?'

'Knock yourself out.'

The sombre conquistador waited … an air laden with perplexity smothered the pair like a cheap overpowered scent.

'You're excused.'

As she marched out the galley Rick began to question what he'd just done. The crew weren't going to be happy about this, bah, they'd settle down after cash began to flow, hell they just had a big score thanks to Annyah.

Sonnet's stanchions creaked as she pushed off Hyades-92's second planet. Clouds of dust obscured Rick's vision, thrusters whipped up tornados of grit. Once they'd gained enough height her engines decided to kick in. To his right Annyha filled Sam's position, translating his old console, this might take some time.

'Destination Captain?' asked Annyha.

The cockpit crew, Dyson and Peters, stopped what they were doing and gave a queer look.

Rick replied in a rather uncomfortable tone, 'Piraxis.'

'Acknowledged Captain,' she paused, 'Navigation officer set course for Piraxis immediately.'

Dyson's eyes widened.

'Is there a problem?'

'I … no, there's no problem,' he turned to his console and plotted course for Piraxis.

'Is that affirmative or negative?'

'Sorry?'

'You are deaf?'

'What the hell?'

As Sonnet moved through upper atmosphere into space Dyson exited his seat, he wasn't taking this crap not from a negg-head. Rick moved between him and Annyha, 'That's enough.'

'I ain't putting up with this!'

Annyha, rather befuddled by Dyson's reaction to her orders, narrowed the pits of her eyes, 'You refuse to execute orders?'

'Fuck off!' shouted Dyson.

It wasn't obvious to Annyah who Dyson was verbally abusing but that was immaterial, for his behaviour, in Annyah's opinion, was mutiny resulting in but one course of action. Peters watched the whole palaver from his station, quite aghast.

The gothic soldier rose, 'Captain, does this vessel possess a stockade?'

'No.'

'I will confine the Navigation officer to his cabin.'

'Forget it.'

The alien pulled an incredulous visage for in her society Dyson's behaviour was unacceptable. To address your superior in such a manner, to disobey his orders and verbally abuse him before subordinates. If Dyson were negz he'd be purged for social indecency. Even more curious were the Captain's actions. Rather than discipline his wayward subordinate he attempted to make peace. None of it made sense to Annyha, these aliens were mere barbarians shouting and screaming at one another, how they'd managed to reach space was beyond her comprehension.

'I'm paying you to get us to Piraxis so you'll fucking do it, clear?'

'Not with her giving orders,' he pointed at Annyha.

'Grow up and punch in the fucking co-ordinates.'

Dyson ground his teeth, his gaze trapped in Annyah's orbit. The gravity of her dark eye sockets engulfed his fury as blackholes with tiny glimmering singularities.

'I said get us to Piraxis, NOW!'

Dyson moved back to his seat steaming with anger. He smacked the dashboard in a rebellious manner as if the devil himself rammed his hands in an act of defiance.

'Co-ordinates set,' stated an angry man.

'Co-ordinates confirmed Captain, portal on your order,' said Annyah.

Dyson was pissed, certain she was an evil alien usurper, antagonising him to the point she'd throw him off the ship.

Rick nodded at Annyah, she spoke into her headset, 'Engineering officer open portal, immediately.'

There was no reply from Graham nevertheless compressed magnetic waves bombarded a forward area of space. Axions decayed into photons leaving a deficit in space-time, enough of a deficit to open a portal between this and another dimension.

'Let's blow this shithole!'

Dyson took his cue and slammed Sonnet into hyperspace as hard as possible garnering a disparaging glance from the new tactical officer.

'How long?' asked Rick.

'Nine days if the weather holds.'

Their new crewmate thought to herself, 'these kumuns employ such odd terms. Why would one describe hyperspace in terms of weather and: "let's blow this shithole"? What could that possibly refer to?'

She consoled herself in the thought this war would soon be concluded, yet kumuns are so unhygienic ... Annyah feared disease might take her before Earth was vanquished.

Chapter Eight

Rick entered Sam's old quarters, in each cabin a smooth cut from Sonnet's hull formed a bed. A table bolted to the floor filled the space between bunk and hatch. To his left a closet, right wash basin and sink, the whole area perhaps three times the size of an average prison cell. It wasn't soft living but room was available to personalise. Sam vacated it in a decent state yet Annyha found more than one point of contention.

'Your suite Madame,' said Rick with open hand.

She followed his arm inside, her nose crinkled as a hound tracking prey until it reached Sam's bare mattress, 'Remove it.'

'Decorate your own cabin.'

Annyah brandished her staff, its blade slipped out and she thrust lifting her quarry above its alcove.

Annyha turned to Rick, 'You are blocking my path.'

He moved aside permitting passage into the slim corridor.

'Where is your waste disposal unit?'

'The same one you used before.'

She marched to the cargo hold with raised eye and old mattress at spear's length. Mechanized jaws chewed swallowing the bedding before pressure compressed it to many fractions of its original size. Annyha returned satisfied to be rid of it. She looked around, her cell until the end of the war, a price she was willing to pay in exchange for innocent lives. Besides, she's negz and negz don't require freedom to live or so her tutors insisted.

He'd kept his word, nevertheless Annyha remained as cautious of humans as they of her.

'So what do you think?'

'It will suffice.'

'You okay sleeping on hard surfaces?' asked Rick in a suggestive tone.

Annyah replied, ignorant to his innuendo, 'I am familiar with frugality.'

'You can get some gear at Templeton's.'

'Clarify Templeton's?'

'You'll never find a more wretched hive of scum and villainy!'

Her eyes widened at his comment.

Rick sighed, 'Bad joke, Templeton's is a stripper station.'

'Clarify stripper?'

Rick thought of another bad joke but spared her, 'We're strippers, that includes you for the duration of your stay so you'd better start acting like one.'

'A thief and a murderer?'

'Listen Madame, I've never killed anyone that didn't threaten me or one of me crew first and we don't steal, we salvage abandoned wrecks.'

Her eyes narrowed within armoured sockets her voice doused in negz spirit, 'Hidden from battle descending upon the dead. A cowardly scourge rummaging through the remains of noblemen.'

'You need to pick up some diplomacy skills.'

'For what purpose?'

'Your attitude's pissing me off.'

'I do not comprehend, pissing off.'

'To irritate.'

Figurative speech was an alien concept to her, 'Also a bad joke?'

'You need to be polite, try using names and don't bark orders.'

'In Kych a clear command structure is obeyed if not chaos would prevail.'

'What's Kych?'

'One of two pillars civilization does rest upon.'

'Well Sonnet's my ship and I'm telling you how it goes here.'

'How would Dyson know to …'

'Dyson's been doing his job for years he knows what to do and when, barking down his ear won't help.'

'Affirmative Captain.'

'And stop calling me Captain me name's Rick.'

'Acknowledged,' she paused for it took some effort to override decades of training, 'Rick.'

'Well settle in and when you're ready come to the galley and get some snap.'
'Affirmative ... Rick,' just saying his name instead of rank made her feel awkward but this was an awkward situation. Light years from home stuck on board a ship of thieving, murdering barbarians, pressed into slavery until war's end. Annyha was counting the days until Earth's annihilation for it couldn't be more than a year after which Rick would release her from her contract, and if not ... she'd release Rick from his mortal coil. She'd been schooled from childhood that freedom and liberty were not a requirement to live, in fact they diminished its potency yet Annyah felt something significant. She quickly buried those feelings within her ordered mind, a talent negz held supreme.

Keeping the peace between his tactical officer and crew had been exhausting. Graham slept with a loaded rifle. Dyson had gone from terrified to carrying a personal grudge. The rest were downcast at best. Allenby didn't say much but Rick could see it written over his face. He thought Rick had finally lost his marbles not that Rick held anything against that judgement. If you'd told him a couple of weeks ago he'd be signing a negz soldier as his tactical officer he'd have called you crazy.
Peters was in the Galley eating a meal. Rick pulled a tray out the dispenser and ripped off its metallic coating to reveal his favourite, tandoori chicken with rice and naan bead. He opened the fridge took out a can of brachian double strength bitter and sat opposite Peters. Shovelling curry and rice onto his naan Rick opened his mouth as a shark emerging from ocean water to engulf a baby seal. Peters winced at his full-on view of Rick's tonsils. Rick chewed away, yet before spicy curry might overcome defunct taste buds brachian bitter washed it down, eerily similar to a waste disposal unit. Rick let out a deep burp then spoke to Peters, 'So what do you think?'
'Ah, I give it a four, four and a half tops.'
Rick shook his head, 'Not me burp you fucking spastic! I meant the negg!'
'Well she's got a tight ass that's for sure.'

119

Rick started to laugh along with Peters, 'I haven't been in space that long mate!'

'Dude, I was on a ship, six months in hyperspace with tracking computers blacked out, we were completely lost. The engineer became the first mate's best mate forever if you know what I mean, and they left that port straight as a die.'

Rick chuckled as he pushed hot curry and rice onto half-eaten naan, 'I bet you were glad to make port.'

'I changed my cabin codes every night.

This negg looks okay to me, I mean we're about to get a second big score in a row, like pure urillium no middle man bullshit.'

'Her attitude stinks but Madame knows more about negg ship systems than anyone in Earth space.'

'If she walks onto Templeton's you know there'll be a shit storm.'

'She can watch the ship while we visit Red Sector,' he grinned like a schoolboy.

Annyah walked into the galley, 'I require nutrition.'

'Over there,' Rick pointed at a wall slot dispensing food trays, 'Drinks are in the fridge.'

'Clarify fridge?'

'A refrigeration unit,' he pointed to a metallic block welded to the wall.

Annyha took a tray and picked a bottle of water. She sat beside Rick, ripped back its cover to be assaulted by an aroma of tandoori chicken for the first time in her life. Her nose crinkled up, Annyah moved her face from the tray placing the outer metallic film in a nearby trash can. She sat, back straight as a board, her nose retracted like a tortoise into its shell, an ability that on observation caused Rick to feel the bite of envy.

'Something wrong?' asked Peters.

'What is this?'

'It's tandoori chicken.'

'Clarify tandoori chicken?'

'Well they're only rations but it tastes better than it looks.'

'That is poor assurance based on initial impression, are these larvae?'

'That's rice it's a vegetable rich in carbs. Chicken is a flightless bird on Earth, it tastes good, trust me.'

Her visage was overwhelmed by a cloud of horror, Annyah's cavernous blue eyes pierced Peters', 'You consume rotting flesh?'

'It's fresh ... well safe to eat.'

'I cannot eat rotting flesh.'

Rick smirked, 'I'm sure the chicken won't hold it against you.'

'This chicken is in no position to hold a grudge nor am I willing to consume its corpse.'

'Well look amongst the trays, when you see one marked quorn take that.'

'Clarify quorn?'

'Sam was a soy boy he used to eat that stuff.'

'Answer my question kumun.'

'It's a vegetarian meal, give me that tray if you're not eating it,' Rick greedily snapped up her tandoori chicken.

Annyah returned to the dispenser, searched for a tray lid marked quorn and returned. She ripped back its metallic film to be greeted by a hot meal of rice, vegetables and micro-fungus masquerading as meat.

'You are certain this is not corpse?' she pointed a plastic fork.

Peters interjected, 'It's made from micro-fungus. Sam was very fussy about his diet.'

'Sam is not aboard?'

An uncomfortable silence permeated the room. Annyha sensed awkwardness, 'Sam is deceased?'

'No,' replied Rick, 'not yet.'

Annyah sampled her quorn, 'Similar to xolim.'

'Is that good?'

Annyha let the right corner of her mouth move upwards, the tiniest of tiny smiles, 'It is Captain.'

'Don't call him Captain it might go to his head and then he'll want us calling him sir,' stated Peters.

'What do you call him?'

'Asshole, on a bad day, on a good day I just call him Rick.'

Rick smiled yet Annyah was confused for if this conversation occurred within the strict hierarchy of a negz military unit Peters would be purged. These kumuns were so flippant concerning rank and command structure it truly was alien.

Annyha had spent her entire life living in structures, not physical buildings built by men but constructions far more ridged, towering monuments to discipline, self-sacrifice and frugality ... prisons of the mind. From childhood she dwelled within these confines her every breath and thought controlled to serve the group, it was the negz way.

Negz are creatures of order and self-control, that is their strength and their weakness. Unfortunately, they understand this quandary and in the fashion of their physical make up, rather than focus on defence, they bolster offence, beshadowing weakness in awe of unwavering will. This philosophy of focusing mind and body together as a group has worked in their favour for the past three millennia. Unknown to humanity the galaxy has long held a proverb: When negz go to war the stars do tremble. Mankind was to meet this revelation the hard way, for in three thousand years no culture, no species, not even an ideology had survived a negz onslaught.

On reading my brief description and observing Annyha's actions you'd have assumed by now that negz are a supremacist species but you'd be wrong. For they've never gone to war without provocation. To see a negz outside its home space is a rare thing often considered an ill omen amongst other aliens. They prefer to be left alone, satisfied within their borders, maintaining embassies only on key worlds. So why would they go to war you ask? It's simple, the Hyades cluster has several systems containing the richest known deposits of urillium in the galaxy. The kicker is negz refuse to mine the richest of these systems. With that being so, many species over the last three thousand years have said to themselves, 'Hey, if they don't want it, why can't I have it?' A few refused to accept a polite (by negz standards), 'Negative' and sent mining ships guarded by war fleets, that's when the stars did tremble.

What of those arrogant empires who thought themselves too titanic for a closed culture lacking means to expand beyond its tiny cluster? They were annihilated, but over time new empires rise and forget. Even holo-vids are brought into question, no doubt cooked up as a hoax years ago. Eye witness reports are lost or scoffed at as old wives tales and so the cycle begins again. Mankind was aware of tales but they were obscured against a bounty of urillium. Brachians warned and Admirals laughed, if they weren't going to exploit that urillium Earth Corps would. As for stories of these negz? They were stories, Earth Corps wasn't going to let old wives tales come between them and the largest deposit of urillium in the known universe!

'So, what did you do before you came here?' asked Peters.

Annyah consumed her meal as if she were royalty, eating from the outside of the plate. Slicing with precision before gracefully bringing the fork to her mouth, 'I am Oci-sebe.'

'What's that mean?'

'In your language it translates to lightning wave.'

'Sounds dangerous.'

'It is, we are deployed during the first wave of ground assault. It is our purpose to throw the enemy into disarray, confuse them. We are not intended to triumph alone yet it has been known.'

Rick downed a gulp of bitter before asking his question, 'So how come a sweet lass like you ends up in the Marines?'

'It is my duty. In my culture the first son enters the Kych the first daughter enters the Suum, those between enter civil service.'

'What's the Suum?'

'It is our religious order.'

'So how come you're in the military?'

'In negz culture couples are restricted to six children. Without a son the first daughter assumes his place. I was raised to be Suum until my mother gave birth to her final child, a daughter, from that day I was Kych.'

'How long have you been Kych?'

'This is my fifteenth year.'

123

'And you're still alive?'

She placed her knife and fork on the tray besides one another and wiped her dainty blue lips with a napkin, 'Is that a question or a declaration?'

'I'm just surprised anyone could survive that long.'

'Unlike kumuns, negz are not perpetually engaged in war. We spend the majority of our time training, executing manoeuvres and meditating. Oci-sebe can be quiet a mundane task, many look forward to battle as a release from its day to day tedium,' she peered at Rick the left corner of her lips rose in an oriental smile, 'Tell me, how did you become a stripper?'

'That story's not nearly as grand. I saved enough to get a ticket off Earth, travelled the core doing odd jobs.'

'Clarify odd job?'

'It's a figure of speech, the jobs weren't odd they were inconsistent.'

'In what manner?'

'Well nothing you'd do for a career just something to get to the next place you're going, if you see what I mean.'

'You were a wanderer?'

'Something like that. Well after a few years I got a job on a stripper ship. I worked cleaning the galley, the shithouse, just about anything. I didn't intend to stick around until one day we found a wrecked brachian freighter, I got into me first fire fight that day.'

'Clarify fire fight?'

He made a pistol with his hand, 'Gun fight. Well I got shot but Max wasted the alien bastard before he could finish me off … no offence.'

Annyah was rather captivated by Rick's tale of living day by day with no plan going forward. For the first time in her life she felt the negz spirit dimmed by that of kumuns, well, one kumun. Listening to Rick, living his past by proxy, she felt free as air, 'Negz do not take offence,' smiled Annyah.

'Well we got away with the swag and I was going to quit. Then we got back to Piraxis, Max divvied up the loot and it was a small fortune, for a young lad anyway. He offered me a permanent position, I said yes and started me apprenticeship in salvage. That was twenty years ago, when Max died he left me Sonnet, so here I am.'

'Max was a good person?'

Rick took a sip of double strength bitter, 'Definitely not a murderer or a thief.'

'That I do not know.'

Rick lifted his leg a little, *PAARRRRPPP*, he broke out with a self-congratulatory laugh. Peters laughed with him.

Annyah leapt from her seat throwing her napkin aside, 'Mister Peters, leave us,' stated the gothic conquistador in a forceful tone.

Peters wiped his mouth, 'I was going on duty anyway,' he stood up and exited the galley.

'What was that about?'

'As Captain of this vessel you are required to set an example, puerile behaviour must cease.'

'You what?'

'Kumuns have an annoying habit, they request I repeat that which disagrees with them. I am still speculating as to whether it is a learned or genetic stupidity.'

'I heard you and the answer's no.'

'Why make a fool of yourself? A crew must respect its Captain, seek to attain his virtue and when the time comes execute his orders without question, every shred of will focused on the purpose set before them.'

'Because this isn't Earth Corps and it sure as hell ain't the negg version of the Waffen S.S.'

'Clarify Waffen S.S.?'

'It's a long story.'

'Nevertheless, a Captain must set an example to his crew.'

'That's not how it works here.'

Her angular face shed a layer, peeling back as an onion to reveal a deeper more caustic skin, 'It does now.'

Rick remained calm, sipping his bitter, yet he wondered how many layers existed beneath that which berated him, 'How's that exactly?'

125

'I refuse to assist a Captain I have no respect for.'

'Oi, we had a deal!'

'According to our contract I am bound to provide my service. It does not describe that service nor when I am bound to engage it.'

Rick shook his head, 'That's not what the contract means.'

'Exactly why negz never sign contracts between one another. Contracts are legal documents to be wriggled out of, the very use implies lack of honour.'

'So you refuse to help us salvage negg wrecks unless I stop farting?'

'Amongst other things.'

'Other things?'

'Again you echo my words is this taught to kumuns at an early age?'

'What other things?'

'I find the unnecessary expulsion of wind from the body to be not only offensive but demeaning towards my Captain and his crew, it must stop.'

'I thought you said neggs don't take offense?'

'There is an old negz proverb: words cannot be offensive for they are the foundation of civilization.

Expelling stale wind from one's anal passage at the meal table is another matter.'

Rick chuckled like a schoolboy.

Annyha's forehead gripped slightly, a furrow by human standards, 'You are mentally retarded?'

'No!'

'Yet you find the most base and vulgar actions humorous, something a child rejects by age seven. If not, it is sent for re-education.

Should you enjoy my compliance in matters of salvage you will abide by my requirements.'

'I can't tell the crew to ...'

'Only you.'

'No farting and burping, will that be all Madame?'

'It is a beginning.'

Sonnet sailed the blue ocean of hyperspace tacking toward her destination. Tides and eddys that pushed her quickly toward the Hyades cluster resisted Sonnet's progress home.

The forces of Mother Nature are not something technology can oppose directly. Man is but a part of nature thus he does his best to bend rather than oppose her will. When he and Mother Nature are of the same mind anything is possible. When not, caution and patience in equal measure are order of the day otherwise disaster follows.

Rick had been on watch while his crew slept, feet on the dashboard, lager in the chair's felt cup holder, rollup smouldering between his fingers.

'Good morning Captain,' came that bloody accent, it could have been Russian but he recognised it as negz.

'Morning.'

'What are you reading?'

'There's plenty on the board.'

Annyha sat down, checked her station then picked a magazine at random. She was taken aback by its cover. Upon opening the glossy publication her jaw quickly did the same, 'This is disgusting!'

'There's plenty of others,' stated Rick puffing his wiry cigarette.

She picked a different magazine then another and another. Annyah realised a constant theme ran through as threads twisted to form a piece of revealing lingerie, 'Captain, you cannot read this.'

Rick chuckled, 'Who said I read anything?'

'These females have been enslaved, forced to debase themselves in the most profane fashion!'

'They do it for money.'

'By the Elders, why would a female accept money to degrade herself?'

'It depends how much's being offered.'

'And where do THEY find this money?' she shook a magazine in her hand.

'These mags aren't given out for free.'

'This is immoral!'

'What the hell's immoral about it? No-one's forced to do anything they don't want.'

'And that qualifies this as moral? To display naked women as vegetables in a market?'

Rick shrugged his shoulders while turning his publication 90 degrees, 'Yup.'

'Kumun delinquency exceeds my initial speculation! Engaging in every base immoral pleasure and if exhausted they create additional corruption!'

'A lonely boy in hyperspace has needs. Tell me what do negg men do?'

'They meditate.'

'That explains a lot.'

'CLARIFY?'

'It explains why they all look like a bank manager who found the postman fucking his wife.'

'A crewman cannot have respect for a Captain who employs such profane language, it ends now.'

Rick threw his magazine on the dashboard, 'This is my ship and I'll be fucked if some negg-head's coming in here and telling me how to run me life!'

Annyah sat in her chair with folded arms, 'As you wish Captain.'

Rick felt nervous, she gave way to easily, 'Okay what is it?'

'Nothing, you are quite correct Captain,' she placed the magazines delicately back on the dashboard.

Annyah was planning to screw him over but he wasn't going to kowtow to a woman. He got back in his seat, with one eye Rick scanned his magazine the other monitored his tactical officer. She sat with arms crossed in that calculated fashion and a contemptuous oriental smile. She irritated him to no end but Rick wouldn't be moved, he'd show her. No free bachelor would be oppressed by a woman not on his ship.

They visited the Bank of Altan, deposited urillium into accounts. A confounded Annyha took her cut, confounded since negz society didn't require money in any form.

On Hemzih evils such as currency were outlawed, for they maintained a collectivist society, albeit through sacrifice. In her culture little existed but work and prayer. Family units are allotted meagre housing by government, every man lives as his neighbour, clothing distributed once every six months on a strict basis. A single set of clothing served every occasion. There were no fashion designers, catwalks or shoe stores. Food is rationed, each family receiving the same as the next. Rations are restricted to no more than six children for government won't provide enough to support a seventh. Entertainment doesn't exist in the form we know it, no holo-vids, no bars, no holidays to weird and wonderful star systems. Negz spent their lives on career, praying and family.

Negz are the minimalists of the galaxy at least on a personal scale but when it comes to great efforts they move as one and their star doth shine brightest in the night sky.

It was not always this way, once a society much like ours existed, living, loving, suffering and trying to make it big … until the plague.

They'd set foot on their closest planet, unlike Venus or Mars it was able to support life.

Negz felt great times ahead, what they didn't feel was a micro-organism burrowing into the lungs of their astronauts. The six heroes travelled the globe to fanfare and celebration. Ten years later thousands of negz died each month, week, day, then each hour, Armageddon was upon them. Scientists struggled to find a cure before civilization was destroyed for none were immune to this hell. Men, women and children collapsed in the streets suffocating on blood filled lungs. It struck so rapidly that dead and dying littered the villages, towns and cities of Hemzih. A modern day black death, negz call it the Xar ukhel, the foreign death. It wiped out ninety percent of their population, those who survived did so through constant prayer sparking a religious resurgence.

What separated survivors from dead was the traditional incense used in church, when inhaled it destroyed the parasite. In one fell swoop the bug had installed a single faith on Hemzih leaving less than a hundred million in population.

Survivors gathered together and took it upon themselves to set the first stone of a new society, one based on the tenets of duty and sacrifice, where none would go without, where every child would have an education. Not everyone was pleased but after your planet has been ravaged by an alien plague you stop asking questions. Burning corpses, securing a food source and clean drinking water are more relevant.

The bug long gone, a vaccine created, they should have returned to the ways of individualism but negz are stubborn creatures. They held onto collectivism as a shipwrecked sailor grasping a rock while sea lashes his body with salt spray.

To this day they remain a collectivist society, a house propped up by two pillars, Kych and Suum, beneath which all flourish, at least that's the propaganda for if a human visited Hemzih it would look glorious on first sight. Great golden constructions, orbital lifts maintained to perfection, neither poor nor unemployed but it covered a great darkness, a secret negz defended with their lives.

A great man once said: since all are born with different qualities to be true freedom there has to be inequality, for true equality there cannot be freedom.

Despite advances in science, religious reflection and self-sacrifice they are a stubborn people who refuse to accept that which rests stark before their eyes.

In a perfect socialist society, no money, no reward for your job other than the fact you enjoy it, there sits a gaping hole ... who does the crappy work? The first son drafted into the military the first daughter given to god but how do you get someone to empty trash compactors or clean toilets when there's no incentive financial or otherwise?

Have you ever heard a kid say: 'I want to be a toilet cleaner when I grow up'? You haven't because no-one wants to do it, no-one likes cleaning other peoples' turds. Well maybe some do but there aren't enough to keep all the toilets clean in every government building on the planet. So how does this "perfect society" get the dirty jobs done? Well you've got two choices, you pay people a lot of money to do it or you press them into service. Since negz don't believe in financial incentives, yeh, you guessed it, in every city, every town, every quarry, every sewer, every mine, every plantation they have an army of slaves working around the clock to maintain utopia, an underclass of aliens beneath the whip so no negz need ask for anything.

First negz pressed their own into service then they met other species. On discovering a market for slavery negz purchased slaves on the premise they did so for charitable purposes ... they were sent straight to Hemzih to be bred.

For millennia millions of aliens have existed in bondage on Hemzih, this is their secret or as negz call it, qarangqui ... their darkness.

Chapter Nine

One by one Sonnet's crew entered Templeton's docking arm. Annyah remained aboard. Her presence, though not prohibited, would only lead to conflict. In Rick's opinion she couldn't function in a normal society. Interaction with aliens, aliens of worlds negz had previously ravaged would create friction. She handed Rick a piece of note paper, 'Obtain these items.' Rick observed her rather odd shopping list, a sewing machine, cloth presumably to repair her uniform, several pieces of hardwood, a hand plane. 'What're these?' he highlighted three unfamiliar items.

'The first is Burquan Nom, our holy book. The second Kych Nom a book of military regulation. Third, qulusu buse, a padding which absorbs menstrual bleeding.'

Rick's visage mixed both revulsion and surprise, 'You get that too?'

Her eyes narrowed inside heavily armoured sockets.

'I mean negg women?'

'Clarify your question.'

He replied in an awkward tone, 'Well you know?'

'I do not.'

His voice dropped so no-one might hear, 'Periods.'

'Periods of what?'

'Women's periods,' he looked over her shoulder for fear Dyson or Allenby may be close.

Annyah turned but saw no-one, perhaps this kumun was truly demented? Years in space alone with only a few of his kind for company. An animal caged for public spectacle with but a tiny filthy living area. Over time he'd slipped into mental retreat, swaying back and forth, observing apparitions existing only in his twisted thoughts, 'You are healthy Captain?'

Rick decided this subject was best abandoned, 'Yes, you can pay me back later.'

Now it was Annyah's turn in the discomfort chair, 'How?'

'After I've bought your gear just transfer the Altan to me account.'

She stuttered for the first time since Rick had met her, 'I, … you will have to demonstrate this process.'

'Remember that card you got at the Bank of Altan?'

From a pocket inside her tunic she produced a gold card, 'I have it here.'

Rick pulled out a scanner, a slim device about the size of a Kindle reader, 'You slot the card into the bottom, when it lights up enter the amount to transfer and where. Certify with a thumb then retina scan and voila!'

'Voila?'

'It means there you go, job done.'

'I am uncomfortable with this process, on my world possession of any unit of transaction is punishable with re-education.'

'Well you better get used to it because outside the Hyades cluster it keeps food in your mouth and clothes on your back,' he folded her list, 'I'll be back in about 12 hours.'

'Twelve hours?'

'I've got things to do, people to meet.'

'Who?'

'That's none of your business Madame,' Rick smiled and winked, 'see you tomorrow,' he left the fore section exiting Sonnet through an airlock in her midsection.

Rick's primary pit stop was always Shaniqua's, if her hands didn't get first dips she'd be upset. Not that she hadn't bled Rick for thousands over the years but Shaniqua was a business woman, she had enough spacefarers on the go to make Earth Corps think twice.

Shaniqua kept herself looking young and beautiful thanks to anti-ageing products purchased from all over the galaxy, after all this is business not charity. The Queen of Red Sector made sacrifices in maintaining youth, not only monetary but morally and I'm not talking about what she did in her establishment. That anti-aging injection shipped every month from the arm of Perseus not only cost in credits but lives. A species far from Corps space on a different galactic arm farmed its own children to pay their way in the universe.

The blood of sacree children had a rejuvenating effect similar to stem cell therapy but one hundred times more effective. One shot and wrinkles were gone in days, breasts rose, bingo wings were decimated and cottage cheese thighs, you know what I'm talking about, vanished in hours. The sacree drug was truly a wonder but it came at a heavy price. At least half of Shaniqua's profits went to stocking this drug, illegal under Corps jurisdiction but out here anything goes, another reason Shaniqua stuck around Templeton's. She could easily retire but there's no way a 64 year old broad with the vanity of Beverly Hills and ego of Hollywood all rolled into one was quitting this gig. She was staying young and beautiful even if it meant a few kids had to die while tubes leeched away their existence. Hell, this is Shaniqua we're talking about, she'd had a damn hard life. It's time someone else suffered and the best part of it was she didn't have to see those drained kids tens of thousands of light years away.

Though she never revealed her age Rick guessed she was in her late twenties, early thirties tops. He'd known Shaniqua ten years now, she looked twenty one but that wasn't possible. Maybe he'd work it out one day but since his genitals rarely asked questions that was unlikely.

Shaniqua sucked on split, clad in a golden mini dress, tassels skirted knees while eyes purveyed her empire. The largest single establishment in Red Sector it was amongst the top five earners on the entire station, since the war anyway.

Women moved semi-naked bodies to the music, some on the central stage others dangling from clear carbon cages others on the floors above as a DJ played dance hits from around the galactic arm. Her opera house of vice was packed thanks to the latest battle in the Hyades cluster. The establishment heaved with men who'd risked their lives for that big score. They indulged in well-deserved pleasure and Shaniqua's girls were more than willing to provide, for a price.

134

Shaniqua smiled, heels clinking on polished composite stone floor. She saved her time for the big players while young guys vied for her girls' attention. Shaniqua's vision scanned like a falcon surveying a field below. The falcon remaining high on thermals not willing to expend her energy for anything less than the fattest pig, time was money. In walked Rick and the falcon swooped its talons clutching the scruff of his neck before he was even aware, 'I've been waiting for you baby,' she pouted sucking split suggestively.

Rick's face lit up, 'Drink?'

'Sure honey, you got me anything?'

'Stories of daring and danger!' smiled the old sailor.

Shaniqua ceased to pout and raised her eyebrows, 'Huh!' came a derogatory noise through her mouth and nostrils.

Rick got the drinks, 'You want to hear?'

Shaniqua rolled her eyes, 'I guess so.'

He ushered Shaniqua to her corner, an alcove with a comfortable divan upholstered in red velvet. Shaniqua stepped behind him sceptical eye on the back of his head and sexy wiggle each time one of her long silky brown legs strutted forward.

They sat down, Rick's face glowed with happiness. Shaniqua wasn't impressed by his lack of tribute. Even that small bottle of what was it called? Alien mystery? Even that beat nothing! She'd have to punish him somehow for his faux pas. There was a short rather awkward pause as Shaniqua sucked her split locking him in a sceptical gaze.

'Is something wrong?'

'Something wrong honey? Stories don't put food in mouths.'

He looked disappointed, 'Okay, how much?'

'One hundred credits an hour.'

'A ton!'

Shaniqua lifted a long perfectly sculpted leg crossing it with the other in an ominous fashion, Rick got the message.

'One hundred credits it is.'

She smiled while spinning straw in her mouth, 'Now why don't you tell me your story, honey.'

Rick relaxed and began his tale. They spent hours talking, well, Rick talked and Shaniqua listened. She wasn't just a hooker she was his therapist except a real therapist would've been cheaper. By the following morning his bank account was a thousand credits lighter and Shaniqua a happy girl, well, a happy pensioner but no-one knew that, certainly not Rick.

Walking the outer ring, Rick combed through his pockets for Annyah's note paper then headed for the market place. Templeton's had many large bazaars, Rick visited more than one to acquire both books on his list, a pair of leather bound tomes. The book on military regulation was much as he expected. A short handbook of wiggly script similar to Chinese or Japanese. The bible was larger yet slipped comfortably within a single pocket. After a few hours of shopping he checked in at customs, they passed large cuts of hardwood before sending him on. Rick travelled down the docking slip, Sonnet parked to the right, her belly exposed to the arm.

Sonnet's artificial gravity assumed sovereignty as he climbed its ladder his head emerged into her mid-section. Annyah had awoken early to check each station.

'Morning,' said a jovial Rick.

Annyah's angular face shed that negz mask of melancholy permitting her sparkling eyes to brush against his flesh and for a moment her porcelain blue lips betrayed a smile.

Rick double checked and it quickly disappeared.

'Good morning Captain.'

'I got your gear,' he offered the sticks and a bag containing her books, woodworking tool and you know what.

'Excellent,' she took her goods then sniffed the air, pointing her armoured nose at Rick.

'Something wrong?'

'Clarify your previous endeavours?'

'Like I said what happens on Templeton's stays on Templeton's.'

136

'You stink of hu'ugai dabqua,' her nose wrinkled, retreating within its armoured shell.

'What the hell's a hu'ugai dabqua?' bellowed Rick.

Rick was unaware but Annyah had been running Sonnet's translation computer through a few checks before he arrived. Upon blasting his statement a cold bland voice replied, 'A rotten fish, similar to Earth's kipper.'

Rick gave the computer console an iron stare, 'Who asked you?'

'You did Rick,' replied the computer.

For the first time Annyah's visage formed a full, yet wicked, smile. Rick was too annoyed to make something of it, he stormed off into his cabin to get a shower. Had he always smelt like you know what on returning from Shaniqua's? Did the guys just refrain from saying? Maybe neggs had a better sense of smell than humans? Yes, that must be it, either that or she was yanking his chain. Nevertheless, he decided to clean Shaniqua from his body and chuck on his other flight suit. The smell would die down over time and he could wear it again in a couple of weeks.

In the next days fresh supplies were loaded into Sonnet's cargo bay, food, medical supplies, shelters, blankets and so forth, items readily traded in warzones.

Some believed it immoral to use others' hardship for profit. Rick believed he was doing them a service, if not he who would bring relief? Earth Corps? Don't make me laugh! Even negz left their people behind, look at Annyah and those workers, how long before they'd have burnt up in that planet's atmosphere or been killed by strippers? The great noble negz were nowhere to be seen. Rick saved their butts and all for the price of some urillium destined for Vulcan's pit. Yet his profession was looked down upon. Sure, not every stripper would have saved them. Some would've killed them outright, a few would've tortured them for information. But Rick couldn't be responsible for the actions of everyone with a salvage operation.

Before they were to leave Templeton's Rick boarded the station one last time. Moving through Green Sector (habitation decks) he travelled a rather dank metal corridor. Its claustrophobic walls dripped an oily substance Rick dared not scrutinize. He stepped in puddles of stagnant water on his way to meet an old friend. On reaching the correct door he tapped the wall beside. A chime rang to no answer, he rang it again, then again. Exasperated, Rick banged the metal door with his fist and shouted, 'Hey Chang, it's Rick, open the fucking door!'

The door disappeared into its wall. A worried fellow about five and a half feet dressed in a grey alien suit with a white mandarin collar shirt stuck his head out scanning each end of the hallway, 'Get in, quick!'

On entering the brachian flashed a modern coil pistol, very different to Rick's old school P-38. The door slid shut locking immediately.

Brachians are humanoid, no ears, no eyebrows with saggy and blemished skin, these are common brachian traits. Humans have great difficulty guessing their true age but a seasoned spacefarer such as Rick need only observe the neck and recognise his genetic heritage. The neck carried a set of openings for long redundant gills, on noticing their condition a keen observer could discern gender and age of a brachian. Brachians are descended from amphibians and, as many have pointed out, their facial features betray those origins. Saggy skin set on wide lips and jaws with bulging eyes, they aren't the most attractive of species, their reputation as toads is well earnt.

Changar pointed his coil pistol, 'You came alone?'

'Chang you've got to stop being so bloody paranoid.'

'Brachian's are always paranoid, besides, sometimes the paranoid ARE being followed!' said the alien in a deep gruff tone.

The residence was quite plush for this level of Green Sector. A large king size bed in one corner along with a shower and bathroom all partitioned with smoky carbon glass. The remaining area an open plan lounge/kitchen. In truth it wasn't single quarters, Changar had bought two and knocked out the separating wall. Rick wasn't sure if you could do that without applying for a permit and if that were so he was certain Changar hadn't applied for one.

'So why'd you drag me down here?'

'You took a couple of big scores lately,' Changar's droopy skin tightened up, that's what happens when a brachian smiles.

'Big scores?'

'Please Rick don't insult me and embarrass yourself,' he holstered the pistol.

'Fine I've had a couple of big scores so what?'

Changar offered him a seat, Rick sat on the leather couch keeping a wary eye on Chang. The room had that thick tarred scent of brachian tobacco. Rick's senses heightened, triggering memories. In fact, this fragrance and the couch reminded him of his favourite smoking club on Templeton's. Rick ran his hand along the arm to realise he'd sat on this couch before. Chang had probably lifted it, he never paid for anything he could steal.

Chang, in his common brachian manner, was blunt and to the point, 'Who's paranoid now?'

'Get on with it Chang I don't have all day!'

'You have infinite time until your fleet is turned into scrap,' brachians are also cunning in thought or as many prefer to describe them, devious.

As Changar sat down Rick let out a loud huff, 'I didn't know you cared.'

'I care as you care … here,' he opened his hand to reveal a data chip.

Rick tried to be dismissive, 'You stole a shipment of brachian porn?'

Changar smiled his skin dragged an inch up his face in a ghoulish fashion, 'Rick, don't fuck with me.'

Rick rolled his eyes doing his best to disguise curiosity, 'Wouldn't dream of it!' he replied in a sardonic tone.

Chang began to laugh in that gruff stuttered fashion all brachians met humour, 'Hah … hah … hah, a kumun joke, most amusing!'

'Alright Chang what's on the fucking chip?'

'Co-ordinates, co-ordinates of one negg supply post, abandoned.'

'There's plenty of them …'

'Full of urillium and data crystals?'

'We both know getting into one of them bunkers is impossible without destroying everything inside unless …'

'You have codes?' Chang's skin lifted another inch.

'I'm not buying that without …'

'Consider it an advance.'

Rick fixed his eyes on those yellow dots brachians call eyes, 'So what happened to the real Chang and who are you?'

'Hah … hah … hah, a kumun joke, yes?'

Rick sighed, 'Yeh, yeh.'

'Changar make an advance, Rick loot post, Changar receive ten percent gross.'

'Gross?'

'Changar take risk getting codes. Rick take risk plundering outpost, ten percent is fair.'

'And what if it's empty?'

Chang shrugged his shoulders, 'Changar receive ten percent of nothing,' he stretched his arm out offering the chip, 'accept?'

'What if I ripped you off?'

'Changar trust Rick.'

'I wouldn't want to find it empty only to earn a grudge.'

'Changar never hold a grudge.'

'Why's that?'

'All my enemies are dead.'

Rick took the chip, 'Brachian humour, right?'

Changar's face drooped back down, 'No.'

Back aboard Sonnet Rick placed the chip on a pad and examined Changar's information. An outpost in the Antares system, the heart of the scorpion, 550 light years from Earth but just as far from the negz home world. Rick pondered the question, 'What would neggs want with an outpost out there?' Antares is a dying sun, it could collapse at any time, its supernova would reach the Earth in 550 years casting shadows during the evening. A dangerous place to build and maintain a supply post. As he reasoned on the subject Dyson stepped into the cockpit and glimpsed Rick's pad, 'You can't be serious.'

'I got some good intel.'

'That's suicide.'

'You sound like an old mare.'

'Old mare? I've got a psychotic alien barking orders at me and you're thinking about going to Antares.'

Rick peered over his shoulder, 'You've made a pretty penny until now, haven't you?'

'Yeh and I'd like to be alive when it's spent!'

He went back to the pad, 'Stop being a pussy, you're starting to sound like Sam.'

'I'm just one of those pro-retirement crowd and when I say retirement I mean sitting on a beach drinking Pina Coladas with 20 hula girls blowing my dick all day!'

'You could do that now.'

'But I want really nice hula girls.'

Rick started to chuckle.

Annyah stepped into the cockpit, 'You are amused?'

'It's nothing.'

She grabbed the pad from his hand, 'This is not amusing.'

'Like I said it was nothing.'

'You intended to steal from my people?'

Rick sighed as he leant back in his chair, 'It's an abandoned supply post, YOUR PEOPLE can file a complaint.'

She dropped the pad in his lap, 'A weak justification for theft.'

'I'm sorry Madame but we're going to Antares.'

'Antares is highly unstable.'

Rick spun his chair to face Annyah, 'So when it goes nova YOUR PEOPLE won't be any the wiser, will they?'

'Where did you procure this information?'

'A friend.'

'Who?' asked Dyson.

'Chang.'

Dyson groaned, 'Fuck my life!'

'He's never let me down.'

Annyah crossed her arms, vision shifting between Dyson and Rick, 'Who is this Chang?'

Rick answered with a tiny bite in his words, 'A friend, it's a human concept … imagine a person you don't kill on sight for being inferior.'

'I comprehend friendship, I do not comprehend why a friend would provide you this.'

'Profit, another concept beneath the higher thoughts of your remarkable people.'

'This kumun is a friend yet would risk your life?'

'He's a brachian and no he's given me the option to risk me life … our lives. This isn't a gulag it's risk versus reward.'

'Clarify gulag?'

'A forced labour camp.'

Annyah's eyes widened, Rick sensed shock. Annyah unfolded her arms and returned to her cabin, 'Affirmative Captain.'

Dyson watched her back quickly disappear into the mid-section, 'What was that about?'

'Buggered if I know. Call the crew we need to discuss this before cast off.'

An hour later all members of the crew gathered at the galley table. Graham glared at Annyah, hand out of sight stroking his pistol. Rick tapped a circular plinth at the centre of the table, a 3-D hologram of the Antares system appeared. It focused on a gas giant with several moons some distance from its star. Antares had expanded and contracted several times consuming its closest worlds. Rick spoke in a serious tone, 'Our mission, should we choose to accept it, is to strip a negg supply post on this planet's third moon.'

'Don't tell me the projector's gonna burn up!' joked Allenby.

Rick grinned, 'No, but Dyson's worried we might so we decide together.'

'What's in this supply post?'

'I don't know,' Rick peered toward Annyah.

The crossed armed conquistador replied in a sharp tone, 'I possess no information concerning this system.'

'How about an educated guess?'

'Kych do not guess.'

Rick sighed, 'Okay let me put it another way, if you were to go there now what would you expect to find in that supply post, within reason.'

'Other than a group of stinking kumun thieves, ship parts, fuel, food and water.'

'In what quantities?'

'Enough to resupply and refit one heavy cruiser.'

'Anything else?'

'No.'

'What about computer crystals?'

'Such instillations always hold three command and twelve communication crystals provided it has not been evacuated.'

'Why'd you say that?'

'I do not trust brachians.'

Rick grinned, 'Even brachians don't trust brachians. We can scan it from orbit, if it's empty we'll leave.'

'Provided there is no interference from Antares.'

Rick pointed at a hologram of Sonnet circling the third moon, 'The supply post's on the dark side of this moon. Its gas giant has a powerful magnetic field which should shield our scanners from Antares,' he turned to Peters, 'What do you reckon?'

Peters examined the data on his pad then replied, 'It'll work, if there's no discharge from Antares or anything.'

'Let's vote,' Rick leant back awaiting a decision for as the Captain he didn't get a vote.

'I'm in,' stated Allenby before sipping a beer.

'I say no,' voted Dyson.

'I say go,' said Peters.

Graham sneered at the gothic alien, 'No,' Graham stood up.

'Oi Graham, where you going?'

'Checking the field emitters.'

'There's still one vote.'

His eyes narrowed in disbelief, 'You're gonna let that negg-head vote?'

'She's a member of the crew, she gets a vote just like the rest of us.'

'But she's a negg!'

Rick pulled a rollup from behind his ear, produced a book of matches from his chest pocket, lit the end and discarded the match after a puff, 'Every crew member gets a vote, no exceptions.'

Annyah looked up from Rick's burnt match and peered around the galley. A temple to the human bachelor, used trays decorating shelves, its floor littered with discarded waste.

'Well?' asked Rick.

'I possess the deciding vote?'

'You got it,' he exhaled a cloud of tobacco that circled her armoured eyes in an antagonistic fashion.

'I vote yes … with one provision.'

'It doesn't work that way.'

'Then I vote no.'

Graham let out a sigh of relief.

'Hold on, hold on, what's the provision?'

'If we travel to Antares you will purge all rubbish from communal areas of the ship.'

Rick didn't take her demands well, 'That's extortion.'

'When my people required food and water did you not employ similar tactics?'

'That was different.'

'Then we remain at Templeton's.'

Allenby grinned, 'She's got you by the short and curlies mate.'

'Fine I'll clean the galley up.'

'You will purge the fore AND mid-section including the lavatory while I serve as a member of this crew… Captain.'

144

Graham scoffed at her statement, 'He'll never …'

'Fine,' stated Rick sending not only Graham but the entire crew into shock. 'Do you give your word, Captain?'

Rick ran his fingers through long brown hair, 'Yeh, you got me word.'

Like the lip of a Ming vase Annyah's mouth curled on one edge, 'Then I vote yes.'

Rick looked at Dyson, 'Okay set course, we leave as soon as the ship's clean,' he turned to Peters, 'You got the cockpit,' turned to Allenby, 'You and Dyson have got the galley,' fixed his eyes on Graham in a gaze of cold, hard, unforgiving steel, 'Graham, you're cleaning the shit house.'

Dyson and Allenby were going to complain before realising they nearly had the toilet.

Graham didn't take Rick's orders well, 'I ain't cleaning no shit house.'

Annyah sat back, arms in a calculated fold. Her mouth curled as an oriental sadist, inspired by perfumes laden with misery, she was good but not perfect at disguising gratification.

Rick stood face to face with Graham. Graham was a broad and intimidating man yet Rick felt secure in the fact Sonnet was his ship. He blew a puff of smoke in Graham's face, 'I spent five years on Sonnet cleaning her galley and cleaning that shithouse. If you think you're too good to clean that bog you can fuck off me ship right now, if not I'll show you the brush and detergent.'

Graham stuttered, 'I … I …'

'I want to see that shit house so clean I can eat me next curry off it and I don't give a fuck how many sick notes you've got from your mummy, understood?'

Graham was dumbfounded his mouth gapped. The engineer gazed at a grinning Annyah then a deadly serious Rick, something you didn't often see, 'Okay,' he stated in a subdued tone before leaving.

The rest of the crew let out a sigh of relief for Graham would've rearranged their faces had they challenged him.

Peters cleared the cockpit of men's magazines, empty beer cans, cigarette ends and all trash in between. Rick considered whether it was Annyah or did all neggs look so smug after they'd won an argument? Nevertheless, she was getting what she wanted. Sonnet would be cleaned before they set off on another adventure. Once complete Annyah inspected Sonnet, she took a good look around the toilet bowl much to Graham's ire. On deciding it was adequate they departed for the scorpion's heart. Sonnet's reactor fired up burning rings of plasma inside its magnetic field before ramming them into one another. The fusion reaction created was hundreds of millions of degrees hotter than the innards of the sun.

Back in the 20th century they were named Tokamak reactors, Russian for Toroidal Chamber with Magnetic Coils. Scientists at the Kurchatov institute put together the first Tokamak. They did so with powerful magnetic fields and an ingenious design. A cigar shaped metal object packed with powerful magnetic emitters maintained an unbreakable field while plasma encompassed the cigar in the shape of two separate halos. The halos were rammed into one another then pulled apart causing a fusion reaction. Today, centuries later, its principles remain the same, major changes being super alloys used in construction and a new method for creating plasma.

In the past it took great power to heat hydrogen-boron gas to high enough temperatures before it was useful. Sure, the return was way beyond any cost but Sonnet is a small space craft about the size of a world war two U-boat. She didn't have the means to heat plasma whilst maintaining a magnetic field … that is until urilliuim was discovered.

Urillium, discovered by accident on Io, is a solid form of exotic matter, that is matter with negative mass. When the rover identified a sample scientists believed its instruments had failed. An inert brown lump which resembled a giant dog turd with negative mass.

Usually it'd have a mass of say 1kg but instead it read as -1kg, the Einstein's scratched their heads. They tested it again, same result, they tested a lump of volcanic rock nearby, results demonstrated a positive mass. It took weeks to work out what'd happened but finally they got there, the world had just done a back flip. After much wrangling backers gave the green light and the rover dispatched a sample, a year later it arrived.

That brown stuff did have weight. Like negative pressure pulling sap up inside a plant, negative mass pulled mass toward it, unaffected by gravity in the way normal mass would be. The sample was refined of impurities to form what resembled a dry yellow clay. It was named urillium after the probe that'd discovered it on the Jovian moon. A corporation looking for ore deposits had made the scientific breakthrough of the century.

Urillium Corp had long since gone out of business but the strange yellow substance remained. A mere oddity on the periodic table, an interesting note for children in science class until the day scientists used it to fire up a Tokamak.

Another Einstein wondered what would happen if he put a little urillium with his usual hydrogen-boron mix. It took years to cut through red tape and finally get his hands on a few negative grams but when he did the world pulled another back flip. Once injected into a gas chamber and subject to pressure urillium did something quite fabulous, it super-heated the hydrogen-boron mix to temperatures thought impossible.

Instead of 10 million degrees he observed 100 million degrees and rising, not only that but the raw power waiting to be tapped dwarfed every power station on planet Earth. It opened not only the door to free energy but permitted many scientific experiments that until now were resigned to theory. Energy companies went broke. The world went mad for urillium, a few negative pounds of it guaranteed a nation's energy independence. The urillium age had begun but as with every new age of man its misery came first, costing lives of hundreds of millions in war, disease and famine. Eventually Earth Corps took control, permitting survivors of this new age to reap its benefits.

Before the urillium age or Earth Ring's construction or Earth Corps, a corporation funded an exploration craft. Their theory being this new dimension (hyperspace) was much like our space-time. You could enter it, move around in four dimensions, and emerge at your destination.

Completing the journey from point A to B in a fraction of the time it would take in normal space, the question was what was in there.

After a week of traveling they found nothing but poor weather and an irritability when confronted with the colour blue. They opened the portal back to Earth, something tested on remote time and time again, to find themselves hundreds of light years away from their intended destination. Fortunately, they were close to another system, in their excitement they decided to survey it and discovered brachians, the most paranoid species on the galactic arm.

Weeks later they were able to communicate in a broken language and with assistance returned home to a hero's welcome. Thought lost, the crew had not only returned but discovered the first sentient life and acquired a half decent map of hyperspace. Shortly after celebrations brachians appeared in the system and raped planet Earth. A hidden transmitter on the exploration vehicle led them to their target.

And so the Earth Ring was constructed, its purpose a first line of defence against brachian attack fleets. Along with the Ring's construction Earth Corps was founded, their mission to defend mankind from an alien horde besieging Sol.

Ten years later Earth corps vessels were refitted with urillium tokamaks, for the first time they possessed the capability to enter hyperspace whilst carrying enough firepower to vapourise any xenos on the other end … namely brachians … it was time for sweet revenge.

After a bitter two decade war concluded, Admiral Harwood signed a peace accord. At the signing when asked by a brachian reporter what humanity would learn from this historic day Harwood stared him straight in the eye and said, 'Shoot first, make peace later.'

Chapter Ten

The scorpion's heart lingered a month away, perhaps more. Despite Mother Nature's plot to deter Sonnet, one way or another, they'd empty that outpost.

Each crewman had his method of passing hours with as little friction as possible. Peters went through a broad collection of stamps until he dozed off. Allenby leafed through investments, the man spent most evenings working out gearing ratios better known as debt to equity ratios. He'd often sit at the galley table revealing some new pearl of financial wisdom, pestering Rick to buy stocks, he never did. Not that Allenby didn't make profits it's just the subject repelled his interest.

Graham remained a mystery spending time alone in his quarters, doing what? Nobody knew. Dyson considered himself a film noir buff, a second subject Rick found intensely boring though unlike Allenby's pastime totally pointless. A constant stream of black and white movies shot at night filled with miserable people, usually French, bitching about the pointlessness of existence in the rain. A few weeks of that and Rick would be on suicide watch, as to how Peters managed not to do himself in before now was a mystery. Annyha spent her free time between reading and a woodwork project in the corner of Sonnet's cargo hold.

Annyha came on duty for the night shift, sat at the breakfast table with Dyson and Allenby, Allenby was about to retire.

She inquired after Rick, 'Is our Captain healthy?'

'He's fine,' answered Allenby.

'I expected to witness his ritual guzzling of curried corpse.'

Allenby smirked as he twisted spaghetti around his fork, 'He decided to GET OFF early.'

Dyson sniggered.

Annyah was mystified as to Allenby's implication, 'Clarify?'

'I think he misses Shaniqua.'

'Clarify Shaniqua?'

Allenby and Dyson sniggered like a pair of schoolboys.

'I was not being humorous.'

'Right,' replied Allenby recovering errant strands of spaghetti.

'Answer my question kumun.'

At this point Dyson was barely able to hold the laughter in. Allenby choked on his ready meal but Annyah was determined to get full disclosure. She folded her arms in that signature fashion, meal set before her.

'Forget it,' stated Allenby before he chewed and swallowed.

'Where is our Captain?'

'In his cabin.'

Annyah stood but before she could exit the room Allenby blocked her path, 'You can't disturb him.'

Annyah circumvented the salvage operator straight into the habitation module. Poised before Rick's door she chimed its bell, judging by the noise emanating from inside he was unaware.

'Computer,' barked Annyah.

'What may I do for you Annyah?'

'Release Captain Katusa's cabin hatch.'

'I'm sorry Annyah I may only comply if a crew member's life is in danger.'

'Captain Katusa is not responding, I believe his life to be in peril.'

'As you wish Annyah.'

The hatch creaked open, Allenby and Dyson observed from inside the galley. Annyah's eyes were attacked by thick smoke, ears assaulted by music. A viscous cloud quivered in harmony to the noise of a steel guitar. An image pulsed through wispy twilight. A topless female hologram clad in uncomfortably tight and stringy pieces of cloth danced on the table, if you could call it dancing. In Annyah's opinion it executed a string of advanced meditation positions broken up by the wiggling of breasts.

She moved in closer, close enough to make out Rick's figure on the opposite side. Annyah examined his upper torso, rollup in one hand, bottle of metaxa in the other, eyes fixated on Shaniqua as she enticed him back to Templeton's.

Suddenly his vision caught on to a smoky figure mutating in and out of tobacco born murk. He jumped liked a caveman witnessing a beast approach his subterranean grotto during the night, its figure barely visible through the smoke of his bonfire. Annyah's bright blue glare sparkled like a spectre in the night so much so he cracked his head on the hull above.

Rick turned his music off, 'WHAT THE FUCKING HELL ARE YOU DOING?'

She folded her arms, 'I might ask you the same!'

Rick's expression was one of incredulity, 'What?'

She moved in closer as he pulled his pants up, the sound of plastic striking the floor drew her eyes. A strange nozzle lay on the ground, Annyah's vision pursued it to its point of origin … the holo-projector.

Smoke began to clear, wafting into the hallway. Annyah aimed her porcelain finger at the projector and snapped, 'This is degrading filth!'

Rick buttoned his pants, stubbed out his rollup and replied, 'It better be I paid a hundred fucking credits for it!'

Annyah gazed into vacancy with a disposition of utter shock. Such activity was unacceptable in her culture, any negz caught engaging in vice would be purged from the group completely. She picked Shaniqua's nozzle from the floor as the hologram did a slut drop, 'Clarify its purpose?'

As she squeezed the nozzle began to contract sending ripples down its outer skin. Annyah ogled in horror as the smutty appliance inhaled Rick's fumes before her very eyes, it didn't take a PhD in xeno-biology to work out this gadget's purpose.

'YYYAAAA!' screamed the gothic warrior.

From outside you'd have guessed Annyah was going into battle but this was a cry of revulsion as she discarded the foul device.

Annyah, overwhelmed by a furious storm of negz duty snatched Rick's projector by its base.

'Hold up, what'd you think you're doing?'

'You are Captain of this vessel you must set an example,' she marched, governed by negz spirit, out of Rick's cabin with Shaniqua in hand.

Rick stumbled out half dressed to be greeted by Allenby and Dyson's red faces, 'OH FUCK OFF!' he snapped before pursuing Annyah.

Moving down the corridor he heard a crunch followed by the waste disposal unit ejecting its contents into hyperspace, 'OI! WHAT THE FUCK HAVE YOU DONE?'

He reached the rear and turned left to witness Annyah beside the waste disposal mechanism. She was doing it again, her lip curled on one side provoking an urge to strangle the bitch.

'What'd you do with it?'

'As kumuns would say ... I took out the trash.'

'That was my personal property.'

'Captain is not only rank, it is responsibility to set a morale example to your men. Lingering in one's cabin gratifying one's self in pornography is unacceptable. As your Tactical officer it is my duty to guide you on these matters.'

'What the fuck are you talking about woman?'

'In the Kych it is the duty of all soldiers to maintain morale clarity. We observe the universe through our own eye glass, if its lens becomes cracked how are we to perceive the actions of our enemy?'

'This is my ship, you don't have the right to take anyone's personal property without permission.'

'A concept which frequently culminates in violence.'

'What if I took your books and trashed them?'

'Feel free to do so, you are my Captain.'

'Well you're not free to take me stuff and that's an order, understand?'

'I comprehend yet I cannot permit you to degrade yourself in the eyes of this crew, it undermines your position and skews your decision making.'

Rick groaned, turned around to see the rest of the crew quickly scarper. He trod along cold metal floor and into his cabin, as the hatch closed everyone heard a scream, 'FUCK MY LIFE!!!'

For the next few days Rick did his best to ignore Annyah, his only communication with her or the crew being strictly utilitarian. Sonnet's atmosphere was tense to the point it became uncomfortable.

Rick stepped into the galley ready to start his shift. Graham and Dyson were eating supper, they observed Rick take his breakfast tray from Sonnet's wall dispenser and a can from the fridge. He sat down, pulled the cover back to reveal a steaming curry. His instinct was to toss the film aside, he halted, hand hovering over table edge.

Rick sneered at his crewmates, got up and placed it in the bin before returning to his seat. He shovelled chicken korma into his mouth with a chapatti, even the taste of curry failed to cheer him up. Rick chewed, swallowed then opened, an ice cold bitter washing it down his gullet. He set the can down *BUUURRRPPPPP* came a vile wind before wiping his mouth with his cuff.

'Our Captain is conscious.'

Rick looked toward the entrance but only for a moment. Annyah stepped in, they were going to be on duty together for the next eight hours. His eyes moved back disregarding her presence.

Graham chewed on his fake steak, 'What you got stuck up your ass?'

Rick's gaze was hard to pin down it lay somewhere between the executioner and executed. Those grey eyes, a window into a usually happy go lucky soul reflected a deep well of animosity and frustration. He and Graham locked gazes, their sight grappled like a pair of sumo wrestlers.

'Fuck me, you're starting to look like one of them!'

Rick ate in silence as Annyah sat adjacent removing the film to one of Sam's vegan meals. Rick attempted to ignore her presence.

'What's the matter you not talking to anyone?'

He maintained silent running, opening his mouth only to accept curry, beer or release wind.

Graham grinned, 'I hear Shaniqua got dumped.'

153

Rick's face went stone cold, a murderous glare fixed on the opposing diner. Graham failed to receive the signal though Dyson wasn't so ignorant, he kept his head down and tried to finish his supper.

'I tell you what, you can use a CO2 scrubber on one of them EVA suits, stick it in the tube and think of that black slapper, ha, ha, ha!'

Rick leapt off his seat, with one step he loomed over Graham, 'You've got a big mouth.'

'Calm down, you can buy another in a couple of months.'

'And maybe you can buy a new face at the same time.'

Graham stood up, he wasn't the kind of man to back down from anything, 'Was that a threat?'

'That's a fact.'

'Why don't you go to bed and stick your dick in the waste dispenser.'

Rick threw the first punch, he jabbed Graham in the face knocking him back three steps. Graham was dazed, not from the power of the jab but the fact Rick had punched him.

Graham felt something warm drip from his nose, he looked at his fingers with a startled visage, blood, his blood. Graham raised his fists to form a guard and moved back in to punch it out.

Graham, the larger of the two men, made strike after strike but Rick dodged each one before replying with a hard body shot. Graham was getting frustrated, he grabbed Rick in a bear hug and head butted his Captain. Dyson pled for order yet neither cared for his petition.

Annyah observed with curiosity, was she evaluating their combat ability or was this just an interesting chain of social interactions to be logged for future consideration? Probably both, either way the gothic alien remained quiet.

Now Rick had a bloody nose and Graham was about to crack him again. Rick moved his left arm under, outside then above Graham's right arm. He grabbed Graham's face simultaneously disabling Graham's right arm.

Rick stuck his fingers in Graham's eyes pushing his head and forcing the man to bend over backwards. Next, he stamped his heel on Graham's foot, the

154

human foot has many small bones making it a target for anyone who might wish to quickly immobilize an enemy.

Rick brought the heel of his boot down resulting in a spine chilling crunch even Annyah felt. Graham howled in pain but Rick wasn't finished. As Graham bent over at a rather perilous angle Rick delivered the finishing blow, his knee made contact with Graham's groin. The engineer let go and hit the deck, bloodied face, shattered left foot, hands nursing throbbing genitals. Dyson ran to the infirmary to retrieve a gurney, Rick sat down to finish his breakfast.

'How long will he be off duty?' asked Annyah.

Rick refused to speak to her.

'What if engineering encounters difficulties?'

'I was running the engines long before that stupid cunt came aboard.'

Dyson returned and started lifting Graham onto the gurney, 'Can I get some help?'

Rick wiped his nose and carried on with his meal.

Before assisting Dyson Annyah stated to her Captain, 'At least you are speaking to me.'

Rick looked her in the eye and snapped, 'Why don't you fuck off and leave me alone.'

She nodded her head before helping Dyson peel Graham off the floor and onto a gurney.

A few days into the voyage Rick lay back on his pilot's seat smoking a rollup and listening to music while the others slept. He was careful to clean his ash lest Annyah complain, her constant nagging every time a speck of dust hit the dashboard played on his nerves. He hadn't spoken a word to her since the galley punch up nor did he intend to but today they shared a shift and he was certain she'd try to engage him.

Annyah walked into the cockpit and sat in the co-pilot's seat. Rick swivelled his chair in the opposite direction. He continued tapping his foot to the beat until the music was switched off in the middle of a guitar solo.

'That is better,' stated Annyah.

Rick did his best to ignore the alien and her actions, unknown to him his pretence fell woefully short of convincing its target. Annyah checked her console certifying Sonnet's course for Antares. Cheap and nasty brachian tobacco smoke wafted across both stations, the gothic lady began to cough as she fanned the soot from her face, 'Must you burn that foul plant?'

Rick feigned oblivion staring into the deep blue of hyperspace, alone in his world, as if he existed in an Annyha-less bubble. His mind completely at sea in the deep void of hyperspace, ignorant to all things negz.

'There is an old negz proverb: good health cannot be purchased,' Rick didn't reply, 'Why squander such a valuable resource?'

Rick took a long drag and blew smoke into Annyah's face. She coughed and spluttered, 'Why do you ignore me?'

Rick spoke in a hushed tone, 'There's an old human proverb: silence is golden.'

'That is logical for a species who worship gold and all its degenerate corruption. I must speculate if your people are related to brachians? Perhaps you are interbred? it would make sense that one barbaric property orientated species would find another attractive. Perhaps your mother and a brachian ...'

'Watch your mouth.'

'Affirmative Captain.'

'Why don't you shut the fuck up? That way we can both do our jobs and go to bed.'

'You seem somewhat agitated, would your condition be related to Shaniqua's demise?'

'And don't mention Shaniqua.'

'Affirmative Captain. Perhaps you should find another method to release your anxiety?'

'What are you the ship's fucking therapist too?'

'Clarify therapist?'

'Never mind.'

'I have a suggestion, it requires a partner and we must vacate the cockpit.'
Rick's eyes moved nervously, was she about to suggest what he thought she was about to suggest?
'Are you interested, Captain?'
He took a puff on his smoke, 'Interested in what?'
'Relieving your anxiety in the cargo bay?'
'I don't think so.'
'Why not?'
She noticed a sweat break on his forehead. Annyah was mystified as to why since the cockpit maintained a cool 18 degrees Celsius.
'I'm not that easy Madame.'
'Clarify?'
He looked at her from the corner of his eye, 'An easy screw.'
'Clarify easy screw?'
'Easy to get in bed.'
'Why would I desire to get you in a bed?'
'For sex.'
Annyah's top lip curled up, not in amusement but revulsion, 'Sexual intercourse with an inferior species?'
'Inferior to what? Some negg who wears her anus for a collar!?'
'Why would one wear her anus for …'
Rick did his best impersonation of Annyah, that is, his best impression of a condescending Russian female, 'Are you trained not to comprehend metaphors or is it a genètic stupidity?'
An uncomfortable pause followed.
Annyah took a moment to centre herself, 'The objective is to discover your partner's weakness and exploit it.'
'You sure you're not desperate for a piece of the Katusa?'
'You have an over inflated opinion of yourself,' she peered at his fat gut, 'I am shocked you have not burst!'
Rick nodded his head, 'Not bad, this time next month we'll have you onto oxymorons.'

157

'I was referring to the curxaj-tayag.'

'The what?'

'The staff weapon, practice will release anxiety and clear one's mind.'

Rick let out a massive sigh, 'Oh, that.'

She saw sweat break upon his brow, 'Are you healthy?'

'I'm alright.'

'You are sweating profusely in a cool environment, for your species.'

'I'm just peachy.'

'Then you will join me in the cargo bay?'

'No.'

'I see,' she raised the corner of her mouth in that oriental fashion. Rick wasn't certain if she'd always done it or applied it exclusively for his personal irritation.

'See what?'

'You fear defeated at the hands of a woman.'

'What do I care?'

'Then why resist?'

'One: I don't know how to use one of them sticks and second: I can't be arsed.'

She fixed her eyes steadfastly on his burgeoning belly, 'That cannot be denied.'

Rick dropped his feet to the floor, 'What's that supposed to mean?'

'I do believe Mr Allenby said it best when he stated you are too fat to be gay. I am uncertain his exact meaning but the crew agreed.'

'Cheeky fucking cunt!'

'Considering the pace at which you consume provisions I would be shocked if you had not brought an extra flight suit for fear you outgrow that one.'

'Are you saying I'm overweight?'

That irritating cobalt lip curled before she snapped, 'Yes.'

He stood up, infuriated by Allenby, 'Right, I'm going on a diet!'

Annyah let out a little snort, 'Pah!'

'What now?'

'I doubt you possess the discipline to deny your gastronomic urges let alone master the curxaj-tayag.'

Rick chewed over her words, she was right, he'd be a soy boy for a day or two before crashing back onto curry and beer and probably adding another ten pounds to his already ample frame.

'A single shift, every day, and I shall train you in the curxaj-tayag by the time we reach Antares. I guarantee your stomach will diminish.'

Rick thought it over, he wasn't going to give up curry, beer, smoking and metaxa so he may as well get rid of his burgeoning waistline another way. If this skinny alien woman was as good as Graham kept warning, Rick would be so knackered by the end of his shift he'd drop to sleep without a thought for Shaniqua, what the hell, why not?

'I'll give it a go.'

In the cargo bay Annyah lay down a thin mat, took two pieces of hard wood both nearly six feet in length and tossed one to Rick, tapered at either end it stood the same height as him. He noticed Annyah's staff poked above her head. It was hard to believe that one so short could control a stick so long.

'You are holding your curxaj-tayag incorrectly hold it like this,' Annyah held her weapon right palm down and left palm up, 'correct, for your first lesson you shall learn naym,' Annyah began to make a figure eight by sweeping the staff to one side, sweeping its end in a circle then sweeping back to her other side and doing the same. Rick's first attempt was unsuccessful, he resembled a man swimming more than anything else.

'You are holding the curxaj-tayag incorrectly!'

'Well you can't expect me to get it right first time.'

'This way!' She pushed her staff out for him to observe.

Rick turned his left palm up by grasping the opposite side of the staff.

'Imagine your curxaj has a paddle on one end, now paddle your boat,' she displayed the technique her right hand slowly guiding the paddle while her left gave the staff momentum. She would paddle one side of the boat then bring the paddle up to her centre and come down on her left to paddle that

159

side. Once sped up the action of paddling a canoe along a steady line resulted in a figure eight pattern.

After a few false starts Rick managed to master the action, it brought a smile of satisfaction to his face, 'Easy peasy lemon squeezy.'

Annyah struck out, cracking the end of her staff on his right hand. Rick screamed in pain and dropped his weapon. Annyah attacked thrusting her staff as if it were a spear. By the time Rick's attention shifted from his throbbing hand he witnessed a thin piece of wood hovering before his neck.

'What the fuck was that for?'

'Over confidence breeds death!'

'I've only just started woman!'

'It is in your best interest to learn this lesson now before entering combat, gather your weapon.'

Rick bent down to retrieve his staff from the mat, as he did Annyah struck the back of his head before sweeping his legs from under, landing him on his back. Grasping the rear of his skull Rick shouted, 'WHAT THE FUCK WAS THAT FOR?'

'Your eyes left your opponent, a fatal mistake.'

Rick got to his feet never breaking eye contact with Annyah, 'I thought this was supposed to relieve anxiety?'

'It will, gather your weapon.'

'This is stupid how am I supposed to pick it up if you whack me every time I try?'

'Squat.'

Rick gave a huff of displeasure and squatted while fixing his gaze upon Annyah. As he squatted a loud noise erupted from his behind *PAAARRRPPP*.

Rick laughed wafting the stench away, 'Fuck me I bet that could hold off an army of neggs!'

He rose staff in hand, Annyah lurched forward cracking his hand then his mouth. Rick dropped the staff to nurse his throbbing mouth, blood dripped from a split lip, 'What the ...'

Her staff's tapered end moved in a blur stopping just before his nose, 'You have two holes on your body, both as filthy as the other, they shall remain shut unless furthering your education, is that clear?'

Rick nursed his bloody lip, 'Fuck this.'

'Very well Captain you may leave and remain too fat to be gay,' her lip curled in Asian sadism.

Rick may be overweight but he never quit on something he set out to accomplish.

Rick squatted down and retrieved his staff, 'Let's do this.'

After a few hours Rick swept his staff in a figure eight, he lacked grace, nevertheless, Annyah discerned it sufficient, 'You have acquired a feel for the curxaj-tayag very quickly, I am impressed.'

'One martial art lends to another.'

'You are trained in martial arts?'

'Boxing.'

'Clarify boxing?'

'Fist fighting.'

'Were you fist fighting with the engineer a few days ago?'

'Yeh, I've always been good at it.'

'Where did you study fist fighting?'

'A friend taught me, he called it the school of hard knocks.'

'What level did you reach in your discipline?'

'There are no levels.'

'How might one judge their skill?'

'By your last fight.'

'You may stop naym now.'

Rick ceased, he could feel muscles in his arms he'd not used for years.

Annyah noted his discomfort, 'Time for stretch movements, we shall do these each day before training to prevent the pain you experience.'

Rick nodded, Annyah held her staff before her, one hand grasped its top half the other end propped on the floor a few feet in front. She stepped forward torqueing her arm until the staff stood in a straight line before her. She did

161

the same with her other arm stretching muscles and ligaments. Rick mimicked her movements, once mastered she demonstrated several different stretches. Annyah was impressed by his ability to pick up on her movements, a trait she'd not expected from a kumun.

After training was complete Rick poured himself into bed and dropped to sleep immediately. Drained to such a degree he skipped his usual curry and beer. Annyah was right, this training took his mind off Shaniqua and stuffing his mouth with calorie laden crap.

As days became weeks Rick advanced in the staff. Stress levels reduced along with his waistline. A paunch that once mounted regular escape attempts from his flight suit vanished. The man began putting basic combat moves together. He had rough edges and it'd be a while before he achieved true fluidity but Annyah was proud of her achievement … and his. She watched him practice a set movement broken up with some fancy staff spins, he did the figure of eight without a problem and to someone who didn't know better Rick resembled one hell of a bad ass.

'Enough,' stated Annyah, 'time for praktik,' she picked a practice staff propped against the hull, stepped on the mat and stood in a fighting stance. One leg in front of the other about a foot apart, her knees bent, right hand by her side clutching the staff, left hand forward on smooth wood. Rick had practiced this stance over and over. He stood legs apart, knees bent with staff pointing toward his opponent. The pair moved as hands on a clock face. Always pointing toward the centre, when one changed direction the other did likewise.

Annyah's hands had a wider spread than Rick's, most of her weight rested on her back leg. The cobalt conquistador's front only touched the floor for movement, the rest of the time it waited like a cobra poised to strike. Rick stood in his traditional boxing stance, it's what he felt comfortable with. Rick lunged forward thrusting his weapon as a spear. Annyah stepped back, tapped it away with ease and thrust toward his face, 'YEEEEAAAHHHH!'

Her weapon stopped an inch short of rearranging his kisser. Rick examined the hard wood with a gulp, 'I guess that means you win?'

'That means you are dead.'

They reset positions and started again. Annyah had a wide hold on her staff best for making blocks and counter attacks. Rick, being a novice was unaware of this fact. He was unable to read his opponent's moves and swung his weapon in a figure eight while moving forward. He thought it might confuse Annyah as to the direction of his next attack. Instead of retreat Annyah struck out and cracked his right hand, 'YEEEAAAHHH!'

In reply Rick screamed out in pain, 'FUUUCCCKKK!' he dropped his staff holding a throbbing hand, 'Do you always have to do that?'

'If I do so sufficiently perhaps you will learn, again,' she pointed her staff at him.

Rick squatted down to retrieve his weapon, sight fixed on Annyah. He realised this was going to be a painful lesson, painful for him. Annyah had an evil curl on her lip, she took pleasure in knocking him about with that stick, well Rick wasn't taking it any longer, he decided to teach HER a painful lesson.

They moved around one another, each staff adjusted to be a little over its user's height. A couple of feet of air between them. Annyah waited like a panther, ready to block Rick's first strike then make him pay for it. Rick had worked this out but he also knew a few rules of savasraga esreg, stick fighting in English. Negz are sticklers for rules yet Rick wasn't so burdened. He thrust forward and as she went to block he brought his weapon down with full force on her front foot sandwiching it between the mat and his staff. Annyah blocked the air and he struck her toes. She hobbled back as Rick pushed forward.

'HALT!'

Rick was rather disappointed. The first time he had the upper hand and she called a stop, 'What?'

'That was an illegal move.'

'What was?'

'Foot strikes are not permitted in the school of Zorxo nor any legitimate school for that matter!'

'Are you telling me when two of you get into a scrap you always play by the rules?'

'Of course.'

'So if a negg comes home and finds some bloke shagging his missus he wouldn't break the rules?'

'Clarify shagging?'

'Sexual intercourse.'

'No negz male or female would act in such a manner.'

'But if they did.'

'Your question is irrelevant.'

'Yeh but that stick on your foot isn't,' Rick smirked.

'You will refrain from transgression of rules, do you comprehend?'

Rick was happy enough to have got one over Annyah, 'Oui Madame.'

'Your weakness is you attack before proper preparation. Tomorrow we shall work on technique and eradicate your failings. Lest they become permanent fixtures leaving you forever open to counter attack.'

Annyah left the mat to propped her staff in a corner, 'However, your skill with the curxaj-tayag has exceeded my expectations.'

'I'm full of surprises.'

'For a primitive species. If you were negz your family would have received a letter of rejection.'

Rick furrowed his brow, 'Rejection for what?'

'The Kych of course. A negz is taught to fight with the curxaj-tayag from the time he can stand. On entering the Kych he will have mastered at least one school.'

'Well you didn't learn to use one of these sticks from the day you could stand.'

Annyah sighed, betraying a tiny amount of regret, 'I was meant for the church. I trained without rest until I had mastered a combination, a stance, a block, an attack.'

164

'How'd you manage it?'

'My father is a revered master, he prepared me. If not for him I would have been rejected.'

'And then?'

'Shame … shame on my family for three generations, yet despite passing the examination I was mocked.'

'Because you're a woman?'

'Because I was a priestess. Kych look down on other paths as inferior … I was inferior to all of them.'

'They sound like a bunch of arseholes.'

Annyah gave Rick a tiny smile, 'They know no better.'

'If it makes you feel any different you're the best soldier I've ever met.'

'Thank you Captain.'

'Me name's Rick and it's time for a beer, what do you say?'

'I could do that,' smiled Annyah.

In the galley Annyah rested her foot and Rick cooled his throbbing hand by clutching a cold bitter beer, 'Here try it,' he sat down and plonked a beer before Annyah.

'I see you drink this every day, what is it exactly?'

'It's brewed from barley, fermented until it produces enough bacteria to kill themselves and voila you've got beer,' he pulled open the ring on his tin and took a swig, 'Ahhh.'

Annyah opened her tin and took a sip, her face screwed up as she swallowed, 'This flavour … it is similar to urine!'

'Don't tell me you people drink piss?'

Annyah hobbled to the sink and washed a turbid foam negz produce when something nauseating enters their system. After she was done the gothic lady looked down on Rick, 'You enjoy drinking that?'

'I'd hardly drink it otherwise.'

'It is vile.'

'It's what we call an acquired taste.'

'In that case I am not certain I wish to acquire such a palate.'

'Come on, sit down and give it another go,' he pulled her seat out.

'As you wish Captain,' Annyah returned, took a sip and grimaced.

Rick laughed, 'There you go we'll have you on ten pints a night before you know it.'

Annyah was half way through the can when she began to detect something odd. The ship seemed to sway and dip yet Rick was unconcerned. Another fifteen minutes and her vision began to blur, words slurred here and there, maybe she was having a stroke? It would be odd in one so young but perhaps the combination of a hard work out and this alien beverage had brought it on?

'Captain ...'

'Rick.'

'Rick, I am in need of medical attention.'

'What's up?'

'I am dizzy, my vision is impaired and I am slurring my speech.'

Rick relaxed, 'That's just the booze, I was like that after my first pint.'

'Clarify booze?'

'Alcohol.'

'This contains alcohol?'

'Didn't you know?'

'Alcohol is expressly forbidden on my world! No negz may partake in any substance which may alter his or her perception of reality!'

'No wonder you're all so fucking miserable.'

Annyah placed her near empty can on the table, 'I have committed a morale and cultural sin.'

Rick raised his can and in a merry tone declared, 'Feels good doesn't it?'

'I have demeaned myself, my family and my people.'

'Jesus Christ you've gotta let your hair down some time,' he looked at a small patch woven into a plait on the rear of her odd shaped skull.

'Why?'

'It's a figure of speech it means to relax and have fun.'

'Negz meditate.'

'What's wrong with a few bevies anyway? You look fine to me.'

'I am losing self-control. I have not experienced this since I was a child, it is most concerning. I cannot see nor speak properly. I do not recognise the pleasure in releasing this poison into my body.'

'Do neggs tell each other jokes?'

'No.'

Rick grunted, 'Here's a good joke, a horse walks into a bar ...'

'Clarify horse?'

Rick looked up at the ceiling, 'Computer?'

'Yes Rick?'

'Please translate the word horse into negg.'

'Mor.'

Rick looked at Annyah, 'You know what a mor is?'

'You refer to a four-legged riding beast?'

'Yeh, that's it.'

'Clarify bar?'

'An establishment for the consumption of alcoholic beverages,' stated the ship's computer.

Rick looked up again, 'Alright computer that's enough.'

'As you wish Rick.'

He carried on, 'So, a horse walks into a bar and orders a beer. The barman says to the horse, why the long face?' Rick waited for a reaction but nothing. Annyah pulled a quizzical expression, 'I do not comprehend.'

'What?'

'Why is it amusing?'

'Why the long face, you get it?'

'No.'

'A long face is a figure of speech, when someone has a long face it means they look miserable.'

'I do not comprehend.'

'Well he's a horse isn't he, he's got a long face.'

167

Annyah thought for a moment, 'I see, traversing from literal to figurative is a source of kumun amusement, yes?'

'Yeh.'

'But why would a horse enter a bar and request a beer?'

Rick took another swig, 'Never mind.'

Allenby entered the galley and slipped on a puddle of water spilt by Annyah a moment ago. He stumbled ramming his groin on the corner of the galley table, 'FUUUCCCKKK!' Allenby grabbed his genitals and winced in pain.

Annyah burst out laughing, 'HAH, HAH, HAH!'

Rick smiled, 'Now you're getting the hang of it.'

Chapter Eleven

Dyson tacked opposing currents while the great blue conspired against him. After three months Sonnet emerged from the blue dimension above a glowing Antares. She burned bright, her magnetic field flailed in all directions punching out as a drunk at closing time. She wasn't going to fade away, she was set on destroying all before collapsing into a long dark sleep.

Peters scanned Antares, instruments fighting her powerful radiation. The scanner eventually found his moon, rotating so one side remained hidden from Antares' radiation. Dyson plotted a course and Sonnet fired maximum burn pushing crew into seats.

Rick peered out at a gas giant mimicking Jupiter's belts, girding the brown planet's waist. The only difference being, this giant wasn't surrounded by mining operations sucking her atmosphere away for the good of Earth Corps. They moved from above Antares' elliptical plane into the orbit of a moon just a little smaller than Earth. Perhaps this was once a planet captured and held hostage by a mighty giant?

Peters used Chang's chip to find the outpost, he discovered something else, 'Gov there's people down there.'

'You sure?'

'There's sentient life. I'm picking up early fission generators.'

'Neggs?'

'I'll have to launch a probe but I'm not detecting any satellites or a space port.'

'Do it.'

Sonnet made orbit, Peters launched an adapted mining probe. It searched for more than metal ore. After 30 minutes he received telemetry, 'No neggs, but I don't know what they are.'

'They got anti-air?'

'Nothing comparable to us … these guys are living in the middle-ages.'

Rick turned to Annyah, 'Do you recognise them?'

169

'Negative Captain.'

'Can we get to the supply post without being seen?'

'Probably not, they're spread out all over the place.'

'Put us down somewhere safe, we'll walk to the post. Maybe they'll think we're a meteor and hide in their homes.'

Sonnet broke dry atmosphere, buffeted by upper winds she rattled as a toy in a child's hand. Dyson monitored wire frame boxes, Sonnet's computer passed each as thread through a needle. They stretched in a slow descent pattern, velocity diminished as she traversed each box. A landing zone came in sight and thrusters kicked back bringing Sonnet to a crawl until she hovered above her destination. Landing claws protruded from stanchions as she descended. The ship creaked and groaned under gravity while landing systems endured their burden, blowing off compressed gas, steadying the craft above dry cracked earth until all fell quiet.

Rick unstrapped himself, 'Okay, Allenby and Annyah are coming with me, Graham's in charge until we get back. Peters, is that atmosphere breathable?'

'Yeh, but take suits anyway it's pretty chilly out there.'

Rick, Allenby and Annyah suited up in the airlock. When it came to put her helmet on Annyah was unable to squeeze inside, 'Do you stock negz exo-suits?'

Rick opened an armoury locker and pulled out a rifle, 'No, can you survive out there?'

'The atmosphere is quite comfortable.'

'Then take this,' he handed her a rifle, 'Fifty rounds of polonium fired via a magnetic coil.'

She took the assault rifle and checked it, 'I am familiar with this weapon. It is satisfactory.'

'I'm sure Earth Corps' flattered, you can lose the staff.'

'The curxaj-tayag accompanies me wherever battle is a possibility.'

He picked another rifle out the locker passing it and two clips to Allenby, they exchanged looks, 'Have it your way.'

An airlock opened from Sonnet's belly, a metal ladder dropped down and three figures exited. Two in exo-suits bearing Earth Corps regulation assault rifles the other in gothic garb.

This side of the planet faced away from Antares, a cold dry desert, its ground hard and cracked with little room for vegetation. Rick looked upon a bleak landscape it was difficult to understand how any humanoid might scratch a living. Rick glanced at a GPS built into his exo-suit's wrist and pointed forward, 'This way.'

Sonnet's team moved across broken ground, the supply post was about a mile ahead. Annyah took a deep breath, particles of dust raced up her nose and she sneezed.

'Keep quiet,' snapped Rick.

Dry dust lashed their suits with every gust of cold wind. Eventually Rick noticed a dwelling on the horizon, he checked the charge on his weapon's rails and pushed its butt into his shoulder, 'There she is.'

Allenby and Annyah took Rick's lead. As the team closed in it became apparent they were not alone. Inhabiting the area were more than a hundred aliens wearing animal furs, their long hair, pale skin and stark white eyes made Rick nervous.

'What do we do now?' asked Allenby.

Rick zoomed in on the enemy through his exo-suit visor from half a mile out. 'We press on,' said Rick.

'Are you serious?'

'Serious as cancer,' Rick marched ahead.

He'd observed no weapons other than spears and bows, they were armed for hunting.

Annyah followed, she wouldn't openly question her Captain's judgement before crewmates, it wasn't the way of the Kych.

On approach Rick's suit counted more than 300 humanoid hunter gatherers. They had thick leathery skin bearing a tapestry of burns and scars, no doubt a combination of cold desert nights and Antares' increased solar radiation. Rick

171

didn't recognise the species off the top of his head, that was Sam's job. There was a long silence as each party examined the other until Annyah stepped from behind Rick. With that each alien dropped to one knee, discarding their possessions they exposed their palms to Annyah and spoke as one, 'Aqur.'

Rick turned to Annyah, 'What does that mean.'

'It means elder.'

'Why're they kneeling?'

Annyah spoke to the mass, 'Sabsa minii keuked.'

The mob of filthy men, women and children rose, heads bowed.

'What did you just tell them?'

'I instructed them to rise, they speak my language.'

'How?'

'Someone taught them.'

'I know that but who?'

'Probably those who built the supply post you wish to loot, we should leave.'

'Why?'

'These savages were taught my culture, we can be sure they will be evacuated. It would be foolish to steal their property.'

Rick shook his head, 'I thought you neggs didn't believe in property.'

'We believe in collective property.'

Rick grinned through his exo-suit, 'So I'm collecting it.'

Allenby laughed through his mic.

'Can you keep these cavemen under control?'

'They will not hinder us.'

'Good, let's do it.'

'Captain, entering the outpost would be a mistake.'

'Why?'

'I believe it will set off an alert signal.'

'We'll be long gone before they arrive.'

'Then permit me Captain.'

The supply post was no more than a black metal dome rising perhaps ten feet above the earth. It had no discernible means of entry yet Annyah moved

172

around its cold skin seemingly intimate with its construction, in discourse with long gone architects. Locals watched in awe of Annyah, it troubled Rick as to why. In a moment she'd not only taken control but hypnotised an entire group of strangers. Something fishy was going on but as long as they spoke in a foreign tongue its true nature remained a mystery.

Annyah dragged her naked palm along the dome's side until its skin emitted a burst of light through three cracks, mimicking a doorway, scruffy hunter gatherers collectively drew breath. A section of the building, large enough for a man to walk through, shifted inside, Annyah fixed her gaze on Rick, 'It is done.'

Before further conversation might occur Rick received a communication, he tapped his wrist, 'What's up?'

Peters spoke in that high urgent pitch, 'We've got a ship on our scanners.'

'Course?'

'Here.'

'When will it arrive?'

'In a few minutes.'

'Why didn't you see it before?'

'It just came out of hyperspace.'

'How the fuck can it be arriving in only a few minutes?'

'It's negg, it looks like a cruiser.'

Rick turned to Annyah, she replied with an "I told you so" visage.

Rick thought for a moment, 'Fuck.'

'What should we do?'

'Nothing, shut everything down maybe they won't notice Sonnet.'

'What about you?'

Rick looked at the locals, 'We'll try to blend in,' his eyes fell on Annyah, 'or not.'

A golden eagle made orbit emitting a pure light clearly fitted to preserve grace and awe. A beautiful spacecraft assembled by the finest craftsmen in imperial shipyards older than the Roman Empire. A drop ship landed close by the indigenous population, ramp lowered and a platoon of negz shock troops in full battle armour exited. Savages knelt with palms out, overwhelmed by a negz spirit to which so many had succumb in the past. Dark graphene armour blended with tradition garb, it bent and compressed as they marched toward a humble population. Light reflecting from the gas giant's surface and onto this world bounced off these warrior's pale blue heads. Like Annyah they held hard expressions, the visage of conquistadors on a quest, knights determined to slay a dragon, crusaders ready to destroy infidels who dare desecrate their holiest sites.

The landing craft, its skin a stunning gold, reflected a gilded light in all directions which soaked into the inhabitants' eyes. For these simple hunter gatherers the gods had arrived.

Their leader directed his men to search the savages, as they did so he approached the supply post pressing his bare hand upon its entrance. Aladdin's cave shifted open then lit up inside to reveal Rick, Allenby and Annyah.

Rick recognised that hard boney face as negz, the battlements of his brow protected deep fire within two embrasures which served the negz species as eye sockets. A thick ridged nose and heavily plated jaw line surrounding a pair of straight blue lips. Negz are built for all intents and purposes like a Russian tank. Frightening and foreboding so much so that women and children hide while grown men step from its path lest they are flattened.

The fellow had lines running along his forehead as far as Rick could see, it gave him bellyache just considering how many confirmed kills might be there.

The warrior eyed Annyah and spoke sharply, 'Tailbarlakh.'

Before Annyah might reply Rick stepped forward peeling back his exo-suit helmet, face to face with a powder blue T-72, so close he could sense this creature's loathing, 'Anyone talks they talk to me.'

Allenby shook his head, 'Rick, let her talk to him.'

'I'm in charge here.'

Several negz in gothic body armour gathered behind their commander. Rick peered around the warrior's shoulder, these fellows meant business, 'Maybe Annyah should speak to him first.'

Next came a greater shock, the negz spoke English, a broken English inferior to Annyah but with the same Russian accent, 'Speak for yourself kumun.'

Rick glanced at Annyah, she had nothing to offer, he returned to the iron warrior, 'Well we were in the area and thought you'd abandoned this place what with Antares being unstable, but since you're here we'll just let you get on with it.'

Rick tried to exit the bunker but the negz blocked his path, 'Excuse me.'

The T-72 looked down at Rick, his spine erect and indrawn nostrils, 'You are a murderer and a thief.'

Rick rolled his eyes, 'Listen, we take stuff but only after it's been abandoned, like derelict ships.'

The tank's eye sockets expanded by such a tiny amount you'd have to be standing toe to toe to notice. From the time Rick had spent with Annyah he understood this to be an indication of scepticism.

'Alright, we get creative sometimes, but we don't murder people and we don't steal from them. I thought this place was abandoned so yeh I'm here to salvage its contents. I didn't come to steal, that's the truth.'

The tall negz shifted his armour-plated visage at Annyah, 'What of her?'

'What about her?'

'She is yours?'

Rick was about to answer but Annyah cut him off, 'I am his.'

Rick furrowed his brow at her.

The tall warrior retreated permitting them passage into the light. As they stepped out thirty Oci-sebe, lightning wave troops, scrutinized them. After Annyah appeared they began to mumble amongst themselves.

'Talbaj,' said their leader, 'Ene ul-Annyah.'

A warrior stepped forth and spoke to his commander, 'Tere minii.'

Annyah's eyes sparkled, sapphires peeping tentatively from nature's armoured caves. She was worried, not for herself but Rick and he was about to find out why.

The leader smirked, 'Kumun, you have stolen the property of another. He requests siguku.'

'You what?'

'You do defend your claim to Annyah?'

'And if I don't?'

'Plina will take possession of his property and you will be executed.'

'I thought neggs didn't believe in property?'

'Kumun, you defend your claim?'

'What have I got to lose?'

The commander spoke, his troops made a noise of approval. Their eyes heavy and hypnotic, brimming with blood lust.

A tall negz warrior handed his plasma rifle to a comrade, drew his staff and stepped onto to dry earth before Rick.

'You possess a curxaj-tayag?'

'No.'

The platoon commander drew his own and offered it to Rick, 'Take this.'

'Why?'

'Should you desire to escape with your ship, you must take it.'

Rick's eyes narrowed, 'What ship?'

The battle-ready T-72 looked down his nose, 'You are also a liar?'

Rick took the staff, 'Just gimme that thing and tell me what to do with it.'

'You must meet Plina's challenge, to the death.'

Plina stood at the ready, shock troops formed a circle defining the arena's limit.

'This is crazy.'

'A coward and a liar, do kumuns possess a single virtue?'

Rick glared into the commander's bitter blue eyes, 'You calling me a coward?'

'Affirmative.'

Rick handed his pistol and rifle to the negz commander then moved into the circle, curxaj-tayag in hand. Allenby's forefinger nervously stroked the trigger guard of his rifle. Annyah's eyes flicked from Plina to his commander then to Rick and finally Allenby, 'Your weapon will serve no purpose.'

Allenby removed his helmet so he might whisper back, 'He's gonna kill us anyway.'

'Not if Rick is triumphant.'

'Are you kidding look at that guy, he's built like a brick shithouse, probably learnt to use that thing before he could feed himself.'

'Rick is a quick learner.'

'But he's only been doing it for a couple of months.'

'Rick has an advantage.'

'And what might that be?'

'Plina believes Rick ignorant. Rick will use that to his benefit ... and claim victory.'

Allenby shook his head in disbelief for he was certain this was the end of the road for him and Sonnet's crew. Negz weren't known as a merciful species, quite the opposite.

The commander passed Rick's weapons to his first then peered at Plina, 'Belxen?'

Plina replied with fire in his eyes and steam in his breath, 'Belxen.'

The commander addressed Rick, 'Ready?'

'As ready as I'll ever be.'

The commander held his arm in the air and called out, 'Ekhlekh!'

A crowd of negz warriors exhibited nothing but grins of satisfaction, awaiting the inevitable ... Rick's bloody and violent demise. For them this was little more than a blood sport, men on horseback with hounds chasing a fox through a forest. However, none were aware Rick had been taught some rudimentary moves in Zorxo. Zorxo being the school of defensive staff combat, to defeat your enemy with blocks and counter attacks ideally after he over commits to an aggressive thrust or strike. But this wasn't everything in Rick's armoury for as a child he'd learnt the skill of gutter fighting,

177

Doncaster rules, as in anything goes, knees, elbows, gouging, strikes to the groin. He'd had a hard childhood but it prepared him for life outside Earth's cradle.

It was Rick's intent to block this guy as best he could, close in and inflict some real damage. As he'd learnt on the streets of Doncaster, a dystopian inner city, once close to an enemy the most vicious and ruthless always claims victory.

Rick held the staff as if he had no idea, cultivating Plina's confidence until it blossomed as a daffodil in bright Spring sunshine. Plina conceived no sequence of events by which this primitive might defeat him, victory was pre-ordained by the Elders.

The negz warrior decided to play with Rick making strikes to his staff, intended to frighten Rick and demonstrate his utter superiority. Plina's strikes were slow and lazy, his commander, the T-72, displayed a typically passionless expression.

Plina's comrades smiled in anticipation of Rick's gory death. As Plina moved in he struck Rick's staff from his hand, unknown to Plina Rick intentionally dropped it. He wasn't going to win with that staff but he could use it to draw his enemy in, use Plina's arrogance against him.

Rick dropped to his knees and with face to floor he pled for mercy, 'Please, please don't kill me, please, I've got so much to give …'

A cobalt grin filled Plina's face stretching from ear to ear. He held his staff aloft as comrades cheered, egging him on to finish this pathetic beast.

Tremors of horror crippled Annyah mentally and physically, how could Rick have forgotten everything so quickly? She knew he wasn't a coward yet he lay paralysed by fear before Plina.

As the crowd cheered and Plina bathed in glory Rick stopped his pleading, peered upwards, eyes fixed on Plina's groin. It was an old trick employed against newbies back in Doncaster and he was about to use it five hundred light years away on Antares.

Rick thrust upwards around Plina's graphene groin guard grabbing the conquistador's soft testicles. Plina's visage changed from one of jubilation to that of dread as he felt Rick's hand slide around his armour and squeeze. The crowd went from roars of victory to silent shock as Rick held Plina in a painful grasp, right hand on his balls and left forearm under his chin. Rick stood behind his opponent who dropped his staff and screamed like a girl, this wasn't how a conquistador was supposed to fight! Rick clutched onto Plina's nuts and with a great tugged ripped them off. Plina lost consciousness, collapsing, face in dirt. Rick retrieved his staff pressed a button on its centre handle releasing a spear blade. He pointed his blade at the soft rear of Plina's skull, brittle as a powder blue Ming vase, comrades were aghast yet his commander remained emotionless.

'Finish him,' demanded the negz tank.

Rick hesitated.

'Kumun, finish him.'

Rick retracted the spearhead, 'Forget it.'

'You possess victory.'

'Victory's enough, I don't need to kill a defenceless man.'

'Show mercy today your enemy will take revenge tomorrow.'

'True and maybe while he's getting his nuts sewn back on he'll decide against being a dick in the future.'

'The first tenet states: mercy is for the weak.'

'I only kill when I have to, I'm not a murderer,' he handed the commander his staff.

The commander glanced at Plina's staff lying in the dirt beside him, 'It is yours, take it.'

'No thanks ...'

Annyah spoke up, 'Take it ... please!'

Rick looked into her eyes, anxiety rested in her face twitching like a herd of antelope stalked by lions. She'd never said please before now.

Rick walked over and picked Plina's staff from the ground.

The commander gave orders and Plina was peeled out the dirt along with many dark glares, sharp enough to cut flesh.

'You have iron,' the tank pointed toward Rick's head, 'here,' then his heart, 'and here, but if we meet again I will kill you, do you comprehend?'

'I comprehend.'

The T-72 with more tattoos than a ship's crew exposed his open palms to Rick, 'I am Agricola, War Master of Kych.'

Rick wasn't sure what to do, Annyah spoke under her breath, 'You must do the same.'

Rick handed her his staff and exposed his palms, 'I'm Rick, Captain of the Sonnet.'

Agricola dropped his palms, 'You may depart unmolested.'

'I don't suppose we can have a look in the bunker?' replied Rick in a cheeky tone.

Agricola's eyes widened, his men stopped and the atmosphere tensed with an air of passionate cynicism.

'Bad joke,' Rick took his weapons and returned to Sonnet empty handed.

On returning from their excursion Rick attempted communication with Peters only to receive static. He carried his rifle in one hand, staff in the other.

'Do you think they destroyed Sonnet?' asked Allenby.

'I don't think so,' replied Rick.

'Why'd you say that?'

'He could've killed us there and then.'

'He might have destroyed Sonnet and ...'

'Allenby, give it a rest.'

'I don't know why you're so calm.'

'Calm? I was shitting me pants!'

'Well you looked pretty solid.'

Rick winked an eye, 'That's why they call me the man stallion.'

A wind full of sand blew into the man stallion providing him with a mouthful of alien grit, 'Fuck! Wish I had me fucking helmet.'

'Maybe we should turn around and ask for it back?'

'Fuck that,' stated Rick, spitting particles to his side.

Annyah was silent yet her expression spoke satisfaction, a negz mask of terror had fallen aside to betray glittering blue jewels.

Rick raised an eyebrow, 'Something wrong?'

'Negative.'

'You're quiet.'

'Affirmative.'

'I thought you'd start pissing and moaning.'

'You did what was necessary to save your crew.'

'And me own life.'

Her lip moved up a little, 'Of course.'

Rick chuckled, igniting Annyah's curiosity, it puzzled her that one should find humour after such a traumatic event, 'You are amused?'

'He spent years learning to fight with that thing and I kicked his arse with one of the oldest tricks in the book.'

'Certainly unorthodox, tell me, that was the school of hard knocks?'

Rick peered at Annyah with a glint in his eye, 'Bloody right.'

'Typically kumun, brutish and savage.'

'But you learn fast.'

'Plina will not be trounced by that tactic again.'

'I'm not planning on meeting Plina or any of those psychos again.'

She smiled, 'Perhaps.'

'What's that supposed to mean?'

'There is an old negz proverb: the best plan must change to suit the future not the other way around.'

They reached Sonnet, Rick stood at the ladder's base, he looked up and waved at the camera. Sonnet's airlock opened inviting them inside. The others made their way up, Rick slung his rifle over his back and tied his opponent's staff onto his back with a medical bandage. On entering Sonnet, Peters, Dyson and Graham awaited, anxious to discover what occurred. Allenby, Annyah then Rick climbed out of the airlock and onto the deck. Rick shook his head scattering dust in all directions as he removed his environmental suit. Annyah was not so inhibited, her clothing seemed to

181

have evaded the atmospheric grime, no doubt constructed of fibres designed to serve that very purpose.

'What the hell happened?' asked Dyson in a concerned tone.

'We met a platoon of neggs but they let us go.'

'Let you go?'

'He gave his word.'

'Who gave his word?'

'The negg commander.'

'Are you crazy? He's probably waiting to shoot us out the sky.'

'War Master Agricola would not do that,' stated Annyah.'

'You know him?' asked Dyson.

'He is Dajin Xagan.'

'Daj what?'

'War Master, the highest rank within Kych, his word bears more value than finest gold.'

Rick looked at Graham, the engineer shrugged his shoulders. He'd been boarded and seen Kych fight like men possessed but had no idea if Annyah spoke the truth.

Despite hesitations Rick believed Agricola's word, why lie? After all he could've blasted Sonnet from orbit, he could've executed him, Allenby and Annyah with but a word.

Negz are a direct people confronting their foe head to head, to do otherwise is a disgrace and a negz officer wouldn't disgrace himself in the eyes of his own men.

Everyone prepared for take-off, Rick's confidence reassured his crew into performing their duties. He sat in his pilot's chair beside Annyah, she still had a smile on her face, 'I don't know what you're so happy about.'

She checked Graham's data, 'Tokamak core certified, thrusters certified, main engines certified,' she glanced at Rick, 'Nokhor ... certified.'

Rick's gaze met her smiling eyes, 'Nokhor? What's that?'

'A conversation for an appropriate time.'

'That's if Agricola doesn't decide to blow us out the sky.'

'He will not.'

Annyah was in a decidedly upbeat mood, hysterically joyous for a negz, the question was why. She spoke to him in a soft tone not the usual short abrasive snap. It was unsettling enough to lift off observed by a negz cruiser but doing so whilst she spoke in riddles wasn't a help.

'Engage thrusters,' stated Rick.

'Thrusters engaged, Nokhor.'

There was that word again but he didn't ask, it was time to concentrate on getting out of Dodge. The ship began to shake as thrust increased, stanchions creaked while pressure decreased until she lifted. Landing claws retracted and she entered the upper atmosphere.

'They're tracking us,' worried Dyson, monitoring negz, monitoring Sonnet.

'Steady as she goes.'

'Their weapons are activated!'

'Only point defence weapons are active, main beam weapons are inactive,' stated Annyah.

'Still enough to blow us to pieces on reaching orbit,' replied Dyson.

Everyone fixed their eyes on Rick.

'Steady as she goes.'

'You better be right Rick.'

Sonnet broke orbit and passed the golden cruiser, its body and wings a finely sculpted piece of art representing a great bird of prey. The cruiser tracked them all the way above the elliptical plane until Sonnet entered hyperspace. Sonnet travelled the great blue divide while her crew gave a collective sigh of relief. Annyah grinned at Rick, he observed the gothic lady with a quizzical expression, 'Have you been doing split or something?'

'I am proud.'

'Why's that?'

'Despite inbred inferiorities you defeated an accomplished warrior trained in the curxaj-tayag since he was a boy.'

'You knew that bloke?'

'We were, as best I can clarify in your language, betrothed.'

'He seemed to believe he owned you is that true?'

'It is … was.'

'But neggs don't believe in property.'

'In my culture a woman is bound by her father. He decides her mate and makes necessary arrangements. I was bound to Plina since the age of seven and he twelve, that was twenty years ago.'

'So how come you're not married?'

'Had I not been forced into the Kych we would be joined.'

'I get the impression you weren't pleased with the arrangement.'

'The Kych or Plina?'

'Both.'

'It is not my place to be displeased with such an arrangement, it is tradition. I am bound to my duty which I will always realise. When this war ends I will be retired to an inactive post.'

'Paper pushing?'

'Clarify?'

'It's a human expression, you move official forms from one tray to another for the rest of your career.'

'That would be a fair assessment. I would have joined Plina's house. My duties would have changed to filling the ranks of the Kych and Suum.'

'And you've got no say in it?'

'It is tradition.'

Rick shook his head, 'That's one fucked up life.'

The dark blue of deep hyperspace danced on Annyah's fair skin as an Earth-bound aurora in the night sky. Her smile was not a smirk of satisfaction but an expression of jubilation. She opened a box in her soul to find elation and for the first time it emerged through her flesh onto Rick. Today Annyah had slid away from tradition into the realm of liberty. Released from tradition's chains freedom overwhelmed her senses more so than any narcotic, leaving her ordered mind in disarray, 'There is an old negz proverb: one does not need freedom to live.'

'So you're not Plina's property anymore?'

'Thanks to you.'

'How come that cruiser was so close to Antares?'

'I am unaware.'

Rick could see the lie on her face, 'Don't lie to me.'

'I am not lying.'

'Then make a guess.'

'I believe they were transporting the population to safety.'

Rick rubbed his chin, 'Interesting isn't it,' Annyah didn't say anything, 'interesting that a bunch of primitives all spoke your language so fluently and recognised a negg on sight. They revered you.'

'I am a soldier not a seer.'

'So what was a military cruiser doing that close in hyperspace? Perhaps they were on the way already? You know what my guess is?' again Annyah said nothing, 'I reckon they weren't on a mission of mercy, I reckon they were transporting goods … slaves.'

'You accuse my people of slavery?'

'Why not? They do it to their own.'

'Negz do not enslave!' snapped Annyah.

Rick narrowed his eyes locking them with her deep sparkling blue wells, 'What about: you don't need freedom to live?'

Annyah was outraged, 'Kumuns are …'

'I'm not talking about all the shitty things humans get up to I'm talking about the shit your people pull and I find it hard to believe they were rescuing those people. In fact I'd bet that they'd been shifting them off that planet for some time. The only question is where they're going? Since neggs trade very little with others I'm gonna bet they …'

'SILENCE KUMUN!'

Dyson and Peters stopped what they were doing to peer at Rick and Annyah, the pair nearly at each other's throats.

'What you gonna do? Do me in with that staff?' whispered Rick.

'Do not mention this again if you wish to live.'

185

'Bollocks, you wouldn't murder your Captain not with all that negg duty and respect.'

She rose from the co-pilot's seat and placed her communication headset on the panel, 'Wars have been fought and civilizations destroyed over less.'

Rick followed her slim back with a cold eye as she exited the cockpit.

Dyson spoke to Rick, 'What was that about?'

'There's an old human proverb: truth is treason in an empire of lies.'

Dyson and Peters gave each other puzzled looks as Rick leant back … boy did that guy know how to kill a good mood! No wonder he spent so much time at Shaniqua's.

Chapter Twelve

Sonnet floated through tides of ice blue sea, meanwhile her crew took time out. Graham delved within his tokamak, displays offered an accurate rendition of urillium enriched plasma halos. Heat greater than the sun itself throbbed within. Glowing doughnuts smashed into one another supplying Sonnet's power requirements. It was a wonder to behold. Graham knew this reactor so well he could spot trouble just by observing the reaction chamber, he didn't need readouts. Perfect halos traveled up and down a cigar shaped core, so beautiful it were as if he'd captured angels.

Whenever down Graham relaxed, beer in hand, and beheld their dance, one angel taking the other in its arms to forge a new burst of energy greater than the sum of its parents. For Graham a tokamak was divine art, the ceiling of the Sistine Chapel in motion, trapped within the walls of a reactor core. Here his problems washed away before the grace of angels, his doubts crushed by the hand of God.

Allenby slept, catching up on well-deserved rest after a traumatic encounter on Antares. Peters went through his stamp collection. Some believed it an odd coincidence but species all over the galaxy at one time or another issued stamps, many still did. Perhaps it was more than coincidence, perhaps a divine mandate had been written into their D.N.A. so no matter how far apart no matter their ignorance to the greater universe they issued stamps.

Peters had some pretty hot stamps, so he said, a first issue brachian green boy, a moxai black scale with three less perforations on one side, a matted golog issued on celebration day 300 years ago, finally his pride and joy a British Penny Red. He spent hours going through his collection, upon discussing the subject the room quickly dissipated. Allenby swore that stamp collection was a cure for insomnia.

Peters took it all in good humour, stamps made him happy and his were worth a fortune at auction. Rick refused to believe that in this day and age anyone would stump up the kind of cash he was talking about for a paper square in worse condition than a sheet of used toilet roll. Rick was wrong, stamp collectors existed across the galaxy buying and selling at auctions, fortunes passed hands for tiny flakes of paper and right now Earth stamps were hot. Sol would soon be annihilated taking with it many rare stamps. If you could get your hands on Earth stamps, any, they'd erupt in value. Just as a rock star's autograph doubles in value after death, the same held true with stamps and dead civilizations. The deader the civilization the rarer the stamps the greater their value at auction.

Dyson relaxed in the galley watching a holo-vid before dropping off in his cabin. He enjoyed his 3D film noir, something else that befuddled Rick. Why would a man watch a black and white movie shot at night during the rain, filled with French people moaning about the bleakness of existence? It was hardly relaxing, characters were always whining about relationships and complaining about how miserable their lives are, what pleasure could one possible get from that?

Dyson said they were "intense", whatever that means. Rick pointed out that taking a 3lb shit was intense though not an experience he looked forward to reproducing. Nevertheless, Dyson sat down cigarette in one hand beer in the other watching men and women complaining about life for two hours. Then he'd watch another holo where men and women moaned about life for two hours.

Rick was about to go to bed when his door chimed. He put a pair of boxer shorts on and opened the door. He was surprised to see Annyah holding a book, 'What's up?'

'I thought we might spend time together.'

'I'm going to bed.'

'I will join you.'

'What?'

'I said I will join you.'

'Look I'm a bit tired after what happened on the planet maybe another time.'

'You cannot read?'

He noted the book, 'I'm a bit old for bedtime stories.'

'This is no bedtime story it is the Kych Nom.'

'Kych Nom?'

'May I enter?'

'Oui Madame,' he moved aside and the gothic lady crossed the threshold, she wasn't taking no for an answer.

Annyah surveyed his living arrangements with a disparaging visage, 'Your cabin is disgusting, I will clean it.'

'Hold up!'

'Why not?'

'I like it this way.'

She handed him the book, 'Read this while I clean your sty.'

Rick sat down bewildered, he peered at the book, a small leather-bound tome of fifty pages, 'How come most of it's blank?'

'The Kych Nom is a living work, each War Master is permitted a paragraph. A great War Master who has led us to victory is permitted one tenet.'

'I can't read negg.'

She looked up from his dirty clothes and smiled, 'It is pronounced neegzz … and you will.'

In the following months Rick spent his free time between study of the curxaj-tayag and Kych Nom. A book revered by negz military. Each War Master was permitted to author no more than a single paragraph to be added on his death … War Masters don't retire. With Annyah's help Rick managed a basic understanding of their language. Her written language, devoid of punctuation, was a long script of characters similar to Chinese or Japanese in appearance. It took much concentration to garner meaning. Maybe that's why each War Master was limited to a single paragraph? From Rick's understanding each paragraph put forth words of wisdom concerning the negz soul and military philosophy. A few concentrated on a military campaign pointing out its opponent's vulnerabilities and strengths, lauding successful strategies and tactics while berating failures in equal measure.

The front page was blank save two vertical lines, tenets of war written by their greatest War Masters both long dead. A War Master who fought and won a holy war was permitted a tenet in the Kych Nom, a rare distinction awarded but twice in negz history. These tenets were something like commandments ... the two commandments of war. Translated into English the first commandment read: Mercy is for the weak. Rick couldn't say he was surprised, a very negz tenet for a very negz book. The second commandment read: Never display emotion. According to Annyah a warrior should never permit his enemy to read his true emotion. Plina learnt the hard way.

The most recent paragraph was written by a deceased War Master. Rick found its description of brachians quite entertaining providing not only combat advice but a psychological assessment of the enemy. To be fair the guy was pretty much on the money, a bunch of paranoid, sneaky liars that'd step over their own mothers. While Rick chuckled over the account Annyah's forehead rippled as miniature waves on a negz pond, 'You are amused?'

They were sat in his quarters free from dirty laundry spent beer cans and half-finished curries. Rick kept his nose in the book, frequently conferring with Annyah, 'Brachians.'

'Ah, Kanut Galus Tettidius, War Master of the brachian defence.'

'Defence? I find it hard to believe brachians would attack neggs.'

'They attacked kumuns, why conclude their degeneracy with you? Brachians are scum, liars and cheats who respect nothing. We had a trade agreement for centuries until they defrauded us,' she looked him dead in the eye, 'such an indignity could not pass.'

'You went to war because they screwed you?'

'Screwed ... as in sexual intercourse?'

'They ripped you off,' Rick strained not to use a figure of speech, 'Burned you.'

Annyah transmitted a bewildered visage, if you understood negz facial expressions that is. Negz communicated their emotions in such pitiable calculations upon their mien, it wasn't easy for a human to interpret.

'Fleeced, diddled, stiffed ... cheated.'

A wave of revelation washed over Annyah and as a child playing in the morning rain she smiled to the heavens for a short time.

'Something funny?'

'For a species you possess far too many expressions of financial fraud yet I find fleeced to my fancy.'

'So why go to war over being fleeced by brachians? I mean it's what they do.'

'Without retribution what further indignities must my people suffer? Perhaps murder? And what if but a single life lost? Perhaps that is not enough, perhaps one hundred? one thousand? A million?'

Rick sighed, 'I get it but you guys killed a lot of brachians in that war. A lot of innocent people died because one deal went bad.'

'As you are so fond of reminding me it is the school of hard knocks, is it not?' Annyah learned quickly.

'I suppose so but I still think it's a bit extreme.'

'I find it odd you would mourn brachian life, their people are disgusting animals who eat their own young.'

'Come on, that's not true.'

'It is a known fact that a brachian unable to support its new born will sell it into slavery. If unsuccessful he will boil it and serve it to his family.'

'That's crazy.'

'You are very naïve kumun.'

'I don't suppose you guys have any similar stories about humans?'

Annyah fell silent on the question.

'Come on, I'm a big boy.'

'They say … they say kumuns worship an evil God they name Sutun. They say kumuns drink bodily fluids in ceremonies sacrificing children to Sutun, the God of murder and theft.'

Rick laughed.

'You are amused?'

'You believe that load of old bollocks?'

She glanced from side to side, 'You ARE murderers and thieves.'

'There's criminals but they're punished.'

191

'You are a thief yet you are revered.'

'Strippers aren't revered by any stretch of the imagination. Besides, you can't just classify humans as if they're underpants or socks.'

Annyah didn't reply, she seemed ill at ease. Rick put the book down got up and sild open his chest of draws. He produced the golden idol he'd taken off that negz ship, 'Here, I thought you might like it.'

Holding it to the light she examined the idol, 'Where did you acquire this?'

'A derelict ship.'

'Clarify?'

'A frigate, maybe.'

'Where?'

'Luyten's star, she'd been abandoned by her crew so we took a nose around. It would've burnt up anyway, do you like it?'

She smiled, 'I like it.'

'What is it?'

'An Elder.'

'A God?'

'Elders are revered for their wisdom but they are not gods.'

'I've never seen an alien like that, where do they come from?'

'No-one knows, what we do know is that on discovering the Elders their wisdom changed our society. We were once barbarians, murderers, thieves and liars until we sent astronauts to our nearest star system in an attempt to test a hyperdrive, they discovered Elders. They said they had waited millions of years for someone to reach them. The Elders returned with our people and revealed the truth. Negz society changed forever, each house set aside its differences and isolated violence to strive for peace and knowledge.'

Rick shook his head, 'And in doing so bitch slapped everyone who got in the way.'

'Clarify bitch slapped?'

'To easily overcome another with force.'

'I did not say we are perfect.'

192

Rick grinned, humility from a negg, surely a moment to savour, 'So what do you think?'

'It is beautiful, this was cast in the early days perhaps four thousand years ago when all precious metals were gathered and crafted into Elders. Jewels which formally adorned wealthy citizens became eyes.'

'Why would they melt all the gold into idols?'

'So it may not be employed for corrupt purposes. This is a rarity from the early days, thank you Rick.'

'You're welcome, oh I got something else you might be interested in,' he produced the gothic tunic he'd taken from the same vessel, 'What do you think of that?'

She put the idol aside to unfold the soft black garment. Annyah eyed animals on each side transmitting to which house its owner belonged, 'You retrieved this from the same ship?'

'Yeh, they had to abandon her pretty quick.'

'I know this house, Lucanus was Captain aboard a frigate lost in battle some months ago,' she looked up from the tunic and at Rick, 'he would not have abandoned his ship.'

'We did run into one bloke.'

'A negz?'

'Yeh.'

'Did he identify himself?'

'No.'

'What occurred?'

'He threatened to kill Sam so I took him out.'

'Clarify took him out?'

'I shot him in the head.'

As a vessel might fill with wine before being sent to the banquet table Annyah's visage filled with horror, 'You murdered Lucanus?'

'He threatened the life of me friend.'

'You murdered a great warrior.'

'It was self-defence.'

'Murderers and thieves.'

'I didn't say I was perfect.'

There was an uncomfortable silence allowing Annyah to centre herself, 'I must leave.'

'Hey what about the book?'

'Another time … I must pray for Lucanus.'

She handed back the tunic and exited with elder in hand. Rick sighed, she'd be over it by tomorrow … hopefully.

The Kych Nom documented every negz interstellar war since the dawn of space travel. After meeting the Elders negz focused on self-sufficiency, self-enlightenment and self-defence. The only area which confused Rick was economy. There was no such thing as a socialist utopia despite the fact every socialist he'd ever met believed in one.

Here's the deal, utopia has these gimmicks called bills just like every other form of society. We can't all live like kings because someone has to take away the trash. Someone has to put their hand up a prisoner's anal passage to check for drugs. So, the question lurked in the back of his mind, who did do all the crappy jobs that no-one wants to do?

He hadn't made the connection yet but those people on Antares had been taught subservience many years ago. Rick witnessed their masters come to the rescue as angels swooping down from the heavens. Scooping them up and transporting them to paradise where they may serve their Gods with a smile.

In truth the foundation of negz utopia was based upon creatures such as those. The dirty work was theirs which they did with a happy heart, at least that's what Annyah had been taught.

Negz considered themselves subservient to the Elders and in turn all other species were beneath them. Since the wisest beings in the universe revealed themselves to negz first it made sense that negz are superiors on a hierarchy of lesser species. This logic justified slavery, preventing its immorality from burdening the negz soul.

Despite persuading themselves it was moral and preordained by Elders they hid it, for in their hearts the truth lurked. The darkness chewed like an animal gnawing at a man's side until one day it draws blood.

Annyah wasn't so different from Rick in this respect, she suffered great guilt, not of her own actions but her society. It was the negz way, society took responsibility for the actions of the individual and vice versa. One citizen's dishonour was every citizen's dishonour and so forth. Negz identified as a group not as individuals.

Within this immoral system of group accountability she felt complicit despite having neither say nor hand in it. Those who were directly involved equally felt their responsibility dispersed throughout the group identity. Similar to guards at a death camp, they were merely following society's orders. This collective liability resulted in the authorization of all manner of atrocities. Annyah hated herself as though she were another person, it was her twisted method of assuming obligation as an upstanding negz warrior. An odd frame of mind considering her species had such difficulty deciphering metaphors, maybe that's why the subject hampered her thoughts?

A totally collectivist society cannot function without forced labour, from the days of the Spartans to the Negz it was the only way. Humans had tried it many times and failed miserably. Perhaps the greatest example was in the first American colonies. Americans celebrate thanksgiving when starving colonists were taught to farm by local Indians and a bountiful crop ensued breaking their hunger.

The truth? Those colonies had started out as collectivists, every man went to work, the fruits of his toil ended up in a big barn from which colonists took what they needed and when. Women made clothes for all inhabitants, when required.

Young men began to stay home rather than work fields for crops, why work when I can sit on my backside and get it for free at the barn? Women became angry, they felt it wrong to sustain a single man when they had husbands and children. Husbands, their toil supporting feckless work shy young men, agreed with their wives and everything ground to a halt. Soon there was no food in the barn not because of poor weather or because they didn't have the knowledge but because hard working people refused to support those who'd rather live as parasites.

After a poor crop and starvation the governor decided to change policy. He dropped collectivism, allotted families their own land permitting citizens the bounty of their own labour. By the following year starvation had disappeared, another year and they were exporting grain at a profit. There were no Indian saviours, Indians lived hand to mouth barely surviving one year to the next. The colonists merely dumped socialism for property rights and free trade, suddenly there was a motive for those young men to work and wives to make clothes.

On the negz home world they used forced labour to fill that gap, for without slaves work would never be done. The church held civilians in line while the military kept barbarians from the gates.

When examined objectively it was a twisted culture so deeply entrenched in its traditions and beliefs it couldn't see its own immorality yet you could say that about most alien cultures to one degree or another. It's just negz are such a stark example of a society gone wrong.

Dyson was grumbling at the galley table, they'd gone all this way, months in hyperspace for nothing except a big refuelling bill. They'd had a couple of lucky finds recently and he was hoping this'd be the hat-trick but it wasn't in the stars. Rather than focus on fortune he centred on failure, a true film noir aficionado, 'Do you know how much it's gonna cost in urillium?'

Rick looked up from his evening curry, 'You want an answer or you just pissing and moaning?'

'Five months in hyperspace without a penny to show for it, that's fucked up and you know it.'

Annyah stepped into the galley, 'You escaped with your life, be thankful kumun.'

Dyson snarled at the gothic lady, 'PUH!'

'She's right,' snapped Graham nursing a bitter beer, 'I still don't know why that psycho let us go.'

'War Master Agricola is not a psychopath.'

'Well I've never seen a negg show mercy, why'd he?'

She pulled a tray of quorn protein from the dispenser and ripped away its film. Steam rose from the tray carrying the scent of a rather bland meal. Annyah delicately sliced her meal with knife and fork, 'Perhaps you are prejudice?'

Rick stepped in before an argument might ensue, 'Look on the bright side, we're alive.'

'And what about those people we left behind on Antares?' asked Dyson.

'Since when did you give a shite about anything outside your bank balance?' asked Rick in an incredulous tone.

The crew quietly chewed their meal waiting for Dyson's reply.

'I don't but ...'

'Then shut the fuck up, we'll get back to Templeton's and wait for the next score, okay?'

Dyson shrugged his shoulders.

Over the next hour Sonnet's crew dispersed, Dyson and Graham took the first shift. As Rick relaxed his doorbell jingled, he got up expecting Dyson. Rick leant on the wall and opened the door, 'Dyson for fuuu ....' Standing before him was Annyah out of her usual uniform.

He ogled ... lost for words.

'I wish to speak.'

'Yes.'

'In private.'

'Be my guest,' he stepped aside.

Annyah had let go of her exterior uniform to reveal a pair of pants and soft pullover, a very soft and very tight pullover which stunned his senses.

She entered his cabin, turned back and spoke softly, 'There is a draft.'

197

Rick broke from his hypnosis, 'Obviously,' hit the panel closing the hatch, 'So what's up?'

'You are my nokhor.'

'I don't understand.'

'On Antares you released me from bondage and now I am yours.'

'Can we talk about this?'

'Are we not talking?'

If Rick were to be honest with himself she had a pretty tight body something you didn't see every day, certainly not in deep hyperspace. Then again how many men had seen a female negg disrobed before now? There might be all manner of horrors lurking beneath those fibres.

'I meant another time.'

'Do you find me repugnant?'

'After five months in hyperspace even Allenby's ex-missus looks good.'

'I do not comprehend?'

'I've got a lot of things on me mind and ...'

'That is why I am here.'

'I'm busy.'

Annyah's visage became quizzical, 'How odd, you will spend hours alone with a hologram employing a suction hose to ...'

'What's your point?'

'I wish to, as kumuns would say, take a weight off your mind.'

'Have you been drinking?'

'I have not,' she glided over to him as if he were in a dream. Annyah held his hands, 'Relax Rick Katusa, let your troubles fall away and think back to when you were truly happy.'

Her soft fire devoured his senses, but was it good or evil? Annyah went on her toes presumably to kiss him, instead her forehead touched his, the moment it did so he fell out of this world. Her mask of negz dignity appeared to fall away. The room blurred leaving only Annyah's presence ... emotion came over him, emotion he'd not experienced in decades. Rick's ears pricked up as music played, an old dance track he first heard as a teenager and then Annyah's lips began to move as she sang the words,

'When I'm going state to state,

Drivin' in my '68,

Feelin' like it's '64,

With my foot down on the floor,

Passing through the 808,

Like I'm stepping through your bedroom door.'

She began to move her body to the beat as he recalled the feelings of a lad in Doncaster dancing with his first girlfriend.

Annyah was still Annyah, a compact and definite entity, Rick was still smelly old Rick but he was in a time and place of pure bliss. A time of care free days and nights with young easy-going girls.

Rick's mind had been tricked, traveling back to his youth and onto the dancefloor of "The Den" an upscale club he'd saved for weeks to get into, Tracy couldn't say no to a date there.

Annyah moved and swayed, his subconscious took control while they shared his past. She felt the rush of abandonment, tasting his emotion, a forbidden ambrosia disavowed by her species. All that negz tradition was chased away by human independence. Feelings flooded his upper thoughts blocking all else. Annyah maintained eye contact on the man in her grasp just as Zeus held his thunderbolt. She danced, channelling emotion, sharing a time held dearly to his breast. Slipping into the past by degrees Rick shifted his body like the stupid kid he was. Annyah leaned back shaking her shoulders as she enjoyed the moment. Rick started playing the bongos on her midriff, it was a very odd sight. On reaching the end of the song Annyah slowed down guiding Rick back to reality. Holding his head straight she sang the last lines softly, went on tip toes and kissed foreheads.

Rick awoke, reality cleared as layers of cloud peel away on making orbit. Emotions from the past remained suspended in his mind as the scent of a woman after she's exited the bedroom, while he was brought forward into his cabin aboard Sonnet, 'What happened?'

'I will explain tomorrow,' Annyah turned to leave but before she might Rick grabbed her frame. She chirped in surprise and their lips met. Perhaps the first time in history a negz and human made such a gesture. Two workmates previously unaware abruptly recognised they were in fact man and woman. She was silent waiting on his desire. He was confused, between one world and another, a slave to instinct. That evening he existed inside her, another first between the species.

On detecting an odd noise those on duty didn't need much of an imagination. Initially Graham ran a diagnostic on Sonnet's boron piping, after eliminating them as the source of an unrelenting knocking permeating every bulkhead on the ship he went on a personal hunt, ending outside Ricks quarters with the rest of the crew.

'What the bloody hell's going on in there?' stated Graham.

Allenby fixed his gaze on Graham, 'Either he's killing her, she's killing him or Shaniqua's gonna kill 'em both!'

Graham looked at the rest of the crew eavesdropping with glee. Dyson had a beer glass against the hatch, 'Fuck they're getting right into it!'

Graham snatched the beer glass.

'Hey, give it back!'

'Get the fuck outta here, all of you!'

The crew dispersed.

Dyson shook his head at Graham, 'You're no fun!'

As the crew scattered Graham looked at the cabin door, 'Who'd have thought it?'

The morning after the night before Rick awoke. Annyah lay her head on his chest. His aching eyes focused on her delicate rear skull, its powder blue iridescence splashed on his celluloid eyes … Rick groaned. His nose detected a scent of alien ambergris and for a moment he wished he were someone other than the guy waking in Rick Katusa's bunk this morning.

She moved from her slumber, Annyah's vision cast light from her mind as hot blue coals piercing armoured caves. This morning those armoured arches seemed soft almost vulnerable. Her lips curled as two fluffy cushions pushed together, 'I am surprised you woke so early.'

'What did you do to me last night?'

'That should be clear,' smiled Annyah.'

'When you touched me with your head I went back at least I felt I went back.'

'As a priestess one of my duties would have been to cleanse citizens of erroneous emotions.'

'Like what?'

'Guilt, lust … compassion.'

'Is that what you did to me?'

'What I did is forbidden on Hemzih,' she made a cheeky grin, 'but we are not on Hemzih.'

'What did you do exactly?'

'Negz women possess a small empathic ability but it must be trained and developed. In the past a father would have his daughter trained by the clergy so she might bring a greater dowry. Today it is used to remove undesirable emotion and intensify the focus of society. I mastered a rudimentary understanding before entering the Kych.'

'Is that why Plina wanted you so bad?'

Annyah batted her eyelids, 'The most prized mates are priestesses for behind closed doors they will perform what you experienced last night … but only for husbands.'

'Run that by me again.'

'Last night we joined making us one, until the day we die.'

'That's a joke, right?'

'On Antares you bound with me. Last night I offered myself and you accepted my offering, in doing so we joined as husband and wife.'

Rick sat up in his bed, 'I'm a gay bachelor.'

Annyah lay her cheek on his chest and spoke softly, 'You were not gay last night.'

'I mean a happy singleton.'

'Did I not make you happy?'

'How could I agree to marrying you if I didn't know about it at the time?'

'There is an old negz proverb: ignorance is not a defence.'

'Is that negg humour?'

'Are you unhappy?'

'I don't like having me status as a bachelor usurped by a crafty woman.'

'Clarify crafty?'

'Cunning, scheming, devious, slick, need I continue?'

'Why would you fight Plina if not for my possession?'

'I fought Plina to get off that world in one piece. I had no idea you came as a package deal.'

'And if you had?'

Rick folded his arms and grumbled, 'I suppose I'd have done the same.'

'And last night would you have joined?'

He let out a great sigh, 'Look as far as humans go we're perfectly single with no obligations.'

Annyah's face lost its joy, her tone became devoid of all softness, 'I comprehend,' she stood up and slipped on her top and bottom, 'I will be on duty in two hours, Captain.'

Rick leapt up, 'Hold on.'

'Yes Captain?'

'I didn't mean to be sharp.'

'Acknowledged, Captain.'

She slapped the door mechanism and marched back to her quarters. Rick stepped outside in a pair of boxer shorts. He saw her slim back disappear into her cabin. Rick turned around to witness his crew sitting in the galley staring back at him, 'Something wrong?'

They said nothing, turning heads away in an air of awkwardness.

That day tension filled the breakfast table more so than a king's banquet. Annyah ate her meal in total silence ignoring those around, unknown to the crew she felt totally humiliated.

Rick looked at Dyson, 'How long until we make Templeton's?'

'Two weeks maybe less if the weather improves.'

Two more weeks of Annyah's cold shoulder, he wasn't sure if he could bear it. In the past he might not have even noticed but today he felt her dissatisfaction wherever she might be on the ship. Rick remembered why he'd labelled Annyah the ice woman for upon entering a room in one of her moods a noticeable decline in temperature was detected. Right now it felt like Antarctica during and ice age.

Rick cut his eggs and bacon then turned to Annyah, 'It'll be nice to get back.'

'Acknowledged Captain,' said the ice woman in a hard monotone.

Dyson excused himself quickly leaving a half finished tray.

'Not hungry?' asked Rick.

'I lost my appetite,' replied Dyson before putting his tray in the trash compactor.

Dyson exited the galley for a good night's sleep. Next Allenby stood up, 'I think I'll turn in early too.'

He left leaving Rick and Annyah, 'Annyah,' there was no reply, 'Annyah.'

'Yes Captain.'

'What's the matter?'

'Nothing Captain,' she chewed a piece of microbial protein.

'If it's about this morning I'm sorry.'

'Sorry?'

'I might have over-reacted. I didn't mean to be rude.'

'Affirmative Captain.'

'Stop playing silly buggers will you?'

'Affirmative Captain.'

'There you go again, stop calling me Captain.'

'You are my Captain are you not?'

'Yeh but when you say it you sound like Darth Vader's evil sister.'

'Affirmative Captain.'

'I'm ordering you not to call me Captain.'

She looked him in the eye with furious blue stoned vision, 'Affirmative ... SIR.'

'Look, maybe I didn't think before opening me mouth.'

Annyah's armoured wells widened permitting more light to reflect off blue pools beneath.

'I wasn't ready for what happened, you have to understand I've planned on living out me life as a gay bachelor, sailing the stars with a lass in every port.'

Annyah's visage became one of disgust her top lip shot up like a cobalt roller blind.

'It's a figure of speech it means I'm a free man, unattached, a gay bachelor. No man in his right mind would give that up.'

'What if he fell in love?' asked Annyah.

'Love? Love was invented by credit companies to turn sensible men into financial retards. I've seen blokes lose their ships because they fell in love.'

'I am yours just as this ship is yours, you may ignore that fact but it remains so until I die.'

Rick looked up at the ceiling and whispered to himself, 'Jesus Christ don't tempt me.'

'Captain?'

'Nothing … and cut the Captain crap I told you I don't like it.'

'Affirmative sir.'

'Call me Rick.'

'Affirmative Rick.'

'Fucking hell are you gonna apply for the job of ship's parrot or something?'

Annyah said nothing probably because she had no idea what a parrot is.

'Listen I appreciate what happened last night but I just don't need a wife.'

'What do you need?'

'I've got everything I need.'

'That is a lie, I have observed you over the last six months, festering on this vessel is not enough for a man such as yourself.'

'So what's your solution Dr Phil?'

'I am not a doctor but you are a man of principle. You lie to yourself every day while your people teeter on the precipice of destruction. While others suffer you have hoodwinked your mind into believing only Rick Katusa is worth saving yet your actions tell a different tale.'

Rick scoffed whilst rolling his eyes.

'You cannot dismiss me as you dismiss your conscience. You are a better man than the Rick Katusa you put on show for the universe. You refuse to be joined for fear you might have to care for someone. I would force your hand, prevent Rick Katusa from hiding away in his shell of self-imposed indifference.'

Rick clapped his hands slowly, 'Great job, you should apply to Earth Corps I hear they need all the psyches they can get.'

'Then why are you afraid of being joined?'

'I told you, I want to stay single.'

'Sitting for months on end in a filthy cabin watching a hologram with your genitals in a suction hose?'

'When you put it that way you make it sound seedy.'

'It is pathetic and beneath you. Do not be afraid you will want for nothing,' she held his hand in hers.

Rick looked down those wells and saw the purest blue water he'd ever seen in his life, so pure it reached out and touch his soul purging his self-enforced stain of indifference, 'What's the negg word for divorce?'

She shook her head, 'There is none.'

Rick groaned, 'Fuck my life.'

Chapter Thirteen

Sonnet emerged from the blue ether her engines firing for home with little to show for recent endeavours. Rick and Annyah were at peace, he'd accepted ownership as a man would a piece of property.

She didn't need freedom to live yet he was different. What was a man without his independence? No more than a slave.

The negz say to become truly free one must win liberty and then have courage to renounce it on the altar of society.

In Annyah's opinion he'd done everything to be free. All that remained was for him to renounce freedom itself. A barmy notion in Rick's opinion, he'd persuade her otherwise, given enough time.

Sonnet floated into dock, clamps latched to her body, airlock fixed to mid-section. Rick was relieved to be back, Templeton's, the closest he had to a home outside Sonnet. Although he wasn't a citizen he'd been knocking about for the last twenty years. Rick was here when it was a real shithole, before Templeton bought out the brachian brothers Lapong and Ganik.

Dishing out property rights and citizenship turned it about and into a beacon of prosperity. Best of all, strippers were given a pass, they paid nothing in the form of docking fees. Templeton's plan brought in strippers attracting corporations, merchants, casino operators, smugglers and everything attached to a virulent economy. Soon Templeton's rode the number one spot in Piraxis. The Bank of Altan opened a branch close by quenching its thirst for currency.

Today Templeton's is one of the largest most powerful non-Corps stations in human space. Creatures from across the galaxy live, work and die here. Strippers are a major part of that economy especially since the war brought disaster to Earth shipping. Stripping one of few trades to garner a net positive from this madness. Smugglers no longer attempt to slip past Earth Corps patrols but dodge negz, delivering ammunition and urillium to the Ring, a more dangerous state of affairs since negz fire first and scan debris afterwards.

While Sonnet and her crew travelled hyperspace the alien grip had tightened. Negz attack fleets penetrated the outer core to within 10 light years of Earth, as each day passed they struck closer and with greater frequency. Earth Corps fought a pyrrhic rear-guard action, negz cruisers trashing system defences on a daily basis. Earth cruisers and destroyers waited in hyperspace to counter attack yet each counter dashed itself against a greater force. Those who could fled Earth, taking anything not nailed down. Rick had become a multi quadrillionaire over the last five months, in Earth credits that is. With each passing hour currency rates drastically changed. Earth credits dropped like a stone in a lake on their way to oblivion as people traded them for precious metals, food, fuel, a ticket out of harm's way or one last drunken party before the inevitable. What was a civilized society had become a pathetic scramble for self-preservation. Passengers on the Titanic finally charged for the life boats only to realize they were woefully short.

To their credit Earth Corps stood fast ready to meet the coming storm no matter what. For a moment Rick felt something within his soul as he watched a General announce evacuation of civilians from the Sol system along with a promise to stand between them and the enemy.

'Is it not magnificent?' stated Annyah as Sonnet waited on Templeton's to certify airlocks and permit entry.

'Magnificent? It's pathetic,' replied Rick as he relaxed in his pilot's chair.

Annyah observed General Bradley declare his intentions, a sacrifice any negz would be proud of, 'He is prepared to put himself in the way of death so your people may use his shadow to slip away.'

Rick scoffed, 'Puh, he knows that one way or another those neggs'll hunt him down. It's the poor bastards who've suffered for years so he can live the good life I feel sorry for! That piece of shit deserves to get vapourised, the sad part is innocents will die with him!'

'You hold no respect for your military class?'

'They're a bunch of jackboot pigs about to get what they deserve.'

'I do not believe you Rick.'

He furrowed his dark brows.

'You have a friend in Earth Corps, I do not believe you wish him death.'

Rick put his feet on the floor and picked a coffee off the dashboard, 'That's different.'

'How so?'

Rick took a sip, 'He's not one of them jumped up twerps.'

'Why attribute negative traits to all Earth Corps barring Sam? Could it be there are many noblemen in Earth Corps and you are merely prejudice?'

Rick put his coffee down pulled a hip flask from one of his pockets and poured metaxa into the cup. He put the flask away and swilled down a mouthful of coffee, 'Ahhhhh.'

'Ahhh, is not an answer.'

Peters started to chuckle as he and Dyson awaited Rick's reply. Rick leant back peering over his left shoulder, 'Something funny?'

'Nothing at all.'

Rick looked over and observed that oriental smile. She enjoyed these philosophical arguments, he didn't because she always won, 'Maybe I was a bit harsh ... satisfied?'

'Somewhat,' Annyah returned to her console, 'we are cleared to board Templeton's Captain.'

'And stop calling me Captain!'

Her lip curled, 'Yes sir.'

'Or sir!'

'Yes my nokhor.'

Peters and Dyson laughed.

Rick grabbed a rollup from behind his ear, 'Fuck my life!'

The crew scattered onto Templeton's for a well-deserved break. The mood had changed since Rick's last visit. Today an air of uncertainty hung above every inhabitant for negz bore down on Earth with full force, in preparation for a spectacular death blow.

208

Mankind and negz stood erect as two gladiators in a galactic arena. Mankind a savage uprooted from his barbaric hinterland and dropped amongst a baying crowd of outraged negz. Menacing gestures demanding blood for the crimes of his tribe. While this confused savage tries to make sense of his situation a negz gladiator appears. Golden armour reflecting the noon day sun, his bright spear symbolising justice soon to be delivered to the mob, his shield embossed with the eyes of Phobos, the god of fear.

As Phobos injects despair into humanity onlookers gain excitement in equal measure. A naked mankind whisks up dirt to discover a short sword and buckler. The horde scream to their champion as he advances, integrity his shield, due process for a lance. Battle ensues and the primitive finds himself at negz mercy. All eyes turn to the emperor perched upon his golden throne, he makes a fist displaying a long boney thumbs down, the final thrust ends in annihilation of an inferior species.

Rick didn't have time to worry about what may, his concerns were more immediate. While Annyah was trusted with Sonnet he made off to visit Shaniqua. It was time to break off their relationship, it seemed the right thing to do. He stepped into Red Sector, nothing had changed, business was booming as men expunged the inevitable from their minds. Music played, women danced, alcohol flowed as a turbulent spring river while sticks of split bobbed up and down its icy waters.

A smile filled Shaniqua's face as she swooped on Rick, she was doing a roaring trade now Earth was in mortal danger. Another alien invasion and she could afford to retire … that was joke … she wasn't going to retire!

'Rick, is that you?' squealed the gold clad Queen of Red Sector.

He entered the largest temple to vice in the Piraxis system, 'The one and only.'

She threw her arms around him cocktail in one hand split in the other, 'You look fabulous, I hardly recognised you!'

'Thanks.'

'I thought they'd got you, I was so worried!'

'They?'

'Those nasty negg-heads,' she pointed to her corner, 'take a seat, I wanna hear what my hero's been up to,' split in mouth she snapped her fingers at the bar tender, 'Metaxa for Rick.'

Rick didn't move, 'Look I just dropped in to …'

'Don't be a silly billy,' she grabbed his arm drawing him into her cloistered divan, 'you're gonna tell me all you been doing.'

Before he realised Rick was chatting to Shaniqua as if what'd occurred aboard Sonnet over the past months were a distant memory. To be fair she had far more practice stroking egos and manipulating men than Rick in resisting feminine whiles.

Despite his good intentions to break it up and return his loyalty card, events took the opposite course. It's not that Shaniqua didn't know what was up, she'd seen clients come in with that look. They think they've found a woman and it's time to call it a day, HAH! She'd dealt with these losers for decades, they were little else than insects caught in her amber, the greater they struggled the deeper they plunged before she squeezed out their final credits. She saw that look in Rick tonight, it scared the life out of her, not that you'd have noticed for she was as devious and crafty as Lucifer himself.

Dyson returned to Sonnet, he'd decided to save himself the cash on accommodations and sleep in his cabin tonight. As he boarded the vessel Annyah waited by the airlock, arms folded in her signature fashion.

'You good?' asked Dyson wondering what he might have done to annoy the gothic lady.

'I was expecting Rick.'

'Ah, yeh, sorry,' Dyson tried to slip away but Annyah saw it written on his face, he knew something.

She stepped in his path preventing the navigator from entering Sonnet, 'Where is the Captain?'

'I don't know.'

'You are a liar, tell me where he is or I will force it from you kumun.'

'Don't tell him I told you …'

'WHERE?'

'He's at Shaniqua's.'

Annyah was puzzled, 'I believe I …' after a second she worked it out, her visage brought forth a fury as yet seen by a human. There was good reason negz spent so much time and energy in meditation for if uncontrolled their emotions led to terrible ends.

Dyson put his head down and shuffled to his cabin. Shortly after locking his hatch he heard a long shrill shriek of frustration sending a chill down his spine. Dyson felt comfort in the knowledge he wasn't in Rick's boots. Next thing he heard the airlock open and close.

Annyah marched onto Templeton's, a woman on a mission, surgical strike and retrieval.

No species were banned from Templeton's, the station was open to anyone with cash and a pulse … scratch that … cash will do. Nevertheless 99.9% of its inhabitants had not seen a real life negz, those who had considered themselves fortunate to be breathing.

She marched into customs with obstinate authority. Silence befell the room, all eyes captured in her orbit. Agents nervously clutched shock sticks. Annyah approached a customs terminal, 'Please step inside for a scan,' spoke its female operator.

'Clarify scan?'

'It's mandatory … Miss?'

'Very well,' Annyah stood in an archway for a few seconds before a bleeping noise filled the air.

'I'm sorry Miss but you'll have to leave your weapon with us.'

'Unacceptable.'

The terminal operator nodded and two agents brandishing shock sticks moved in. Annyah exited the arch and drew her curxaj-tayag swinging it from side to side, 'Who is first?'

One agent glanced at his partner, the sons of Mars travelling up and down his anatomy, 'She's all yours Mike.'

Mike took a deep breath as electricity danced on the end of his shock stick in a frightening ballet. Annyah wasn't nearly as impressed as the onlookers. She swung her staff striking the agent cleanly in his stomach. Mike bent over her rod as a groan emanated from a deep dark place rarely visited within the human frame. She raised her weapon and struck the back of his head, knocking him out cold. Mike fell to the floor like a sack of potatoes while his superior observed in horror.

'And you?' snapped Annyah.

The agent holstered his weapon, 'My shift just ended lady.'

Annyah sheathed her curxaj-tayag in one sweeping move, 'Where may I find Shaniqua's?'

'That'd be Red Sector,' he pointed at a station map laid out on the wall.

Annyah committed it to memory in a glance, 'Remove this obstruction,' snapped the dark conquistador zeroing in on the terminal.

After an uneasy pause the customs agent nodded to the operator and the bars disappeared into the floor as Annyah stormed onto Templeton's.

'You're welcome Ma'am,' replied the agent in a sheepish tone.

The terminal operator took off her glasses and stated in a distinct Bronx accent, 'My hero!'

Shaniqua charmed Rick via whiles crafted over years of professional practice. He was trying to explain his position but couldn't find the words, it must have been an all-time record. The motor mouth of Doncaster searched for five hours without luck. Shaniqua saw his pained soul wringing, 'What's wrong honey?'

'I sort of came to tell you something important.'

She smiled rolling split around her mouth, 'You wanna take me away from all this?'

'Not quite.'

'Oh? What you got for me, a present?'

'Not really.'

Shaniqua rolled her eyes, 'Well spit it out before I die of old age!'

Rick closed his eyes tight … he just couldn't do it … he couldn't bring himself to throw away all those years, all those memories, all those good times. Music stopped, chatter of customers and prattle of workers screeched to a dead silence, only a clink of glasses here and there could be detected. The flow of booze and split came to a screeching halt. Rick opened his eyes, Shaniqua was taken aback by something directly over his shoulder, what could it possibly be?

'Rick will no longer frequent this den of perversity.'

SHIT! Terror kicked him in the head like a mule, ejecting Dionysus back to Mount Olympus.

Shaniqua's visage had gone from one of an adoring woman to that of an executioner, 'Who the fuck are you?'

'That is superfluous, your services are no longer required.'

Shaniqua's stare locked onto Rick as a heat seeking missile, ready to rip him to pieces for this faux pas, 'You been fucking some negg bitch behind my back?'

Rick lifted a shot glass of metaxa to his lips sloshing the muscat brandy down his neck in an attempt to stabilise his mind.

Shaniqua looked past Annyah, 'LEROY! Get this bitch out my bar!'

A tall man dressed in a suit approached Annyah from behind, 'It's time to leave.'

Annyah turned to observe a man over a foot taller, heavily built with wide shoulders. To Shaniqua's patrons it seemed an impossible mountain for this gothic conquistador to climb. She was elegant slim and neat to the point of insignificance when compared to the broad brutish physique before her. Annyah whipped her staff, in a single easy sweep its point rested beside Leroy's neck. She squeezed and a spike pressed into him. On observation Annyah noted a familiar barcode tattoo, 'You are a Marine?'

Leroy looked down her spear and swallowed, 'Was a Marine, got boarded around Beta Librae. Neggs killed most of my company.'

'If that is so you comprehend the markings above my eye.'

'I do.'

'Do you wish to see your soul carved into my brow?'

Leroy peeked over the abyss only to see an alien conquistador glaring back, her stark blue eyes etching fate into his soul. Annyah was prepared to satisfy the Keres with another victim. He'd battled negz before, they don't flinch, they don't second guess and they never show mercy. Not many men became an ex-Marine without a body bag entering the equation first and he wasn't giving these psychos a second chance.

'LEROY!' shrieked Shaniqua, 'Get that bitch outta here, NOW!'

Leroy peered into needle eyes resting within sockets plastered by hard bone and thick skin. This breed of psychopathic killer, feared throughout the galaxy, held a spear point to his jugular. Leroy stepped back from the fray causing Shaniqua to shriek at the top of her voice, 'WALK AWAY AND YOU'RE FIRED!'

Leroy couldn't feed his kids impaled on a negz spear. He picked up his coat and silently left the establishment to the shock of customers and Shaniqua's frustration.

Annyah's gaze returned to Shaniqua's annex. Rick sloshed down anything left on the table. Shaniqua stood up and strutted to the bar, 'Gimme the bat.' The barmaid produced a baseball bat, rusty old nails protruding its bulge. Shaniqua placed her split on the bar and took the bat, 'You ain't the first skinny little bitch to try and steal my customers.'

Annyah squeezed her staff retracting its spike, 'I came only to retrieve Rick.'

'He's mine, if you want him you're gonna have to get past me.'

Rick attempted to stop this madness from escalating, 'Ladies, let's just calm down.'

Annyah and Shaniqua barked as one, 'SHUT UP!'

Rick tapped his table waiter ordering another bottle of metaxa, hell, if he was going out he was going out with a tab.

Shaniqua swung, a brutal uncoordinated attack, the gothic conquistador dodged with ease. Unfortunately, a rubber necking bar patron was not so nimble. He thought he was getting the cat fight of the century at no extra charge but Shaniqua missed her intended target, striking him dead in the gut.

She pulled her bat from his stomach, he groaned before collapsing to the floor. Shaniqua showed no concern for the man, moving on as if he were little more than a broken glass. Rick had seen her make more fuss over unpaid tabs than this poor son of a bitch bleeding to death on her floor. What Shaniqua lacked in skill she made up for in cold brutality. After the fifth strike Annyah realised this woman wasn't going to stop until one of them was defeated. Raising her staff she spun it above her head before making that figure eight and moving in. Shaniqua lashed out again lodging her weapon in the side of the bar, Annyah struck Shaniqua in the ribs, a muffled crunch passed around the establishment. Rick opened his metaxa and took a good swig.

Uncharacteristically for a negz Annayh withdrew in an act of mercy. Shaniqua was bent over in pain spitting blood onto the floor. The Queen of Red Sector wiped her mouth then from underneath her tasselled outfit she pulled a pair of daggers. With the devil in her eyes Shaniqua charged. Annyah waited for her to enter striking distance and in one motion smashed Shaniqua's jaw with a solid and substantial sweep. Shaniqua's limp body slammed against the bar head, her wig flew onto a barmaid while a set of false teeth skated across the bar top, much to Rick's wide-eyed horror.

Annyah surveyed the joint, all fell calm, 'We are leaving.'

Rick stood metaxa in hand.

'Leave it!'

In a daze he put it down and followed Annyah, 'Jesus Christ! I can't believe it!'

'What can you not believe?'

As they stepped over the threshold he glanced down at Annyah, 'She had false teeth?'

Before Annyah might reply a detachment of station security armed with assault rifles appeared. Five men in battle dress took up positions in the courtyard leading to Red Sector's many establishments, 'HALT!'

While red laser dots ran up and down Annyah's body the officer in charge spoke, 'Get on your knees!'

215

Rick looked up at Annyah, 'Get down.'

She followed instructions.

'Lay face down on the floor.'

They both lay belly down as Red Sector filled to capacity observing the strange event.

'Cuff 'em Keith.'

The pair were cuffed and led from Red Sector to the wonderment of Templeton's population. As they were taken into custody Rick muttered to Annyah, 'Fuck my life.'

As Hypnos faded away Rick was greeted by a set of metal bars and a headache. He lay on a mattress atop a wire frame welded to the floor. A toilet and wash basin projected from the wall, all the amenities of home. Rick rubbed his eyes and groaned, 'Jesus, did I get pissed again?'

'Are you feeling better?' came a familiar voice.

Through his cell bars over a narrow corridor behind a second set of bars sat Annyah, legs and arms crossed like a genie.

Rick leant on the wall and searched his mind, oh dear, as Hypnos retreated to Olympus the situation became worse and worse, 'Sweet Jesus say it ain't so.'

'If you are referring to last night I am afraid it is.'

'Did you have to?'

'I was concerned and when informed ...'

'Informed?'

'It is superfluous.'

'Don't lie, who told you I was at Shaniqua's?'

Her eye sockets widened, causing those sapphires to twinkle from their caves a little more than usual. Annyah still took offense to being accused of lying, even when it was true. Negz are funny creatures, holding themselves to a higher standard despite committing the same transgressions they disparage others for, as if the logical part of their brain drops its gates with a big: ACCESS DENIED. Living with Rick forced Annyah to face her inadequacies whether she liked it or not, the latter being the usual case, 'Dyson informed me of your,' her visage changed as if she were looking down at a pile of dog excrement, 'safari.'

'Safari?'

'An expedition to observe animals for one's personal gratification.'

Rick wasn't going to argue the toss, his brain throbbed like an amplifier at a Stones concert.

Rick lay down to rest his aching head.

'What will become of us?'

'We'll be brought before a judge and fined, if we're lucky.'

'If not?'

'At worst Shaniqua will sue me for everything I have.'

'I fought in self-defence.'

'Yeh, but you're not a tax paying resident.'

'What difference does that make?'

Her intelligence was like her beauty, it held an illusive quality with the odd explosion of naivety when viewed in the right light.

'Templeton's puts property rights above human rights. You damage property, especially that of a tax payer, it's the same as damaging them physically.'

'That is ridiculous.'

'No more than sending your twelve year old daughter to the military.'

Annyah didn't reply for he was correct, even in her society it was an oddity. Usually special provision would be made and she'd received a desk job yet Annayh refused for she wished to honour her family name.

A guard walked into view, he ran his truncheon across Rick's cell bars sending a stinging pain into his hungover brain, 'Rise and shine kids!'

Rick massaged his temples, 'Do you fucking mind?'

The guard lowered his voice into a tone of sardonic pity, 'I'm sorry is there something special you want for breakfast?'

Rick sat up and fixed his glazed eyes on the guard, 'I'll have eggs, bacon … tell you what why don't you just call your wife she knows what I like.'

Annyah's lip rolled up in disgust while a ripple of laughter flowed throughout the cell block. Guards and prisoners alike cracked up at Rick's line, the man stallion had earnt himself another enemy.

The guard glanced at Annyah then back on Rick, 'I hope your negg bitch is laughing when I beat her ass,' he ran his hand up and down his truncheon.

'That's a lot of pent up anger you've got towards women. I guess I'd be the same if me son was half brachian.'

Another round of laughter filled the cell block much to the guard's fury yet before he might reply a door leading out the block swung open, 'John? What the fuck's going on? I asked for both prisoners.'

'Yes sir, I'm cuffing them right now,' he pulled out a set of cuffs, 'give me your hands.'

Rick stepped up placing his hands through vertical bars. The guard took a set of cuffs clamping them on, a light went green indicating they were locked. He did the same with Annyah.

The guard tapped Rick's cell wall, its bars retracted into the floor, 'One step forward.'

Rick stepped into the corridor, to his right the hall stretched another fifty feet with cells on both sides, at the end a jail master waited for his prisoners. Two men stood in full battle dress with loaded rifles, Annyah's species demanded their presence.

'Follow me,' the guard walked toward the door, Rick and Annyah in the middle, armed escort watching their backs.

Prisoners quietened down to examine a real life negz.

After ascending for a few minutes an elevator reached the very highest level of Templeton's and they exited into a small white hallway. After thirty feet it ended in a cul-de-sac. Their guard spoke into his headset, 'They've arrived sir.'

A few seconds later tall wide double doors opened and the criminals were ushered inside. A man in his sixties sat behind an ornate desk carved from ivory. He was absorbed, finishing up that morning's business, 'Unchain the prisoners.'

'Sir?'

'Release them Captain.'

'Yes sir,' he tapped his wrist unlocking their chains.

Rick passed his cuffs to the guard.

'You may leave us Captain.'

'But sir …'

Templeton looked up, a full head of boyish brown hair skilfully crafted above a pair of, how can I put it? Experienced eyes? For they were not those of an elderly man. They held a sparkle of youth yet spoke of years beyond his looks, 'Is there a problem?'

'No sir,' the guard exited, double doors swishing shut behind him.

Rick peered around the room, a large office decked out in the style of a 19th century study. Items from all corners of the galaxy adorned its beige walls in a menagerie of personal glory, occupying every available piece of real estate. A hologram of Templeton standing over a dead space whale caught his eye. The owner of this station was a noted huntsman travelling the galaxy for big game. In the holo he and several men posed on and around the corpse of a space creature within the cargo bay of a very large spacecraft.

Templeton smiled with pride, 'You're looking at my desk,' he turned his work hologram off and tapped his desk.

A curxaj-tayag mounted on the wall behind him caught Annyah's eye.

'It's a real one,' smirked Templeton. He believed the hunt kept him young, that and his weekly trips to the station's top salon.

'No doubt looted,' replied Annyah.

'Not at all, I only display trophies I risked my own life to acquire, what would be the point otherwise?'

'You fought for this?'

'I led an expedition, we raided a small military outpost and came back with a few trophies. You'll be pleased to know that that curxaj-tayag cost a lot of men their lives.'

'Not as pleased as you.'

Templeton chuckled for Annyah's insight into the human psyche easily outstretched that of any negz he'd encountered and Templeton had met a few, 'Smart girl, but on to more pressing matters, you attacked one of my tax payers last night, why?'

'That is false I defended myself.'

'That may be but she's a tax payer and you're not, the law must side with Shaniqua.'

'That is unreasonable.'

Templeton opened his desk humidor to produce a Churchill cigar shipped from Havana, 'On my station paying your taxes on time is nine tenths of the law that's just the way the cookie crumbles.'

Rick chirped up, 'Look whatever the fine …'

Templeton cut him off, 'You're lucky I haven't seized your ship.'

'Sonnet's safe?'

Templeton clipped his cigar before toasting its foot, 'Shaniqua could sue you and take everything you have right now.'

'You mean she hasn't pressed charges?'

'Oh no, she did.'

'Then?'

Templeton stood up, dressed in a cream two-piece suit matching his ivory desk, his face betrayed irritation, 'You were on your way to court and the poor house then I get a message, a personal request, seems you've got friends Captain Katusa.'

Rick furrowed his brow, 'Who?'

'My wife.'

'I don't …'

'Here's the deal, Shaniqua's popularity doesn't spread much beyond the male of the species,' Templeton became animated moving his hands in circles paired with odd fluctuations indicating frustration at it all, 'in fact the female of the species, especially the married type, despise the woman and

220

everything she stands for. So, I get an ultimatum, I let you and your negg off the hook or I'm sleeping on the couch permanently.'

Rick let out a sigh of relief.

Templeton picked a pad off his desk, approached Annyah and held it out, 'I need a palm print.'

'For what purpose?'

'Just do it.'

Annyah placed her palm on the tablet, it scanned her D.N.A., palm print and blood vessels. The tablet bleeped and Templeton placed it before Annyah's face, 'Look into the tablet,' as she did a beam scanned both her eyes then bleeped.

Templeton pulled an identity card from his pocket, slipped it into a port on the tablet and waited until a bleep informed him its operations were complete. He presented the card to Annyah, 'Congratulations you're a citizen of Templeton's.'

Rick opened his eyes in wonder, now he could dodge a ton of tariffs. Annyah looked at Templeton with a quizzical expression.

'Complements of my wife, it seems you've gained quite a following since you sent Shaniqua to intensive care.'

'Send your wife my gratitude, I am at her service in the future.'

Templeton looked Rick stone cold in the eye, 'I don't know if she's your slave or what but you keep her under control on this station, you got me?'

'Yes Mr Templeton.'

'Just call me Templeton,' said the famous adventurer his finger pointing in Rick's face, 'and don't let this happen again,' he looked at Annyah, 'you can retrieve your curxaj-tayag at the desk on the way out.'

Annyah's lip curled up at the side in her signature smile, 'Thank you Templeton.'

The pair left through giant double doors. As they stepped over the threshold Templeton muttered under his breath, 'And they call me crazy.'

Chapter Fourteen

Rick and Annyah passed through a stretched airport lounge circling the outer edge of a city in space. Here many comfortable restaurants littered a causeway with small duty-free shops. They passed a Merchant's guild and sat down for breakfast. After ordering a familiar face approached, 'How ya doing buddy?'

'Rough as a bear's arse, what you up to?'

'Visiting Templeton's biggest celebrity,' smiled the stripper.

'You what?'

Vince pointed at a panel above the restaurant doorway playing last night's brawl in Shaniqua's along with commentary, 'Oi, turn that up!' blurted Rick as the waiter served him.

'The Piraxis system was considered safe from alien invasion, that is until last night, when a negz soldier burst into Red Sector and laid waste to Shaniqua's bar. I must warn you the footage you're about to see is disturbing. If you're faint of heart or easily shocked please turn away now ....'

The screen greyed out to be filled by a shaky shot inside Shaniqua's. It began somewhere at the start of the confrontation just before Leroy attempted to throw Annyah out.

Rick shrivelled in his seat, Vince sniggered, Marie shook her head in disappointment. The waiter's gaze swung between the panel and Annyah's angular features before he exclaimed at the top of his voice, 'HEY! THAT'S YOU!'

All eyes turned on Annyah the air twitching with electricity as citizens gathered.

The crowd drew oxygen as one when Annyah's staff pressed on Leroy's neck, they released as he walked away, they breathed in again as Shaniqua took a spiked baseball bat from the barmaid. With each swipe gasps became louder until the first hit, Annyah whacked Shaniqua hard in the ribs and every woman on the causeway cheered. Shaniqua's popularity languished somewhere beneath rabies, far lower than Templeton had intimated.

The whore of Red Sector was getting its butt kicked and they didn't care who discharged her foul person. Several men looked as if they were attending a funeral, others hooted in joy observing the cat fight of the century.

Shaniqua pulled her knives and the crowd collectively sucked air from Templeton's causeway. Shaniqua received another beating her teeth projected in one direction, wig the other. Screams and howls of normally modest human beings filled the air as they pummelled Shaniqua by proxy, 'Fuck that bitch!' and laughs of 'Eat shit you dirty whore!'. Rick was worried who their hostility might befall next, yet on Shaniqua's demise into a pool of blood the Keres had been satisfied for the crowd erupted in applause.

A young mother previously hypnotised by Annyah's fracas turned her vision on the party. She pulled her daughter by the hand, a young girl obviously afraid of Annyah, 'Excuse me,' said the lady dressed in a polite skirt suit, no doubt on the way to dropping her daughter off at a nursery.

'Yes?' replied Annyah.

'Was that you?'

'It was.'

'Would you mind a selfie?'

'Clarify selfie?'

'A holo, would you take a holo with my daughter and I?'

Annyah queried Rick who nodded his head. The heroin of Red Sector smiled, 'As you wish.'

The lady lifted her toddler onto Annyah's lap, the girl squirmed but didn't cry. Her mother, attired for an office, dragged a chair beside Annyah then pulled a tiny globe from her pocket and let it hover in the air, 'Say cheese.'

Annyah held the child in an awkward manner while circled eyes observed the globe, 'Cheese?'

The globe took several snaps before returning to its owner who picked it out of the air and into her pocket. The child leapt behind her mother's legs.

'Thank you Miss ...?'

'Annyah, my name is Annyah.'

'What a beautiful name, I'm Sophia and my daughter's Grace.'

'Hello Grace,' smiled Annyah.

Grace hid as best she could.

'I'm sorry but she's afraid of neggs.'

'I comprehend.'

'But after you beat that skanky ass bitch last night things might change …
pardon my French. I'm usually a pacifist but …'

'There is an old negz proverb: though one may be a pacifist one is not obliged
to respect sentient life.'

'I'll have to remember that, thanks,' she smiled, 'The girls are gonna be so
jealous when they see this.'

Before waving the woman gave Rick a long derogatory snarl.

Rick's back straightened at her holier than thou stare, he felt quite insulted.
Yet before he could reply Annyah kicked him under the table.

'See you later,' the lady left with daughter in hand, from behind her a long
line of women unfolded by many degrees, prolific as fish, waiting to chat with
the heroin of Red Sector, the woman who'd kicked out Shaniqua's teeth,
something on every female citizen's bucket list.

'Maybe we should charge for these selfies?' stated Rick.

Annyah gave him a rude stare sending Sonnet's Captain into quiet mode.

A long line of people waited some to meet a negz in the flesh others to thank
the lady who'd brought down the bane of their existence. Vince chatted with
Rick, during his five months in hyperspace the war had neared Earth. A
request had gone out to every space vessel capable of making the journey,
report to the Ring. Accounts came in daily as systems closer and closer to
Earth were ravaged by a terrifying war fleet. At its head a ship rumoured to
be made of gold, cast in the image of God. Rick scoffed at such stories,
probably colonist exaggerating their plight or religious fanatics predicting
Armageddon. That is until Vince played back footage from the last system
burnt to the ground and sure enough a warship larger than any he'd either

seen or heard of, even in legend, preceded a group of negz battleships, cruisers, carriers and every supporting vessel that might travel with such a fleet.

'It's doctored,' stated Rick.

'This isn't the only capture it's real for sure.'

'Why the hell would you build a warship that big? It doesn't make sense.'

Annyah peered at a hologram emanating from Vince's pad, 'That is the Hammer of God.'

All eyes fell on Annyah once more, 'Say what?' asked Vince.

'The Hammer of God, destruction for those who stand against the Elders.'

Rick looked again, 'I know that ship.'

Annyah nodded her head, 'In veneration my people assembled this. It remains in negz space, a place of pilgrimage where Elders rest. During war it is mobilized for final destruction of our enemy. My people revere it as yours should fear it.'

In the footage all kinds of ships, freighters, tankers, liners, shuttles sped across space preceding an Earth Corps' battle fleet. Loaded with fuel they made runs at negz warships detonating reactors on impact. It held them back, even took down cruisers and set battleships aflame but only to delay the inevitable.

'Kamikazes,' groaned Vince as Earth Corps' request became clear.

'Clarify kamikazes?'

'A nation on Earth was saved from an enemy invasion fleet by a storm, they named it the sacred wind or in their language kamikaze.

Centuries later a fleet of war ships they had no means of stopping approached. So, every young man joined up to become a pilot of the sacred wind. Planes loaded with fuel deliberately crashed into enemy ships to save their people.'

Annyah was spell bound by Vince's story, 'Were they saved?'

'No, we dropped two atomic bombs on them before they surrendered.'

'But such a noble sacrifice should be lauded.'

Rick pulled a rollup from behind his ear and scoffed, 'Pah! They got what they fucking deserved!'

Annyah fixed her cindered caverns on Rick, 'And do your people deserve to be vapourised from orbit?'

'Whatever.'

'It also begs the question, why are you not defending your people today, why do you not become the sacred wind?'

'Are you joking? I'm not getting vapourised while some cock sucking Admiral sits behind me!'

'Why?'

'Because after me and Vince have given our lives that jackbooted brown shirt'll shoot off into hyperspace and we'd be none the wiser!'

'You can be so very selfish.'

'That's what's kept me and me crew alive this long.'

'What of those men who sacrifice themselves in the hope humanity might survive?'

'Humans call it natural selection, the dumbest load up and try to ram a negg warship, lowering the genetic tendency toward suicide and increasing the species' average intelligence in one fell swoop.'

'Sometimes I feel ashamed to be your wife.'

Vince's eyes expanded as if a cactus entered his anal passage, 'Whoa dude! You're married to a ... negg-head?'

Rick groaned, 'Sort of.'

'Sort of? I mean you've either got a ten inch dick or you ain't.'

'It's a long story.'

'What's the short story?'

'According to negg tradition we're ... what's the word?'

'Joined.'

'Right, but according to my tradition we're friends with a future, maybe.'

Vince peered at Annyah, 'So that's why you beat Shaniqua's ass?'

'I was protecting my lord from danger.'

'Lord?' stated Marie.

'Why yes, in negz tradition I am now Rick's property it is my duty to protect him.'

Rick rolled his eyes , 'Lucky old me,' then sipped his coffee.

Marie was rather averse to Annyah's description of a negz marriage, 'That sounds awfully one sided.'

'Clarify?'

'Well he's like your owner, I mean, that's not fair.'

'Forget it,' sighed Rick, 'I've been trying to tell her that for months and it hasn't worked.'

'You are only attempting to slither out of your vows. Sometimes I wonder if you are not brachian.'

'I didn't make any vows, I fought some bloke on a planet so that we could get away in one piece. How was I supposed to know I was bonding with you? As far as I'm concerned I was duped into it, isn't there a court of appeal or something negg men can go to?'

'Rick?' snapped Marie. As an outsider for so long she felt the pain his words inflicted. The gothic lady may have a hard exterior but inside she suffered injuries no different to any human.

'What?'

'Apologize to Annyah.'

'For what?'

'You're so fast to display your own distasteful resentment whenever you see injustice, yet you'll humiliate a woman who obviously loves you.'

Rick peered toward Annyah, up until this moment he'd not considered she could love him or likewise. On reflection if she left his ship he'd miss her not only as his tactical officer but his companion, the only woman he'd got this close to that wasn't interested in his bank account, 'Sorry.'

Annyah nodded her head, 'You are forgiven,' something she'd learnt from being around Rick, the capacity to forgive, not a common negz trait.

A list of casualties ran down as the presenter commented on the last battle at Proxima Centauri, their next strike would certainly be Sol. The word Crusader caught Rick's eye, he stood up to scrutinize the list while Annyah met locals.

227

Rick searched a list of dead and missing aboard the Crusader, she had several dead including the first officer and nearly 100 injured, fortunately Sam wasn't among their number. Rick felt relief wash over him, his friend wasn't dead but he soon would be. Nothing could stop that fleet, even if every ship mankind had ever built made a stand they'd fail.

As a reporter commented on the battle of Centauri he sensed his heart pull against his head. Rick wanted to help yet it was a lost cause, whether he was present or not the end result was cut in stone. The man from Doncaster felt a slave to his own freedom for now was his opportunity to renounce it, become one of the many and defend his people. Yet freedom held him down, for freedom has its own principles, self-determination one of them. If he were to join Earth Corps and sacrifice his right to choose his path he'd no longer be free but if he didn't he'd be no more than a captive to the tenets of liberty, just as Annyah was to her Kych Nom and its tenets ... could he say he was truly free and she not?

Annyah stood behind him, 'You are concerned for your friend?'

'Stupid kid, thought he could change the world and signed his own death warrant instead.'

'It was his choice and a noble one at that.'

'No-one will remember that after he's been vapourised.'

'You will.'

Rick shook his head, 'He just wouldn't listen.'

Hours later Annyah was still taking holos. Rick discovered Vince was planning to join the fleet, he couldn't believe it. Vince was the last guy to do something this idiotic. Marie was 100% behind it which made the notion even more ludicrous. If she were captured they'd retire her personality, a politically correct word for execution. Why the hell would she want to save those who wished her harm?

Five months in hyperspace and the galaxy had gone mad, a plague of lunacy had struck down humanity. Vince did his best to convince Rick, according to him Earth Corps needed every ship to turn back the negz tide. Rick was stunned that a normally rational human being had transformed into a suicidal fool in such a short space of time.

'With enough ships we can make the neggs think again maybe sue for peace.' Rick had studied the Kych Nom and at no point did it mention suing for peace as an option. Negz ploughed forward leaving but a smear on a formerly habitable world, if you believe otherwise you're either naïve or a smear in waiting. In the same manner Annyah had identified Shaniqua as a threat, charged bold as brass into her bar and ripped her face off that war fleet was going to do exactly the same to humanity.

'Neggs don't sue for peace and there's nothing we can do to change that.'

'We gotta do something.'

'Why? What did Earth Corps ever do for you?' he looked accusingly at Vince and Marie.

'It's not about the Corps anymore it's about all of us, mankind.'

'Mankind's fucked, the best you can do is not be there when it hits the fan.'

Marie spoke to Rick in a soft tone, 'What happened to make you so bitter?'

'I owe nothing to those jackboot scum. I fought every inch of the way to get off that planet.'

'Can't you forgive?'

'Fuck forgiveness, fuck dying in some lost cause and most of all fuck Earth Corps!'

Vince broke them up, 'Listen I'm gonna be on my ship for the next few hours, we'll be leaving at sixteen hundred. If you change your mind let me know, it'd make a difference if you helped out.'

'I guess I'll see you in hell.'

Vince made a half-hearted chuckle, 'I guess so buddy, see you around.'

They stood up and walked away, Rick sipped his coffee.

Annyah's queue had come to an end, all the time she'd eavesdropped on Rick's conversation, 'What if I said you could make a difference?'

'Then you'd be crazy.'

'But if you could, would you go?'

'I've spent years paying into that bank,' he peered across the street through a hull port and pointed to the Bank of Altan glimmering in the distance, 'I plan on being around to enjoy it.'

'Rick Katusa you are a poor liar.'

'You telepathic now?'

'No but when your head is in conflict with your heart you will surrender to your heart.'

'I've got no idea what you're talking about.'

'Another friend has joined this sacred wind. I believe that if you could sacrifice yourself to save them you would.'

'Who told you that? Doctor Phil?'

'I know of a method to end this war without sacrificing a single ship.'

Rick betrayed curiosity, 'How?'

'Siguku.'

'What the hell's that?'

'You have read the Kych Nom, it is ritual combat for ownership such as your disagreement with Plina on Antares.'

'You can do that for a civilization?'

'I see no reason it would not apply to our situation.'

'Has it been done before?'

'Did that stop you in the past?'

Rick didn't answer he just picked a piece of toast and chewed on it while footage of the Proxima Centauri cluster fuck played out.

'My people could learn from kumuns.'

'Really?' stated Rick in a sceptical tone.

'Yes, you are individualists yet you sacrifice your lives for one another not out of obligation or tradition but because you believe it the right thing to do. After a short time by your side I have come to the conclusion, individualism is morally superior.'

'We might be good as individuals but as a group we suck. If we took responsibility for our actions like neggs we wouldn't be in this bloody mess.'

230

Annyah was surprised, for the first time he conceded her species may be superior on some level, 'I do not wish to see kumuns become a drifter species but I cannot prevent it, only a kumun who comprehends and respects our traditions might do so.'

'Good luck finding him,' Rick washed down dry toast with a swill of coffee.

Annyah fixed her gaze on Rick, the corner of her mouth lifted in that signature grin.

'You don't mean me?'

'You have already fought and won siguku, you are the perfect choice, you are the only choice.'

'I'm not some bargain basement hero love.'

Annyah narrowed her eyes and rippled her brow in an attempt to wring a semblance of comprehension from her mind.

'Never mind,' stated Rick.

'Well?'

'Well what?'

'Are we travelling to Earth?'

'No.'

She held his hand across the table, 'Sam needs you, Vince and Marie need you. I know you would not forgive yourself if they died when you could have saved them.'

'Strippers don't save the universe they chop it up and sell it back to whoever built it.'

'Perhaps it is time to teach the builders how to manage their creation?'

Rick groaned, 'When I was a kid all I wanted to be was a rock and roll star.'

'Why would one wish to be a star that rocks and rolls?'

'Never mind, let's get back before Vince's gone.'

Rick held council on Sonnet explaining his intended return to Earth for the final battle. In exchange he received startled expressions, they couldn't believe their ears. Dyson was waiting for the punchline ... this had to be one of Rick's stunts. All Rick cared about was making a profit while sticking it to the man and now he was going to risk it all for Earth Corps? A bunch of Nazis who screwed him at every turn? They only allowed him in Sol because they needed alloys more than they despised him.

'Let's do it,' said Allenby.

'DUDE!' yelped Dyson.

'I got family on Earth, I ain't letting those negg-heads kill 'em without a fight.'

Rick peered at Graham, 'You in?'

Graham scowled, 'Has she addled your brain man?'

'I intend for everyone here to be alive when it's over.'

'At what cost?'

'It isn't always about profit.'

'You've fucking lost it.'

'I need you Graham, I need you all, you're the only people I trust.'

'Why don't we just stay here and let the neggs do what they want?'

'At some point a man has to hold his principles above his pockets, besides being a hero can have its benefits,' Rick let a smile hit his mouth.

'Yeh, you get the best lot in the graveyard,' snapped Graham in a sardonic tone.

'No-one's gonna die.'

'You can't guarantee that.'

'I can't but it's no different than any other job and you came back from them in one piece. I'm asking you to trust me, trust me and this'll be the ride of your life. Afterwards you'll be able to get laid anywhere in the core just by showing your face.'

'I'm in,' shouted Peters in his high tone. The crew gave him odd looks, 'Why not? Sounds like a blast ... figuratively.'

That was just Dyson and Graham left, Rick waited for their reply.

'I'm in,' sighed Dyson, 'What the fuck would I do if you guys were dead anyway?'

Rick smiled before turning to Graham, 'You in?'

'Did I ever tell you you're an arsehole?'

'Every other day.'

232

'That pussy better be waiting when this is over or I'm gonna break your face!' Rick grinned as he shook hands with Graham, 'Okay, get her ready for cast off we'll be leaving in a couple of hours.'

The crew dispersed to their stations leaving Rick and Annyah in the galley. Annyah smiled in pride, 'That was a sight to behold.'

'What's that?'

'My people cannot comprehend how individualists might achieve even the simplest tasks without what you call cohesion.'

'You mean communism?'

'We prefer cohesion.'

'If a man acts willingly he'll do a better job than forced.'

'Individualism is so alien to my culture, it is a wonder to observe your crew and the people of Templeton's. To witness chaos form cohesion without structure.'

'We haven't won yet, get Vince on the blower let him know we're ready to cast off.'

'Clarify blower?'

'I mean communicate with him.'

She dipped her head, 'Affirmative Captain,' Rick groaned and Annyah corrected herself, 'Affirmative, Rick.'

Vince was over the moon, Rick was coming, now they had a chance. He didn't have any logical reason as to why Rick would make a difference against a negz war fleet, what he did know was Rick never lost. Rick took the greatest risks and often claimed its rewards, with him on side those negg-heads didn't stand a chance.

Rick had always instilled confidence amongst Sonnet's crew for he prioritised their well-being above profit. He may be a slob with poor personal hygiene that drinks too much but he cares for his crew. Besides, thanks to Annyah he was fighting fit wearing a clean flight suit with a fresh ambergris emanating from his person rather than the stench of yesterday's beer and curry.

The Black Dog departed Templeton's, moments later Sonnet mirrored her path into hyperspace. It wouldn't be long before they exited the great blue dimension into Earth space. During that time Annyah prepared Rick, the tunic he'd taken from a negz frigate last year now adorned his body. He wore a pair of black cargo pants, work boots and a thick cotton shirt. He and Annyah were in his cabin, she shaved his head while he spoke, 'Do you think they'll accept?'

'There is nothing in the Kych Nom to exclude aliens, provided they recognize tradition.'

'Is that a yes?'

'Probably,' she ran the razor over his head dropping swathes of hair to the floor.

'I don't see why shaving me head makes a difference.'

'If you demonstrate respect my people will recognise you, besides I think you look good.'

'Well, I suppose when you bury me you won't need to pay for a hair stylist.'

'Only a kumun could be both an optimist and pessimist at the same time.'

'It beats being a pessimist all the time.'

'I inquired into a rock and roll star, Dyson advised me to listen to AC/DC, do you comprehend?'

Rick smiled as Annyah ran an electric razor over his head, 'Computer?'

'Yes Rick?'

'Play rock and roll singer by AC/DC.'

'Yes Rick.'

As guitars played he spoke over his shoulder, 'Listen carefully.'

Annyah listened dutifully while sculpting Rick's new look. She wasn't exactly certain what rock and roll was but it was very human for it advocated individualism and rebellion, the opposite of everything her species stood for. Since joining Sonnet's crew the gothic lady had acquired an interest in many things, rock music being one of them. She'd heard a hundred different ways to "fuck the man" yet her ears still found it shocking. A life of cohesion, conformity and tradition didn't vanish after the first Jimi Hendrix track.

"Well you can stick your nine to five livin',
And your collar and your tie,
You can stick your moral standards,
'Cause it's all a dirty lie,
You can stick your golden handshake,
And you can stick your silly rules,
And all that other shit,
That you teach kids in school,
('Cause I ain't no fool)."

Annyah's eyes widened, 'On Hemzih such material would warrant imprisonment.'
'Don't you have rock and roll stars on Hemzih?'
'They populate our re-education centres.'
'So there IS dissent against the system?'
'There, I have finished,' she switched the razor off, 'That is preferable, is it not?'
Rick examined his shiny head in the mirror, 'I'll have every woman on Hemzih kicking me door down.'
'For what purpose?'
Rick sighed, 'It was a joke and you didn't answer me question.'
'Yes?'
'You have dissenters on your home world?'
'We do not speak of it.'
'I didn't advertise me bowel infection but it didn't stop me from speaking to the doctor.'
'Again, only a kumun could compare ideological dissent to a bowel infection.'
'The way I see it those Earth Corps arseholes are the bowel infection.'
'And dare I ask how you came to that conclusion?'
'Without them we wouldn't have a fleet of negg ships about to burn Earth to ashes.'

'Earth Corps does serve a purpose.'

'Really?'

'I do not witness any rock and roll stars fighting to save mankind.'

Rick turned around and snarled, 'Annyah ...'

'Yes?'

'You do piss me off sometimes.'

She put the razor down, pulled his tunic into shape then peered into his eyes, 'Only because you are cute when you are angry.'

'Can I take this stupid get-up off?'

'Of course, I will adjust it before we reach our destination.'

'I'm gonna look like a prize prat when I step off this ship,' Annyah offered a vague smile forcing Rick to chuckle at the lunacy of their situation, 'but I'll be in good company.'

Sonnet exited hyperspace a few days later, her tokomak throbbed to the rhythm of Graham's tune. Rick peered out the cockpit, he'd never seen so many ships gathered in one place. Vessels of every shape, size and purpose floated just off Earth's docking ring. Earth Corps brandished what military ships it could muster, ready to engage anything bearing ill intent. Her warships didn't look so good, many were scorched, probably by nearby explosions. Some displayed heavy damage taken in battle from negz beam weapons. Additional armour had been welded onto every vessel ... an extra five seconds before the negz struck atmosphere.

'Peters, get the Crusader.'

'What should I say?'

'Say you want to speak to Lieutenant Ward.'

'Sure,' he sent the communication across Earth Corps' fleet.

Rick scanned every ship on his console eventually locating the Crusader. He locked on and expanded her image. The Crusader was blackened across one side. Her armour melted and mottled by super-heated shrapnel perhaps?

'I'm being directed to another ship.'

236

'Give me that!' Rick took communications on his dashboard, 'Crusader this is the Captain of the Sonnet.'

'What do you want stripper?'

'I want to speak with Lieutenant Sam Ward he's a tactical officer aboard ...'

'I know who he is, you need to hail the Ring they'll answer any questions.'

'Tell him it's Rick and I've got a way out of this cluster fuck.'

'You'll have to dock with the Ring and receive your orders there.'

The line went dead.

Rick leant back in his chair, 'Dyson set us on a collision course with the Crusader.'

'Are you fucking crazy?'

Rick, concealed in dark garments with shaven head except for a short brown plait hanging off the rear of his skull, fixed his gaze upon Dyson, 'Right now I'm the craziest bastard in the galaxy.'

Dyson shook his head in disbelief, disbelief he was carrying out these orders. He punched in co-ordinates, Annyah certified and Rick engaged engines.

'Rick, message from the Crusader they want to talk.'

'Really,' Rick made a self-satisfied grin, 'put them on.'

'This is communications officer Brown third class, please reduce speed and adjust your course.'

'After I've spoken to Lieutenant Sam Ward.'

'If you maintain course you WILL be shot down.'

'Fine.'

A voice could be heard in the background, 'He won't do it.'

Rick barked into his headset, 'What've I got to lose? We'll all be dead in a few days!'

There was a pause for a minute before a familiar voice came on the line, 'This is Commander Samuel Ward, reduce speed and adjust your course.'

Rick nodded to Dyson who let out a sigh of relief as he brought the Sonnet to a halt.

'Commander? Sounds like a lot of boot licking to me kid!'

'Rick? Is that you?'

'The man stallion himself.'

'What the hell are you doing here?'

'Saving your backside, AGAIN.'

'Rick this is serious, the negz will be here in a couple of days.'

'The sooner you let me dock the sooner I can tell your Admiral his new battle plan.'

'I can't do that Rick.'

'Jesus Christ, you're a fucking Commander, command those arseholes!'

'Just because I have a rank doesn't mean I can do what I want. Besides, there's no way you'd put your ass on the line for Earth Corps.'

'Tell your Captain I've got a negg aboard me ship and she has information on the enemy fleet.'

'Show me.'

Peters activated a visual feed of the cockpit. Sam and several Bridge officers looked on in amazement, 'Why isn't she restrained?'

'She defected.'

'Negz don't defect.'

'They do now ... well? Do you want to question her or not?'

Another minute went by as men mumbled in the background, 'Fine, you can use docking bay 5 the others are non-operational right now.'

'Thanks Sam.'

'Don't exit the Sonnet until you see me, understood?'

Rick made a Nazi salute, 'Understood mein Oberst-Gruppenfuher!'

Sam shook his head, 'See you in a minute,' the screen went blank.

'Dyson, you heard the man, take us in.'

'Ya mein Oberst-Gruppenfuher!' barked the navigator clinking his heels.

Rick relaxed into his chair as the burnt Destroyer loomed closer, her scars cut deep, she was lucky to be in one piece.

Chapter Fifteen

Search lights coursed Sonnet's body, automatic docking clamps guiding her to an alcove. An airlock attached to her mid-section. Once atmosphere certified lights flicked green both sides. Rick uncoupled his straps, at a distance indistinguishable from a negz warrior. Curxaj-tayag slung over back he and his counterpart made for the airlock. Before opening its hatch Rick thought to himself, 'Here goes nothing.'

He spun a wheel unlocking Sonnet's hatch and moved down its ladder, Annyah followed. As Crusader's artificial gravity took precedence Rick went from a vertical stance to horizontal, instead of dropping down in a straight line he dropped off Sonnet's ladder at a right angle onto his feet. Sonnet sat in Crusader's docking bay, belly facing onlookers. Annyah dropped through a decontamination mist and Crusader's welcoming party quickly braced. Marines dropped to one knee and took aim. Red dots danced on her chest as playful fairies turning a waltz of death. Rick raised his hands and thought, 'Nice to see some things never change.'

'Move aside,' armed men parted to reveal a tall fellow in his early sixties grey hair absent but for the sides of his head, shaved to within an inch. He had the look of a man who'd been to hell and back. His tunic and trousers fit well, bolstering an authoritative air, 'What the hell's this scum doin' on my ship?' an accent perhaps somewhere in the southern parts of the United States. The Captain paused when he realised Annyah wasn't human but a real negz, 'Sergeant, arrest her!'

Rick stood between them, 'That won't happen.'

'Son, you got three seconds to move your hippy ass before I have you shot, 3, 2 ...'

'Captain!' came a familiar voice, 'If I may intervene?'

Sam dashed to the quarrel dressed in a navy-blue uniform and white shirt, ribbons decorated his chest as did a golden badge of rank on his cuff and shoulder.

'What is it Commander?'

'I permitted this ship to land.'

'Why?'

'The Captain has information that may be useful in our upcoming battle.'

'You know this filthy piece o' shit?'

Rick was about to say something when he felt Annyah punch him in the back.

'I was his tactical officer for three years, sir.'

'What?'

'He is, I was a stripper, sir.'

'Why wasn't I informed of this?'

'I was going to inform you but he docked before ...'

'Why wasn't I informed you were a stripper?'

'I never found the time.'

'What the hell are you talkin' about?'

'We were either fighting, running or evacuating civilians. My former employment just wasn't pertinent to our situation, sir.'

The Captain grumbled, 'So who is this asshole?'

'Captain Rick Katusa of the Sonnet.'

'PUH! Captain my ass! And the bitch?'

'I've not seen her before now, sir.'

Annyah removed herself from Rick's gallant shadow, 'I am Annyah, Oci-sebe rank twelve and tactical officer aboard the Sonnet.'

The Captain's face screwed up, his eyes ran up and down the gothic lady, 'Neggs don't draft women!'

'A typically ignorant kumun statement.'

'So what are you? A spy?'

'If I said yes I would not be a very good spy, would I?'

'Just tell me why you're here before I have you and freak boy shot in the head!'

'I am here to avert a catastrophe.'

'What catastrophe might that be?'

'Extermination of the kumun species.'

Moods changed throughout the docking bay, the impending attack weighed heavily on each man's mind.

'We got a few tricks up our sleeve sister.'

'Kamikazies loaded with atomic weapons and urillium?'

'Have you contacted your fleet with this information?'

'You underestimate my people, the Doli were the last species to employ such a tactic.'

The old man furrowed his brow, 'Doli? Never heard of 'em!'

Annyah folded her arms, 'Precisely!'

There was an awkward pause before the Captain spoke again, 'So what's your solution sister?'

'Siguku.'

'You want us to kill ourselves?'

Sam whispered into his superior's ear, 'Siguku is a negz form of traditional combat. When all channels have been exhausted they settle disputes with a one to one death match.'

'How does that help us?'

'I believe the negz ... Annyah ... is suggesting we invoke siguku sparing our fleet the Ring and humanity in exchange for gambling a single life.'

'Will it work?'

'I've only read about it, I've no idea if the enemy will accept our offer.'

Cronin looked Annyah in the eye, 'You're sayin' you'll fight for us?'

Annyah shook her head, 'Only a kumun may represent mankind, Captain Katusa has volunteered.'

Sam raised his brow, he didn't believe it in Rick's character to make such a sacrifice. For years he'd bitched and moaned about Earth Corps and the hell of growing up in a town called Doncaster. He'd sworn to look out for himself and screw the bastard Corps.

Rick noted Sam's reaction, 'Don't say it kid.'

'Say what?' replied Sam.

The Captain examined Annyah, red dots scurried up and down her body awaiting the order to smear her frame against Sonnet's hull, 'Why'd you help us?'

'I am joined to this kumun.'

Sam gasped, 'Rick!'

'Don't say it kid!'

'Commander, what the hell's this bitch talkin' about?'

'She means to say that she's married to Captain Katusa.'

'Married? To a negg-head? You been doin' split boy?'

Rick had a moment of inner reflection before Annyah's elbow cajoled a response, 'It's a long story.'

'I'm supposed to go to the Admiral and tell him some beatnik stripper that married a negg-head's gonna defeat an undefeated war fleet ready to jump in at any time?'

'I haven't come to win, I'm just here to make sure we don't lose.'

'What's the difference?'

'If we lose we all die.'

The Captain looked stoic for a second, that stripper didn't seem so crazy anymore, 'I've had more than one of them fights.'

'Then you'll call the Admiral?'

'I'm sorry but ...'

Sam cut in, 'Sir, if I may, I can vouch for this man. I'm prepared to guarantee that what he's saying is true.'

Captain Cronin fixed his tired gaze on Sam, a gaze that'd endured many battles, a gaze which had witnessed the destructive power of a negz cruiser, a gaze that relied on his tactical officer to out think and second guess his enemy, 'You sure he's legit?'

'I served with him for three years sir, he saved my life more than once. I trust him just as anyone on the Crusader, sir.'

Cronin looked back at Rick, 'We'll see what the Admiral thinks.'

A sergeant leading the security team spoke from within his battle helmet, 'What should I do with the prisoners, sir?'

Sam spoke up again, 'Leave them in my custody, I'll take full responsibility.'
Cronin nodded his head, 'Have it your way Sam, just make sure they don't
cause any trouble … not that they haven't already.'
Captain Cronin and his security team dispersed from Crusader's dock, two
men armed with automatic rifles remained on duty.
Sam grinned at Rick.
Rick pointed his gloved finger, 'Don't say it.'
'Who'd have thought? Ready to put everything on the line for the Corps?'
'I couldn't care if they all got vapourised by neggs tomorrow.'
'So why're you here?'
'Someone has to save your stupid fucking arse!'
'I've done pretty good so far.'
'I can see that, brown nosed your way up the rank and file and now you're
first officer AND a Commander. You must've taken it to the hilt!'
'It's good to see you too Rick,' Sam expected no less from his old friend
besides there's no way Rick would admit to undertaking a totally selfless
deed, it just wasn't his way, 'You can move down, one of the guards will take
you to the galley.'
Rick moved past Sam, 'You brown shirts serve decent snap?'
Annyah approached Sam, 'Thank you Commander.'
Sam exposed his palms to Annyah, 'Zugeer (You're welcome).'
Annyah smiled and replied with palms open, 'Gyalailaa (thank you).'
'Please, this way,' he led her toward the galley, both smiled at Rick striding
defiantly whilst questioning the parentage of Crusader's security guards.

Admiral Jones was ushered through docking and onto Crusader, he returned
Captain Cronin's salute, 'Okay Robert where's this mysterious delegation?'
Captain Robert Cronin led his friend through the ship and into her galley.
Men turned heads to catch a glimpse of the Admiral, a man famed for leading
several victories in this war. He was duly promoted and put in charge of their
last stand. Jones had beaten the negz more than once … perhaps he could do
it again?

In truth the situation weighed heavily upon the Admiral's mind. The fate of every man and woman in the fleet alongside billions inhabiting planets below wasn't easy to bear. He suffered the responsibility of formulating a strategy to defeat the golden horde about to appear from another dimension. Armed with beam weapons centuries beyond any technology available to him, scanners with a greater active range, targeting systems so precise they could carve an Earth cruiser as a Japanese chef might slice and dice raw fish.

Each time he'd defeated the negz he had the advantage. Admiral Jones, Captain Jones at the time, used surprise to ambush his enemy, jumping from hyperspace close to their space docks. Annihilating negz structures before defence systems might respond then disappearing into the blue dimension. Today negz possessed the advantage, they would choose the time of attack, they'd strike with absolute force against every last ship he could muster. Admiral Jones understood the odds went against him. He couldn't predict where, but they'd probably exit hyperspace above the elliptical plane, an impossible area to cover, forcing him to spread his fleet so thin he'd only assist those xeno scum. He could but counter with their tactic of striking head on, employing maximum force until your opponent cracks. A thankless and impossible task yet the Corps held faith in the Admiral.

They walked into the galley and Jones nearly had a heart attack, staring back at the old man was a young negz warrior, a shock troop with a dozen confirmed kills. Sitting down was another slobbering over curried chicken, spoon in one hand and chapati in the other. Admiral Jones observed the one eating and whispered to his friend, 'My God look at that filthy animal eat … have they been interrogated?'

'No sir, they've come to assist us.'

'Are smoking split? Those devils would rather die,' the Admiral had a few thoughtful moments and turned to the Captain, 'You mean you didn't capture them?'

'No sir, they requested to come aboard.'

The Admiral nodded, 'Advanced scouts evaluating our fleet.'

'My first officer disagrees, apparently he used to fly with one of them.'

'Your first officer flew with neggs?'

'The male is human.'

'You mean a BEATNIK? Dressing up like xenos, sucking split and brachian cock?'

Men in the galley were hypnotised by the conversation, Captain Cronin gave the order to clear the Mess and so they filed out. Rick looked up and the Captain quickly spoke to him, 'You two stay.'

Rick was happy to do so, these Earth Corps Nazis made a damn good curry. Annyah spoke under her breath so only he would pick it up, 'Must you stuff yourself?'

'Every condemned man gets a last meal,' he fixed his eyes on her disgruntled gaze and winked, 'it's tradition.'

Captain Cronin spoke into the Admiral's ear, 'Commander Ward is the best tactical and first officer in the fleet, I've already staked my life and that of my crew on it, he knows his stuff when it comes to neggs. He says I can trust that man claimin' he can get us out this shit storm in one piece. I thought you might want to hear 'em out before we have no choice.'

'If this were anyone else I'd have him sectioned and those two interrogated ... like we did in the old days.'

'I know.'

'Fine I'll hear them out but I want some privacy.'

'We can do it in my office.'

Admiral Jones examined Annyah and Rick then shook his head, 'Rob, why the hell would any man in his right mind sign up for Earth Corps?'

Captain Cronin shrugged his shoulders, 'When I find out I'll let you know.'

Sitting in the Captain's office Admiral Jones examined the two intruders with a hard gaze. Their clothes, her angular face, his acceptance of it all, it unnerved him, he'd fought these evil creatures over distances beyond the comprehension of man just fifty years ago. Yet truth be told those boney faced devils had run his fleet ragged, he just couldn't get a break.

A win here and there helped boost morale amongst the rank and file. They were certain Jones had a grand plan to lure his enemy into a deadly trap before assembling the pieces of his puzzle, forming harmony from chaos, a victorious jigsaw to which only he knew the solution.

In truth he'd been hanging to the precipice by his fingernails for a year as the enemy pushed relentlessly, a biting winter storm. Now they were to jump in for the final blow and his best stratagem was a kamikaze attack, that and faith in the almighty.

The Admiral eyed Rick, 'Crazy must run pretty deep in your family Captain.'

'I know what it looks like but you don't … we don't have a choice. They won't stop until they have justice.'

'Justice? What the hell does a negg-head know about justice? They're cold calculated murderers.'

'They say the same about us.'

'Who cares what they say? We need to stop them now before another catastrophe takes place.'

Annyah spoke up, 'There is an old negz proverb: he who fights, dies; he who does not fight, dies as well.'

'What's that supposed to mean sister?'

'It means that my people will fight to the death … yours or theirs.'

Admiral Jones undid his collar and grabbed a glass of water, 'I need some meds.'

'That is why Captain Katusa is here.'

'And you, what do you care if we get exterminated?'

'I have come to comprehend my enemy … even love one of them. He cares for his people therefore I must do all I can, it is my duty as his emgen.'

'Emgen? What's an emgen?'

Rick looked over at what he could only think to be a blushing negz, hard skin smoothed for a moment softening her brow. Only after a year observing Annyah in detail could he pick up on her minuscule alien mannerisms.

From the corner, Sam, a quiet observer up until now, said in a surprised tone, 'A wife, sir.'

'Wife! You mean you two are ....' The Admiral's long grey face contorted in revulsion before popping several pills out a container and into the palm of his hand.

Annyah dug her elbow into Rick's side, 'It's complicated.'

'No kidding, so let me hear this proposal,' the weary spacefarer sloshed a colourful array of pills down his neck.

'Neggs are a tradition based culture they respect traditions like a religion. Now, they have a tradition where two men with a dispute, when all other avenues are exhausted, sort it out through combat it's called siguku.'

'Like a duel?'

'Something like that.'

'This is war Captain not some fight over a piece of ass.'

'In negg culture it doesn't matter what the fight's over, siguku was created to avoid war on Hemzih.'

'So they do fight each other?'

'A long time ago but like we stopped war with the Ring and Earth Corps they created siguku. All factions on their planet came together and fought it out until a dominant House emerged.'

'How the hell do you get a whole planet to agree to that shit much less abide by the results?'

'The Elders, a race of creatures from the stars landed on Hemzih. They offered a new way of life, each faction agreed to the principles of siguku since the Elders were obviously wise beyond any negg.'

'What do these Elders look like?'

'You will see,' stated Annyah in a stoic tone.

Rick carried on, 'A representative for each faction fought it out and the winner, the winner represented the Elders and their cultural traditions.'

'A coup?'

'That's what I thought but the Elders don't rule they just enforce tradition. The Kych Nom for instance ...'

'Kych what?'

Sam spoke from behind the Admiral, 'Something like the Bushido Shoshinshu, sir.'

'But it's more than that, it's a code of honour and a way of life. After this war another chapter will be added, it'll become tradition and the Elders will enforce that tradition. In the same way Kings and Queens of England enforced parliament's will, they enforce tradition.'

'I don't see how this helps me.'

'When they arrive I'll invoke siguku.'

'That's crazy.'

'What've we got to lose? If I fail we go to your plan.'

The Admiral ran his hand down a grim visage before speaking, 'Ah, has it come to this Robert?'

'What's that sir?' replied the Captain of the Crusader standing behind a seated Admiral.

'I'm so screwed I'm actually entertaining some split freak and his negg-head wife?'

'I admit it sounds pretty out there.'

'Pretty out there? It sounds preposterous.'

'I spoke with my first officer he says it's worth a shot.'

The Admiral swivelled on his seat and peered at Sam, 'Son, I've got pairs of socks older than you.'

'Understood sir, but I flew with this man for three years and I can guarantee his sincerity.'

He peered back at Rick, 'So how do you propose we execute this plan?'

'When the enemy exits hyperspace I'll send a communication on a recognised frequency. If they accept I fight for possession of everything in this solar system.'

'You think you can win?'

'The devil's in it if I can't.'

'Fine, if it doesn't work I'll sue you afterwards.'

Hours later an alarm howled throughout Earth Corps' fleet as the largest group of warships witnessed by man emerged from hyperspace. Rick and Annyah were escorted to the Bridge where Admiral Jones and the crew watched in awe.

The Admiral's eyes fixed on a single ship at the forefront, a golden craft constructed in the image of an alien approached. Rick recognised the ship for it resembled that idol he'd given to Annyah. It dwarfed the entire negz fleet.

Admiral Jones spoke to Captain Cronin, 'What the hell's that?'

'It is the Hammer of God,' replied Annyah.

'What is it?'

'The greatest warship in the universe.'

'Why the hell would you build a warship that's such an easy target? Besides I don't read any weaponry, barely enough manoeuvring thrusters and its slowing down their entire fleet.'

'Many have attempted to destroy it Admiral, they all failed miserably. If you are curious as to the appearance of an Elder, observe.'

A creature with a high forehead long stalky fingers and tiny beady eyes, humanoid in form, sat on a throne flanked by a fleet of elite ships. On observing his foe the Admiral realised he was going to need more suicide vessels and about double the cruisers just to hold his ground against this golden horde. As for that flagship, any other situation and it'd be subject for humour, but today, right here, right now, it was a daunting sight. If they were willing to field such a vessel and move at its leisurely pace from above the elliptical plane toward the Ring they must be confident of victory … on consideration he'd feel pretty damn confident if he were them.

'Sir they're heading straight toward us, ETE one four three minutes,' spoke an Ensign on the scanner station.

Admiral Jones turned to Rick, 'Send your message.'

Rick moved to the communications station and punched in a code on a frequency the negz would recognise. Once it was ready to send the officer nodded his head, 'You're good to go sir.'

Rick stared into the monitor below him and spoke using his best negz, 'Dotona Kych Nom taivan kekesun. Bi dur-a shiidverlekh damjij siguku (Inside the Kych Nom it is written. I request settlement via siguku),' he tapped the console ending the communication.

'Is that it?' stated the Admiral.

'Now they consider his request,' whispered Annyah.

'Consider?'

'He is kumun.'

'Why didn't you make the request?'

'Only a kumun may represent mankind, my request would have been ignored.'

All swung on tender hooks for a few moments until a communications officer yelped causing staff to leap out their skins, 'I'm getting a reply from the enemy fleet, on the same channel!'

'Put it on.'

On the main viewer a visage familiar to Rick and Annyah made its demonic appearance. Increased to ten times its normal size he filled the screen, every crack and line betrayed in full detail, 'Dur-a bolzo. Ta nar ukhel daga gazryn zurag (Request acceptable. You will follow these co-ordinates),' the screen went blank.

The navigation officer went over the download, 'It takes us right up to their flagship sir.'

'Take but a single ship and have the fleet power weapons down,' stated Annyah.

'That's suicide.'

'No different than flying into your enemy loaded with atomics.'

He conceded the point, 'You think they'll buy it?'

'Clarify?'

'They won't blow us out the sky before we get there.'

'We are not brachians dear Admiral. Be assured War Master Agricola will keep his word, you need but keep yours.'

'Fine we'll take my ship to ship,' he fixed his eyes on Captain Cronin, 'Robert bring your first officer he seems to know what the hell's going on even if I don't!'

The fleet powered down weapons as did the negz. Earth stood aghast. Earthlings had not witnessed before, nor would they after, such a titanic mass of warships. Two sides poised to fight and no-one knew why, it were as if Satan did savour the moment, feeding off their distress, torturing humanity with imminent destruction, throwing back his head in laughter while those over which he held dominion writhed in fear an terror. Today hell was silent for every fallen angel had risen to persecute mankind.

Confusion reigned on Earth and Mars, if only they were privy to Admiral Jones's thoughts. The man was going spare, he had no idea whether this entire situation was just a heap of crap or had a chance of success. He'd led some crazy missions in his time but this one took the biscuit.

A massive effigy in space loomed closer until it covered the cockpit window. Nothing but a golden skinned elder was visible, sunlight reflected off the monolith's skin causing their window to automatically dim.

'Sir, I'm getting another set of co-ordinates I think they want us to dock … with that.'

'Do it.'

The shuttle moved closer and so detail did unfold. As a pilot flying through fog will see his destination much later than usual. Due to the size of this craft and their directions it was only obvious at the last moment where one might land.

Somewhere on the finger of its right hand a port opened permitting the party of five entry.

Rick smirked, 'That's about right.'

'What's so funny Katusa?' asked the Admiral.

'They just gave us the middle finger.'

'You're a barrel of laughs you know that?'

'Kiss my arse.'

'If you were in the Corps I'd have you spaced for that.'

'If I were in the Corps I'd have hung me-self before now.'

'What's your problem?'

Sam groaned inside, 'Here it comes.'

Rick turned away from an expanding docking bay full of automated arms and robot AI buzzing back and forth, 'My problem's shit heads like you!'

The Admiral's eyes expanded at the speed of light, the Ensign navigating their shuttle didn't know where to look while a total stranger ripped into Earth Corps' most esteemed commander.

'No-one speaks to me like that.'

'It's because of dick heads like you people die. If you'd have kept your greedy fucking mitts off their urillium everything'd be fine but you thought no-one could stop you and now WE'RE ALL FUCKED!'

Sam looked at his Captain, 'Is that true?'

'Partially,' replied Cronin in an uncomfortable manner his military collar began to itch on his skin.

'Well which part IS true?' demanded Sam.

Cronin peered over at the Admiral who nodded to his friend, 'We discovered a system rich in urillium, enough urillium for millennia. We sent some government mining vessels to do a standard economic assessment and well it turned out someone else had laid a claim.'

'The negz?'

'They attacked us ...'

'Attacked us? Out of the blue? With all respect I don't believe that sir.'

Cronin began to sweat and the Admiral cut in, 'This is classified so no-one heard it,' he looked at the Ensign,

'Understood sir,' replied the pilot.

Jones looked back at Sam, 'They laid claim to the system. They didn't seem that advanced ... so we ... we opened fire and destroyed their vessel.'

Annyah spoke in a cold tone, 'A civilian vessel shuttling pilgrims to ancestral burial grounds.'

'You killed innocent people for urillium?'

'We didn't realise the consequences at the time.'

'Who cares about consequences? They were innocent people and you killed them.'

'It was surmised they'd recognised our superior strength and cede the belts.'

'So how's that working out for us Admiral?' he snapped in a sardonic tone.

'Watch your mouth kid!'

'Or what? You'll demote me?'

'Are you sure this kid's stable?' The Admiral asked Cronin.

'Maybe we shoulda told our officers the truth.'

'The truth? Neggs are our enemy, that's all they need to know.'

Sam cut in, 'I don't know about you but I'd appreciate knowing what it is I'm supposed to be fighting for.'

'Robert, shut that kid up.'

Sam snapped back, 'Fuck you!'

Admiral Jones was in shock, the Ensign feigned ignorance, Rick enjoyed every moment of it, 'Commander you're on suspension!'

'I quit!'

'You can't quit the Corps!'

Sam leant over and snarled at the Admiral, 'Eat my shit!'

Admiral Jones went for his side arm, Captain Cronin tried to calm Sam down, Rick pulled out his curxaj-tayag, a blur transformed to a spike that broke a little skin on the Admiral's neck, 'Put it away or I'll cut you to pieces.'

Suspended in time the Ensign went for his side arm until Annyah caught his eye. The sight of a dozen souls plastered above her armoured ridge changed his mind.

The Admiral stained his navy-blue collar with wine dark blood before holstering his weapon, 'After this is over I'll have you tried and executed you know that Katusa?'

'You'll have to buy a ticket and get in line.'

There was a deep clunking noise followed by small vibrations as the shuttle locked into place. Rick sheathed his staff to peer out the cockpit window. For miles and miles he saw nothing but endless docking slips with fighter craft fuelled and ready to go. The rectangular bay was a brightly lit three-dimensional highway, trucks parked in laybys resting left, right, above and below.

'We should greet our hosts,' stated Annyah.

Everyone exited the craft except the Ensign. One by one they stepped through a decontamination mist onto a golden floor, reflecting light cast from fifty feet above. Over a background noise of fighters and bombers preparing loads their heels clinked.

Rick perceived but a black line on a golden horizon. After a few minutes he made out individuals then faces, soon he read confirmed kills on individual eye ridges. Conquistadors concealed by dark garments with staffs slung over backs, his welcoming party felt far from it. The visage on each and every man as serious as a tax bill, these guys weren't playing around.

Amongst the party he recognised two individuals. A year ago all negz looked alike but since his time with Annyah, observing her face night and day, his perceptions changed. Rick's brain was able to discern one negz's facial features from another as naturally as a human. He recognised Agriciola and his former opponent Plina. The horde halted behind Agricola, there was a pause.

Rick fixed his eyes on Plina, 'How's it hanging?'

'He does not comprehend your language,' stated Agricola in a solemn tone, lines stretched back where men once lived.

Rick smiled at Plina, 'Sonin bain tere elgu?'

His jest was met by odd looks.

Agricola spoke again, 'He does not comprehend your humour.'

Annyah whispered into Rick's ear, her voice carried down the giant echo chamber of a docking slip, 'Rick you must demonstrate proper respect.'

'You may not speak,' snapped Agricola.

Annyah bowed her head in acknowledgment of her War Master. Agricola approached Rick, as he did the Admiral became nervous reaching for his side arm. The gothic War Master noted his reaction, 'You will not be harmed.'

'How do I know that?'

'You have my word.'

'The word of a negg? You must be joking!'

'Negz do not joke.'

The Admiral's hand shifted from his holster. Agricola returned to his prior subject, his eyes scanned Rick's tunic, 'Where did you acquire this?'

'I was at a church jumble sale and ...'

'Speak plainly kumun.'

'I got it off a negg ship in a decaying orbit.'

'Which system?'

'We call it Luyten's star you call it ...'

'I am familiar with your designations,' his sparkling eyes, protected by a pair of armoured sink holes, melded with the structure of his jaw line, formed a frightening face no man would take lightly. Agricola's vision traced Rick's tunic, 'I am familiar with the warrior who wore this, clarify his fate?'

'He's dead.'

'Clarify?'

'I shot him.'

Agricola's eye sockets expanded as if Charybdis did open to draw in Odysseus, 'You murdered Lucanus?'

'It was him or me tactical officer.'

'You should not have come kumun.'

'Me name's Rick.'

'Soon to be forgotten along with your inferior species.'

'Eat my shit fuck head!'

Annyah spoke in a hushed tone, 'Rick ...'

'YOU WILL REMAIN SILENT DEVIANT CHILD!' roared Agricola as he marched toward Annyah.

She hung her head again. Rick gallantly stood in his way placing a single hand on the War Master's chest. The entire delegation was aghast. Agricola's voice lowered to one of repressed anger and hatred, 'Remove your diseased hand, kumun filth.'

Rick dropped his hand, 'Just keep away from her.'

'She is yours?'

'We're joined.'

Agricola's lips tightened, a cobalt insect disappearing into an impenetrable visage. He betrayed emotion, namely that of distaste, something a War Master rarely did, 'You comprehend our tradition?'

'I do.'

'Silence your female.'

'You don't need to tell me twice.'

'You will be escorted to our hall of worship.'

'He who dares wins.'

'We shall see, kumun.'

Chapter Sixteen

At the heart of God's Hammer a vaulted roof of gold welcomed Rick with trepidation. One hundred metres down, at its far end, an altar of solid gold steps rose three times the height of a man. What occupied its plinth remained a mystery for its sides were solid gold, with but a single veiled opening.

Agricola led them inside what can only be described as a gilded cathedral, a place of great significance to his people. Rick's party reached golden steps, a veil receded to reveal an alien on a throne constructed of the same auspicious metal. The wrinkled being was familiar even to humans for it resembled the effigy they'd docked with. This was the Hammer of God, the brilliant idol he'd recovered more than a year ago.

Every negz in the room dropped to one knee in reverence, exposing soft rear skulls. A stoic being surveyed its faithful, eventually those beady eyes inside a leathery old head fell upon Rick. The creature was light skinned, its forehead towered as a condominium. Rick recognised large hands and long boney fingers, it was dressed in a blue robe, shimmering in the presence of purity. Negz neither moved nor spoke, the creature rose traversing steps to Rick's level, it must've been seven feet tall. Chronos had spent many years ploughing lines into its visage. Its head towered as a rocky keep, white hair sprouting from battlements. A chin reached down as its head did push up, thick wrinkled leather stretching into wispy white candy floss hair. Its lips were small in comparison to its features yet no larger than a human. His nose and eyes could have been those of an old man, 'Had a rough night?' cracked Rick.

The stoic alien spoke with a negz accent, 'I slept comfortably.'

Rick was shocked to hear English come from its mouth, it betrayed the beginnings of a grin.

'Those who serve say you are murderers and thieves, what do you say?'

'I've only killed in self-defence and took what was abandoned.'

The alien's dark beady eyes focused on Rick. Rick wasn't aware but it possessed an ability to view another's aura, an electromagnetic field cast by all living things. It examined Rick's brain as he answered, 'You are a liar.'

'Excuse me?'

'You have taken possessions not abandoned.'

'I've bent the rules once or twice.'

'That is the truth. Tell me, why you are here kumun?'

'I'm here for siguku.'

'Why YOU?'

Rick thumbed over his shoulder toward Earth Corps officers, 'Someone needs to save the rest of us from this bunch of fuckwits.'

The alien stroked a clump of long wispy grey hair on the end of its droopy chin, 'Clarify fuckwit?'

'A zondoogerch.'

There were rumblings amongst every negz, heads facing floor. The Elder, for that is what he was, contemplated the phrase. Rick had appropriated two words and married them in a fashion quite alien to negz but on reflection its meaning became clear. The Elder let out a small chuckle, 'I take it you blame your kych for your imminent destruction?'

'I do.'

'Have you considered kumun nature to be your enemy?'

'Yeh but the good guys are supposed to keep the bad guys in check.'

'Negz achieve this via tradition, what method do kumuns use?'

'Morality I suppose.'

The Elder nodded his head, 'A poor substitute for tradition, especially in an individualist society where laws apply to the weak yet the powerful escape justice,' the Elder's eyes scanned Earth Corps officers, 'Why sacrifice yourself to save your oppressors?'

'First off I haven't lost yet.'

The Elder spoke in a tone of pity and warning, 'Your fate is certain you must realise this?'

'I'm doing it for the people on Earth, Mars and every colony in the solar system. They don't deserve to die because a bunch of greedy scumbags couldn't keep their hands in their own pockets.'

The Admiral went to speak, the Elder halted his tirade, 'I believe it is fair to warn you, our meeting is being transmitted throughout your solar system.'

Admiral Jones closed his mouth and looked around the great hall, he couldn't see any recording devices.

'There will be no siguku lest I approve.'

Rick opened his arms, 'Won't you throw a poor boy a bone?'

'Throw a bone?'

'Give me a break.'

'A break?'

'Give me a chance.'

'Ah I see, an interesting language, a pity I will not have further opportunity to study it.'

'It ain't over 'till the fat lady sings Gandalf!'

The Elder's long lines and furrows contracted in puzzlement.

'It isn't over until it's over.'

'We shall see … savage,' the Elder turned his back, ascended golden steps and rested upon a polished throne, 'Sabsa!'

With absolute co-ordination and compunction every negz rose to his feet, 'Dajin Xagan!'

Agricola knelt at the first golden step eyes toward his ruler, 'Tiim Xutag (Yes Majesty).'

'Ta nar ukhel koloolokh Hemzih Negz (You will represent the negz).'

'Az ta nar khusel Xutag (As you desire Majesty).'

'Sabsa, khangasan tany orsoldogh (Rise, meet your opponent).'

Agricola rose, bowed his head and moved toward Rick. Negz soldiers moved away, Annyah looked to the Admiral and his men, 'We must make space.'

'For what?'

'Our challenge has been accepted,' she moved back thirty feet followed by Earth Corps officers, clearing room for the final battle.

259

Rick and Agricola stood face to face, to most humans Agricola's face was an emotionless block of stone, an edifice of unwavering will yet Rick distinguished pleasure deep behind that redoubt. In his short time with Annyah he'd learnt subtle betrayals which we call emotion, 'Don't start celebrating yet,' whispered Rick.

'I look forward to skewering your frame while an Elder looks on.'

'I get the feeling you're trying to compensate for something, what with extra-long staffs and the authoritarian get up. It wouldn't surprise me if you had a pair of socks stuffed down the front of your trousers.'

'Before you die, what attracts her to you?' his eyes locked on Annyah for a moment.

'You can ask her when this is over.'

Agricola narrowed his vision on Rick, he'd inadvertently betrayed his strategy. Rick had no intention of winning this contest. This savage was prepared to sacrifice his life despite the corruption and evil within kumun society. He'd learnt just enough to invoke siguku and lose. Agricola was impressed, no brachian would do such a thing. A brachian would watch his home system burn provided he was safe and sound, 'I comprehend.'

The Elder spoke from his golden perch, 'Yamar sool? (Which school?)'

'Zorxo!' replied Agricola.

The Elder waited for a few seconds then addressed Rick, 'And you?'

Before Rick could answer Agricola spoke, 'Hard knocks your Majesty.'

'Hard knocks? I have no knowledge of such a school.'

'A kumun school.'

'How intriguing, mash sain kumun ukel sool ni khatuu togshikh (very well the human shall use the school of hard knocks).'

Agricola stepped back and drew his staff, Rick did likewise, both stood still until the Elder spoke, 'Ekhlekh!'

Each fighter circled the other, on Earth, Mars and every colony in the solar system people were glued to their screens. This was the World Football Cup times one million playing out before their eyes with the Pope and all his minions praying for their team in the streets. Jews in synagogues, Christians in churches and Buddhists in temples imploring their deities with fervour as the day of Armaggedon befell a wicked mankind.

With a short thrust Rick probed Agricola's defences, making sure not to over extend himself, to test rather than attack. Agricola answered quickly, slapping Rick's staff, the strength of his counter action caught Rick by surprise. He'd trained for months with Annyah tempering his combat to her strength and speed, Agricola hit harder and with greater aggression. Rick's staff crossed his body exposing his left side. Agricola took advantage striking hard and fast into his opponent's ribs. A crack of bone reverberated around the cathedral's golden walls and vaulted ceiling. Rick moved back returning to a defensive position. Oddly negz soldiers and priests betrayed satisfaction in this base brutality. As Annyah had once said even they aren't perfect.

Admiral Jones winced, 'Jesus, that's gotta hurt.'

Fighters circled one another as two birds of prey. Rick ignored his broken ribs, he could piss and moan later, if there was a later.

Agricola feigned an attack. Rick leapt back in a defensive stance, negz onlookers perceived fear, approving their champion's intimidation with mumbles. This was Rick's metaphysical death by a thousand cuts before his material slaying. The Elder remained expressionless, no more than an objective observer in all of this.

After a minute of Rick disentangling his staff from combat Agricola decided to test his foe. He moved hard and fast at his target with a combination attack, waving the point of his staff from side to side confusing its target. Once in range Agricola, who by now stood side on, staff along his chest, one end pointed out toward Rick the other behind him suddenly pushed the end upwards at Rick's face then downwards toward his legs. Rick moved back, successfully blocking both attacks, unbeknownst to him they weren't intended to meet their target. Agricola quickly pulled his forward foot back a few inches, withdrew his staff point, took aim on Rick's body and brought his foot forward into his usual fighting stance at the same time thrusting the point of his staff into Rick's chest.

This whole combination of attack, defence, withdrawal, attack, was executed in short seconds. Rick was still on his feet thanks to Annyah's training but fighting a crippling chest pain, he gasped for air.

Agricola withdrew, why was anyone's guess. Admiral Jones believed he was dragging it out, those damn negg-heads siphoned a perverse pleasure from human pain as if panning for gold. Annyah was relieved Rick had scrounged another shot, perhaps he could carve victory from a stone edifice of certain death?

Negz soldiers called out, Rick ignored a cohort of dark conquistadors cheering in a restrained fashion for their War Master. His display of mastery over this primitive enforced their beliefs of superiority, chosen ones picked from a galactic primordial slime of species for enlightenment.

On Earth and Mars groans of dismay made the rounds of people in bars, streets, huddled in homes and places of worship praying judgement day might be staved off until tomorrow.

Rick held himself together drawing oxygen into his lungs, engaged in an atmospheric tug of war with nature. He couldn't move too fast thanks to his broken rib but his tunic kept it in place, clever design.

Admiral Jones knew little of stick fighting yet realised Agricola was the superior, Jones had already made reservations in hell, a penthouse suite, he's an Earth Corps Admiral after all.

Rick held his staff loosely, his right hand close to its tip with the remainder of his weapon resting on the floor behind. He looked tired and ready to be put out of his misery, like an old pack animal sent to the donkey farm ready to end his fate, turned into glue so he may cure a dry throat somewhere in China.

Agricola moved in with a second combo a diversionary swing with another straight thrust, this would be to the head. Agricola entered range and Rick swung his staff its tip moved as a pendulum from behind his body, beneath, then before him and into his opponent. Thanks to the fact Rick held his weapon close to its tip he was afforded superior range, striking Agricola's genitals with a great thud. Rick pulled his staff from between his opponent's legs, his hand once close to the forward point was now at the rear of the stick, his left hand held the centre to provide power. Rick pulled his staff back a little, raised it to Agricola's gut level then with all his might pushed, resulting in a deep dark grunt.

All around the solar system the sound of humans celebrating filled the heavens, a negz just got smashed in the nuts live on air. Even Admiral Jones felt the touch of hope chase pessimism from his old soul, maybe he'd put that penthouse on hold for now?

Negz were horrified for Rick's attack was explicitly unsanctioned by any rules of combat. Agricola placed his hand in the air, 'Zogsookh! (Halt!)'

Rick moved to his corner, Annyah tended his wounds while the Admiral gave encouragement.

The Elder stared down Agricola.

Agricola caught his breath still recovering from the groin strike, 'Beleg ajil tavian khuuli! (Groin strike is illegal!)'

The Elder looked disappointed with his War Master, 'Burru, dotana siguku tavian ugui khoriglono (Incorrect, within siguku it is not prohibited).'

Agricola's face screwed up much to his master's displeasure. The creature snarled from its elevated throne, 'Ta nar ashiglakh neg zogsookh ... ekhlekh! (You have used one halt ... begin!)'

Agricola moved stiffly into the centre of the arena. Admiral Jones patted Rick on the shoulder, 'You've got him upset kid now KICK HIS MOTHERFUCKING ALIEN ASS!'

Rick ignored Jones, he looked to Annyah for a nugget of negz insight, 'Your advantage is the unexpected use it to throw him off balance, remember the school of hard knocks.'

Rick nodded his head and returned to the centre, matching his opponent curxaj-tayag to curxaj-tayag. Before Rick could prepare a defensive stance Agricola attacked in what negz consider a most un-gentlemanly (though not illegal) fashion. He struck Rick on the arm with a baseball bat swing.

Pain shot along Rick's left side but rather than withdraw he grasped Agricola's staff wrapping his left arm around it. In the same move he approached and kicked down, his right boot squarely met Agricola's kneecap. A horrific crunch bounced around the hall, Agricola was momentarily exposed, vulnerable to any assault. Rick struck with what he knew … a vicious head butt. There was a crack and Rick staggered back, his mind swirling in confusion. This steadfast combo worked fine on the streets of Doncaster, unfortunately Agricola's armoured skull forced Rick into a painful retreat on that bargain. Worried noise filtered through gothic soldiers observing what should have been a simple victory. Their War Master, leader of the greatest military in the galaxy, the deadliest negz with a curxaj-tayag, the most qualified man to represent their people had been taken advantage of. In fact, it was a distinct possibility he may not win against this unorthodox human school of combat.

Despite its tenets, tradition won't protect you against a shattered kneecap. Agricola watched Rick stagger back, head swimming in a stormy sea of grey syrup. He wanted to move forward and finish the kumun yet his knee refused to be his associate in such a bold action, Agricola could but observe, his mind fired with frustration.

Rick recovered, he was still alive … but wait … THE KNEE! He flew back at Agricola with only a single thought. Curxaj-tayag in a neutral position Rick swung left and right, up and down. Agricola blocked each attack with skill and finesse yet he portrayed a bear chased into its cave by huntsmen, his back to the wall, fighting for his life with everything God had given him.

Agricola lifted his fractured leg a couple of inches off the floor and shuffled into Rick employing all his might. With the grip of his curxaj-tayag held between his hands he punched Rick in the face knocking him off balance. This time Agricola took advantage. As Rick turned away Agricola manoeuvred behind to hook his curxaj-tayag over his opponent's head and around his throat. Rick felt Agricola's staff crush his windpipe, cutting oxygen from his bloodstream.

'C'MON KID!!!' screamed the Admiral.

Annyah was a nervous wreck, the ice woman had shattered, she visibly shook watching the last moments of the man she loved.

Rick made a gaging noise for a second before the streets of Doncaster returned ... he lifted his right leg. Resting an Earth Corps Marine issue boot heel softly on Agricola's shin, with all his weight and power Rick thrust down tearing fabric and skin until it reached his enemies foot ... *CRUNCH*.

Agricola grimaced in pain, released his grip and fell onto his back with an almighty thud. Rick staggered forward coughing and spluttering, Achlys's grey curtains drawn across his eyes.

'FUCKING KILL HIM!' screamed a ruddy faced Admiral Jones pointing to a crippled Agricola now writhing on the floor.

Rick turned, his situation revealed itself, the grey mist of battle dispersed to betray a wounded and immobile opponent. Rick moved in, staff fixed on his quarry. On approach Agricola grabbed one end of his curxaj-tayag with both hands and thrust the other into Rick's crotch forcing an excruciating halt.

The Elder's visage changed to that of shock, well as shocked as a stone carving could be, for never in his existence had he witnessed gutter fighting, it just simply wasn't done. The stoic being felt rather uncomfortable observing his War Master adopt this kumun school of dirty fighting in order to survive.

Rick stopped in his tracks as lightning shot through his testicles and around his entire body. Agricola, trained from birth to ignore the most crippling pain, with the assistance of his staff as a prop, hopped up from the floor.

He found a neutral combat stance by balancing most of his weight on a single foot, pivoted his body with curxaj-tayag and whacked Rick full in the face. A devastating right to the jaw sent Rick to the floor like a sack of potatoes, he was out cold, it was over.

Agricola shuffled as fast as his broken bones permitted, the dark conquistador's curxaj-tayag extended its spearhead, victory was his.

'AAV!!!' screamed Annyah at the top of her voice.

Agricola paused as every negz anticipated the final blow.

The Keres, spirits of death, hovered over the battlefield poised to gorge on the dark blood of another fallen warrior. Delight shone in their eyes while lust dripped from their teeth as saliva drooling from a hungry lion's jaws before devouring a fawn.

'DAHIN AAV!!!' shrieked the ice woman.

Agricola's spearpoint retracted, he leant on one foot and retrieved Rick's staff, draining a pool of blood it previously dammed. Grasping both weapons Agricola hobbled toward Admiral Jones, as he did negz warriors exchanged obstinate looks with one another. Mystified as to why their War Master had not skewered this kumun, ending the war.

The daughters of Nyx gnashed their teeth above Rick's body, ready to satisfy their hearts on wine dark human blood. Poised to dine on him just as they had since ancient Greece, hovering over the walls of Troy, waiting for their banquet of death to commence as two sides charged into battle. Yet it was not to be.

The Elder observed, his clairvoyant confidence abandoned to cynical fate. Eventually Agricola stood before Admiral Jones as every human in the solar system watched with bated breath, 'Your fleet, your planets, your people.'

Admiral Jones looked toward Annyah, she whispered, 'You must accept.'

The Admiral was about to say something when Sam cut him off, 'She's right, you have to keep your word, sir.'

Jones straightened his tunic, if he didn't accept they were going to exterminate every human in this system but what was stopping them from doing that anyway?

'If I accept will my people be safe?'

'Keep your word kumun!'

'Fine I accept defeat,' Jones pulled back his cuff and tapped a communicator on his wrist, 'the fleet's standing down, here are the command codes,' he began to remove his officer's bracelet.

Agricola thrust his hand forward offering Rick's curxaj-tayag.

Jones peered at Annyah.

'Take it, quickly!'

With trepidation he took possession of the staff, as he did every negz soldier spoke with his neighbour to the point they might become a rowdy mob.

'Nam Guum!' snapped the Elder, silence prevailed.

'I return your fleet, your planets and your people with one caveat.'

'Yes?' said a startled Jones.

'Your people may not enter negz space without prior permission.'

That wasn't so bad, Jones was prepared for a sermon but instead he received a service, 'I can't control every human in the galaxy.'

'I comprehend, but break your word and there will be no second siguku.'

'Agreed.'

Agricola looked down at Annyah, 'He will survive,' then hobbled past an unconscious Rick to kneel before a perched Elder.

'Ene (this one),' he peered at Rick, 'Liudol? (Lives?)'

'Taivan kekesun: dejile bain elbeg (It is written: victory is enough).'

'Bi da ugui ulne sonun a mordol (I do not recall such a passage).'

'Tavian te sarn sucur (It is the third tenet).'

The Admiral whispered to Annyah, 'What're they talking about?'

'History.'

'What's that got to do with us?' Admiral Jones was none the wiser yet he held his staff and listened, what else could he do?

'Te Kych Nom khudij bu song sucur (The Kych Nom contains but two tenets).'

'Tere nahor khudij a sarn ... toolya tany bolzo (It contains a third ... with your tolerance).'

You could cut the atmosphere with a knife. The cathedral was filled with anal passages capable of strangling an amoeba to death. The only sound came from Rick as he groaned in and out of consciousness. The Elder scanned his devoted soldiers, on making eye contact they knelt, each one produced a copy of the Kych Nom from inside his tunic, something no gothic conquistador was without.

The Elder observed the human delegation and its single negz, 'Mash sain, te sarn sucur nit e Kych Nom: dejile bain elbeg. Kekesun bo Dajin Xagan Agricola Titanus Augustua (Very well, the third tenet of the Kych Nom: Victory is enough, authored by War Master Agricola Titanus Augusta).'

267

Annyah was down on one knee with the rest of her people scribbling the new tenet in her copy of the Kych Nom. The Admiral remained both upright and perplexed. On diagnosing his dumbfounded mien the Elder enlightened Earth Corps' leader, 'Today a tenet is joined to the Kych Nom.'

'I see,' replied the Admiral, none the wiser.

'Their Bushido Shoshinshu,' said Sam into his ear.

The Elder almost smiled at Sam before continuing in his enigmatic way, 'A holy war permits a Dajin Xagan to propose a tenet, it has been blessed.'

'Tenet?'

'The first tenet: Mercy is for the weak, authored by Dajin Xagan Remus Cluadius Severus. The second tenet: Never display emotion, authored by Dajin Xagan Lucius Vitellus Brachanius. Today the third tenet authored by Dajin Xagan Agricola Titanus Augusta: Victory is enough.'

Captain Cronin mumbled to himself, 'Sounds like McArthur.'

'I'm certain he wouldn't mind,' replied Admiral Jones in a hushed tone.

A week later

Reality began to unfold, Rick emerged from hibernation as a bear recovers from a cold winter. Full of aches and pains, it moves slowly with blurred vision, the sound of wind rushing in and out its wintertide cave. He turned his crusty eyes toward the draft and observe an iron lung pumping oxygen through a tube, one of many machines surgically inserted into his rib cage. Something clasped his hand … he could feel his hand … that must be a good sign. Rick's eyes turned to the opposite side of his bed. As the mist of Hypnos dispersed he recognised a face. Annyah stood by him, her hands clutched his, anxiety fled his frame, he was alive. Rick tried to move only to sense restraints pressing his body against the bed.

'Rick, can you hear me?' stated the gothic lady in a soft tone

He relaxed his body, 'Yeh,' cracked a dry throat forcing out words for the first time in seven days.

'Do you recognise me?'

'Annyah.'

She smiled, 'Do you know where you are?'

'Up shit creek,' groaned Rick as his body ached.

'You are on Earth Ring.'

'It worked?'

'Yes, it worked.'

'What happened?'

'You have been in a coma for one week.'

'I feel like shit.'

'They say it will be another two weeks before you can walk.'

Rick heard a pair of heels clinking on a polished floor. Sam stepped into the small room where Annyah had been at Rick's bedside for nearly a week. The room was brightly lit, with but a chair and bedside table, on the table rested the negz holy book on the other side of Rick's bed computers and all sorts of equipment were installed into the wall. Tubes linked his body to a central mainframe maintaining and monitoring life signs.

On approach Sam displayed a big grin.

'Don't say it,' groaned Rick.

Sam was dressed in civilian shirt and pants, whenever off duty he'd visit to check on his mentor, 'Say what?'

'You know what I mean.'

'I never thought I'd see Rick Katusa put it on the line for a bunch of Earth Corps assholes.'

'Someone had to and besides I expect to be reimbursed!' he coughed as his iron lung pumped oxygen, 'Someone turn that fucking thing off!'

A fat man in a white coat with thin wire frame glasses stepped through the door of Rick's spacious hospital suite. Earth Corps had spared no expense in keeping Rick Katusa alive. A young nurse followed him and immediately moved to the opposite side inspecting readouts on Rick's medical station.

'Excuse me,' he stepped through Sam and Annyah, 'Mr Katusa?' he shone a light in Rick's eyes.

'Turn that off!'

'Can you hear me Mr Katusa?'

'Of course I can fucking hear you!' Rick felt a static charge zap his anal area, 'WHAT THE FUCK??!!!!'

'I'm sorry,' said a blushing nurse no more than twenty years of age.

'What the fuck was that?'

'Your anal feeding tube had feedback Mr Katusa.'

'ANAL WHAT?'

'You've got a tube up your ass,' sniggered Sam.

'Well take the fucking thing out!'

The Doctor removed his glasses and spoke in a serious tone, 'Mr Katusa you've just awoken from a catatonic state, your body needs to heal and you need to relax.'

'Forgive me Mr?'

'Doctor Shaw.'

'Well forgive me Doctor Shaw but considering I'm tied down with a tube up me arse end I don't see how I CAN relax!'

The doctor gave Rick an odd look then turned to Annyah, 'Is he usually like this?'

Sam and Annyah replied in unison, 'Yes.'

'I see,' Dr Shaw brought out a tablet and began to download information from the medical station, 'Hmm nothing here, nurse will you inspect the rectal rehydration tube?'

'Yes Doctor Shaw,' the lady turned Rick's bed sheets back over his feet and moved his legs apart.

'NO DOCTOR SHAW!' barked Rick.

'Lungs seem healthy enough despite years of abuse,' noted the doctor tapping his tablet.

'Abuse?'

'You do smoke?'

'I have a rollup every now and then.'

The Doctor raised an eyebrow.

'What is this a fucking inquisition?' Rick felt another zap, 'JESUS CHRIST WILL YOU STOP THAT!'

'Come on Rick you've paid for worse,' sniggered Sam.

Rick watched as the nurse's eyes popped over his feet and ogled him, 'Get back to ya bloody job woman!' snapped Rick sending her down and out of sight.

'Could you move your feet for me Mr Katusa?'

Another shock penetrated his rear forcing Rick's feet into the air, 'FUCK ME!'

'Excellent Mr Katusa it seems you're on the road to a full recovery.'

'Not if she burns me fucking arse off first!'

'Yes I'll send a technician to replace that.'

'Technician?'

'Gregg's our best man.'

'Hold on, I'm not having some shirt lifter putting his hands up me arse!'

'Don't worry Mr Katusa he'll be wearing sterilised gloves.'

'I don't care if he's wearing Frank Sinatra's favourite suit and singing New York, New York. HE'S NOT putting his hands near my arsehole.'

'Why ever not?'

'I'm no fucking queer.'

'What does Gregg's sexuality have to do with it?'

'YOU MEAN HE IS A SHIRT LIFTER?!!'

'Really Mr Katusa that term has been prohibited for some years now.'

The nurse giggled somewhere below Rick's vision.

Rick looked up at the ceiling, 'I died and went to hell.'

Annyah spoke to Dr Shaw, 'I shall remove his tube.'

'I'm afraid that's not possible.'

Sam placed his hand on the Doctor's shoulder, 'I think you can make an exception in this case, can't you?'

A grumpy Doctor Shaw put his tablet away, 'As you please Commander.'

Admiral Jones stepped into the room looked down at Rick's tubes and his eyebrows shot up, 'Jesus Christ, it looks like they put your flight suit on upside down!'

The Admiral returned Sam's saluted, 'At ease, could everyone leave the room. I have something to discuss with Captain Katusa, in private.'

Doctor Shaw gestured toward the door and his nurse exited, 'Certainly Admiral,' Shaw left the suite.

Annyah and Sam waited outside while the Admiral spoke with Rick, 'How's it hanging?' smirked the Admiral one eye on the pipes straddling Rick's rear end.

'Do you mind?'

Jones turned the sheets down, covering a monstrosity responsible for sustaining Rick's life this past week.

'What do you want?'

'I want to give you medal.'

'I didn't know they gave awards for good looks and charm.'

'You're a hero and heroes have to be honoured no matter how foul mouthed and ungrateful they may be.'

'How am I a hero?'

'Every man, woman and child saw you fight that negg-head and to cut a long story short you could walk into just about any bar, snap your fingers and every woman would drop her panties.'

'I'll put that theory to the test as soon as this octopus is out me shitter.'

'Naturally Earth Corps has decided to award you the gold star. The problem is we only award medals to men and women who are or have served in Earth Corps.'

'My heart bleeds in agony.'

'It does?'

'I was being sarcastic.'

'Oh, right, so while you were in a coma we signed you up.'

'YOU DID WHAT?'

'You're a civilian advisor with the rank of Captain.'

'How the fuck can I join the Waffen fucking S.S. while I'm fucking comatosed?'

'The decision fell to your next of kin. Annyah being your legal guardian agreed and signed the paperwork.'

'I need a drink.'

'As soon as you're standing we'll send a tailor to fit your uniforms.'

'Uniforms?'

'The award ceremony will be public, everyone'll be watching.'

'I'm not doing it.'

'Why not?'

'Fuck Earth Corps!'

'I don't understand where all this hostility comes from?'

'It's you that turned me country into hell, you turned most of planet Earth into a living hell.'

'I'm sorry to break it to you son but they did that themselves. If it weren't for us up here they'd have nuked each other long ago. You see, I just keep the peace, I don't force them to live the way they do.'

'Well you nearly did the job for them didn't you?'

'That wasn't my call and I regret it to this day.'

'You mean you regret losing.'

'My son died fighting that war and I swear on his grave it was a war Earth Corps never wanted. While I'm Admiral of the fleet it won't happen again, you have my word.'

'Pah, your word?'

'The future of humanity depends on my word so I intend keeping it. Will you attend the ceremony ... no bullshit.'

Rick pushed his head into a fluffy white pillow and closed his aching eyes in an attempt to de-stress his mind.

'What will take?' asked the Admiral.

Rick thought for a minute.

'Anything ... within reason,' pled Jones.

'Annyah gets a medal.'

'I can't sign a god damn negg-head!'

'Then fuck your gold star.'

273

'Be reasonable son.'

'Your choice.'

'They'll hang me by the balls for even suggesting it.'

'That's your problem.'

Admiral Jones stood up, pulled back his sleeve, tapped his officer's bracelet and chatted into a mic embedded in his collar. There was a long discussion with longer periods of silence, eventually he tapped it again and pulled down his sleeve, 'It's done, she gets the honorary rank of Ensign and a bronze star, satisfied?'

'Do I have your word?'

'You've got my word.'

'I'll let you know when I'm ready.'

'And by the way, how'd you know they'd hand everything back?'

'I didn't.'

'So what was the plan?'

'If I lost they'd enslave us.'

'What if they decided to kill us?'

'They wouldn't break the rules of siguku, Neggs aren't murderers.'

'And if they enslaved us? What then?'

'There's an old negg proverb: you don't need to be free to live … or something like that.'

'Well, good job Captain.'

'And another thing, it'll be a cold fucking day in hell before I salute you!'

The Admiral nodded his head before marching out the recovery room.

Chapter Seventeen

The ceremony had passed away yet Rick remained. Just as Sonnet scanned battlefield remnants he surveyed empty paper plates, used cups, napkins, knives and forks, all this had been for him.

He peered down a crisp white jacket, his hand lifted a gold star awarded by Admiral Jones two hours ago, he was a hero … what a load of crap! A fake speech for a fake gold star surrounded by a bunch of Earth Corps krishnas … millions dead for this?

'Be careful your vanity.'

Rick faced her with a smile, 'Where were you?'

'Admiral Jones thought best I not attend.'

'The only real thing here.'

'You are not authentic?'

'I was lucky. I made it by the skin of me teeth.'

She set arms on hips like a slim gothic vase, 'Is that not the point?'

'Of what?'

'A simple feat does not require a hero.'

'Whatever.'

'That uniform wears you well, I am certain it will find future use.'

Rick chuckled, 'I'm not signing up for the S.S. anytime soon.'

'I refer to your observations concerning kumun females.'

'Oh right, a woman in every port?'

'That and poorly constrained undergarments.'

Rick laughed, 'I suppose there has to be an upside to keeping one set of clothes clean.'

Annyah smiled and offered her hand.

Rick examined it with a perplexed visage, 'What's this?'

'My hand.'

'I know it's your hand.'

'Our contract is concluded.'

A dazed Rick shook her hand, the past rushed back as melt waters breaking a river bank to flood a Spring valley. In truth Rick hadn't considered their contract for months nor did he believe it still applied but Annyah was a serious woman, she was negz. For once the motormouth of Doncaster was devoid of wisecracks or comebacks, Echos removed his abilities in one fell swoop.

'Good fortune Captain,' Annyah turned and walked away. Now when I say walked away she made the smallest steps possible at the slowest pace without betraying her true desire.

Rick was stunned, eyes locked the back of Annyah's head. His heart pounded slow and hard emulating the dull rhythmic thuds of a crank shaft. Rick hadn't considered this scenario, surely her home was aboard Sonnet ... maybe he should've spoken to her about it? As Rick choked on air searching for words Annyah strode into the distance each step more painful than the last until finally he spoke, relief washed over her hardened visage. The gothic conquistador reset her face so not to betray her true emotion and turned, 'Did you say something Captain?'

'Well I ...'

'I am leaving for Hemzih within the hour, please be punctual.'

'Don't you want to stay?'

She folded her arms, disguising emotion so great it would overwhelm as a tsunami rushing a sea shore, 'Stay where?'

'Here,' replied Rick as his throat battled an obstruction. Anxiety had vacated Annyah's frame to reside in Rick's.

'For what purpose?'

'Well I,' he wrung his hands, 'I still need a tactical officer.'

Her upper lip curled back in disdain, 'I am certain many kumun females are desperate to serve alongside the brave Captain Katusa!'

Annyah turned her back and began to march out the hall. Before she got very far Rick called out, 'I thought we were married?'

Annyah stopped moving yet maintained her back to his face, 'I thought we were shipmates with benefits?'

'Okay, that was me being an arse.'

'A state you achieve frequently.'

'Yes, yes, you're right,' Rick had barely moved yet he was out of breath, his heart beat like a hammer in a blacksmith's. The fear of Annyah leaving had not struck until this moment and now that it did, it did so with the intensity of Vulcan's forge. She on the other hand had contemplated this conversation for weeks. In negz tradition it was Rick's responsibility to make a move and forcing him to do so when not inclined is a challenging task.

Rick removed his cap and wiped sweat from his brow, 'Don't go.'

Annyah remained silent her back to his face, waiting on words, words he'd forced down so long yet now struggled to release. Annyah had unlocked the door, she stood waiting for Rick to open it yet it pained him to do so. To fight Agricola in a death match required less courage than Annyah asked of him now ... 'I love you.'

Another wave of uncertainty flushed from her soul into his forming a tear. A lone waterfall trickled along a dry creek until the ice woman wiped it clean and regained her composure. Annyah faced Rick, she did her best to hold back for the words she sought were plainly spoken, 'What did you say?'

'You heard.'

'Do not be weak.'

'I'm not.'

'Then answer my question.'

'I said I love you.'

'I am supposed to be flattered?'

'Now you're the one playing silly buggers!'

'I do not comprehend,' she did but Annyah couldn't make it straightforward. Rick wasn't turning this one around so easy.

'I want us to be married, properly.'

'One of us is.'

Rick pulled a face befuddled as to her meaning.

'The other belittles our union with indiscreet … base humour. I am no longer obliged to remain here and be humiliated as if I were no more than a harbour slut.'

Rick groaned inside, she was right, he'd been a dick about this negg marriage thing far too many times. Even Sonnet's crew had declined to laugh on the subject for some time now, 'I'm sorry.'

'You are sorry and I am leaving.'

He grabbed her arm before she might move, 'Alright I'll stop making jokes, you've got me word.'

Annyah raised her brow to cajole the rest out.

'I want to get married, a tradition human marriage here then go home and get married on Hemzih, if that's alright by you.'

It was, it's what Annyah wanted all along but Rick had to pay for being an arse, 'Who will be there?'

'Well me and you.'

She closed her eyes, passionate and frustrated, 'It would hardly be a marriage otherwise!'

Rick could think fast when it came to stripping. It was his profession to solve those problems, but when it came to women he hit an impasse, 'Well, whoever you want.'

'Admiral Jones is permitted to wed individuals is he not?'

'You can't be serious?'

Her caves opened to let those bright sapphires glare with full intensity.

'Okay, Admiral Jones, anyone else?'

'Commander Ward will be your best man.'

'Best man … hold on how do you know about that?'

Her eyes intensified again as she strategically crossed her arms.

'Alright, anything else?'

'Sonnet's crew and families are to be invited.'

'How the fuck am I supposed to pay for that?'

'My passage to Hemzih is yet to be cancelled.'

'Fine whatever you want, just promise me you'll stay.'

She moved in closer and smiled, 'You have my word Captain Rck Katusa.'
Rick's bones let go, permitting Phobos passage to his father's side. Rick
thought he'd faced his greatest fear on the Hammer of God, that was nothing
compared to what he felt when confronted with the idea Annyah might
desert him. To face death and survive is a simple task for a man like Rick, he'd
done so many times before. To face love and surrender is a feat he'd never
attempted. Something happened between him and this crazy alien woman
out there in space and he'd not discovered its intent until this moment, he
was in love and he'd nearly thrown it away. Rick would've torn himself apart
until his dying day had he allowed Annyah to walk out on him and so he
found himself in a situation undreamt of in the past. The gay bachelor begged
the most diametrically opposed woman in the universe for her hand in
marriage. It was funny, after all the women, all the ports and Shaniqua, all he
wanted now was to be with Annyah. They embraced one another and Rick
whispered into her ear, 'You're the only real thing in me life.'
Annyah didn't comprehend his full meaning not that she wasn't smart but it
was going to take more than a year of living with kumuns, especially with this
figurative speech. Despite her lack of sophistication concerning human
intercourse she reached the assumption based on contextual situation and
tone Rick was making a solely optimistic statement … truly an oddity for the
Captain. She replied by embracing his slimmed down frame and whispering,
'As are you in mine.'
The scent of regret dissipated to be replaced by that of tranquillity, finally,
the universe had come into balance.

Three months later

'Entering normal space, universal hail received.'
'I see her,' stated Rick as crew dashed to stations.
'What should I do?' asked Peters.
'Permit me,' Annyah activated her mic informing a golden vessel of their
intent, a short conversation, co-ordinates downloaded and Dyson set course.

Sonnet entered the solar system of Annyah's home world, Rick and his crew would be the first humans to set foot on Hemzih. Very few aliens had made the journey to Hemzih unchained ... spoils of war or tribute being the traditional path.

Rick was here to do what he must, tradition demanded they join on Hemzih. Another first, a negz would join with an alien. Though Rick wasn't exactly enthused after Annyah described his fate. A traditional bachelor party consisted of two weeks meditation, fasting and praying before lashes with a thin stick ... no wonder they all looked so bloody miserable!

A great elevator, one of many, reached from the surface as the arm of God clutching an orbital station, holding its position within his mighty grasp. Rather than a ring, many such elevators and stations were held together with a web of nano-tubing to prevent sway. Encompassing the entire planet this web regulated sunlight, maintaining perfect conditions across Hemzih.

A glint of golden light caught Rick's eye, he looked up to see the Hammer of God sitting above the northern polar region. Floating in space it remained vigilant as its children worshipped below.

'Is it not glorious?' whispered Annyah.

Rick felt its eyes searching his mind for truth, 'Terrific,' stated Rick in a sardonic tone.

Annyah smiled before making contact with the station, a metallic diamond in the grasp of Zeus. Engines cut and powerful electro magnets shepherded a lost warrior back to its people. For Rick's crew it felt rather ominous entering a negz cavern. Armoured gates shut swallowing any hope of retreat.

Ships rested in docking slips as cars in a parking garage. Sonnet was led down several levels before being placed out of sight. Sonnet's landing gear dropped, stanchions squealed, pressure valves discharged force created by her mass. Once the procedure was over latches came down holding her hull fast.

'It is time,' said the gothic lady rising from her seat, she approached the airlock eagerly.

Rick got up and exchanged tentative glances with Peters and Dyson, 'Let's go.'

They met up with Graham and Allenby, both considered the chances of a firing squad or welcoming committee, perhaps they were both on this world?

Annyah unlocked the safety, 'Sonnet, open airlock.'

'As you wish Annyah.'

A hatch opened beneath them, 'If they shoot us I'm gonna fucking kill you,' whispered Graham.

'You can have me last case of metaxa.'

Annyah peered at Rick her battlements ground against themselves, eyes burnt with the fire of accusation.

'I saved it for the bachelor party.'

'We will have a traditional negz joining.'

'I was kidding.'

'I'm starting to wonder if my ex-wife was a negg spy!' quipped Allenby.

The men laughed, except Rick.

Annyah looked Allenby up and down, 'If that were so your table manners would not be so loathsome.'

Graham chuckled to which Allenby shot a dirty look.

The hatch opened, a single negz in brown robes flanked by two gothic conquistadors were barely visible past a thick grey decontamination mist.

'Not much of a welcoming party,' mumbled Rick.

Annyah climbed down Sonnet's steps, the station's gravity slowly took precedence over Sonnet's, a very primitive vessel by negz standards. Her heels tapped the floor, she raised her palms, 'Sain baina uu.'

A brown clothed negz greeted her likewise, 'Sain baina uu,' the fellow turned his hard exterior to Sonnet's crew, 'Sain baina uu.'

Rick raised the palms of his hands, 'Sain baina uu.'

The station operator lowered his hands and eyed Sonnet as if he were doing an audit, 'Ta nar irjee dotona ene? (You came in this?)'

'Bloody right I did!'

'He does not comprehend,' said Annyah in a low tone.

'Fine, tiim, bi irjee dotona ene (Yes, I came in this).'

The operator was taken aback at Rick's emotional response, emotional for a negz anyway, 'Daga nada kumun (Follow me human).'

Escorted from their docking slip the crew scrutinized a wonderous structure, light bounced of walls plastering gold on the bewildered foreigners. Grand corridors built from perfectly flat facades rising more than three metres above their heads met to establish a ceiling. This place was created by a minimalist yet it's size emitted impressions of grandeur and audacity. At intervals walls broke to connect with a corridor or form a white panel its purpose to light the way, the interior of negz vessels brighter than that of human constructs. Rick assumed it was due to evolution but in fact it was spiritual, gold and piercing light were symbols of purity and truth. Gold the purest of all elements and shining light God's vessel of truth.

Sonnet's crew dressed in their best clothes but Rick's officer's uniform with cap and shining gold star garnered special attention, I guess being in Earth Corps had its upsides. Negz stepped away so they might observe this carnival without distraction.

The staff of this station all dressed in similar pants and shirt with odd amalgamations of robe and jacket. These were those who served, civil servants if you will. Those who didn't serve the people in some fashion wore pure white, usually children or the infirm since those who could do something were put to work. Rick sneered his way toward the sky lift since they represented everything he despised. He was eager to get a look around the surface for communism had never worked on Earth nor anywhere else to his knowledge. As far as he knew the only thing socialism exceeded at was starvation, there must be something Annyah wasn't telling him.

The party were led to a carbon glass elevator its golden struts created a cage worthy of a King. The men followed Annyah, stepping inside they leaned against its wall to be grasped by a brace. Four fingers, two on each side, closed in with a thumb rising between the legs.

'Jesus Christ!' shouted Rick as the thumb caught him by surprise.

'Relax,' said Annyah.

'Pretty hard to do that with a robot grabbing me balls!'

'You found it pleasurable in the past, did you not?'

Graham laughed through his bushy beard. Rick turned to face his engineer, 'Keep it up arsehole.'

Everyone secure, the lift released from its station cutting artificial gravity. For a while Rick was weightless until acceleration pulled him from his alcove. A few more minutes and the planet below influenced their bodies. Like creeping vines, one by one taking hold, gravity slowly pulled them down. Their whole journey took just under ten minutes from leaving the station in a burst of speed to a descent into Hemzih.

Rick peered outside the booth, the arm of Zeus was not one solid structure but many separate towers and nanotubes of a single mind, it mirrored negz society to a tee. Between those structures Rick observed a tundra planet with many cities. Unlike human cities they weren't dense pieces of land squashing men and women against one another in a constant battle for real estate. Negz cities, at least from orbit, looked to be sparse with a wide circumference. As Earth gave off a blue/brown colour this world was grey/white with no discernible ocean. He would learn that Hemzih's oceans were hidden beneath thin ice sheets. On approach Rick noted purple blobs forming on a landscape of grey. As Earth has forests and plains so this planet possesses large areas of fungal growth where cultivation of its main food source takes place. Annyah was looking forward to eating fresh moogon. Negz lived on a diet of what humans would describe as fungus in one form or another. It was difficult to preserve and only tasted good when fresh, well that's what Annyah said. The thought of it turned Rick's stomach.

They entered the clouds, a glass elevator attached to a nanotube. The men felt ill at ease for the whole endeavour of coming to Annyah's home world seemed precarious enough. Now they were strapped into a glass box falling at speed into the planet's atmosphere with no visible means of deceleration. Cloud broke, Sonnet's crew took a collective breath, stunned by a perfect golden circle on a grey landscape transmitting colour and purity toward observers. It was impossible not to stare in awe for detailed placement of buildings created an image of what one might describe as a radar dish, in its centre a mega structure reached out. After a moment of surprise Rick realised they were headed toward that central tower, it was the orbital platform's ground station. On making orbit he'd counted more than twenty orbital stations. In truth there were probably hundreds, each one connected to a glorious golden city the size of New York.

The antenna closed in devouring Rick's view, he wondered if they were going to crash. Just as every human had underestimated these aliens he'd underestimated its size. The golden spire's pinnacle gobbled them up. It went dark for a moment with only a murky yellow light illuminating their glass box. He looked to his left, Annyah smiled back. He looked down to see a distant bright dot, it must be miles high. After a few minutes the dot expanded to envelope him, he looked around and a bustling port revealed itself. A line of cargo containers travelled up one of the many parallel nanotubes and shot into orbit.

Their box passed several floors before picking a stop, its door swung open to reveal another delegation. Restraints retracted and Peters staggered up to a tall negz flanked by gothic soldiers, *HUUURRRRRRRRAAAAHHHH*.

Seven brown negz looked on in horror as their master stood in a puddle of human vomit. Conquistadors guarding this poor fellow stepped back, they didn't want to be anywhere near that toxic alien mess.

'Sorry buddy,' gasped Peters as he wiped his mouth on the cuff of his new suit, 'I've been feeling shitty since I got up.'

Annyah quickly apologised as a hazardous waste team ran to neutralise the health threat. Many believed it outrageous to permit these aliens on Hemzih unchecked, but this was intolerable. Annyah bowed her head pointing out they were mere savages and knew no better ... igniting Rick's temper. In a moment he took over the conversation using his best negz. As with all port security Rick managed to bring the nature of the official's birth into question along with some choice remarks linking the disproportionate size of his genitalia to his job. The surrounding soldiers and civilians were shocked by such candour. Had it come from a negz they'd have beaten him to within an inch of his life but Rick got away with it. After the battle in Sol he was to be respected, none dared challenge his vulgar language, disappointing the wayward Captain no end.

Rick enjoyed bucking authority figures because it provoked a reaction. After the initial shock these damn neggs wrestled control of their emotions and stood as obelisks gazing through him until his tirade ceased. The scene reminded him of a holo-documentary on Easter Island.

'Are you satisfied?' snapped Annyah.

Rick pulled out a hip flask of metaxa, 'No booze, no smoking and a lifetime diet of fungus it's no wonder you people are all so fucking miserable!'

His bride to be snatched the drink from his hand, 'You promised to show respect while you were here!'

Rick snatched his flask back, screwed off the cap then took a swig, 'Whatever.'

Annyah moved close and spoke in a hushed tone so only they might hear, 'Please Rick.'

When she said please he melted like butter on a sunny day. Rick screwed the cap down handed her the flask then peered over his shoulder, 'Come on lads, let's blow this shithole,' and walked out of customs.

The group split up to indulge in the delights of Hemizh. A planet bathed in golden light, its great shining towers punched the sky in every direction. Truly this was a wonderous city where everyone walked or travelled sky trains built upon invisible rails twisting and intersecting in the sky without bumping into one another.

After pulling into their station Rick followed the gothic lady off the train car. Every negz observed with deafening silence, it made Rick's skin crawl. The escalator walls were decorated with shards of crystal, thousands of tiny prisms splitting truth, a feat both humans and negz excelled. Rick was not only in awe of how their public buildings were decorated but also the fact he'd yet to notice graffiti. He guessed any negz caught defacing a wall would be punished as if he did so every wall on the planet and promptly flogged to death … he wasn't far off.

After an hour's walk through what felt like a pleasant Japanese garden, interspersed with small single floor dwellings made of wood and white clay they reached their destination. Rick checked his Earth Corps Captain's uniform, guaranteed to get a blowjob in any Corps system bar, before knocking the door. Annyah stopped him, 'Only women are permitted access to this area of the residence.'

He stepped back and shrugged his shoulders, 'Go for it.'

While Annyah met with her mother for the first time in years Rick examined his surroundings. Sand and smooth stones met green moss, trunks of tall spindly trees gave shade from the soft sun of Hemzih. Despite being a residential area he felt very relaxed. Citizens in brown, white and the odd negz dressed in gold (the religious class) walked level stone paths to and fro, his presence turning heads. Rick contemplated their destinations since this strange city made little sense to a human. Negz are a species capable of quickly turning their hand to violence and extermination without remorse, yet this place didn't fit that narrative. Here rested tranquillity and order at its greatest expression, if first contact with negz were in this city the result would have been a very different impression of these creatures.

In the distance buildings of gold rose around a great orbital elevator, pieces of art crafted over generations. Earth's orbital ring was crude in comparison, a utilitarian construct of grey metal and black nano tubes that broke down more often than a brachian selling out his compadres. This orbital web was a placid work of art, a reflection of the planet and its people below. Comparatively his home was a wretched cesspool of misery and toil. Not for the first time since meeting Annyah, Rick had learnt to respect these creatures, their capabilities and accomplishments.

'Good morning Captain,' came a deep familiar voice. Rick broke from the spell of Hypnos and turned his head. Within his mind the Captain girded his loins.

Agricola raised the palms of his hands toward Rick, 'Sain baina uu.'

It took a few seconds for Sonnet's Captain to recover. He didn't expect his would-be killer to show up, the question was why? Revenge? If Annyah was anything to go by these aliens were just as capable of holding a grudge as humans.

'Will you not greet me?'

Rick paused his contemplation and raised his palms, 'Sain baina uu.'

'Your pronunciation has improved, I am impressed.'

Agricola was dressed in the tradition gothic black of a military man, staff peeping over his shoulder. An armoured visage mimicking only the fiercest of Russian tanks. A line of tattoos stretched above his forehead, a tally of confirmed kills to which Rick favoured ignorance. This "chance" meeting stank of payback.

'That uniform wears you well.'

Rick cleared his throat, 'Why're you here?'

'Once a Dajin Xagan authors a tenet his presence becomes, as kumuns would say, a hot potato.'

'A hot commodity.'

'Ah so it is Captain,' he chuckled.

Agricola secretly enjoyed this kumun penchant for figurative speech though he'd never admit it to his fellow negz.

'And you just happened to be passing by, right?'

A sage masculine smile manifested upon the old warrior's face, 'I must confess another motivation.'

Rick stood back his hand slipped inside his jacket drawing his pistol from its holster, 'I knew it!'

'Clarify?' asked Agricola staring down the wrong end of a barrel.

'I'm not that stupid mate,' he loaded a round into the chamber and flicked the safety off.

A door behind Rick opened and Annyah emerged with her mother. Annyah exposed the soft rear of her skull to Agricola, 'Sain baina uu, aav.'

Aav, that's negg for father ...

Agricola replied to Annyah, 'Sabsa minii keuked.'

Her gold clad mother did the same before all eyes turned to a stunned Rick, 'What are you doing?' asked Annyah.

'Nothing,' said Rick holstering his weapon.

'You are invited to my Triumph, kumun.'

'Triumph?'

Annyah smiled, 'Dajin Xagan Agricola will ride through each city to the celebration of all negz.'

Agricola stretched out his hand, 'Welcome to the house of Augusta, kumun. Treat my daughter with respect and we shall … get on like a dwelling under bombardment, yes?'

Rick slowly reached out and shook the tall warrior's hand, 'Annyah, pass me the flask!'

The End

www.ingramcontent.com/pod-product-compliance
Lightning Source LLC
Chambersburg PA
CBHW021334250626
47155CB00002B/694